Praise for the O[...]

"*Rosemary and Rue* will surely appeal to readers who enjoy my books, or those of Patricia Briggs."

—Charlaine Harris,
#1 *New York Times* bestselling author

"Fast-paced, without ever being frantic, with excellent characterization.... McGuire is a dab hand at dialogue, and the bantering between Toby and everyone—especially Tybalt—is one of the highlights of the book." —*RT Book Reviews*

"The plot is strong, the characterization is terrific, the tragedies hurt ... and McGuire's usual beautiful writing and dark humor are present and accounted for. This has become one of my favorite urban fantasy series, and I can't wait to find out what happens next." FantasyLiterature.com

"An urban fantasy detective series featuring a resourceful female detective ... [October Daye] should appeal to fans of Jim Butcher's *Dresden Files* as well as the novels of Charlaine Harris, Patricia Briggs, and similar authors." —*Library Journal*

"It's fun watching [Toby] stick doggedly to the case as the killer picks off more victims and the tension mounts." —*LOCUS*

"With *Ashes of Honor*, McGuire has crafted a deeply personal and intense story that will keep you on the edge, hoping to be pushed over. In my opinion, it is, hands down, the best Toby to date." The Ranting Dragon

"These books are like watching half a season of your favorite television series all at once.... More than anything else, it's the fun of it all that's kept me returning to McGuire's books, and to this series, long after I've stopped reading other mainstream titles." —SF Signal

"I love that Toby is a strong, independent—yet still vulnerable—heroine. I love that this is a world where people die, where consequences matter. I love the complex world-building and mythology. I love the almost film noir tone of the series. I love that each book leaves me wanting more. If you dig urban fantasy, this is one of the best out there." —CC2K

SEANAN McGUIRE

CHIMES AT
MIDNIGHT

AN OCTOBER DAYE NOVEL

DAW BOOKS, INC.
DONALD A. WOLLHEIM, FOUNDER
375 Hudson Street, New York, NY 10014

ELIZABETH R. WOLLHEIM
SHEILA E. GILBERT
PUBLISHERS
www.dawbooks.com

DAW TRADEMARK REGISTERED
U.S. PAT. AND TM. OFF. AND FOREIGN COUNTRIES
—MARCA REGISTRADA
HECHO EN U.S.A.

PRINTED IN THE U.S.A.

For Jude and Alan,
and all the staff at Borderlands Books.

But especially for Ripley. We miss you.

ACKNOWLEDGMENTS:

Chimes at Midnight marks the start of what I view as the second stage in Toby's journey, and I am grateful and a little awed that you're all here with me, watching it happen. Writing these books is forever a labor of love, and a big part of that is all of you. Seriously. Thank you all. Thanks also to the Machete Squad, as always, since without them, I would probably still be hiding under the bed rather than facing the tangles of draft two; to the Disney Magic Bitches, for putting up with endless trips to Disneyland; and to Vixy, Amy, Brooke, and Shawn, for being extremely forgiving of the fact that no matter where we go, Toby goes there too.

I remain utterly delighted with my agent and personal superhero, Diana Fox, with my editor and savior, Sheila Gilbert, and with my eternally fantastic cover artist, Chris McGrath. Thanks to Christopher Mangum and Tara O'Shea for website design and maintenance, and to Kate Secor for keeping my email from eating me alive. I know it's hungry . . .

We have come so far, and we have so far yet to go, and I am honored to have you all here with me to see where we wind up. I hope you'll continue to stick around.

My soundtrack while writing *Chimes at Midnight* consisted mostly of *Prepare the Preparations*, by Ludo, *Carry the Fire*, by Delta Rae, *Fairytale*, by Heather Dale, endless live concert recordings of the Counting Crows, and *Journey's Greatest Hits*, by Journey. Any errors in this book are entirely my own. The errors that aren't here are the ones that all these people helped me fix.

Now remember: You must not look at goblin men. You must not buy their fruits . . .

All pronunciations are given strictly phonetically. This only covers races explicitly named in the first seven books, omitting Undersea races not appearing in, or mentioned in, book seven.

Afanc: *ah-fank*. Plural is Afanc.
Annwn: *ah-noon*. No plural exists.
Bannick: *ban-nick*. Plural is Bannicks.
Barghest: *bar-guy-st*. Plural is Barghests.
Blodynbryd: *blow-din-brid*. Plural is Blodynbryds.
Cait Sidhe: *kay-th shee*. Plural is Cait Sidhe.
Candela: *can-dee-la*. Plural is Candela.
Coblynau: *cob-lee-now*. Plural is Coblynau.
Cu Sidhe: *coo shee*. Plural is Cu Sidhe.
Daoine Sidhe: *doon-ya shee*. Plural is Daoine Sidhe,
    diminutive is Daoine.
Djinn: *jin*. Plural is Djinn.
Dóchas Sidhe: *doe-sh-as shee*. Plural is Dóchas Sidhe.
Ellyllon: *el-lee-lawn*. Plural is Ellyllons.
Gean-Cannah: *gee-ann can-na*. Plural is Gean-Cannah.
Glastig: *glass-tig*. Plural is Glastigs.
Gwragen: *guh-war-a-gen*. Plural is Gwragen.

Hamadryad: *ha-ma-dry-add*. Plural is Hamadryads.

Hippocampus: *hip-po-cam-pus*. Plural is Hippocampi.

Kelpie: *kel-pee*. Plural is Kelpies.

Kitsune: *kit-soo-nay*. Plural is Kitsune.

Lamia: *lay-me-a*. Plural is Lamia.

The Luidaeg: *the lou-sha-k*. No plural exists.

Manticore: *man-tee-core*. Plural is Manticores.

Naiad: *nigh-add*. Plural is Naiads.

Nixie: *nix-ee*. Plural is Nixen.

Peri: *pear-ee*. Plural is Peri.

Piskie: *piss-key*. Plural is Piskies.

Pixie: *pix-ee*. Plural is Pixies.

Puca: *puh-ca*. Plural is Pucas.

Roane: *row-n*. Plural is Roane.

Satyr: *say-tur*. Plural is Satyrs.

Selkie: *sell-key*. Plural is Selkies.

Shyi Shuai: *shh-yee shh-why*. Plural is Shyi Shuai.

Silene: *sigh-lean*. Plural is Silene.

Tuatha de Dannan. *tootha day danan*. Plural is Tuatha de Dannan, diminutive is Tuatha.

Tylwyth Teg: *till-with teeg*. Plural is Tylwyth Teg, diminutive is Tylwyth.

Urisk: *you-risk*. Plural is Urisk.

ONE

August 22nd, 2012

We have heard the chimes at midnight, Master Shallow.
— William Shakespeare, *King Henry IV, Part II.*

LIKE MANY PORT TOWNS, San Francisco is a city built on top of its own bones, one where broad modern streets can exist side by side with narrow alleys and abandoned thoroughfares. It's a lot like Faerie in that regard. Both of them are studies in contradiction, constant wars between the old and the new. I prowled down one of those half-hidden alleys, the sky midnight dark above me and my shoulders hunched against the growing chill. I'm inhuman and borderline indestructible. That doesn't make me immune to cold—more's the pity.

I'd been walking down the alleys of the city since a little after ten o'clock, when most of the mortal population was safely inside and the streets informally switched their allegiance to Faerie. The air around me smelled faintly of cut grass and copper, as well as the more normal scents of garbage and decay. The don't-look-here I had cast over myself was holding, for the moment.

Somewhere in the alleys around me, a tabby tomcat was prowling, and a woman who looked enough like me to be my sister walked shrouded in her own don't-look-here. Quentin and Raj—my squire and Tybalt's heir, respectively—were back at the house watching horror movies and pretending not to resent the fact that we wouldn't let them come along. I've dragged Quentin into plenty of dangerous situations, but even I have my limits.

We were hunting for goblin fruit.

It's a naturally-occurring narcotic in Faerie: sweet purple berries that smell like everything good in the world and give purebloods beautiful dreams. The effect can be concentrated by making the fruit into jam, dark as tar and more dangerous than any mortal drug. What's just pleasant for purebloods is an unbreakable addiction for humans and changelings—the crossbred children of the fae and human worlds. They waste away on a diet of nothing but sweet fruit and fantasies.

Goblin fruit isn't illegal. Why should it be? It doesn't hurt the purebloods who love it, and it's usually too expensive for changelings to get their hands on—which didn't explain why the stuff had been appearing on the streets of San Francisco with increasing regularity. My old mentor, Devin, used to control the city's drug trade. He kept the goblin fruit out . . . at least until he died. It took me too long to realize what a hole his passing would make. In my defense, I was busy trying to keep myself alive.

That excuse wasn't going to hold much water with the people who were already addicted—or with the ones who were already dead.

Word on the street was that half a dozen local changelings had vanished recently, there one day and gone the next. They hadn't taken any of their possessions, if they had anything to take; not all changelings did. They hadn't told their friends where they were going. A few were known criminals—thieves and petty thugs. Others were just kids who'd been bunking in the independent fiefdoms of Golden Gate Park while they tried to figure out what to do with their lives. And then, suddenly, they were just gone.

Changelings are the perfect victims in Faerie. We're a

born underclass, and very few of us have anyone to miss us if we disappear. I might never have heard about the problem at all, if I hadn't been one of Devin's kids, once upon a time. A few of my fellow survivors came to me to see if there was anything I could do. I agreed to try. I'd been out on the streets every night for a week doing just that. So far, I'd busted three goblin fruit dealers, stopped a mugging, and stopped for coffee at half the all-night diners in the city. But I hadn't seen any of the missing changelings. I honestly wasn't sure whether that was a blessing or a curse.

A raven cawed harshly from somewhere overhead. It would have been a perfectly normal sound in the day light, but here and now, this late at night . . . I looked up, scanning the rooftops until I spotted the outline of a large raven perched on a broken streetlight. It cawed again and then took off, flying west. I swore under my breath and chased after it, trying not to let it out of my sight as I ran along the alley.

The uncharacteristically night-flying raven was the animal form of Jasmine Patel, my Fetch's girlfriend. She'd been keeping lookout over the whole area. If she was calling for backup, she'd seen something—and whatever it was, it was pretty much guaranteed to be nothing good.

Jazz's caws guided me through the maze of narrow streets, until I skidded around a corner and into a dead end alley. There was a dumpster at the far end, so overstuffed with garbage that it had practically become a tiny, localized landfill. A figure I knew was standing at the edge of the mess, her head bowed in evident sorrow. She was my height, with colorless brown hair worn short and streaked with neon pink. Her clothes were almost shockingly bright in the dim alley—orange corduroy pants and an electric blue sweater—but somehow, that didn't do anything to lessen the impact of the scene. May knew what death meant, maybe better than any of us. She was a Fetch, after all.

I stepped up next to her, releasing my don't-look-here

as I joined her in looking at the heaped-up trash. She put a hand on my shoulder, sniffling.

"Yeah," I said softly. "I know."

There was a girl lying sprawled in the garbage. Her skin and hair were the ivory color of old bleached bones, with a faint waxy sheen: she was half Barrow Wight. Only half; her height, and the square lines of her jaw, came from her human parent. She was thin enough to look consumptive, and she wasn't breathing.

I walked forward, kneeling to touch the girl's wrist. Her skin was still warm. She'd been alive when we started prowling the streets. There was a faint, sickly-sweet smell to the garbage around her, too dilute to be tempting, but strong enough to make her cause of death plain. Goblin fruit. We'd finally found a changeling who had been killed by goblin fruit. Luck was with us.

Luck was nowhere in the picture.

"Toby?" May's voice was very soft. "What do you want to do now?"

There was only one thing that we *could* do. I stayed crouched beside the girl, my fingers still resting lightly on her wrist. "We wait for the night-haunts."

The soft scent of musk and pennyroyal tickled my nose. "Are you sure that is the wisest course of action?" asked a male voice, sounding faintly concerned.

"I promised not to summon them again. I didn't promise not to hang around and say hello." I straightened, turning to face him. I couldn't quite conceal my relief at the sight of Tybalt, standing there in a wine-colored shirt and tight black pants. Unlike May and I, he hadn't bothered trying to make himself look human: the black tabby stripes in his dark brown hair were clearly visible, and his eyes were banded malachite green, with vertical pupils. His expression, however, was as sorrowful as May's.

If I hadn't already loved him, I think I would have started to in that moment.

"The night-haunts aren't friendly people, Toby," said May. "I know. I used to be one."

"Do you have a better idea?" I shook my head. "It's not like we can break into the county morgue later and examine her body. Even if we had forensic training, it wouldn't matter. This is the only way." If the girl had died a violent death, I could have sampled her blood for clues. This was different. If I tried to do blood magic and ride her memories, I could wind up getting addicted to goblin fruit in the process. I cared about justice. I cared about cleaning up my streets. There were some risks I still wasn't willing to take.

The night-haunts were a risk of a different variety, and one that I had taken before. They were one of the deep, dark secrets of Faerie, the shadows that came for the dead and carried them away, leaving perfect human replicas in their place. The work of the night-haunts allowed Faerie to exist without worrying that the bodies of our dead would betray us. The trouble was, they also made it impossible for me to know how many of the missing changelings had died and been replaced by human manikins. This changeling could be our first casualty. She could also be our twentieth. If the bodies couldn't tell me, I was going to have to go for the next best thing, and ask the dead.

Wings rustled overhead as Jazz came in for a landing, shifting back into her semi-human form in the same motion. She was a tall, black-haired woman of clearly Indian descent, with raven-amber eyes. "I think Toby's right," she said, moving to take May's arm. "That doesn't mean we have to stay if you're not comfortable."

"No," said May, shaking her head. "If Toby's staying, so am I." She hesitated before smiling, very slightly. "It'll be nice to see my siblings again."

Fetches are created when night-haunts consume the blood of the living. Sort of like caterpillars turning into butterflies, only gorier and a lot less likely to wind up on binders designed by Lisa Frank. I grimaced a little. "All right. Tybalt?"

He raised an eyebrow. "Do you even need to *ask* whether I intend to remain here while you engage in casual conversation with a group of merciless carrion-eaters who have little reason to be fond of you? I'm staying."

"Not going to argue," I said, and walked over to stand beside him.

"What do we do now?" asked Jazz.

In unison, May and I replied, "We wait."

Tybalt snorted before casually looping his arm around my waist. I let him pull me a little closer, although I didn't allow myself to relax. The night-haunts are nothing to relax around. The comforting smell of pennyroyal and musk rolled off him like my favorite cologne. All fae have their own distinctive magical odor. I'm more sensitive to them than most. It's all part and parcel of being the first in a new race of blood-workers: the Dóchas Sidhe.

My mother, Amandine, is the daughter of Oberon himself, making her Firstborn and more powerful than anyone as . . . reality-challenged . . . as she is has any real need to be. I'm her daughter by a mortal man, making me a changeling with a rather unusual skill set, combined with the bleached-out coloring of a bad watercolor painting. The fact that I managed to get myself knighted for services to the Crown was practically a miracle. The fact that I had been dating the local King of Cats for three months without discovering that it was all an especially cruel dream sequence was *definitely* a miracle.

The four of us made a strange tableau as we stood there, looking at the body of a dead girl and waiting for her strange eternity to begin. It felt almost disrespectful. The dead should be alone when the night-haunts come. But I'd promised not to summon them, and there was no better way to find our answers than this. No; that wasn't right.

Given the circumstances, there was no other way at all.

Ten minutes, maybe less, passed before we heard the distant sound of ragged wings beating against the night. That was our only warning: immediately after that, the flock descended. They were a ribbon of smoke and dead leaves against the night, an impossible swirl of half-realized bodies and charcoal-sketched faces. Individually, they were about the size of Barbie dolls, but they didn't travel that way; they moved as an all-consuming cloud, too organized to be natural.

They landed between us and the body, the more solid members of the flock standing closest to us, folding their wings behind their bodies and watching us with wary hunger. Several of them had faces I knew. Devin, my old mentor; Oleander, the woman who'd been partially responsible for my spending fourteen years as an enchanted fish . . .

. . . and Connor, the Selkie man I'd loved, once upon a lifetime ago. My mouth went dry. Connor had been alive the last time I'd seen the night-haunts. Somehow, I hadn't allowed myself to consider what his death would mean.

He met my eyes, and then looked away without saying a word. There was nothing left for us to say.

Devin's haunt felt no such restraint. He launched himself into the air with a maddened buzzing of his wings, flying forward to hover in front of my nose. Face contorted with anger, he gestured at the girl in the trash and demanded, "Well, Toby? *Well?* Is this good enough for you?"

"What?" My eyes widened, temporary shock over seeing the night-haunt wearing Connor's face forgotten. "Devin, what the hell are you talking about?"

"For over a hundred years, I kept that shit out of this city, and you—" He laughed, a bitter sound with no amusement behind it. "You may as well have invited it in. Rolled out the red carpet, told the dealers that San Francisco was ripe for the taking. Are you happy now? All these dead kids are on your head."

"What? Devin—"

"You could have stopped this!" He flew even closer, close enough that I could feel the breeze generated by his wings. "You could have done something!"

"Egil, you forget yourself," snapped May, her words suddenly overlaid with an accent that I had never heard before. Devin's haunt and I both turned toward her. Her eyes were fixed on him, and so cold. You could freeze to death in those eyes. "Chastising the living? Really?"

"As if you have any right to judge me, Mai," he snapped. The difference between the name he used and the one I knew her by was subtle, but I could hear it. "You've *joined* them."

"Yeah, well," she said, the accent slipping from her voice to be replaced by her normal Californian lilt. "That's the way the cookie crumbles. Now stop shouting and help."

"You said 'all these dead kids,'" I said, slowly. "Devin ... how many have there been?" I knew that "Devin" was the name of the face the night-haunt wore, and not the name of the night-haunt himself, but I was pretty sure that I didn't have the right to call him "Egil." "This girl is the first one we've found."

He turned in the air to look at me impassively. Then he snapped his fingers. Figures began to separate themselves from the flock, flying forward—not as close as he had come, but close enough for me to make out faces, hair colors, the points of their ears. Some were more human-looking than others, but all of them were changelings. They just kept coming. By the time they stopped, there were more than a dozen night-haunts hanging in the air, wings a blur as they stared at me.

The blood ran out of my cheeks, leaving me pale and lightheaded. "So many?" I whispered.

"Goblin fruit is a killer," snapped Devin. "You may as well have put a bullet in their heads. It would have been more merciful."

"Your memories are of the man who killed me," said May mildly. "Maybe you should watch the murder metaphors, huh?" The last person whose face and memories May had consumed when she was still a night-haunt was a girl named Dare, who'd seen me as her hero. Devin had killed her. That had to be making this pretty awkward for both of them, now that May saw the world as herself, and not through the death-hungry veil of the night-haunts.

I couldn't really appreciate her quipping. I was too busy looking at the night-haunts. Some of them were wearing faces I recognized, changelings I'd seen in Golden Gate Park or at Home before Devin died. Others were strangers to me, and always would be, now. They were dead. These were just their echoes, and all too soon, they'd fade away.

This had to stop.

"Devin . . ."

"Don't you apologize to me," he said, fluttering back, until he was flying just in front of those silent, doomed children. "If you want to make this right, make it stop. The dead are dead. Worry about the living."

"I thought the night-haunts appreciated death," said Tybalt. I glanced at him, startled. I'd almost forgotten that he was there.

"We do," said Devin's haunt mildly. "It doesn't make us monsters. Now leave, all of you. This is not for you to see."

"Not even me?" asked May. That strange accent was in her voice again, turning it plaintive—almost lonely. Just as I'd never considered that Connor would be among the night-haunts now, I'd never thought about how much she had to miss them. One adopted sister wasn't exactly a fair trade for a whole flock of blood siblings.

"Not even you, Mai," said Devin's haunt, his voice softening slightly. "You made your choice."

She nodded, eyes oddly bright, before she took Jazz's hand and turned to walk away. She didn't say good-bye. Maybe that wasn't a thing the night-haunts did.

I stayed where I was for a few seconds more, forcing myself to look at the entire flock—even Connor's haunt, who still wouldn't meet my eyes. "I'm sorry," I said softly. "I knew the goblin fruit problem was bad. I didn't know it had reached this point. And I'm going to make it right."

"Don't make promises you can't keep, girl," said Oleander's haunt, still standing safely on the ground.

"I never do," I said.

There was nothing left to say after that, and too much left to do. Blinking hard to keep myself from starting to cry, I turned and followed after May and Jazz. Tybalt paced beside me, a silent shadow.

Even when I heard the sounds of the flock beginning to eat, I didn't look back. The night-haunt with Devin's face was right: there are things in Faerie that are not for me to see. Not if I ever want to sleep again.

I had work to do.

TWO

THE CAR WAS PARKED behind a convenience store, draped in an illusion to keep it from being borrowed by some enterprising joyrider. May snapped her fingers to release the spell as the four of us approached. None of us spoke, and we held our silence as I unlocked the doors, checked the backseat for unwanted visitors, and slid behind the wheel. My hands were shaking and I was afraid that I was going to run us off the road, but that didn't matter. May doesn't drive, largely because no one is willing to get into a car with her anymore. Jazz can fly. Tybalt mostly uses the Shadow Roads to get around. Unless I wanted to call a taxi, I was driving.

Tybalt grimaced as he got into the passenger seat. I didn't say anything, but I knew how uncomfortable he was, and I appreciated that he was willing to put himself through this for my sake. Faerie: where it's only a little weird to realize that my boyfriend is older than the internal combustion engine.

We were halfway home before anyone spoke. "What are we going to do?" asked Jazz. "All those kids . . ."

"There was no way we could have known." The words sounded sincere. It took me a moment to realize they'd come out of my mouth. "The night-haunts were doing their job, and that meant we never had a chance of finding out about those other kids. Not unless someone told us, and nobody knew for sure." Their names. Sweet Titania, I hadn't even learned all their *names*. How was I going to tell their parents if I didn't know their *names*?

Thinking like that was just going to drag me down into a never-ending spiral of blame and self-loathing. I couldn't afford that. Not right now.

May must have known what I was thinking, because she said softly, "I can try to talk to the flock. Maybe I can get their names."

"That would be good." I glanced at Tybalt as I turned onto Market Street. "Were any of them yours?"

"Thankfully, no," he said. "The goblin fruit has not reached my Court as yet. Given time, it will. My control over my subjects is strong, but it is not absolute."

"Right." Three months ago, right before we started officially dating, one of Tybalt's subjects introduced me to my own intestines. That probably wouldn't have happened if Tybalt had been in control of Samson's actions at the time. "Okay."

"They weren't from the flock, either," said Jazz. "We're not missing anyone."

"Okay," I repeated. I was learning more and more about whose they weren't—and it wasn't helping. The Cait Sidhe and the Raven-maids and Raven-men kept a close eye on their changelings, protecting them the way the larger fae community didn't. But selling goblin fruit to changelings wasn't a crime. The Queen of the Mists had to know that it was happening, and she'd never done a thing to stop it.

Everyone quieted after that. None of us really had anything to say. I pulled into the covered two-car parking area next to the large Victorian house that we had on long-term loan from my liege, Duke Sylvester Torquill. May and Jazz got out as soon as the engine stopped, leaving me alone with Tybalt. He waited until their doors were closed before putting his hand on my shoulder and saying, softly, "He was wrong. This is not your fault."

I kept my hands on the wheel, staring straight ahead

through the windshield. "Are you sure about that? Because it feels like my fault."

"October."

I didn't turn.

Tybalt sighed before saying, more firmly, *"October."* Reluctantly, I turned to face him. He reached out and touched my cheek. "This is not your fault. That does not mean it is not your responsibility. I know that. So my question now becomes ... what are we going to do about it?"

"We're going to stop it." Once again, the words were out almost before I realized they were coming, and once again, they helped. I nodded, slowly at first, then with growing conviction. "People are dying. The Queen of the Mists will have to do something now."

"I do not share your conviction on that matter, but I am willing to follow your lead." He leaned in, fingers still pressed to my cheek, and kissed me.

There was a time when I would have pulled away, feigning displeasure I didn't really feel. That time ended after I nearly lost him in Annwn, and after he nearly lost me at the hands of Raj's father, Samson. The phrase "tumultuous courtship" was practically invented for us.

But that's over now. He kissed me with calm assurance and I responded in kind, taking a brief, sweet comfort in the hint of pennyroyal on his lips. Finally, I pulled away. "Let's go inside," I said. "We need to decide what happens next."

"As milady wishes," he said, smiling faintly, and opened the car door.

A narrow brick path led from the parking area—it's not really a garage, since it doesn't have walls, but it's private parking in the city of San Francisco, which makes it worth its weight in gold—to the back door of the house, which opened on the kitchen. May and Jazz had left it unlocked when they went inside. I pushed it open, calling, "It's just us, don't shoot."

"Toby!" My name was followed by the sound of a teenage boy vaulting over the back of the living room couch. Quentin appeared in the kitchen doorway a few seconds later, practically vibrating with the need to know what he might have missed. "You're home."

"I am," I said, heading for the coffeemaker on the counter. May, Oberon bless her, had started a fresh pot while I was still out in the car with Tybalt. "Where are May and Jazz?"

"They went straight up to their room. May said you'd tell me what was going on."

"Of course she did." My hands were shaking again as I poured myself a cup of coffee. I still forced myself to complete the process before I turned to him and said, "We finally found proof that the goblin fruit problem has gotten bad enough that it's killing people."

Quentin's eyes widened behind the bronze fringe of his hair. I remember a time when that hair was the color of cornsilk, but like many Daoine Sidhe, it had darkened as he aged. "Somebody died?"

"A lot of somebodies died, Quentin." I could see their faces if I closed my eyes. "We found a dead changeling in an alley, and we waited with her until the night-haunts came. We saw the victims, all of them. There have been at least a dozen. Maybe more."

"Oh, oak and ash." He stood a little straighter, unconsciously falling into a formal posture. He was a courtier at Shadowed Hills when we first met, and some habits die hard. "What are we going to do?"

There was something extremely comforting about that "we." I spent so long without any allies that sometimes I wasn't sure I knew what to do with the ones I had. "We're going to take it to the Queen," I said. "This is her land. She should be doing something to keep her people alive."

"Um," said Quentin. "But . . . she *hates* you."

"Yeah, I know," I said dryly. "I appreciate the reminder, though."

"He has a valid point," said Tybalt. "Her dislike for you is rather legendary."

"And she's still the Queen." I sighed before taking a gulp of my coffee. "We work with what we have."

They weren't exaggerating, sadly. The Queen of the Mists had hated me for years, starting when I refused to pretend I hadn't been the one to discover what was currently her knowe. Her hatred had just grown stronger, and more irrational, with time. She'd done some complicated political maneuvering to get me convicted of murder not all that long ago. She nearly succeeded in having me executed over that one.

But this was her Kingdom, and Faerie is a feudal society. If I wanted this to happen, we would have to go through the Queen.

"Quentin, go get changed," I said, topping off my coffee. "I'm going to go find May and Jazz, see if they want to come with us—where's Raj?"

"He went to Helen's," said Quentin, grimacing. "They're fighting again."

Helen was Raj's longtime half-Hob girlfriend. It was sort of a miracle that they were still together, given the circumstances of their meeting, but I wished them luck. Love does best when it has lots of luck to bolster it up. "All right, fine. That means we don't need to worry about him. I want to leave within the hour, got me?"

"Got you," said Quentin, and vanished into the hall, sounding more like an elephant than a teenage boy as he galloped toward the stairs.

I followed more sedately, sipping my coffee as I walked. I was almost to the second-floor landing when I heard Tybalt following. I knew he was letting me hear him, and that dissolved what little irritation I might have otherwise felt; by walking loudly enough for me to hear, he was offering me the opportunity to tell him to go away.

Adjusting to the nonverbal oddities of dating a Cait Sidhe has been strange, but rewarding, and in a way, I think I've been getting ready for this for years. I looked back over my shoulder as I stopped in front of the door to May and Jazz's shared room, flashing him a quick smile. "You okay back there?"

"Yes," he said. "I do believe I am."

"Good." I turned back to the door, knocking as I called, "Is everybody decent? I need to talk to you."

"We're clothed," said May, opening the door. I could see Jazz behind her on the bed, pulling her blouse down in a way that implied "clothed" might have been an exaggeration. I didn't say anything about it. Their sex life is none of my business. "What's up?"

"I'm about to do something I really, really don't want to," I said. "You want to come?"

May pulled a face. "The Queen's Court? Really? Tonight?"

"I don't see another way to take care of this, do you? I can't just sit here and let more changelings die without telling her what's going on."

"Okay." May looked over her shoulder at Jazz, and then back to me. "We'll be ready when you are." She shut the door. I blinked, taking a step back.

"I guess they're coming with us," I said, and turned toward my own room. Tybalt followed, pacing me down the rest of the hall. I flashed him a small smile and said, "You can come in, but you'll need to sit on the bed while I get changed."

"I believe I can manage that," he said gravely.

"Cool." I flicked on my bedroom light, handing Tybalt my half-empty coffee mug before starting for the closet, where I kept my relatively small assortment of Court-suitable formal wear. I shrugged out of my leather jacket, hanging it on the closet doorknob. "I've been assuming, but I didn't ask. Are you coming to the Queen's Court with me?"

"I'd like to," said Tybalt, following my instructions and sitting down on the bed. "I know your Queen thinks little of me, but as she thinks even less of you, my presence cannot help but improve the situation."

"If nothing else, it'll give her something besides me to be pissed off about." I crossed my arms, scowling at my clothes. Most of the time, when visiting a noble who demanded "proper respect," I would just have created an illusory dress for myself, weaving it out of dead leaves and butterfly wings and whatever else I had to hand. The Queen of the Mists, unfortunately, didn't approve of illusions. Whatever I wore was likely to get permanently transformed into something else. Unless I went in assuming she was going to do that. On those occasions, I usually wound up disrespectfully underdressed in front of her entire Court.

"That is admittedly one of my goals," said Tybalt.

"You're a smart guy—ha!" I pulled a low-cut silk gown the color of dried blood out of the back of my closet. It was surprisingly simple, given that it was one of the Queen's designs. It had started out as one of my favorite pairs of jeans. I held it up against myself, checking the fit. "What do you think?"

"I think that, given how often you accessorize yourself with bloodstains, it's for the best that the color flatters you," said Tybalt solemnly. He put my coffee down on the bedside table as he leaned back on his hands. "I also think you should wear dresses more often. They make me itch to peel you out of them."

I raised an eyebrow. "Now isn't the time, but that's good to know." I hung the dress on the back of the door before starting toward the master bathroom, trusting Tybalt to follow. I shed clothing as I went, letting the pieces lie where they fell. "I really don't want to see the Queen."

"I know."

"But I can't handle this on my own, and I can't go to Sylvester when this isn't his demesne. I have to find out whether she's willing to put her dislike of me aside and deal with something that's a real threat to this Kingdom." I bent to turn on the shower.

"I know that too, and I love you for it." Tybalt's hand landed on my shoulder. I straightened, turning to face him. It didn't matter that I was naked and he wasn't; he didn't need to be naked to make my knees go weak, especially when he was smiling at me like I was all that mattered in the world. Still smiling, he leaned forward and kissed me.

I'll never get used to kissing Tybalt. More, I'll never

get used to being *allowed* to kiss Tybalt, to it being a
normal part of my life that I'm not supposed to think
twice about. I leaned into him, reveling in the heat of his
skin and the sweetly musky pennyroyal taste of his lips.
He put a hand on my upper arm, pulling me toward him,
and I raised my own hand to touch his cheek, letting my
eyes close. This was real; this was really happening.

This was why I had to see the Queen. Because for my
life to be a calm enough place to allow for moments like
this one, I needed her to be doing her goddamn job. I
couldn't take care of the goblin fruit problem without her.

"Love you, too," I murmured, as he pulled away from
me.

I opened my eyes to the sight of Tybalt's smile. "I'll
never tire of hearing you say that." He let go of my arm.
"Please allow me to help with the laces on your gown
when you're ready."

"Gladly." The moment over, I stepped into the shower,
pulling the curtain closed between us.

I showered quickly—something that wouldn't have
been possible if Tybalt hadn't gone back into the bedroom; I was angry and worried, not *dead*—and dried my
hair with a towel as I walked back to meet him. He had
the dress unlaced and ready to lower over my head.

It fit like it had been made for me, which technically,
it had been. Tybalt laced me into it, pulling the bodice so
tight that I couldn't have concealed anything in my
cleavage if I'd wanted to. I squeaked in protest, and he
kissed the side of my neck before giving the laces one
last tug and saying, "If you appear to have suffered in the
name of fashion, she will respect you all the more for
your efforts. You are stunning. Now you only need to do
something with your hair, and you'll be the prettiest potential accuser at the ball."

"I feel like a giant Barbie."

"I do not become romantically involved with plastic
people," said Tybalt dryly.

"That makes me feel much better." I turned to kiss
him, planting both hands flat on his chest to keep the

gesture from turning into anything more involved. "Can you get my ankle sheath? It's on the dresser."

"Certainly." As he turned to find it, he asked, "Have you considered how to make your entrance without soaking your skirts?"

The entrance to the Queen's knowe required us to pass through a frequently semi-flooded cave. My gown was floor-length. "Maeve's tits," I swore. "I'm going to get drenched. Again."

"Not necessarily." He smiled as he turned to offer my sheath. "The Queen of the Mists is required by treaty to allow the Court of Cats entry through the Shadow Roads. I believe it would cement me as the target of her frustrations if I were kind enough to allow you to short-cut her watery pranks for the evening."

I blinked, and then grinned. "You're brilliant. Can Quentin pass through the shadows too, or does he have to wade?"

"I believe I can transport you both a short distance." He sighed as he watched me strap on the sheath. "You're intending to drive to the beach, aren't you?"

"I'm not comfortable when I haven't got my car. Besides, you said yourself that you could transport us both a short distance. We're close to the Queen's knowe, but we're not *that* close." I grabbed a hairbrush off the dresser, beginning to brush the snarls out of my wet hair. It was slow going. As I worked, I offered, "You could meet us there, if you'd rather?"

Tybalt paused before sighing again. "I think that might be best, since I'm sure whatever misadventure we're about to embark on will require me to spend more time in that damnable contraption. I should save my tolerance for a time when there won't be a better choice."

"That seems wise." I pulled my hair into a ponytail.

He winced. "*Please* tell me you're going to let May do something *else* with your hair. Something that is not that."

"What?" I lowered my hands, blinking at him. "You said I should put my hair up."

"October, in formal settings, there is a world of difference between putting one's hair up and preparing to go for a run. You have accomplished the latter. You need to accomplish the former if you're trying not to insult the Queen."

"I usually just leave my hair down," I grumbled.

"And you usually manage to insult the Queen in short order. Let's try this without stacking the deck against you, shall we?" He folded his arms. "Please? For me?"

"You know, everyone warned me that getting into a serious relationship would change me, but I thought they meant my habits, not my hair." I turned toward the door, stopping when I realized that Tybalt was openly staring at me. "What? What did I say?"

"You think this is a serious relationship?" he asked.

Sudden panic flooded over me. I forced it down, trying to focus on his tone of voice. He'd sounded surprised, not upset. "Yes?" I ventured.

To my immense relief, Tybalt smiled. "Good. So do I."

"Okay, well, that's one heart attack out of the way for tonight." I grabbed my leather jacket from the closet door. "I'll let May do my hair, since you insist. I'm keeping my sneakers. The gown will hide them until we get there, and I always feel better knowing I can run if I have to." They'd be high heels as soon as the Queen worked her magic, but that was a problem for later.

Tybalt chuckled. "If things go so badly at Court that you have to run, little fish, then I assure you, footwear will be the least of your concerns."

I shook my head at him and led the way out of the room, clutching my jacket against my chest. Maybe this was it; maybe she would listen, and stop the goblin fruit from spreading any further. Maybe it'd all be all right after we visited the Queen.

Maybe, but probably not. Unable to shake the feeling that I was somehow heading for my own execution, I walked down the stairs, and into the inevitable.

THREE

TYBALT TAKING THE SHADOW ROADS to the Queen's Court turned out to be a good thing. He was uncomfortable in the car under the best of circumstances. He would probably have exploded if he'd tried to ride with three people behind him in the backseat, all of them crammed together and complaining. As it was, May and Jazz were able to sit together in comfort, while Quentin rode up front with me, by right of "I'm the squire and besides, you want to ride with your girlfriend."

"You don't have to come, you know." I turned into the parking lot nearest the Queen's knowe. "You can still back out. Go and see a movie or something, and I'll fill you in when we're done."

"What, and miss all the fun?" May shook her head. "No way. I love bothering the Queen almost as much as I love Saturday morning cartoons."

"If you say so." I eyed them in the rearview mirror. "She'll definitely be bothered."

Jazz was wearing a purple sari with a feather pattern around the edges that matched the feathered band in her hair. As a skinshifter, her fae nature was bound into that knotted band. May, on the other hand, was wearing a bright pink dress, accessorized with bright green heels and jelly bracelets. It was like playing chauffeur for Jem and the Holograms, only without the convenient excuse of it being the 1980s.

"Why did you get dressed up?" Quentin asked. "Won't the Queen transform your clothes as soon as you get inside?" He was wearing jeans and a nice button-down shirt, since he wasn't the one the Queen actively disliked. He was also maintaining a don't-look-here over the entire car, sparing us from needing individual human disguises. Sometimes I wonder how I ever got along without a squire.

"Ah, but we're entering separately," said May. "We may be spared her merciless fashion sense, in which case, I get to horrify courtiers with my taste in prom gowns."

"Jazz's dress is actually nice," I protested.

Jazz smiled. "I'm good either way."

"Too late for me to argue now. We're here." I pulled into an open space between an old VW van and a shiny new Prius too nice for the neighborhood and thus almost certainly protected by a stack of anti-theft charms. If the owner was smart, mortals couldn't even see the car. Anti-theft charms don't do anything to stop people from throwing a brick through your rear window when they get frustrated by their inability to touch the car.

My own VW bug was protected by anti-theft, anti-detection, and anti-bird-crap charms. You'd never have known to look at it, but my car had been basically totaled three months ago when an Afanc—a big beaver-looking monster from the deeper realms of Faerie—decided to take a nap on the roof. Thankfully, my friend Danny has a really good Gremlin mechanic, and my liege was footing the bill. After the repairs were finished, I was pretty sure my car was functionally indestructible. That would be a nice change, considering the fates my vehicles normally suffered.

"It'll be fine," said May.

"Tell me that in an hour," I countered. I left my jacket on the front seat as I got out of the car. There was no point in tempting the Queen to turn it into a bolero or something.

We walked across the pavement to the sand and started down the beach in a ragged line. I didn't realize Tybalt was beside me until he took my arm. I jumped, turning to face him. He smiled.

"Good evening, little fish."

"You know, if you were anyone else, you'd have gotten decked just now," I said. But I didn't jerk my arm away.

"That is one of the many reasons I am thankful, each and every day, not to be anyone but myself." Tybalt considered my ballet-style bun for a moment before he nodded. "It's simple, but should avoid the Queen's ire."

"So glad you approve," I said dryly.

"I just don't want this to be harder than it has to be," he said, sounding briefly quieter, more like the Tybalt I saw when I was alone than the hard, brilliant King of Cats. He turned to May and Jazz while I was mulling over the difference, and said, "You both look lovely tonight, but I believe this is where we part company. May I assume I'll be seeing you inside?"

"Unless there's a velvet rope now," said May. "You crazy kids stay out of trouble, or at least wait until we get there to start it!"

"We'll try, but I can't promise anything." I took Quentin's hand in my free one. Tybalt led us forward, into the deepest shadows on the beach. Then we stepped through the wall of the world into darkness, and everything was cold, cold, and there was no air, but Quentin's hand was warm in mine, and Tybalt's body was warm beside me, and we were moving forward . . .

. . . into the sound and light of the Queen's ballroom, where more than a few courtiers turned to look at us, some in surprise, some in more assessing disdain. I pulled my arm away from Tybalt, dropped Quentin's hand, and looked down at myself. Then I sighed.

"You know, since the dress I *was* wearing was her work, I thought she might leave it alone. Silly, optimistic me." My red silk gown was gone, replaced by an equally simple, equally floor-length gown. This one was gray silk, so pale it looked almost white when it wasn't right against my skin. A complicated braid of red ribbons circled my waist. Even my hair had been restyled, my simple bun replaced by a waterfall of layers held separate by a thin net of ribbons. That was going to be hell to take out.

I pulled up the skirt to check my shoes, and blinked as I realized that they were still sneakers: all she'd changed were the laces, which were now red ribbons that matched my semi-belt. My ankle sheath was still in place, undisturbed by the Queen's annoying obsession with changing my clothes. I let go of my skirt. "She left my shoes alone," I said. "That's weird."

"At least she got us all?" offered Quentin, who looked annoyingly comfortable in his tunic and trousers.

I glanced toward Tybalt, and whatever I'd been about to say fled my mind, leaving me feeling more oxygen-deprived than our brief passage through the shadows justified. "Uh . . ."

He was wearing brown leather trousers, a darker brown leather vest, and a silk shirt that matched my dress. The sleeves were almost piratical in style, and the collar was unlaced. His boots were the same shade as his vest, a few shades lighter than his hair.

"Uh," I said again, before managing, "Weren't you wearing that the last time you came to Court?"

"She always dresses me in some variation of this attire," said Tybalt. "I can't tell whether she likes the look of it, or whether she's trying to make a point. This would have been a stagehand's garb, once upon a time, and nothing suited for a King."

"Uh," I said, for a third time.

Seeing my distress, Tybalt smirked, leaned in, and murmured in my ear, "I have a disturbing assortment of leather trousers, thanks to her. I'd be happy to show you, if you like."

I could feel my ears turning red. But with embarrassment came annoyance, and annoyance and I are very old friends. I shook my head as I straightened and stepped away. "Let's go see about talking to the Queen."

It felt like every eye was on me as I led Tybalt and Quentin into the crowd. My sneakers made soft squeaking noises on the marble. A commotion near the main doors told me that Jazz and May had made it inside, but I couldn't see them through the crowd. No matter; they'd find us soon enough. They always did, when it was important.

The ballroom was a study in white that seemed carved from a single piece of ivory. The only difference between the floor and ceiling was where you were standing. Both were polished until they verged on becoming mirrors. Cobweb ribbons of white spider-silk were wrapped around the filigreed pillars, eddying and dancing at the slightest breeze. It was like walking through a forest of ghostly tentacles, and it felt like it could turn hostile at any moment—if it wasn't hostile already.

We walked until we reached a dais, as white as the rest of the room, but set in the center of a wide clear space. No one kept it clear; people avoided it of their own accord, unless they'd come to speak with the Queen. I looked around at the crowd, and realized how few people I'd ever seen come to seek her counsel. They'd come to her Court. They'd do the political dance. But they never *talked* to her, or encouraged her to talk to them. I knew I wasn't the only one who had problems with the Queen. I was starting to wonder how many people *didn't*.

The thought had barely crossed my mind when the air grew cold with the scent of rowan, and mist clouded the air above the throne. People stopped talking, turning toward the dais like flowers turning toward the sun. I stayed where I was, keeping my chin high, and waited.

I didn't have to wait long. The smell of rowan intensified, then shattered, and the mist parted to show the Queen seated on her throne, as comfortable as if she'd been there for hours.

If anyone looked like they'd been modeled on the idea of the perfect Faerie Queen, it was her. She'd grown her hair out again, and it fell in a ribbon of white silk to puddle at her feet, impossibly long, especially since she'd bobbed it less than two years before. Her dress was blue velvet, shading from deep-sea blue at the hem to white-cap gray at the neckline. She was beautiful, as long as you didn't meet her eyes, which were the moon-mad color of the foam on a stormy sea. That shouldn't have been a color, but it was. Faerie is nothing if not creative.

My breath caught. Her beauty was not the kind that human hearts—or part-human hearts—were ever intended to deal with. As I breathed in, I tasted the strange cocktail of her heritage on the air. Siren, Sea Wight, and Banshee. How she teleported in and out of the ballroom was anybody's guess. It's possible to borrow the magic of others through their blood. There was probably a Tuatha de Dannan on her staff who was willing to bleed for her.

She frowned before looking down her nose at me, one perfect eyebrow raised in what looked like surprise. "Sir Daye," she said. There was nothing warm or welcoming in that voice. "I did not expect to see you here again."

Since my visits to the Queen's Court always seemed to end with things going horribly wrong, I shared the sentiment. Still, I wasn't foolish enough to say that aloud. I gripped the sides of my transformed skirt and sank into a deep curtsy. "Your Majesty."

She let me hold that position long enough that my thighs began to ache before she said, sounding almost bored, "You may rise."

I did, forcing myself to lift my head until I was looking at her face. Her beautiful, terrible face. "I came to petition for an audience."

"Did you?" Her gaze flicked first to Quentin, then to Tybalt. "In the company of your loyal hounds, even. Well. How can I deny such a thoughtful petition? You have your audience. What petty trouble have you brought to lay before my feet tonight?"

I had wanted to do this in private if possible. I should have known the Queen wouldn't allow it. She never had before, after all. "Your Majesty, as I am sure you're aware, there has been an increasing amount of goblin fruit in the city of late. It's appearing everywhere. The dealers—"

"Wait." She raised a hand, cutting me off. "Have you

truly come to ask about the goblin fruit? October, really. I'm disappointed in you. I knew your upbringing left much to be desired, but this seems a new low, even for your bloodline."

"What?" I blinked at her, my train of thought utterly lost. "What do you mean?"

"I won't grant you a license to peddle the fruit, October. I'm ashamed for you, that you would even ask."

It felt like the floor was dropping out from under my feet. "I didn't come to ask for a license to sell the stuff," I said slowly. "I came to ask you to help me stop people from selling it at all. It's dangerous. Changelings—"

"Should know better than to imbibe. Those who do not would clearly have become a danger to Faerie, given the time; better they float away like Ophelia, each to their own private river, and drown in peace, rather than continuing such terribly troubled lives." A thin smile touched the edges of her lips. "I am doing this Kingdom a service."

"You . . . you're the source of the goblin fruit?"

"I am not the source, but I am the channel. Those who had need to know—those whose minds were not closed to the possibilities, whose halls were not choked with mongrels—" Her gaze flicked to Tybalt. "—they knew where to come. Perhaps you should question the worth of your allies if not one of them could tell you that."

I didn't speak. I couldn't. I just stared at her, trying to wrap my head around the enormity of what she was saying. *She* was the reason the goblin fruit was showing up on the streets. *She* was the one allowing it. "But, Your Majesty—"

"This is a difficult time for the pureblood community. The mortal world encroaches at every side, and we need what escapes we can find. Surely you, with your insistence on diving into every trial and trouble, must recognize that, sometimes, dreams are better."

"Changelings are dying!" I clapped my hands over my mouth and closed my eyes, the echoes of my shout still ringing through the hall. Conversation around me

stopped dead, leaving the rustle of fabric and the pounding of my heart the loudest sounds in the world. Fearfully, I cracked one eye open and looked to the Queen.

She was smiling. Somehow, that was worse than her anger could possibly have been. "Oh, October. Silly little October. Whatever made you think that a few changelings would matter to me? We can always make more."

I lowered my hands, opening both eyes as I struggled to gather the shreds of my composure. "Goblin fruit is bad for Faerie." If she was going to let my outburst go unpunished, I was going to try to reason with her. "It kills changelings. Your subjects. It makes even purebloods careless. Our secrecy is too precarious right now. I urge you to reconsider your position, and ban the stuff from the Mists."

"Mmm," she said, thoughtfully. Then, sounding almost bored: "No."

"Your Majesty, please. I beg you—"

"You urge. You beg. You *raise your voice to me*." Her tone turned suddenly icy as she rose, eyes narrowed, and spat, "*I* am Queen. *My* word is law. Not yours, not your allies, *mine*. Do I make myself clear?"

"Yes, Your Majesty," I whispered. Her anger was terrifying, and not just because of the notes of Banshee fury that I could hear wrapping themselves around the words.

But she wasn't done. "I have tolerated your disrespect time and again. I have tolerated the disrespect of your so-called 'friends.' I am *done*, Sir Daye. I am done listening to your mewling protests, your demands for 'equality,' your cries for justice you have not earned. You have three days to put your affairs in order. At the end of that time, I will expect you to be outside my demesne." Her eyes were cold. "Flee to your liege, if you like; so long as you remain confined within his Duchy, I will not challenge you. I respect his rights as your regent that far. No further. Should you set foot outside the bounds of Shadowed Hills but within the Mists after that time has passed, I will see you brought before my Court on charge of treason. Do I make myself *perfectly* clear?"

I stared at her in horror, trying to absorb what I was hearing. Yes, I had been disrespectful, but I had also saved her Kingdom over and over again. At some point, that should have earned me a little leeway. Instead, it had earned me a faster path to exile.

"That isn't fair," protested Quentin. "She never disobeyed you."

"It is my Kingdom, little fosterling, and I shall ban whomsoever I like from its shores. Watch that I don't ban you alongside her." She turned toward Tybalt. "And you? Are you going to argue for her?"

Please don't, I thought, wishing desperately that he could hear me. *Please, please don't.*

"No," said Tybalt.

"Good. Uncharacteristically wise." The Queen's eyes swung back to me. "Have you any other questions, Sir Daye?"

"No, Your Majesty." I dug my nails into my palms until it felt like they would break the skin. "May I be excused? I have a great deal of packing to do."

She settled back into her throne. "Yes, you may. You and all your merry little band of sycophants."

I curtsied again, not trusting my voice. Then I turned and plunged into the crowd, not pausing to see whether Tybalt and Quentin were behind me. I knew they would be, just like I knew that May and Jazz would already be moving toward the exit. We all got there about the same time, moving through the clumps of whispering and pointing people, some of whom weren't bothering to be subtle about it. My eyes were burning. I resisted the urge to wipe them. I'd be damned before I let the Queen see me cry.

Tybalt caught my wrist before I could charge out into the cave that connected the Queen's knowe to the mortal world. "Let me see you out," he murmured. "*Please*. I wouldn't put it past her to play some final prank if we were to use her front door."

I looked at him, the threatened tears finally beginning to fall, and nodded.

"We shall see you outside," he said to the others, Quentin included. Then he pulled me into the thin shadow cast by a pillar, and out of the world entirely.

The cold wasn't as bad this time, maybe because Tybalt didn't have to focus on pulling two of us through the darkness. He was able to keep me closer to him. My tears froze against my eyelashes. I let them. This wasn't the time for crying. This was the time for getting pissed.

We emerged into the parking lot after what felt like a dozen steps. Tybalt held on only long enough to be sure that I had my feet under me. Then he let go and took a step backward, giving me my space. I loved him even more in that moment. I'm not sure I could have let him go, if our roles had been reversed.

"October—"

"Not here." I shook my head, scraping away my frozen tears with the heel of my hand before grabbing a handful of night air and spinning it into a thin human disguise that wouldn't stand up to any real scrutiny, but would at least keep me from being immediately fingered as inhuman. I was still wearing the gray silk gown the Queen had dressed me in. It matched my mood nicely, although I really wanted a pair of jeans. "We're going to get the others, and we're going to go home, and then we'll talk about this."

"Speaking of the others . . ." Tybalt draped himself in his own human disguise as he looked past me to the beach. I turned to see May, Jazz, and Quentin running across the sand. I finally realized that May and Jazz were still in the dresses they'd been wearing when we arrived. Apparently, the Queen really *did* have it in for my wardrobe.

And for me. She'd banished me from the Mists. The idea was too big to wrap my head around. Exile was a threat she'd always held in reserve. It was riskier than either imprisonment or execution, because it was the one punishment that left me free to look for new allies. It potentially endangered her safety almost as much as it hurt me. It was just the only thing that didn't require real charges; "I don't like your face" was good enough. I never thought she'd do it . . . and she had. I just wasn't sure why goblin fruit was the tipping point.

"Toby! Are you okay?" May nearly tripped over her own shoes as she made the transition from sand to pavement. Jazz caught her, both of them looking at me anxiously.

"Yes. No. I don't know." I was crying. I dug the heel of my hand into my eye again, trying to make the tears stop. "We need to get out of here before she comes after you guys, too."

"Jazz and I will call Danny to come and drive us home."

I dropped my hand, blinking at May. "I . . . what?"

"You need to go see the Luidaeg." May shook her head. "Take Quentin with you if you want, or send him home with us. But if anyone will know a way to make this go away, it's her."

"I appreciate that you did not even pretend I was going to let her go off without some form of backup," said Tybalt dryly.

"I may be a composite of multiple dead people, but I'm not stupid," said May. She kept her eyes on me. "Go see the Luidaeg. Ask her what you should do from here. Because I really don't have any answers."

Jazz, who had been silent up until then, said, "And if her answer is 'there's nothing to be done,' come home and tell us. Because we're going to need those three days to start telling all the changelings in this Kingdom that it's time to find another place to live."

My exile meant the goblin fruit trade wasn't going to stop. Any changelings who didn't leave the Kingdom would be at risk. I shook my head, trying to wrap my mind around the enormity of it all. If there was a way that I could beat this, I didn't see it. Unless the Luidaeg had some kind of magical solution for me . . .

I didn't see any options at all.

FOUR

WE DIDN'T LINGER ON THE BEACH. We were too close to the Queen's knowe for comfort, and the night was slipping through our fingers, already skating down the long slow slope toward dawn. I put my leather jacket back on, drawing it tight. Then Tybalt, Quentin, and I piled into the car while May produced her cell phone from somewhere inside the candy confection of her dress, raising it to her ear. I didn't worry about them. Danny would get them safely home.

Quentin sat quietly in the backseat for the first part of the ride, mirroring Tybalt, who sat stiff and silent next to me. I was just starting to consider turning on the radio when Quentin said, in a careful tone, "Toby? Can I ask you a question?"

"You just did, but you can ask another one." Anger and dread were warring for control of my emotions, and it felt like they were negotiating a team up. I had to find a way to fight this. If the Luidaeg couldn't help me, I still had to come up with something. But what? She was the *Queen*. I was a changeling with some weird skills and a bunch of allies that I cared way too much about. What if she decided to go after them? Tybalt couldn't abandon his Court. Sylvester wouldn't abandon his Duchy. They were going to be sitting ducks if I was forced to leave.

I didn't want to be in this situation. She hadn't given me a choice.

"Why do you hate goblin fruit so much? I mean ..." Quentin paused, choosing his words more carefully before he said, "I mean you hated it even before you knew for sure that people were dying. Lots of things can kill people. You don't hate them all."

"Most deadly things come with a choice. A changeling who tastes goblin fruit once—just once—doesn't get any choice after that." I frowned at him in the rearview mirror. "You've been watching me chase the stuff all over the Bay Area for months. I thought you'd know this by now."

"Yeah, but you started when you were still ..." His voice faltered as he realized he'd almost mentioned Connor. He glanced guiltily at Tybalt. Tybalt, bless him, didn't say anything.

Purebloods don't like to think about death much. It upsets them to remember that people aren't eternal. Connor's death nearly broke me. But he died to save my little girl, and I couldn't shame him by refusing to go on with my own life. "The goblin fruit started showing up on the streets after Connor died," I said. "I was looking ... I don't even know what I was looking for. I was looking for trouble. I found it."

"I thought you were going to die, too," Quentin admitted in a small voice. I stared at his reflection, shocked. That was something he'd never said out loud, no matter how much his behavior told me he was feeling it. He looked down at his hands, twisting them together in his lap, and said, "It's why I kept telling Tybalt where you were going, and how much danger you were putting yourself in. I hoped maybe you'd listen to him, even if you wouldn't listen to me."

Tybalt nodded, confirming Quentin's story. I winced.

"Oak and ash, Quentin, I'm sorry."

"Yeah, well." He raised one shoulder and let it drop again in a classic teenage half-shrug. "When I had to break up with Katie, I sort of felt like dying for a little while. I guess having someone you love *die* has to be a whole lot worse."

"It is," I said honestly. "It's the worst thing you can imagine." I glanced at Tybalt, who was still looking straight ahead, letting us talk without him. I took my right hand off the wheel and placed it on his knee, earning myself a quick, almost grateful look. "But it gets better."

"That's good. It's just . . . you never told me why you started hunting goblin fruit the way you have been. I'm your squire, Toby. I'm supposed to support you while you train me, and I can't do that if you never tell me what's going on. It's my *job* to be here for you." He sounded profoundly frustrated. "People are dying. I get that. I could have helped, if you'd let me."

I took a deep breath, pulling my hand from Tybalt's knee and raking the hair out of my face. Finally, I said, "Let me ask you something. Have you ever tried goblin fruit?"

There was a long pause before Quentin answered, "No. I mean. Some of the older courtiers back home had tried it, but I wasn't old enough when I came here, and Duke Torquill doesn't allow the stuff in his Court."

Quentin was originally from Canada—somewhere near Toronto, if I placed his faint and fading accent correctly. Where near Toronto was something I didn't know. He was a blind foster to the Duchy of Shadowed Hills, which made his parentage and title, if any, a secret until such time as his fosterage ended or his parents chose to reveal themselves. "So you've never had any, but you've talked to people who have. What do they say about it?"

"That it's like going to the deeper lands of Faerie, even if it's only for a little while." Quentin's tone turned disdainful. "I've *been* to the deeper lands. I didn't like it much."

I had to fight the urge to laugh. It would just have offended his dignity, and it wouldn't have been fair: I didn't like the deeper lands much either. Tybalt wasn't so restrained. He snorted. All three of us had wound up in

Annwn, a realm that's supposed to be long-sealed. Our stay had involved a lot of bleeding, mostly on my part, and a lot of pain, for everyone. I was just as glad to be home. "Yeah, but I bet it sounded pretty appealing before you knew what the deeper lands were like."

"I guess so," admitted Quentin.

"Now imagine how amazing that sounds to changeling kids. They're on the outside looking in. They're never going to have as much magic as everybody else. They're not going to live as long as everybody else. Hell, half the courtiers I knew when I was a kid said even setting foot in the deeper lands would strike a changeling dead." It was pure pixie-crap, of course. The first changelings came about because the fae insisted on abducting mortals and carrying them away to their enchanted castles under the hills. If changelings couldn't survive the deeper lands, we'd have known that millennia ago. "Can you see how goblin fruit would sound appealing?"

"Well, sure, but goblin fruit is deadly to changelings. Everybody knows that."

I sighed. Sometimes my squire was such a pureblood that it hurt. "Quentin, believe me, changeling kids get used to being lied to by people who want to keep the best things for themselves. There's always someone who thinks the whole 'it's deadly' thing is one more lie to keep them from being happy. There's always someone willing to try one little taste. And one is all it takes." No one evangelized for goblin fruit like a changeling on their first high, before the first pains of withdrawal hit them. They were true believers, each and every one, and they'd convince all their friends that the warnings were false.

Quentin frowned, disdain fading into puzzlement. "You hate goblin fruit because it messes with changelings? Not because it kills them?"

"It's not just about that, although it's part of it. Goblin fruit is too dangerous. It kills changelings. It endangers the secrecy of Faerie. The more it infects the streets, the more likely it becomes that someone will slip and hand a jar to a human. What happens then? And yeah, I also don't like that it's one more 'we can have this because we're so pure and awesome, and you can't, because your blood is all tainted and gross' reminder that we can't ever be on equal footing."

Quentin paused before he said, "You sound like my dad. He hates goblin fruit. He says it's a divisive element and that it drains resources that should be going toward preserving unity."

"Sounds like a smart guy." I tried to keep my tone light. Quentin didn't mention his parents often. No matter how curious I was, some rules aren't meant to be broken, and that includes the rules that protect the blind fosters. I wouldn't push. Which didn't mean I didn't want to.

"Yeah," said Quentin. "I guess I understand why you hate goblin fruit. I mean, it makes sense, especially with . . . you know, everything."

"You mean me being the only changeling knight in the Kingdom, and constantly dealing with a Queen who hates me?" I asked dryly. "Oh, and now? Banished. Because exile was so what I needed this week."

"Yeah." Quentin sighed. "I wish this didn't have to be your problem."

"Any chance of that just died."

"I know. But I . . ." He met my eyes in the rearview mirror. "I don't want anything to happen to you."

"Nothing's going to happen to me," I said. Then it was my turn to grimace. "Wow. That sounded about as sincere as a used car salesman, huh?"

"I was thinking you sounded as sincere as someone in a horror movie saying, 'I'll be right back.' You won't be right back, unless it's as a head in a bag."

"I've got to talk to May about the stuff you're watching on television."

"Who do you think keeps showing it to me?"

Tybalt chuckled. "He has a point."

"Don't help. I don't think I could handle it if the two of you ganged up on me right now." I pulled up in front of an all-night taqueria, glancing down at my distinctly nonstandard attire before digging my wallet out of the front pocket of my jacket and handling a twenty dollar bill to Quentin. "Go inside. Get as many burritos as this will buy, and get me a large coffee."

"Yes, sir!" He snatched the bill from my hand and was out of the car like a shot, all anxiety forgotten at the sound of the dinner bell. I smiled a little, turning toward Tybalt.

"The Luidaeg likes it when we bring—" I began. His kiss cut off the rest of my sentence. While I was turned away, he had unfastened his seatbelt and closed the distance between us, and now he was pressed to me like a teenage boy after the prom. I fumbled with my own seatbelt until I found the latch and was able to squirm free, wrapping myself around him in turn. His fingers found the back of my neck, tangling in the small wisps of hair not contained by the net of ribbons. I splayed my fingers against his chest, bracing myself without pushing him away, and kissed him like I thought the world was going to end.

We were still like that when the rear door opened and Quentin said, sounding both amazed and a little disgusted, "Don't you need to *breathe*?"

"Ah, you see." Tybalt pulled his mouth away from my throat, turning a lazy, smug eyed smile on Quentin. "I am a King of Cats, and she was a fish for quite some time. We are both very, very good at holding our breath."

"Off." I pushed him away, shaking my head. "You just had to go to the fish place, didn't you? Quentin, did you get my coffee?"

"I like being alive," he said, and passed me the cup.

"Good." I took it, refastened my belt, and started the car, trying to pretend that Tybalt wasn't grinning wickedly at me from the passenger seat. It wasn't easy. "Buckle up."

I let Tybalt hold my coffee as we drove the last mile or so to the Luidaeg's neighborhood. The area where she lived wasn't exactly what you'd call "upscale." Or "nice." Hell, even "livable" was pushing it, although the definition is different when you're a functionally immortal sea witch who likes to be left alone. San Francisco grew up around the Luidaeg. She could live wherever she damn well wanted to.

The streets changed around us as we drove, careful maintenance giving way to benign neglect, then wanton vandalism, and finally the sort of disrepair that implied the residents had abandoned all hope. It was just another facade. The people living in the Luidaeg's shadow enjoyed some of the lowest crime rates in the city. When we had earthquakes, their foundations didn't crack; when it rained for a week, their roofs didn't leak. The residents of the blocks surrounding the Luidaeg's dockside home were her last passive line of defense against strangers, and she took care of them.

No one lived on the Luidaeg's block. There was maintaining a neighborhood, and then there was putting up with neighbors. One was good sense. The other was likely to get someone killed.

I parked on the street, reclaiming my coffee from Tybalt and letting Quentin carry the burritos as we walked down the alleyway to the Luidaeg's door. It was old, faintly bloated wood, set into a frame that looked so water-damaged it might fall apart at any moment. Appearances can be deceiving, especially where the Luidaeg is concerned. I knocked lightly. Then I stepped back, sipped my coffee, and waited.

"Think she's up?" asked Quentin, rummaging through the bag of burritos.

"If she's not, we're probably all about to be torn limb from limb. Get ready to run." I peered into my cup. "Maeve's tits, I think they pumped this stuff up from the center of the Earth. It's not coffee. It's fermented dinosaur blood."

"Cool." Quentin pulled a foil-wrapped burrito out of the bag and began unpeeling it.

I raised an eyebrow. "'Cool'? That's all you have to say?"

"Be glad he's not grilling you about the comet that

killed them all," said a dry voice. We turned, almost in unison, to see the Luidaeg standing in the alley behind us, two paper grocery bags in her arms. She looked faintly puzzled, but not annoyed. I'd take it. "What the fuck are you three doing here?"

The Luidaeg is fond of human profanity, I think because it tends to shock the purebloods. I shrugged. "We were in the neighborhood." I didn't want to tell her I'd been exiled until after she'd agreed to let us in.

"Uh-huh. Is there a burrito in that sack for me?"

"Lobster, shrimp, and every pepper in the store," said Quentin happily.

"Ew," I said, and took the bag. If I left it alone with the two of them, Tybalt and I weren't going to get any.

"You don't have to eat it." She turned her deceptively normal-eyed gaze on me, considering my dress. Finally, she said, "You reek of the bitch-Queen's magic, and you don't normally bring the kitty-cat here. What's wrong?"

"Can we talk about it inside?" I asked. "Please?"

The Luidaeg smiled, showing too many teeth. "I love it when you beg. Come on in." She pushed past us to the door. It swung open at her touch, revealing a dark hallway. She stepped inside, calling, "Hurry up, I don't have all night," without turning back.

"You know, the first time I came here, she used a key to get in," I commented to Quentin, as we followed her.

"I guess she doesn't feel like she has to pretend as much," he replied, pausing long enough to close the door behind him.

The idea that the Luidaeg wasn't pretending for us anymore was reflected by the hall itself, which was pristine, in that slightly shabby, lived-in way older apartments get when they've been well-cared for and well-loved for long enough. The air smelled like clean saltwater, a scent that implied there was a beach somewhere in the house, if we were brave enough to look. Knowing her, I wouldn't have been surprised to find a stretch of shoreline inside the pantry, waiting for beachcombers and human sacrifices.

It was almost a relief when I saw a cockroach scuttle across the floor. No matter how much she cleaned the place up—or how much of the mess had been an illusion—she was still the sea witch we knew and liked more than was probably good for our health.

We followed the Luidaeg down the hall to the kitchen, where she began unpacking her groceries. Tybalt and I stayed in the doorway, watching, while Quentin moved to help her put away the cans. There was no illusion-sheen in the air around her because she wasn't wearing one: she was the oldest among us, and her nature was protean enough that she didn't need anything as crude as an illusion when she wanted to pass for human. She just changed herself.

She looked like she was somewhere in her early twenties, with the fading ghosts of acne scars under the freckles on her cheeks and strips of electrical tape holding her thick brown pigtails in place. I'd seen her fae nature slip through a few times, but never for long, and never all the way. I was pretty sure that the day I saw the Luidaeg's true form would either be the day she killed me, or the day when I had much bigger things to worry about.

She placed a twelve-pack of Diet Coke in the fridge before turning to face me, folding her arms, and saying, "Well?"

"Well?" I echoed. "What 'well'? Did I miss something that would trigger a 'well'?"

"Well, can I have my burrito?" She held out her hand. "And, well, you want to tell me what's going on? You look like you've just seen a ghost, and you wouldn't have come here like this, fresh from Court and with an entourage, because you thought I wanted a burrito. You're not stupid enough to think I wouldn't realize something was up."

"Gee, you sure know how to make a girl feel good." I straightened, dug her burrito out of the sack, and passed it to her. There was another burrito labeled "chicken w/o beans." I handed it to Tybalt before taking a deep breath, putting the bag down on the kitchen table, and saying,

"We finally found proof that the goblin fruit is killing changelings. At least a dozen so far."

"You found a body and waited until the night-haunts came, didn't you?" She took a bite of her burrito, foil and all. Her teeth had turned sharp at some point, more like a shark's than a human's.

"Yeah," I confirmed quietly.

The Luidaeg took another foil-covered bite of burrito and swallowed without chewing before she said, "They must really like you, or they'd have killed you by now. So the stuff is killing changelings. We knew it would, eventually."

"I went to the Queen of the Mists. I had to tell her."

"You what?" The Luidaeg lowered her burrito, the color draining out of her eyes until they were the color of green driftglass, weathered and worn down by the sea. "Mom's tits, Toby, are you *stupid*?"

"I had to know if she knew."

"Let me guess: she did."

"She's the one who's been distributing it." The depth of loathing in my voice didn't surprise me, although maybe it should have. At some point in the drive, my dislike of her had solidified into hatred. She was a murderer, even if Oberon's Law didn't see her that way.

"And? Kings and Queens need money, too, and people like their drugs too much to care about whether or not they're going to be fatal. Hell, sometimes 'it will kill you' is the main appeal."

"It's too fast," said Quentin. We all turned to look at him. He shrugged. "Almost nothing is addictive just because you taste it once. Goblin fruit doesn't give people a choice. You could make someone a peanut butter and jelly sandwich, if you wanted to be a jerk. And there's no way to quit. It doesn't seem . . . I dunno, fair."

"Faerie isn't fair, kid, and if you don't know that, it's high time you learned it." The Luidaeg shook her head. "Fair was never on the table."

"It's not *right*," I said, suddenly annoyed by her casual dismissal of Quentin's concerns. "It's endangering Faerie.

Even if 'fair' was never a consideration, survival was. Is. As long as we're stuck in the human world, we can't afford the risks goblin fruit encourages people to take."

"Better," said the Luidaeg, and took another bite of burrito.

I was warming to my subject. "How are they even growing the stuff? You can't cultivate goblin fruit in the mortal world. You can barely grow it in the Summerlands without a dedicated team of horticulturists who don't have hobbies. Walther tried to cultivate a bush, just so he could chart the life cycle, and he gave up when even doing the whole thing inside Goldengreen didn't make the berries germinate."

"Where does goblin fruit grow naturally?" asked the Luidaeg.

"Tirn Aill, Tir Tairngire, and the Blessed Isles." The answer was automatic. Back when I lived with my mother, I spent hours being trained on the names of all the lands of Faerie, even the ones that I would never live long enough to see.

"Uh-huh. And they've been sealed for centuries, right?"

"Yes, but during the exodus, people brought soil and stuff. I just don't understand why it hasn't all been used up by now. I mean, how long does a pot of dirt from the Blessed Isles stay a pot of dirt from the Blessed Isles, and not a pot of dirt from Marin?"

The Luidaeg smiled. "Now you're asking better questions. Here's the deal with goblin fruit: it keeps showing up on the street because purebloods with the space and magic to grow the bushes like the berries. And where there's a market, people will find a way to get to the product. I hate the shit. It wreaked hell with the Selkie community about two hundred years back, and I don't like anything that screws with the Selkies. But I wasn't able to stop people from selling it, just drive them off my territory. With the Queen backing them and with me in semi-retirement, there's nothing standing in their way."

"Yeah." The Luidaeg didn't like anything that screwed

with the Selkies, except for the Luidaeg. They were her property, in a messed-up way, because they existed due to the horrible murder of most of her descendants. I tried not to think about that too hard. "Are you going to come out of retirement?"

"Can't. Wish I could, but I can't." The Luidaeg shook her head. "I withdrew for a reason. Don't ask me about it. It's one of the things I'm not allowed to tell you."

"Swell." I was aware that the Luidaeg used to be more active than she was these days—the stories about her confirmed that, even if she'd rarely left her apartment for anything but groceries in the years I'd known her. Why that changed was something I didn't know, and that apparently wasn't going to change any time soon.

"All of this is well and good, but it does not touch on what really brought us here," said Tybalt gravely. "October. You need to tell her."

The Luidaeg frowned, gaze sharpening. "Tell me what?"

"The Queen . . ." I took a deep breath. "I asked her about the goblin fruit. I asked her if she would please stop allowing it on the streets."

"And . . . ?" prompted the Luidaeg.

"And I've been exiled. I have three days to get out of the Mists. After that, she's not going to show any leniency with me."

To my surprise, the Luidaeg laughed. "Oh, is that all?" She put the remainder of her burrito down on the counter before turning to me. Her teeth were back to normal. "See, the trouble here is that once someone has a throne, it's damn hard to tell them they're doing it wrong. Three days is a lot of time, if you know how to use it."

I stared at her. *"What?"*

"I'm just saying, you have more resources at your disposal than you think you do, and she's letting her own prejudices blind her. You're just a changeling, after all. What could you possibly do to hurt her?" She grinned broadly. "You can do a lot. For starters, you can try talking to some of the people who knew King Gilad and find out what they can tell you."

Quentin and Tybalt looked at her blankly.

For once, I wasn't the last one in the room to get what the Luidaeg was hinting at, and I didn't like the feeling very much. I stared at her. She raised an eyebrow, clearly content to wait me out if that was what it took. Finally, slowly, I asked, "Luidaeg, if there's something you want me to know, why don't you just tell me?"

"Because I can't." Her smile slipped, replaced by an expression of deep frustration. "This is one of those areas where I'm bound and counter-bound until I can't see straight. Unless you know the right questions, I can't give you the answers you need."

I slammed back the rest of my taqueria coffee in a long, profoundly unsatisfying gulp. Wiping my mouth, I said, "Just one question, then. Can the people who knew King Gilad help me take down the Queen?"

"Yes."

"Okay, then. So it's time to play scavenger hunt." I looked at Tybalt and Quentin, who were watching me hopefully, and sighed. "Okay. Just one more question."

The Luidaeg gave me a flat, frankly disbelieving look. "Really."

"Yes, really."

"What is it?"

"Can I have one of your Diet Cokes? Because I'm not up for saltwater coffee right now." And if I was going to go talk to the only people who I knew for sure had known King Gilad before he died, I was going to need more caffeine. Hell, I was going to need a caffeine IV.

The Luidaeg blinked at me. Then she laughed, indicating the fridge with one hand. "Help yourselves."

"That's what you're always telling me to do," I said, and went to get myself a soda.

FIVE

WE LEFT THE LUIDAEG'S about half an hour later, after burritos and sodas had been consumed. Give me another six cups of coffee and I might start feeling normal, if not for the whole "counting down to exile" thing. Tybalt didn't even complain as we walked back to the car. He didn't trust the Queen not to have guards out looking for me, and, consequently, he wasn't willing to take the Shadow Roads if I wasn't with him. I wanted to call him paranoid, but after the night we'd had, I couldn't. It's not paranoia if they are really out to get you.

"Can we listen to a good station? Please?" asked Quentin, climbing into the backseat. "Something recorded this century, maybe?"

"Says the kid who listens to country music," I said. I shook my head, starting the car. "No radio. We're going to talk."

Tybalt raised an eyebrow, looking at me. "Talk?"

"Yeah, talk. Both of you: what do you know about King Gilad?"

Quentin spoke first: "Are you asking to test whether I've been paying attention in my history lessons, or because you don't know?"

"Both," I admitted. "I know who he was, but that's about it. Now spill."

"If you get anything wrong, I will know," added Tybalt helpfully.

"Swell," said Quentin. "Um, Gilad Windermere became King of the Mists—"

"King *in* the Mists," corrected Tybalt. I turned to frown at him. "The proper form of the title. Your current regent does not make use of it."

"In, of, whatever," said Quentin. "He took over in 1800 after his parents, Denley and Nola Windermere, died in their beds. No one was ever accused in their deaths, but most people assumed they were poisoned. No fingers were pointed at the Prince, since he was extremely open about not wanting to take the throne yet."

"I knew they were assassinated." I grimaced. "Wasn't Oleander already known here?"

"There had been sightings," said Tybalt. "There was some effort made to blame the deaths on her, but nothing could be proven before she disappeared. It was fifty years before she darkened these shores again."

"Even dead, she can ruin my day." Oleander de Merelands had been a paid assassin and major threat right up to the day I killed her. I didn't want to kill her, but she didn't leave me any choice, and I'd do it again in a heartbeat if it would keep her from hurting the people I loved.

"Well, she ruined Gilad's pretty good, too. He was King in the Mists from 1800 until he died in the 1906 earthquake. His knowe was lost at the same time. Um ... he never married, and there was concern the Kingdom would have to petition the High King to have a new monarch officially recognized when the current Queen appeared, said she was Gilad's daughter, and took the throne. She had the backing of a lot of local nobles, and I guess they just sort of decided it was easier not to involve the High Court in a matter of local succession."

"Not all the local nobles backed her claim," said Tybalt. "She was a haughty thing even then, and she put up the hackles of many of the landholders. Most of them are gone now, fled for kinder political climates."

"Or buried in shallow graves," I guessed.

Tybalt nodded grimly. "Nothing has ever been proven, of course."

"Naturally." I turned onto a side street, listening to the engine whine as we climbed one of San Francisco's many hills.

"Where are we going?" asked Quentin. "Home's the other way."

"Yes, and Goldengreen is this way."

"Ah," said Tybalt. He sounded approving. "The Lordens?"

"The Lordens," I confirmed. The San Francisco Art Museum houses the doors to Goldengreen, the knowe held once by Countess Evening Winterrose, and once by me, before I weaseled out of my promotion. I'd passed my lands and title to Dean Lorden, eldest son of the Duchess of Saltmist, our local Undersea neighbor. His parents, Patrick and Dianda, were also contemporaries of King Gilad. The old King had been an attendant at their wedding—and if there was a way to speak to them without going into the Undersea, it was by visiting their son.

"A good choice," Tybalt said. "Your liege knew Gilad, but he was not part of the royal Court. Patrick Lorden was, before he met his lady wife, and Dianda Lorden was a contemporary who spent a great deal of time in Gilad's halls."

"I'm glad you approve." I started down the winding road to the San Francisco Art Museum, a series of white stone buildings right at the edge of a cliff. Maybe some cities would have looked at the priceless treasures housed in the museum and thought, "Hey, let's put these where a single bad storm can't destroy everything," but not San Francisco. We're a coastal city, and if that means a few expressionist artists get their oeuvres ruined by tsunamis, so be it.

"I just want to see what Dean's done with the place," said Quentin. He sounded almost normal, which I took as a good sign. The more stable we all were, the better.

It was almost three in the morning, and while it wasn't dawn yet, the night was rapidly fading. The museum grounds were deserted. Nothing moved save for the three of us, making our way across the parking lot to a small footpath that led down the gentle slope of the grounds toward the edge of the cliff.

"Are you sure we can't use one of the entrances that *doesn't* involve jumping into empty space?" asked Quentin.

"This is one of the public entrances, which means we don't need a key to use it," I said. "It also means we're not being rude by coming in without an invitation. Come on. I was in charge of this knowe long enough to know where the doors are."

Quentin gave me a dubious look. "You were never in charge of the knowe. You borrowed it from the pixies. How do you know they didn't move the door?"

"Shut up." I grabbed one his hands and one of Tybalt's, pulling them along as I stepped off the edge of the cliff. The world did a brief twist and roll around us, as disorienting as a carnival hall of mirrors, and then we were standing in the knowe's main hall with our knees slightly bent to absorb an impact that had never come. Quentin pulled his hand out of mine and straightened, fussily smoothing his hair. Tybalt did almost the same thing on my other side. I stifled a smile as I straightened in turn and looked around the hall.

I only held Goldengreen for a few months, after the Queen of the Mists essentially tricked me into taking it. During that time, we'd started the process of cleaning up and restoring the place, transforming it from Evening's sterile stronghold into something more welcoming. Dean had continued that process since I'd ceded the knowe to him. The last of Evening's furnishings and ornaments were gone, replaced by potted trees whose branches were alive with pixies. A rug patterned with golden primroses on a green background stretched the length of the hall, and steadily gleaming lights filled the chandeliers.

The walls were softened with tapestries showing scenes from both Undersea and San Francisco fae history. The one nearest where I stood showed Lily, the

Lady of the Tea Gardens, preparing a tea service for my mother. I put a hand over my mouth as I looked at it.

Lily was the last of Oleander's victims. I miss her every day.

"Toby? What are you *wearing*?"

We all turned toward the voice. Marcia, the Seneschal of Goldengreen—my only formal appointment as Countess, and one Dean had been more than willing to retain—was standing in the nearest doorway, a dishtowel in her hands, staring at us. She had fae ointment smeared around her eyes, allowing her to see through illusions. It was necessary; without the stuff, she wouldn't be able to see half of Faerie, including the pixies that plagued her on a daily basis.

I lowered my hand, forcing a smile. "Hey, Marcia. I just came from the Queen. Is the Count in? I need to ask him for a favor."

"Toby!" She slung the dishtowel over her shoulder as she ran over and hugged me hard. Then she hugged Quentin in much the same way. Tybalt didn't get a hug, but he did get a smile and a small curtsy. Only when that was finished did she say, "The Count's in. He'll be thrilled to see you. I think he's pretty much bored out of his skull, but he's being too noble and stupid to say anything."

I laughed. "It's good to see you, too, Marcia. Let's go save the bored."

"Your noblest endeavor yet," said Marcia, gesturing for us to follow her to the central courtyard.

Goldengreen's courtyard was probably intended to host genteel entertainments and noble proclamations. It had been somewhat repurposed by its current inhabitants, who had converted it into a tiered garden, complete with trees, flowers, and beds of moss. Tree frogs chirped from somewhere high overhead as we entered. I looked up into the branches. No frogs, although I did see a bogey scurrying through the canopy, currently shaped like a spider the size of a terrier.

"I love what you've done with the place," I said, looking down again. "I mean, we planted, but you've *grown*."

Dean Lorden, Count of Goldengreen, blinked as he raised his head from the book he'd been reading. Then he grinned, standing. "Sir Daye! I didn't know you were going to visit today!" His attention switched to my squire. "Quentin. You're looking well."

"You, too," said Quentin.

He was right: Dean *was* looking well. Life on land agreed with him. As the son of a Merrow and a Daoine Sidhe, Dean was born with a fifty-fifty chance of taking after his mother. Unfortunately for him, he lost that coin toss, although it could have been worse: he could have been a merman who couldn't breathe water. Instead, he was basically a normal Daoine Sidhe whose mother happened to be the Duchess of the largest local Undersea demesne. Dean had spent the first eighteen years of his life in the ocean, until he was kidnapped as part of a ploy to start a war between the land and sea. The war didn't happen; Dean and his brother, Peter, didn't die; and when it was over, Dean didn't go back to Saltmist. Not to stay, anyway. He was the Count of Goldengreen now, and that meant he finally got the chance to start living on the land.

Dean had his father's hair, bronze with a light sheen of greenish verdigris, and his mother's eyes, the blue-black color of deep water. His skin had acquired some color since he claimed Goldengreen; while he was still pale, he no longer looked like a ghost. He was wearing jeans and a gray pirate shirt which would have looked silly if he hadn't been so clearly comfortable. His feet were bare, exposing slightly webbed toes.

"I didn't know we were going to visit today either," I admitted. "But I've just been to see the Queen, and now I need your help."

"Anything," said Dean. He glanced involuntarily to his left hand. The stump of his little finger had healed cleanly, but it remained a reminder of what he had gone through while he was held captive.

"I need to talk to your parents. Do you think you could call them and see if they can come?"

"Um ... sure?" Dean blinked. "Why do you need to talk to my parents?"

I took a deep breath, stalling while I tried to decide exactly what to tell him. In the end, it was easiest to go with the truth. "I went to talk to the Queen about the goblin fruit that's been flooding the streets. Things got a little ... heated ... and she banished me."

"From her Court?" asked Dean.

"From her Kingdom. I have three days. The Luidaeg told me to talk to people who knew King Gilad. That means your parents."

There was a clatter behind us. We all turned to see Marcia picking up a tray of sandwiches from the floor. "Sorry!" she said. "Sorry, sorry, I tripped over my own feet, sorry."

"It's okay, I do that all the time," said Dean. He was still staring at me, looking a little stunned. "Walking is hard."

"Gravity sucks," I agreed. "So can you call them?"

"Didn't you go to the Undersea on your own last time you needed to talk to Mom? She's sort of land-averse." He hesitated before adding, "And maybe she could let you stay in Saltmist for a while."

I grimaced. "Okay, yes, I went to the Undersea last time, but I had to let the Luidaeg turn me into a Merrow in order to do that. I'm not a big water person. Your mother's land-aversion? Multiply that times a thousand and you've got me and water. Oh, and I'm even less fond of being turned into things. So if there's any chance she's willing to come up here, that would be much, much better." I didn't touch the idea of my hiding in the Undersea. Horrifying as it was to contemplate, there was a very real chance that things could go that way.

"Toby was a fish for a while," Quentin informed him, in a matter-of-fact tone.

"Oh, yeah?"

"Yeah. Fourteen years."

"Yes, I remember when MTV played videos and only geeks had the Internet, okay?" I crossed my arms and scowled, temporarily forgetting that I was supposed to be asking Dean for a favor. People are more likely to do you favors when you're nice to them. "Now can you call your parents? *Please*?"

"Of course." Dean shook his head. "I probably shouldn't be relieved, but I'm *so* bored. It turns out ruling a County full of people who don't want you to tell them what to do doesn't actually take up all that much time."

I bit my lip so as not to smile, having experienced something very similar during my time at Goldengreen. "You don't say."

"I do." Dean sighed. "I'll go call my folks. Be right back."

"We'll be here." I was surprised when I first learned that the Undersea has DSL and phone service. I shouldn't have been. Faerie likes to stay in touch as much as anybody.

Marcia returned with a fresh tray of sandwiches while we waited. She had a large mug in one hand. "I thought you could use this," she said, handing it to me.

"You are a *genius*," I said, before taking a long drink of coffee. "Oh, that's good."

"The Luidaeg didn't have any coffee," said Quentin.

"Well, then, I'm amazed Toby hasn't started stabbing people yet." Marcia looked at me frankly. "It looks like you've been eating, and I can't see any circles under your eyes. Have you started actually sleeping?"

"Tybalt makes her," said Quentin.

"That's wonderful," said Marcia, and handed Tybalt a sandwich.

I raised an eyebrow. "You three realize I'm right here, don't you?"

"Yes, but as you can't be trusted to take care of yourself, we're doing it for you." Marcia thrust her tray in my direction. "Sandwich?"

I sighed. "Sure." I may be stubborn, but I know when I've been beaten. I took a sandwich. Quentin took two. "How are things around here?"

"Good. The Count's getting his land-legs, and he's a thoughtful boy who'll be a thoughtful man someday. Sooner rather than later, if he has his way, but he's only eighteen. We're not pushing him yet." Marcia cocked her head. "How about you? Are you doing well?"

"I am, yeah, except for the whole banishment thing." The admission would have seemed impossible a year ago, when I'd lost my boyfriend and my daughter on the same brutal night. But time heals all wounds, and mine were healing.

"Banished. *You*, by *her*, over goblin fruit. I never thought I'd see the day." Marcia scowled. "It's filthy stuff. The Count doesn't allow it in the knowe, and we've managed to keep everyone away from it, but that can't last forever. Not with the way it's spreading."

"I don't like goblin fruit either." Marcia was a quarter-blood, more human than fae. Goblin fruit would probably kill her even faster than it killed most changelings. I took another drink of my coffee, and said, "I just can't focus on that until I've dealt with the banishment. I'm not sure what King Gilad has to do with my being kicked out of the Kingdom, but when the Luidaeg tells me to do something, I try to do it. If it can get me un-banished, it's worth the time."

"And if not, at least there are sandwiches," said Quentin.

"Way to look on the bright side there," I said.

He grinned. "I know."

Marcia, on the other hand, looked genuinely concerned. "Toby, are you sure that challenging the Queen's declaration is, you know, a *good* idea?"

"No," I admitted. "But it's the only one I've got. She's not going to stop the goblin fruit, and she's not going to let me stay in her Kingdom. Right now, you could be handing out goblin fruit sandwiches in her Court and you wouldn't actually be doing anything wrong."

"Yes," said Marcia bitterly. "I know."

Oberon's Law is supposedly the one unbreakable rule in Faerie: thou shalt not kill. Or at least, thou shalt not kill purebloods. Killing humans is okay. So is killing changelings. As a changeling who's known and loved a lot of humans in my time, I'm not a big fan of the way the Law is enforced. I'm even less a fan of the way the Law is sometimes used: as a weapon. I killed a man named Blind Michael. It was self-defense, which is allowed under the Law. I was still considered guilty of his murder by the Queen, who would gladly have put me to death if I hadn't been pardoned by the High King. At the same time, the bastards who were peddling goblin fruit to changelings could kill hundreds of people and not even get a slap on the wrist.

The Luidaeg was right: Faerie isn't fair.

"Toby will find a way to fix it," said Quentin. "She always does."

"I wish I had as much faith in me as you do," I said.

"Believing in you is not your job," said Tybalt mildly. "It's ours."

"He's right," said Marcia. "So let us work, and eat another sandwich."

"Yes, ma'am." Between the burritos, the sandwiches, and the caffeine, I was starting to feel better—or at least less hungry, which was sort of the same thing. Now all I needed was something to hit, and I'd be doing great.

We chatted about the state of the County, our lives, and Marcia's sandwiches until Dean came back, bare feet slapping against the stone. He looked entirely pleased with himself.

"Mom and Dad are on their way up, and they'd be glad to find you here upon arrival, so don't leave," he said.

"First part, formal message, second part, Dean's addition," I said to Quentin.

He nodded. "Definitely."

Dean's smile didn't waver. "Hey, this is the most interesting thing that's happened all week. Let me enjoy it."

"My apologies, sire, if we endangered your enjoyment." My mocking bow was accentuated by the coffee mug I was still holding in one hand.

Dean laughed. "You should come to visit more often. I think the knowe has missed you. I know the pixies have."

"I've been busy," I said. That, and Goldengreen, pleasant as it was these days, was altogether too haunted by the memories of my dead friends. As someone else's home, I could appreciate it and even enjoy being there, for a little while. Anything longer than that, and I was likely to break down crying.

"Still, you're always welcome here." Dean took one of the last remaining sandwiches from the tray. "My parents will meet us in the cove-side receiving room. Come with me?"

"There's a cove-side receiving room?" I asked, putting my mug down on Marcia's tray and moving to follow Dean into the hall.

"The door was locked when I got here. I guess you didn't get around to opening it."

"I guess not." Or it hadn't been there when I was in charge of Goldengreen. I've long suspected that knowes were not only alive, they were capable of thought, even if the thoughts of a building were incomprehensible to the rest of us. Goldengreen had definitely expressed its preferences to me more than once when it was supposedly mine. Having a new Count who came from the Undersea could have inspired the knowe to form a more direct connection between the land and the water. As long as that was all it did, I was still comfortable walking down the spiraling stone stairway toward the distant sound of water lapping against sand.

There was a large room at the bottom of the stairs, maybe half the size of the central courtyard, with a high ceiling inlaid in quartz and mother-of-pearl. I wondered whether Dean had noticed how similar it was in design to the ceiling in his mother's arrival chamber, or whether he'd dismissed it as being some sort of architectural standard for rooms like this.

The floor was treated redwood, which required more upkeep than marble but would be less slippery when wet. That was a good thing, since only two thirds of the room actually *had* a floor. The wood ended at a narrow strip of clean white sand, and then the water began, extending out into the ocean. Everything smelled of clean saltwater and the Summerlands sea, much like the Luidaeg's apartment.

Tybalt sniffed the air, and smiled. Quentin looked curiously around. "This is a neat room," he said.

"Yes, it is," I replied, directing my comment toward the distant ceiling. Everyone deserves a few compliments. Even a building.

The surface of the water rippled, and the sleek black-haired head of Duchess Dianda Lorden of Saltmist broke through. Her husband was a few strokes behind her. Patrick lacked his wife's natural advantages where swimming was concerned. Honestly, I was impressed he could make the trip at all, even with the aid of the water-breathing potion her Court alchemists brewed for him. Dean grinned and waved when he saw his parents, looking less like a Count and more like an ordinary teenage boy living on his own for the first time.

Patrick stood, waving back, and began wading through the waist-deep water toward us. Dianda remained low, swimming until the water got too shallow, and then pulling herself the rest of the way to the sand. Instead of legs, she had a jewel-toned tail, scaled in shades of purple and blue, which she stretched out as she reclined. Her flukes barely broke the surface.

"Your Grace," I said, bowing to her. "Patrick." He was technically the Ducal consort and not the Duke, which made formality a little less important with him.

Not that Dianda looked that formal. Without legs, she didn't need pants, and her top was made of blue cotton, embroidered around the neck and cuffs with stylized green kelp. "Hello, October," she said, sunny smile entirely at odds with her sour disposition the first time we met. Then again, at the time, her children were being held hostage, so I couldn't blame her. "Forgive me if I don't get up. It's harvest season for us in the Undersea, and I've been in the fields every night for tides. I'm too tired to deal with having legs right now."

"It's cool," I said. "Just don't expect me to come into the water and say hello."

"You need to get over your hydrophobia."

"Hey. I'm standing next to the ocean, talking to a mermaid, not freaking out. I think I'm on my way to recovery." Just to prove my point, I sat down cross-legged on the edge of the wooden dock, putting us on the same eye level. Quentin did the same. Dean, meanwhile, splashed out into the water and sat down next to his mother, not seeming to care that his jeans were getting drenched. Tybalt stayed a few feet back, well away from the shoreline.

"Dean said you wanted to talk about King Gilad." Patrick sat down on the dock as well, although he chose the other side of his wife. We made a funny little line, like a beach party gone weirdly wrong. "I'm a little confused about why you'd need to. Gilad was a great man, and a good friend, but he's been dead for a long time."

"Yeah, I know. That's why I wanted to talk to the two of you. And, well. There's another thing." I took a deep breath. "I've been banished from the Mists."

Dianda frowned. "What?"

"The Queen banished me for trying to get her to stop distributing goblin fruit. I went to the Luidaeg, and she told me to ask about King Gilad. I don't know what talking about the Queen's father is supposed to accomplish, but . . ."

"It would help if he had been her father," countered Dianda, frown fading into her more customary scowl.

I stared at her. "Wait—what?"

"Di . . ." said Patrick warningly.

"No. Don't use your 'honey, play nice' voice on me. If she's looking into Gilad because of that spindrift *bitch* who claimed his throne, I'm going to tell her the truth." Dianda turned back to me. "She's *not* Gilad's daughter. I don't know what kind of whaleshit political insanity went on up here when she stepped forward—I was busy rebuilding my own Duchy at the time—but there's no way she's a Windermere."

"The earthquake did massive damage in Saltmist," said Patrick. "Our air-breathers were trapped for months while we made repairs, and our water-breathers were busy cleaning up the gardens, rebuilding the farms, and a hundred other things. I didn't even know Gilad was dead until after his memorial."

"What do you mean, there's no way she's a Windermere?" I asked. "Is it because she's a mixed-blood? Gilad was never married—"

"My own children are mixed-bloods," said Dianda. "I have no issues with her heritage. Just with the fact that her heritage contains no Tuatha de Dannan. And Gilad Windermere was a pureblooded Tuatha de Dannan."

I didn't say anything. I just gaped at her, feeling like an idiot.

As a Dóchas Sidhe, I have a gift for determining the makeup of someone's blood. All blood-workers can do it, to one degree or another, but I'm what you might call an untrained savant when it comes to identifying the elements of a person's fae heritage. The Queen of the Mists had Sea Wight, Siren, and Banshee blood . . . and not a drop of Tuatha de Dannan. I should have realized that she wasn't related to King Gilad years ago.

"Could the Tuatha have been removed from her?" asked Tybalt, before I could recover the capacity to speak. "There is at least one hope chest in the Kingdom. There is also Amandine to be considered."

Hope chests could change the balance of an individual's blood. So could my mother—and so could I. "Mom might have been able to, I guess," I said slowly, "but why would anyone want to keep three different bloodlines and give up a fourth? It doesn't make sense." The more mixed a person's fae heritage is, the more likely it is that they'll become either physically or mentally unstable. Some types of fae don't play nicely, and when you're talking about people who can exist on the bottom of the ocean or in the heart of a volcano, the fighting can be very literal. Almost every mixed-blood I've ever known eventually snapped, driven to madness by the conflict living inside their own veins.

One day, I was going to offer to shift the Lorden boys all the way to either Daoine Sidhe or Merrow. One day. But Daoine Sidhe and Merrow were both descendants of Titania, which made the boys more likely to be stable than a mixture of Titania and Maeve. And once a decision like that is made, it can't be taken back. I wanted to give them time to figure out who they were and where they wanted to be before I made them any promises.

"Amandine never laid hands on that girl," said Dianda. "When we came to her Court to offer our regrets and our aid, she was already holding herself apart, and your mother was nowhere to be seen. She made it clear that the Undersea was not welcome in the Courts of the land. We left after that. We had our own tides to tend."

"So if Mom didn't mess with the Queen's blood, there's honestly no way she could be Gilad's daughter." The Queen of the Mists, my old nemesis, the woman who once tried to have me executed for murder . . . she wasn't even rightfully our ruler?

If I was distressed, Quentin was downright distraught. "That's not right," he said. "She should never have been allowed to do that. The High King—"

"They never called for the High King, and he was busy elsewhere when this happened," Patrick shrugged. "North America is large, Quentin. It's more than one man, even a man like High King Sollys, can oversee. Sometimes he has to take the Kingdoms at their word. When the Mists said all was well here, he spent his attention where it seemed more needed."

For a moment, Quentin looked like he was going to protest. Then he sighed, sagging, and said, "I don't like politics."

"Then you are a very wise boy," said Tybalt.

"No one likes politics," said Dianda. "On the plus side, it gives me a lot of excuses to shout at people. I like that part."

"Mom's great at shouting," said Dean.

"Hang on," I said, raising my hand in a futile signal for quiet. I was still reeling from the idea that the Queen of the Mists wasn't our rightful ruler. If I didn't focus on something, I was going to scream. "How can you all be so *calm* about this?"

"Because we've had a long time to deal with the knowledge," said Dianda. "King Gilad was a good ruler, and she has done her best to undermine his legacy at every turn. He believed in maintaining strong ties with the Undersea; she cut them as soon as she could. He believed changelings had a place in fae society, that we owed them that much, since we were their parents and originals. She did her best to banish changelings from the Courts. She even took us to war against the Kingdom of Silences because they dared to protest the way the changelings here were being treated. I'm so sorry she's banished you. You are always welcome in the Undersea."

There was a moment of silence as we all considered Dianda's words. Finally, I sighed. "Great. I guess I know what we're going to be doing this week."

"What's that?" asked Quentin.

I tried to smile. It came out feeling more like a grimace. Maybe that was a better reflection of my feelings. "We're going to overthrow the Queen."

SIX

WE EXCUSED OURSELVES AFTER THAT. Once it had fully sunk in that the woman who had banished me wasn't the legitimate ruler of the Mists, there was really nowhere else for the conversation to go. Dean needed some time with his parents. We needed to go home and reassure May and Jazz that we hadn't been arrested, deported, or worse.

It was another quiet drive. We were nearly back to the house before Quentin asked, "Toby? Are we really going to overthrow the Queen of the Mists?"

Tybalt looked at me out of the corner of his eye, clearly interested in my answer. I took a deep breath and held it for a few seconds before letting it out and nodding. "I don't know. But I'm going to try."

"Who would you put on the throne?" asked Tybalt mildly.

"See, there's the stumper. She has no kids, and even if she did, they wouldn't have a legitimate claim, since *she* doesn't have a legitimate claim. She was able to take the throne because there was no known heir. The Windermere line died with King Gilad. I guess that means she'd be as valid a Queen as anyone, if she could get the High King to confirm her as the start of a new royal line, but she's been on the throne so long . . ."

"If she knew she wasn't King Gilad's heir, and she took the throne anyway, that's treason," said Quentin. "We could tell the High King now."

"If we can prove she wasn't Gilad's heir, sure," I said, feeling even more daunted by the scope of this potentially treasonous notion. In the mortal world, contesting someone's claim to a throne after a century had passed might have seemed excessive. In Faerie, it was likely to be filed under "guess it's Tuesday." "But we need something more concrete than the word of the changeling she's just banished if we want the High King to take this seriously. If we make a false accusation, we won't live to make a true one."

"So we find proof," said Quentin.

"I do enjoy a challenge," said Tybalt.

We were quiet for the rest of the drive home. Cagney and Lacey—my half-Siamese cats—were sitting in the kitchen window when we pulled into the driveway. They looked at us disapprovingly as we got out of the car. "You'd think dating a King of Cats would get them to cut me a little slack," I said.

Quentin snorted. "Are you kidding? The cats probably think you're a social climber."

"Something like that," said Tybalt.

"I hate you both," I said, walking to the back door. I unlocked it, pushing it open and calling, "It's us. Where is everybody?"

"We're in the dining room!" May called back.

We found them sitting at the dining room table. May was cutting pictures out of a magazine. Jazz was armed with a hot glue gun, a plaster unicorn head, and a box of artificial gems in various colors and sizes. I stopped in the doorway. "Do I want to know?"

"It helps us stay calm," said Jazz, hot gluing a bright purple teardrop to the unicorn's cheek.

"How did it go?" asked May.

"The Luidaeg told me to talk to people who'd known King Gilad before he died," I said. "So we went to Goldengreen to talk to the Lordens."

"And?" prompted May.

"Dianda and Patrick were happy to talk to us about King Gilad," I said. "The trouble is, that just made things worse."

May frowned. "How could they make things worse than 'we have a goblin fruit problem and I've been banished from the Kingdom'? Is the Undersea being attacked by giant squid?"

"I think the giant squid thing is pretty much normal for them, but no. According to Dianda, the Queen of the Mists isn't King Gilad Windermere's daughter. Which means she's not legitimately our Queen; she's been holding a throne that wasn't hers for all these years, and no one did anything about it."

"Which goes a long way toward explaining her policies regarding the Undersea," noted Tybalt. "Most of the nobility on land was behind her, or was mysteriously absent. I doubt our sea-going cousins would have been so accommodating."

Jazz yelped. I turned. She was sucking the side of her thumb. "Sorry," she said, voice muffled by her hand. "I got distracted listening to you and hot glued myself to my unicorn."

"Right. See, this is why I don't think anyone in this house should be allowed to use power tools." I shook my head. "Anyway, now we need to figure out how to prove that Dianda is right about the Queen. And we have to do it all in three days, since otherwise I'm going to be committing treason by correspondence course."

"We all are," said May. I blinked at her. She laughed, a little wearily. "Do you honestly think Jazz and I will be staying if you go? Oh, and Quentin? He may be fostered to Shadowed Hills, but he's your squire. He goes where you do, unless you decide to leave him behind."

"Which you're not going to do," said Quentin quickly.

"I have a Court to tend to," said Tybalt. My heart sank a little, even though I had already known that would be his answer. Then, to my surprise, he continued, "It will take me some time to hand my duties off to Raj. When that is done, I will find you."

I turned to stare at him. "What . . . ?"

"I am a cat, October. I have a sense of duty, because I am also a man, but no cat can be held down by duty forever. Eventually, we must go where we wish to be, not where we are told." Tybalt smiled slightly at the expression on my face. "A simple banishment is not enough to see you quit of me, little fish."

"Is it just me, or is getting hot in here?" asked May, causing Jazz to break into a peal of laughter. I wrinkled my nose at her, but I was secretly relieved. I would have either thrown myself at him or blushed myself to death in a few more seconds, and neither of those was a great option.

"You are all evil." I slicked the wisps of hair that had escaped their net of ribbons back from my face with both hands, releasing the illusion that had been making me look human in the same gesture. "Okay. We have three problems. If the Queen of the Mists isn't supposed to be in charge, who is? How do we find them? And how do we depose a sitting monarch who has her very own private army?"

"Remember when our biggest problem was 'who turned the laundry pink'?" asked May. Then she sighed. "Yeah. Me neither."

"Your guess is as good as mine on all of these topics," said Tybalt. "Even in my misspent youth, I never attempted to depose a monarch of the Divided Courts. Only my father, and I doubt our means of succession would hold in the Courts of Oberon."

"Probably not, but . . ." I paused. "Maybe we don't need to guess about any of this."

"What?" said May.

"What?" echoed Jazz and Quentin.

"Li Qin has a Library card." I dug my phone out of my jacket pocket. "Maybe she can get me a temporary pass or something."

Tybalt blinked. "That is a surprisingly thoughtful, nonviolent solution."

I stuck my tongue out at him as I scrolled through my

contact list, finally locating the entry for Li Qin Zhou, current acting regent of Dreamer's Glass. She was the widow of Countess January O'Leary of Tamed Lightning, and the adoptive mother of Countess April O'Leary, also of Tamed Lightning. She was also the only person I knew who might be able to get me into the local Library.

The phone rang twice before Li Qin picked up, with a cheerful, "October! I wasn't expecting to hear from you today. Has Treasa turned up?"

"Not as such, no." Duchess Treasa Riordan was technically the regent of Dreamer's Glass. It was a real pity she'd gone and gotten herself stranded in Annwn, leaving Li Qin to mind her fiefdom. And by "real pity," I mean "too bad she didn't do it sooner." "I need to ask for a favor."

"Anything. I owe you."

"Yeah, you do, but you might want to hear what I need before you agree to it. Can you get me a Library pass?"

There was a pause before Li Qin asked, "May I know why you need one?"

"Stuff. Important stuff. I'm not going to burn the place down or anything, I just need to look a few things up, and the Library seems like the best starting point."

There was a longer pause. Then Li Qin said, "I know when you're not telling me everything."

"Fine. The Queen just exiled me from the Kingdom. I have three days to get out. I'm sure you'll hear about it in short order, since neither Dreamer's Glass nor Tamed Lightning were on the list of places it's okay for me to go and hide. I need to get into the Library to find out whether there's anything I can do to keep myself here."

"Why didn't you say so in the first place? The Librarian owes me a few favors, and I suppose it's time I collect. I just . . . have you ever *used* a Library before?"

"Not in the fae sense," I said.

"All right. I'll see what I can do. If I can get her to agree, I'll call you."

"Okay. That's cool. I appreciate it."

Li Qin laughed. "Of all the things I expected you to ask me for, Toby, a Library pass was not high on the list."

"I'm full of surprises. Open roads, Li."

"Kind fires," she responded, and hung up.

I turned back toward the others. "Li Qin's going to see if she can get us into the Library."

"You didn't say 'us,'" said Tybalt, voice suddenly sharp. "You just said you needed a pass."

"Oh, Maeve's teeth. I'll explain when she calls me back, okay?"

Tybalt nodded. He didn't look completely mollified. I'd worry about that later.

"I still can't believe the Queen is doing this," said Quentin.

I wanted to hug him and say that it was all going to be okay. I wasn't going to do that, though. I try not to lie to my friends. "Why not?" I asked. "She doesn't like me. The murder trial should have tipped you off about that, even if nothing else did. I gave her an excuse, and she took it."

"Not a good excuse," said Tybalt.

"It didn't have to be." I plucked at the gray silk fabric of my dress. "I'm going to go upstairs and change. Then we're going to call Sylvester, and—"

My phone rang. Or rather, my phone chirped like a techno remix of a cricket. I pulled it out of my pocket, frowning at the display, which indicated that Li Qin was calling. Motioning for the others to hang on, I raised it to my ear. "Li. *Please* tell me you have good news."

"I got you a Library pass," said Li Qin.

"Oh, thank Oberon." I flashed a thumbs-up at the others. "So how does this Library pass thing work? Do I need to come to San Jose and pick up a note or something?"

"No note—the Librarian is expecting you. I'll text you the Library's current physical address. It moves around more than most knowes, because of the way it's anchored." Li Qin sounded concerned. "Do you want me to read your luck for you?"

"No!" I said, more loudly than I intended. Tybalt and Quentin both took a step forward. I waved them back and repeated, more quietly, "No. No luck. Please." Li Qin was a Shyi Shuai. Her race specialized in manipulating luck. The trouble was, for every action, there was an equal and opposite reaction. The last time I'd allowed her to play around with my luck, I'd wound up getting disemboweled. Twice. Not an experience I was in a hurry to have again.

"I understand," said Li Qin. "Let me know if you change your mind?"

"I will. Look, this Library pass, is it only good for me? Because I'm not sure I want to be running around without some sort of backup just now." More, I wasn't sure my backup would let me get away with it if I tried.

"I made sure you could bring an escort." Li Qin's concern melted into amusement. "I couldn't picture you going out alone. The Librarian is nice enough, and she understood why you might not want to come without friends. Her name is Magdaleana. Play nicely with her."

Not that long ago, I considered myself a loner. It was a little odd to realize that I'd moved so far past those days that people I'd met since then didn't even consider it an option. "I really appreciate this, Li," I said, skirting dangerously close to thanking her.

"I'm gearing up to ask you for a favor to be named later. I'm just adding to my leverage here." Her tone was light, but there was an element of seriousness there.

That was something to worry about later. "I still appreciate it. I'll talk to you soon."

"Please do. Now get yourself un-banished before time runs out. This Kingdom would be awfully dull without you." Li Qin hung up.

"She got me the pass," I said, lowering my phone. "And yes, you can come with me, since she didn't think I'd want to go alone."

"Both of us?" asked Quentin hopefully.

Tybalt didn't ask. He just raised an eyebrow.

Li Qin said "friends" when I asked her about bringing

an escort . . . "Yes," I said firmly. My phone buzzed again as Li texted me. I checked the display. "Lucky us: we're staying in the city. The place is just a few miles from here."

"I don't think you should change your clothes," said May.

I turned, blinking, to see her standing in the kitchen doorway with Jazz. "What?"

"Keep the dress. Most Librarians don't get out much. Whoever runs the local branch is probably a little bit behind the times. They'll find formality appropriate and respectful." May shrugged. "Just a suggestion."

Sometimes it was easy to forget that my silly, flamboyant Fetch had started her existence as one of the night-haunts. They met all the Librarians, eventually. "Okay," I said. "As long as I can keep my jacket. But I don't think we can all go."

"I know," said May. "Jazz and I will stay here and deal with anyone who shows up to tell you how sorry they are. You go and make this exile go away. Find out whose throne that really is, and depose the bitch."

"No pressure," added Jazz, with a sweet, if worried, smile.

"No pressure," I echoed. I tucked my phone back into my pocket. "Come on, boys. Let's go to the Library."

"If I may," said Tybalt. "Were I the Queen, I would almost certainly set someone to watching this house, to see if you went anywhere after you finally came home from racing about the city, looking for aid. Were I the Queen, I would also be quite likely arrogant enough to disregard the fact that you are being courted by a man who can take you anywhere you wish without needing to move the car or, indeed, step outside the threshold."

"Were you the Queen, I wouldn't be dating you, but point taken," I said. "Can you carry me and Quentin over to 5th and Brannan? I'm not leaving him here just so the Queen doesn't follow me."

"Your loyalty will be the death of us all one day, but yes, I can take you both," said Tybalt. "It may not be pleasant. I can still manage it."

"Then let's go," I said, and offered him my hand.

"As you like." This time, Tybalt took Quentin's hand directly, rather than letting him hold onto me. "Both of you, take a deep breath, and hold fast. I would not want to lose you." On that dire note, he stepped into the shadows formed by the meeting of the cabinet and the wall, and pulled us with him, into darkness.

The Shadow Roads seemed colder this time, maybe because we were going farther than before. I held Tybalt's hand, trusting him to see us through the darkness, which was too deep for my eyes to penetrate, but must have been clear to his. I could hear Quentin's teeth chattering. He hadn't traveled through the dark this way as many times as I had, and I wasn't sure he'd ever come this far.

Just as my lungs were beginning to burn, we stepped out of the darkness and into the watery streetlight shining on the corner of 5th and Brannan. There were no people in sight. A few cars moved on the cross streets, but none close enough to have seen our sudden appearance.

"Good aim," I said, stuffing my freezing hands into the pockets of my jacket. "Quentin? You okay?"

"I really, *really* miss living where there's snow," he said, sounding altogether too chipper for someone who'd just been pulled along the Shadow Roads.

"All right, when this is all over, we'll go skiing. Now let's find the Library." I pulled out my phone, checking Li's text. Then I blinked. "This isn't what it said before."

"What?" Tybalt stepped closer, peering at the screen over my shoulder.

"Before, it said '5th and Brannan.' Now it says to turn left." I scowled. "April's been making improvements again. Yippee."

April O'Leary, Countess of Tamed Lightning, was the reason I *had* a cell phone. She's the world's first cyber-Dryad, and she specializes in making mortal technology compatible with fae magic. Phones that could work in the Summerlands, for example, or survive the freezing temperatures of the Shadow Roads without breaking. And now, apparently, phones that could receive semi-sentient text messages.

We started walking. After we had turned left, the message changed again, now telling us to head three blocks down. We kept walking.

Annoying as this was, it probably served a purpose. Many knowes can't simply be walked into: they all have their own requirements for entry, tricks and twists that have to be observed if you want to get inside. There was no reason for the Library to be any different, and a lot of reasons for it to be the same. If Li Qin had started by texting me the address, we'd never have found it. That didn't make the process any less irritating.

The text changed again after we'd been walking for almost fifteen minutes, now reading, "You are here." I lowered my phone and lifted my head, looking around.

"Okay," I said, after a moment. "Where the hell are we?"

Li's directions had led us deep into the sprawling maze that makes up downtown San Francisco, and down a small side alley that was clinging with game tenacity to the title of "street." I'm sure it had the qualifications, once upon a time. But then these silly little things called "cars" came along, and suddenly being wide enough to allow one fairly slender carriage to pass just wasn't cutting it.

Tiny shops lined the alley, obviously clinging just as fiercely to keep from sliding into failure. Somehow, I knew they weren't our destination. That dubious honor was reserved for the two-story building at the end of the alley, sunk back in a vague haze of dust and ancient brick. It was shabby and a little sunken-in, like it was going to collapse at any moment—or maybe last another fifty years. Sometimes it's hard to tell with San Francisco architecture.

We approached the building, passing the blind eyes of the closed and shuttered shops, until we left the last streetlights behind and found ourselves standing in front of a plain wooden door. A sign in the window identified the shop as "Bookstore." A few shabby volumes were on display in the window, with a curtain drawn behind them to hide the rest of the shop from view.

I tried the door. It was unlocked. "Here we go," I said, and pushed it open. I was rewarded with the tinkling of a silver bell and a small shower of pale, translucent dust that fell like rain from the doorjamb, coating us in glitter. I coughed. "Pixies."

"We're doubtless in the right place, then," said Tybalt.

I motioned for the others to follow me inside. It wasn't much better in than out. The room was small, packed with shelves stacked with battered, mildewed paperbacks and magazines that had been old before I was turned into a fish. Everything glittered with pixie-sweat. The door slammed behind Quentin with an ominous "thud." I jumped, turning to glare at him. He shrugged apologetically.

I'm not much for signs and portents. If I went looking for them, I'd find them, and my life is already hazardous enough, thanks. Still, the combination of creaking doors, decaying books, and unseen pixies was enough to raise the hairs on the back of my neck.

Tybalt sniffed, and then sneezed.

Quentin was squinting at the piles of moldy books. "Something's wrong with the titles," he said.

I followed his gaze, and realized I couldn't actually *read* any of the book covers, not even the ones unblemished enough that they should have been legible. My eyes refused to fix on the letters, sliding instead from vivid decay to vivid decay. I slid my hands through the air, summoning as much of my magic as I could hold, and said solemnly, "You all did love him once, not without cause. What cause withholds you, then, to mourn for him?"

A faint gleam snapped into view above the books, clinging to every surface like pixie dust, pale gold and tasting of parchment. Someone had thrown an illusion over the entire room, presumably to keep the merely curious from coming any further. It was a clever piece of work, one I wouldn't even have been able to notice a few years ago.

"I do adore a woman who channels magic via Shakespeare," said Tybalt.

"Flirt later, business now," I said. There was a narrow doorway in the left corner of the room, tucked between two dilapidated bookshelves. I kept my hands up to prevent the illusion from slipping back into place, and started for the opening, Quentin and Tybalt close behind me. The golden haze snapped as we passed into the next room, leaving our eyes unclouded. And what we found was . . . more books. Given that we were looking for a library, that probably shouldn't have been as surprising as it was.

"Um, Toby?"

"Yeah, Quentin?"

"The door's gone."

I turned, and realized he was right. We were standing at a spot where four paths through the floor-to-ceiling bookshelves met. At least I assumed they were floor-to-ceiling; they actually stretched away into the dark above, disappearing toward a point I couldn't see. There were no obvious exits, just more shelves, stretching out into forever. They were spotlessly clean, loaded down with books until I was pretty sure that they constituted a fire hazard.

Judging by the volumes in view, whoever ran the place had been collecting books for centuries without bothering to actually *sort* anything. The Colored Fairy books were shelved next to a pile of torrid-looking romances, several broad, flat art books, and a hefty leather-bound volume with a Latin title. It was like we were standing in the world's largest used bookstore.

And there were no clerks, or Librarians, in sight.

"Hello?" I called, hesitantly. I wasn't sure what Library etiquette was, and I didn't want to start out by pissing off the Librarian. Li Qin had called her "a nice enough sort," but we were talking about Li Qin here. Her definition of "nice" was questionable at best, and at worst included things I didn't even want to think about. Some of us are more naturally tolerant than others, I suppose.

The dusty silence didn't change. I exchanged a look with Quentin and Tybalt. "Should we wait here, or go looking?"

"I honestly have no idea," said Tybalt. He shook his head. "I've always been more interested in oral histories than written ones."

"Waiting, maybe?" said Quentin. "Seems polite."

"Okay." I turned to study a bookshelf. Quentin and Tybalt did the same. Several minutes slipped by, until finally I turned and called again, more loudly, "Hello?"

"Coming!" shouted a cheerful, British-accented voice from somewhere in the maze of shelves. "Hold on a moment, shall you? I'm coming as fast as I can!"

"We'll be right here," I called back. After several more minutes, a small figure slipped out from behind one of the shelves, her arms full of books. Her clothes were dowdy, suited to rummaging through dusty old tomes and cobwebbed shelves: an ankle-length black skirt, sensible shoes, and a tweed sweater over a white blouse. She looked about fifteen years old. There was an odd bulge on her back, like she was wearing some kind of brace.

"Hullo!" she said. "I hope you weren't waiting too long. Time can be a mite squirrelly in here." She dropped her armload of books on the nearest available surface — another pile of books. Near as I could tell, the Library was a paper avalanche waiting to happen. "Welcome to the Library of Stars."

She was short, maybe five-two, with a slim, almost frail build. Her hair was the bright copper color of new pennies, and cut short in a bob that framed a heart-shaped face dominated by enormous dark blue eyes. Something was wrong with the way they focused. I squinted, trying to figure out what about those eyes was bothering me, and then dismissed it with a slight shake of my head. I was jumpy. Being exiled does that to me.

"I'm October Daye; Li Qin Zhou called about me," I

said, offering my hand. "These are my friends, Tybalt and Quentin. Are you the Librarian, or do you know where to find her?" She looked like a teenager, but in Faerie, that didn't have to mean anything.

The girl smiled, taking my hand and shaking it. "If you want the last Librarian, best of luck with that. I'm Magdaleana Brooke, and I'm currently in charge here, inasmuch as anyone is. Call me Mags—it's easier to shout if something's about to fall on you."

"Really?" asked Quentin. "But . . ." Then he caught himself, reddening.

Mags turned her smile on him. "Appearances can be deceiving. I'd tell you to ask my mother how old I am, but I've not seen her in about three hundred years, and I don't know where she is. Off harassing some poor musician, I've no doubt. That was always her favorite game."

"It is a pleasure to make your acquaintance," said Tybalt gravely.

"And yours," she said. "I've never met a King of Cats before."

There was something off about her. I breathed in, trying to catch her heritage, and stopped, blinking. "Wait. What are . . . I mean . . ."

"You mean to ask what I am, and don't want to give offense by saying I don't come across as fae to your blood magic." She reached around to rub the lump on her back, wincing slightly. "I'm a Puca. You've caught me in my street clothes—I was out and about when Li called, and I've not had time to change."

"Oh!" I said, realization dawning. "I'm sorry."

"No need." She smiled again. "Just come and have some tea while I get changed, and then tell me what *you* are, and we'll call it even."

"Sure, but we're also here looking for some information."

"Isn't everyone? Come on." She waved for us to follow her as she turned and headed into the stacks. Not wanting to get lost again, we hurried after her.

She led us through the maze, taking turn after turn

until we emerged into a space the size of a normal living room, if normal living rooms had walls made of bookshelves. A table, two couches, and several chairs were set up in the center of the space, carefully arranged on a faded rug. "I'll be right back; make yourselves comfortable, there's tea and such in the kitchen." Before we could say anything else she was gone, vanishing between two bookshelves.

"On the plus side, I don't think she was offended by my dress," I said.

Tybalt snorted.

Puca are shapeshifters. They have no skill at illusions, but they don't need it: instead of making themselves *look* human, they turn *into* humans, hiding their strangeness under veils of too-solid flesh. Of course, they're not perfect. There's always one thing they can't change, one fae feature that refuses to be hidden. It got a lot of Puca killed, back when humanity still believed in us, and eventually, they faded as a race, nearly becoming extinct.

"I've never met a Puca before," said Quentin.

"Great. This night is already educational." I looked around the little square of furnishings, all of which seemed to be at least fifty years old. "When she gets back, we'll ask for the books on Kingdom history, and we'll get started."

"Kingdom history, is it?" Mags appeared from between a pair of shelves—not, I noted, the ones she'd disappeared between before. "That's an interesting topic. The Mists is a young Kingdom, but it's had its share of troubles."

"Yeah, it has," I said, fighting back the urge to stare.

She was still wearing the long black skirt, but the tweed sweater was gone, as was the lump. Instead, she had pliant-looking dragonfly wings, two on each side, which trailed down to her knees in a wash of translucent rainbow color. They twitched as she walked, making minute corrections in her balance and leaving a thin haze of red and copper glitter in the air. She didn't have a pixie problem. She just had herself.

Mags chuckled as she caught me staring at her wings. "Unlike some of my luckier cousins, who only had to contend with goat's feet or webbed hands, I was born with a full set of wings. It makes travel by public transportation *ever* so entertaining."

I winced, but it was Quentin who spoke, saying, "Binding your wings like that must hurt."

"You get used to it." She glanced aside, expression briefly grim. "You get used to a lot of things, really." The grimness was gone when she looked back, replaced by her earlier amiability. "Li Qin doesn't ask for passes often, and certainly not for such interesting groups of people. You said you were looking for the history of the Kingdom? What part?"

"We should start with the reign of King Gilad," I said. "If there's anything from the later years, that would probably be best."

To Mags' credit, she didn't bat an eye. "King Gilad, is it? What are you looking for? We have the standard histories, of course, and I know where there are a few of the less common ones, although those sections may be dangerous this time of night; better to wait until sunrise, when things settle down."

"See, I'm on a little bit of a time crunch with this research project," I said, picking my words as carefully as I could. "So if we could start with the easy-to-find and move on to the more obscure ones, that would be good."

"Well, you haven't got a Library card, so you won't be able to take anything away with you, but if you're willing to put in the hours, you should be able to find almost anything you need." Mags walked toward the nearest bookshelf, pulling several volumes down and tucking them under her arm. "I'll start you with a few biographies, some books of Kingdom history . . ."

"This is very helpful," I said, following her.

She took down another three books, handing them to me. "I wouldn't have let you come if I wasn't willing to help. Besides, I was curious."

"Curious?"

"I've heard of you—who hasn't? Toby Daye, Amandine's daughter, twice-dead and twice a changeling child—it's fascinating, really. I'm sure we'll be teaching your history in a hundred years. Maybe you'll even tell me how you managed it, if I'm helpful enough."

"That was easy," I said, without thinking about it. "Mom is Firstborn. Surprise."

Mags stiffened, her wings buzzing a new tattoo. Then she took down another book. "I guess I'll have to revise her biography, then. But there's a good way for you to pay your Library fees, if you incur any. We're always happy to take knowledge in trade." She took the books from under her arm and added them to the pile I was holding. "This should get you started, and if I can borrow your young men, I'll let them carry the rest back to you."

". . . right." I looked at the sheer number of books in my hands and managed, barely, not to wince. "It's a good thing I didn't have any plans for tonight."

Mags laughed. "Oh, don't be cross. Knowledge must be earned, and sometimes this is the only way to do it." She waved to Quentin and Tybalt. "Come along, gentlemen. We'll get more knowledge ready for the fight."

"Um," said Quentin. "Okay."

Tybalt paused next to me, murmuring, "If anything troubles you, yell."

"If anything troubles me, I'll stab it to death," I said, and kissed him. "Go with the nice Librarian. Find the book that cracks the case."

He sighed. "As you say." I watched him walk after Mags and Quentin until he vanished into the stacks. What can I say? He was still wearing leather pants.

I walked over to the nearest couch and sat, piling the books around me. They looked dusty, but the dust didn't come away on my fingers, and I had to wonder how much of it had been generated by the Librarian herself. Maybe it was connected to her admittedly eccentric filing system. Navigation via dust.

Reaching into the pile, I picked up the first book my fingers hit, a fat red volume with a redwood tree embossed in gold across the front. I flipped it open to the front page, where the title *The Life and Times of King Gilad Windermere in the Mists, Duke of Golden Gate, Protector of the Western Coast* was written in florid calligraphy.

"I wish I'd packed some of Marcia's sandwiches to go," I muttered, and started reading.

The text was dry, which I expected. It was also dense. By the end of the first chapter, I knew Crown Prince Gilad was an only child; that his parents had been married for more than six hundred years before he was born; that he was a prodigy in every possible way, as befitted a King; and that he really liked climbing trees. Like, *really* liked climbing trees. Once he was old enough to walk and control his natural teleportation magic, he was continually being fished out of trees all over the Kingdom. Mostly in Muir Woods, where the redwoods presented an irresistible challenge.

At the end of the chapter, Gilad was approaching his teens and had adopted the redwood tree as his personal banner, and I was developing the worst headache I'd had in a long time. I groaned, dropping my head into my hands. "Oh, oak and ash, I *hate* history," I moaned.

"History hates you as well," said Tybalt, whisking the book out of my lap as he sat next to me. "It goes out of its way to be complicated and inscrutable for just that reason."

"Right now, I'm inclined to believe you." I eyed the stack of books that he'd brought with him. Quentin was staggering toward us with even more books in his arms. Mags walked behind him, clutching a single massive volume to her chest. "How much history *is* there?"

"Years and years," said Mags, and giggled, like that was the funniest joke she'd ever heard. Sobering, she explained, "Much of what you'll find here is the same information from slightly different points of view. There's little that's unique. Historians are magpies, in their way, and they share things back and forth. Still, if you can find a footnote that points you to an index that leads you to a bit of knowledge you didn't have before . . . librarianship is a form of heroism. It's just not as flashy as swords and dragons."

"Any tips on slaying this particular beast?"

"If you could tell me exactly what it was you were looking for . . ." Mags looked from face to face, catching the sudden guardedness in our expressions. "No, I rather thought not. Well, then, I suppose it's time we reviewed the rules of the Library. Nothing's quite free, you know."

"I figured," I said, and sat up a little straighter. "What's the fee?"

"The fee comes, in part, with obedience. There is no running in the Library unless you're being pursued by something that didn't enter with you. There is no fighting in the Library."

"What about fighting back?" asked Quentin.

"Self-defense is allowed," said Mags. "But aggressors *will* be evicted, and their privilege of passage revoked. Do not taunt someone simply because you think they can't hit you here."

I frowned. "You sound like you're expecting trouble."

To my surprise, she laughed. "Amandine's daughter comes here from the Queen's Court, if the dress you're wearing is any indication, and starts asking for books about a long-dead King? It doesn't take a genius to know that you *are* trouble, and you're likely to cause even more."

"Fair," I admitted.

"Next, I'll need you to tell me about your mum. We can do that part later, once you have the information you need, but it's clear you know something that's not in her official biography, and that could help me quite a bit." Mags looked almost abashed. "The Libraries work on a system of information for information, you see. If I have verified information that no one else does, I can use it to trade for some volumes we've needed here. Undersea histories and the like."

"Done," I said. Mom gave up the right to pretend she was Daoine Sidhe when she lied to me about my heritage, then left me with powers I didn't fully understand. I paused as a thought occurred to me, and asked, "While we're here, do you have any books about hope chests?" They were a manufactured method of doing what my mother—and I—could do naturally. Maybe reading about the hope chests could give me a better idea of how my own magic worked.

And how to hurt people less when I had to use it on them.

"I do," Mags said. "I'll get it for you."

I looked at the heap already building around me, and sighed. "Right. We're going to need to make a coffee run."

Mags smiled. "I like my mochas with extra whipped cream."

SEVEN

AFTER SOME DEBATE—and writing our order on a piece of scratch paper—Quentin and Tybalt were dispatched to get coffee, on the theory that Mags was the Librarian and I was the one who'd actually be banished if I didn't find something useful in these books. I squinted at the one I had open, wondering if it would make more sense after I'd had some coffee. Mags emerged from the shelf-maze with another four books in her arms.

I looked up. "Was this written to be confusing?"

"What's the title?"

"Um ... *A History of the Westlands, volume III.*"

"Then yes. That series was written to the style of the time, which called for absolute heroism on the part of everyone involved, even the villains. It made things a bit difficult to muddle through." She put the fresh stack of books down next to me. "It might help if I knew what you were looking for. King Gilad wasn't a friend of mine, but we met. He came to the Library more than a few times. Never would tell me what he was looking for, but oh, he was a sweet one, when he wanted to be ..."

I looked up, assessing her. Finally, after a pause almost long enough to let me lose my nerve, I asked, "What you know about the Queen of the Mists?"

"Not much. Our biography on her is more like a

pamphlet. 'How to start a war and terrorize your citizenry without revealing your real name.' And she's not Gilad's heir, of course. I'd have been happy to confirm that, if I'd ever been asked." Mags shook her head. "She claimed the throne, the local nobles backed her, and no one ever came here to check her pedigree. Sloppy. But then, succession so often is."

I stared at her.

She blinked. "What? Did I say something wrong? Not that it matters—Libraries are sovereign territories. I can't commit treason unless I do it outside these walls."

"Good to know." I set the book I'd been struggling with aside. "How can you be sure she wasn't his heir?"

Mags blinked again, wings buzzing in a rapid blur that telegraphed her confusion. "Because I met his children."

I was on my feet before I realized I was going to move. "Children? King Gilad never married."

"Marriage is not a requirement for children, nor does every marriage result in children," said Mags slowly. "Do I need to add some books about sexual reproduction to your pull list?"

"No! I mean . . . he was the *King*. Why wouldn't he have gotten married if he was going to have children?"

"As a King, I believe I can answer that," said Tybalt. I turned. He was standing in the opening of the nearest row of bookshelves with Quentin and a tray of take-out cups. "I never introduced my wife to the Divided Courts. My cats knew her because I wanted her to have their protection. But she never met a soul she did not need to know."

He walked over to me, taking the largest of the cups off the tray and holding it out. I took it. He smiled, a little sadly.

"A King learns to conceal what matters most, lest others use it as a weapon against him. I learned that early and held it dear. If King Gilad had children, he did well to keep them from the public eye."

"A little *too* well, since it looks like it netted us the wrong Queen." I turned back to Mags. "Were they too young to claim the throne when their father died?"

"They may have been dead, or injured, or lost in grief," she said. "The Kingdom was in chaos after the earthquake. No one expected Gilad to be killed. If Arden and Nolan lived—"

I went still. "Wait. Arden?"

"Yes. Arden Windermere, the King's daughter."

When Dean and Peter Lorden were kidnapped, their kidnappers hid them in a shallowing in Muir Woods. The Luidaeg was able to convince it to let us in by telling it that Arden lived. The Luidaeg never lied.

The King's daughter was alive.

Quentin's thoughts had clearly mirrored mine. He nodded toward the door. "I'll stay here and keep reading," he said.

"Good," I said. "Mags, if we go, can we come back?"

"Of course," she said. "A Library pass is good for a fortnight, and you owe me information. The Library will not move as long as your pass is good."

"Since that's more time than I have left in the Kingdom, that should be more than enough." I turned to Tybalt. "We need to go back to the Luidaeg."

He nodded. "Yes. I suppose we do."

"Wait!"

We both turned to Mags. "Yes?" I asked.

"Is the Luidaeg still in San Francisco?" Her cheeks reddened as she added, "I haven't heard from her in years. I thought she'd moved on to some other coastal city."

"She's here," I said. "I don't know why, but she's here. And I think she knows where Arden Windermere is, which means I need to talk to her. Quentin, call if you need anything, or if you need us to come and get you, okay?"

"Okay." He sat down on the couch with his coffee. "I'm good at research."

"Compared to me, so are pixies." I looked to Mags. "It's been lovely to meet you. I hope we meet again soon."

"As do I," she said. "Open roads and kind fires."

"All winds to guide you," I replied, and moved toward Tybalt. He put the tray with the remaining cups down before taking hold of me and stepping into the shadows. The last thing I saw was Mags' startled expression. Then the blackness blocked everything else, and we were running through the cold, me trying to hold Tybalt's hand and my coffee at the same time, Tybalt pulling me along at his usual breakneck pace. I thought briefly about drinking the coffee, and decided that would cross the line from silly to stupid.

The sun had come up while we were in the Library; its walls had been enough to protect us from the effects of the dawn. That was a pleasant surprise. We emerged from the shadows onto the street a few blocks from the Luidaeg's apartment. I stepped away from Tybalt and peered into my coffee cup before sighing. "It's frozen."

"That happens to liquids on the Shadow Roads," said Tybalt. He sniffed the air, and frowned. "October . . ."

"Is this where you tell me the Queen is staking out the Luidaeg's place in order to keep me from going for help?"

He paused, frown deepening, before he asked, "How did you know?"

"It's what I'd do, if I were feeling really stupid and predictable." I pulled my phone out of my pocket, dialing half a phone number before muttering, "Pussy-cat, pussy-cat, where have you been? I've been to London to piss off the Queen," and filling the rest of the screen with zeros. The cut grass and copper smell of my magic rose around me as I raised the phone to my ear.

It was ringing. It shouldn't have been, but it was, and that meant that it was working. As expected, the Luidaeg picked up after the first ring, demanding, *"What?"*

"The Queen has troops watching your apartment to make sure I can't reach you. Tybalt and I are a few blocks north, at the edge of your anti-teleportation field. Can you please come get us? I need to talk to you."

"She has people watching *my* apartment?"

"Yes, and I'm feeling sort of exposed out here on the street. Come get me." I hung up.

Tybalt looked at me, one eyebrow raised. "I realize the sea witch is a friend of yours, October, but are you sure it's wise to talk to her that way?"

"My head hurts from trying to read all those stupid books at the Library, I've been exiled, I'm wearing a dress, and my coffee's frozen." I folded my arms and scowled. "I'll talk to her any way I want to."

"Even so."

I paused, and then sighed. "I'm sorry. I don't have much patience left." A suspiciously deep shadow had formed along the wall of the nearest alley. I eyed it before calling, "I'm supposed to have three days. Why don't you scuttle on back to your mistress and tell her I'm not setting anything on fire, okay?"

The shadow split into four pieces, each bipedal and man-sized. I continued to eye it dubiously. The shadow continued to dwindle, until four men in human disguises were standing there.

"Shoo," I said.

"We've got our eyes on you," one of them replied. He was either their leader, or the only one too brave to have any sense. "There will be none of your trickery this time."

Footsteps approached down the street. "I have *never* resorted to trickery, and I resent the implication that I would," I said. "Now if you'll excuse me, I'm meeting a friend." I turned toward the sound, and was greeted by the sight of the Luidaeg, wearing her customary overalls and work boots. She was scowling. I waved. Her scowl deepened.

I glanced over my shoulder to see how the men by the wall were responding. Answer: they weren't. They were looking at her the way they'd look at any random human. I turned back to the Luidaeg. "I don't think they know who you are."

"I didn't think you'd be back here this soon," she said. She glared at the men. "Really? You called me out here for *this*?"

"Well, those four, and however many are between us and your place," I said. "If they don't know who you are,

I'm not sure why they're staking out your apartment, but I didn't feel like getting arrested without doing anything wrong."

"I'm sure you'll do something wrong before the day's out." She stalked past me, heading straight for the four men standing by the wall. They blinked at her, nonplussed. I turned to watch the fun.

"What is she doing?" asked Tybalt.

"I don't know, but I wish I had popcorn," I said.

The Luidaeg raised her hand and snapped her fingers, and just like that, their human disguises disappeared. Two were Daoine Sidhe. The others were Candela and Ellyllon, respectively. All four were wearing the Queen's livery. One reached for his sword. She turned to look at him. Her eyes had gone white from side to side, like fog rolling in over the water.

"I wouldn't do that if I were you," she said, and her voice was an undertow, promising all the darkness and dangers of the open sea. "Let me guess. Your lady told you to watch the places October was known to frequent; told you this was one of them; didn't tell you why. She said you should stand here, and harry her if you got the chance. If not, you were to return to Court, report your findings, and stand another watch. Am I right?"

"Who *are* you?"

"Uh-uh, that's not how this goes. I asked the first question. Am I right?"

The man swallowed. I felt almost sorry for him in that moment. It didn't last. "Yes. You're correct."

"Bully for me. Now here's your answer: I am the sea witch. I am the tide you fear and the turning you can't deny. I am the sound of the waves running over your bones on the beach, little man, and I am not amused at finding you on my doorstep." She took a step forward. He took a step back. "I won't punish you for obeying orders the way *she* would. But I can't let an insult go unanswered. You know how it goes." A smile twisted her lips. "I'm actually grateful. You see, there are . . . rules . . . that govern what I can and can't do. But you broke them first. Now I get to do something I don't get to do very often. Now I get to play."

The man grabbed for his sword. The Luidaeg raised her hand, whispering something I couldn't hear, and all four of them froze. They stayed that way for several minutes. I knew the Luidaeg was speaking—the wind brought me enough of her voice for that—but not what she was saying. Maybe that was for the best. Finally, she turned and walked back to us.

"That's done," she said. "Let's go to the apartment. It's a nice morning, but there's so much traffic on these streets."

Except for the Queen's men, we hadn't seen a soul. "What did you do?"

"Nothing they hadn't allowed by coming onto my territory. Every soul who came here on the Queen's business will go home, go to bed, and sleep soundly, dreaming the sweetest of dreams."

Something about that statement had teeth. I paused, and then ventured, "For how long?"

The Luidaeg smiled brilliantly. "Until something wakes them up. True love, childbirth, and bees are all on the table."

It seemed grossly unfair. I knew better than to say anything about it. As the Luidaeg was so fond of pointing out, Faerie isn't fair, and as a punishment, it was entirely in line with what the stories said she'd do. Instead, I just nodded. "Let's go."

No one bothered us on the way back to her place. I was unsurprised to see that the illusory mess she created for my benefit was back when she opened the door. "Come in. I don't have all day."

"Neither do I," I said, following her inside. "Did you send me to look for information on King Gilad because you wanted me to start looking for Arden Windermere?"

"You mean Her Highness the Crown Princess in the Mists, even if she wasn't formally recognized," said the Luidaeg, and smiled. "Good girl. This way." She started for the living room. We followed her.

She was already on her knees in front of an old oak sea chest when we got there, throwing things randomly to the floor as she dug them out. "Gilad and his lover never married, because he feared that what had happened to his parents would happen to his wife and children, if he ever publicly acknowledged them," she said, as soon as we were close enough to hear. "So he hid her, for her own protection, and they raised their children in secrecy. But some of us knew. Some of us had to know." She looked up and smiled, baring her teeth in a distinctly predatory fashion. "Some of us had to craft the charms that hid them."

"You told the shallowing in Muir Woods that Arden lived," I said. "King Gilad's children survived the earthquake."

"Yes, but they were in no shape to claim the throne, and by the time they were ready, the pretender was already in place." She produced a glass flask from the chest. It was small, the sort of thing that used to be sold off the back of snake oil wagons, filled with unidentified tinctures and too dear by half. She gave it a shake as she stood. It lit up from within. "They were tired, and heartsick, and they'd never expected to inherit the Kingdom that way. They walked away."

"But they did not abdicate," said Tybalt. "They never renounced their claim to the throne."

"And the kitty earns his keep!" The Luidaeg tapped her nose and offered me the glowing flask. "Here."

This close, I could see that it was full of live fireflies. I took it anyway, asking, "What am I supposed to do with these?"

"Find Arden. I know she's alive. I don't know about her brother—I lost track of him after the War of Silences—but she's alive, hidden by charms I helped craft when she was a baby." The Luidaeg smiled wryly. "Magic's a bitch that way. But if you want to stop the goblin fruit, you have to change the law. Since the current Queen won't do that, you need to change the person who *makes* the law."

"And since the Queen has exiled me, this is the perfect time for me to try." I peered through the side of the flask. "So how will these help me find Arden?"

"She'll be in a place that anyone who claims allegiance to the Mists never sees—a place you don't want to go, because it doesn't exist for you. As long as you keep one of those," she nodded toward the fireflies, "with you at all times, you'll see through any illusions in your way. They'll burn brighter in the presence of my magic, to light your way, and if you set them on the wing, they'll do their best to chase it down. I caught them myself, on the moors of Annwn, and bathed them for a full month in the moonlight of Tirn Aill. I made them, so I can't use them, but you can. Each one will glow for a full day once you let it out. If that's enough . . ."

I counted fireflies. "Ten glowing bugs to help me find a missing Princess protected by charms *you* can't see through. After that, all I have to do is depose the current Queen of the Mists, convince Arden to take the throne, and get myself un-banished. Oh, yeah. Piece of cake." I scowled at the Luidaeg. "Don't you believe in easy quests?"

"No." She smiled again. At least this time there was a trace of sympathy in her expression. Not much, but I'd take what I could get. "I don't want you getting bored."

"Right." I looked at Tybalt, and then at the flask of fireflies. "Somehow, I don't think that's a risk right now."

"It never is, with you," said Tybalt.

"Well, okay." I slipped the flask into the inside pocket of my jacket, checking twice to be sure it was secure. "Let's go find a Princess."

EIGHT

"**Y**OU REALIZE THIS IS one of those things far easier said than done," Tybalt said, as we stepped out of the Luidaeg's apartment. "I have some acquaintance with princesses. In my experience, they tend to be either blazingly obvious, or so well-concealed as to be practically invisible."

"Then it's a good thing we have magical Princess-finding bugs to help us, isn't it?" I paused. "I can't believe I just said those words, in that order, like they meant something. I need coffee."

Tybalt chuckled richly. Sadly, that just made it harder not to think about coffee. "Is there any time in your life when you do *not* feel the need for caffeine?"

"Sure. Sometimes I'm asleep." I pulled the flask out of my pocket, peering at the fireflies. "They look pretty happy in there."

"You're concerning yourself with the inner lives of bugs." Tybalt took my arm, walking toward the nearest wall. "Now I *know* you require a cup of coffee. Possibly a pot, if we can find a straw capable of handling the heat. Your squire can wait a little longer for your return."

"I'd argue if you weren't doing what I wanted you to do." I paused. "Wait a second. I just thought of something." I whirled, pulling my arm free as I darted back to the door.

The Luidaeg opened it the second my foot hit the step, leaving me with one hand raised to knock. Our relative positions made it look like I was getting ready to punch her in the face. I froze. She gave my fist an interested look before asking, "Do I need to give that whole 'sound of the waves running over your bones' speech again? Because seriously, I can only do fucking terrifying once a day before I get bored and want to go do a crossword puzzle or something."

"Um. Sorry." I dropped my hand. "The fireflies. Can they survive on the Shadow Roads? That's how Tybalt and I got here."

"Uh-huh." She held up a finger. "They're magic bugs." She added a second finger. "I caught them in Annwn. Winters in Annwn get colder than a Banshee's tit. I wouldn't worry about them. Just don't drop the flask while you're in there, or you'll never get them back."

"What would happen if I let one of them go in there?" The various fae Roads stretched through the empty spaces of the world, at least insofar as I understood them—which admittedly, wasn't that well. But Tybalt and I had been able to use one of Luna's Rose Roads to search for someone marooned in another realm of Faerie. If we were trying to find someone hiding in the mortal world, the Shadow Roads should be able to serve the same purpose.

The Luidaeg looked surprised. She blinked, the edges of her irises doing something so odd and reptilian that my brain refused to deal with it, choosing to shunt it to the side where I wouldn't need to think about it. Then she said, thoughtfully, "You know, that might work. Or it could lose you a firefly before you even have a plan of attack."

"I've gambled more for less," I said. "It's worth a try."

"Important things always are. Don't die," she said, and shut the door in my face.

I turned back to Tybalt, who was watching me with

undisguised bemusement. I held up the flask of fireflies. "I think I know what we try first."

"What, pray tell, is that?"

"Dowsing."

The flask's cap was screwed on tight, and gave way only after I strained hard enough to bite my tongue. Finally, the cap slipped, and I was able to remove it. The fireflies ignored their sudden chance for freedom, choosing to keep buzzing happily around their artificial home. "Um, would one of you like to help me?" I asked, sticking a finger through the narrow opening. Requesting help from a bunch of bugs made me feel faintly ridiculous.

A bunch of *magic* bugs. Most of the fireflies continued to ignore me, but one landed lightly on my finger, glowing momentarily brighter. I pulled my hand out of the jar, holding it against the collar of my jacket. "Just, uh, hang out there for right now, okay?"

The firefly obligingly crawled off of my hand and settled on the leather. I couldn't see it directly, but I could see the glow it cast reflected off my hair, making it look like I was wearing a small flashlight clipped to my shoulder. I put the cap back on the flask, screwing it tight—although not quite *as* tight—before tucking it back into my pocket. Then I looked up at Tybalt. "Okay," I said. "Now we can go and get me that coffee."

He raised an eyebrow. "Were you planning to tell me the precise nature of your plan, or am I doomed to guessing games for the duration of our relationship?"

"These fireflies respond to the Luidaeg's magic. The Shadow Roads compress distance. I figure if I let this little guy go while we're on the Road," I indicated the firefly, "it'll head for the nearest patch of her magic it can find. All we need to do is make sure we don't lose sight of it, and we can at least come out in the same neighborhood, if not actually in Arden's location."

"That is . . ." Tybalt stopped, an odd look crossing his face. Finally, he said, "That is so nonsensical that I believe it stands an excellent chance of working."

I grinned. "That's why you love me."

"Among many other reasons." He moved forward with the lithe, inhuman speed that was the birthright of the Cait Sidhe, slinging an arm around my waist before I had a chance to react. Then, without any further comment, he leaned in and kissed me, sweet and slow and tasting of pennyroyal. The heat of his lips chased away all concern for the chill of the Shadow Roads—and as always, the feeling of his hip pressed against mine made me want to forget about everything else and request a trip back to the house for an hour or so of well-earned relaxation.

Sadly, this wasn't the time. He knew it as well as I did, because he pulled away just as the kiss was on the verge of deepening into something more. My ears were burning, and his pupils were extended to their fullest size—

Shit. "We're getting too comfortable in places like this," I said, raising my hand to my lips and wiping the taste of pennyroyal onto my fingers before dragging them through the air, filling them with shadows. "No guarantee the firefly comes out in the Summerlands. Suit up."

Tybalt blinked. Then he swore and set about weaving his own human disguise. For a few seconds, the air around us was a perfumer's nightmare of mixed scents, copper and musk, pennyroyal and fresh-cut grass. Then the magic dissipated, and two apparent humans stood where two obvious non-humans had been only a moment before.

"Better," I said, glancing down. The firefly on my collar was still visible. It had been enchanted by the Luidaeg. I would just have to trust her enchantments extended to making them difficult for humans to recognize as unusual. Bugs are easier to explain than pointy-eared people with inhuman eyes, anyway. I lifted my head. "Ready when you are."

"Finally," Tybalt said, a rolling chuckle underneath the word. Then he took my hand and pulled me into the darkness of the Shadow Roads.

The Shadow Roads are always going to be a mystery to me, since I'm not Cait Sidhe, and it's not like I can stop and examine them while we're running through the dark, trying to outpace the limits of our lungs. This much I know: that the darkness there is so absolute that even Cait Sidhe can't see for more than a few feet in any direction—enough to navigate, but not enough to let them know what might be surrounding them. That when we run there, we seem to be surrounded by absolute nothingness, but there's ground beneath our feet, and we never run in a straight line. That it's cold, and airless, and if it weren't for Tybalt, I would die there.

Hopefully, I wasn't consigning the first of our fireflies to the same fate. Its light was almost blinding in the absolute dark. I slid the forefinger of my free hand under the creature, brought it to my quickly-freezing lips, and spent precious air whispering, "Find Arden," before I flicked my wrist and sent the firefly flying. It fell, dropping well below the level of what I thought of as the ground. I stopped running, pulling Tybalt to a halt. I hadn't been sure my plan would work, but I hadn't expected to send the firefly quite so quickly to its death—

A blast of light like a signal flare rose from beneath us, leveled out at eye level, and raced into the distance. Tybalt, once he recovered from a split-second's-worth of shock, was almost as fast. He took off running, and I ran alongside him, letting him make up for my slightly less impressive speed by dragging me in his wake. Nonsensically, I wished I'd thought to ask the Luidaeg for some roller skates. It would have been easier on my feet.

We ran long enough that my eyelashes were sticking together and my lungs were one constant, aching burn, screaming out their need for air. I ignored the pain as best I could, focusing on following the firefly through the dark.

And then it stopped moving.

It hovered in place, turning a sad little circle in the air, like it couldn't decide what it was supposed to do next. Tybalt and I stopped behind it. Carefully, I lifted my

hand until the bug was resting on my palm. I closed my
fingers around it, and finally, mercifully, Tybalt opened a
door from the shadows back into the comfort of the
mortal world.

We were standing on the corner of Valencia and 20th
Street, where the spreading branches of some kind of
waxy-leafed tree provided enough cover that no one had
seen us appear. I took a deep, gasping breath that turned
into a cough at the end. Then I did it again. After three
of those, I was breathing almost normally, although the
ache in my chest made it clear that it would be a while
before the "almost" went away.

"You okay?" I asked, still wheezing.

"Mostly," said Tybalt. He released my hand. "Check
your bug, I beg, while I regain my dignity."

I managed a faint smile before reaching up and scraping the ice crystals from my eyelashes. With that done, I
opened my fingers to check on the firefly. It was glowing
more weakly than before, and it willingly crawled back
onto my lapel when I raised my hand and tipped it into
place. "Sorry about that," I said. "Next time, we'll take a
taxi."

"Ah, yes, I forget how eager modern drivers are to
respond to commands like 'pray, take direction from the
bug.' "

"You know *Labyrinth*, you should know 'follow that
cab.' "

"I do." Tybalt smiled. "I just enjoy watching the faces
you make when I become overly archaic."

"Me and my five-hundred-year-old boyfriend." I
raked a loop of hair that had escaped its complex net of
ribbons away from my face. Then I frowned, looking at
the street around us. "We're near the house. This is where
the police station is."

"There's more to a road than a single landmark, especially in this city. What did she say?"

"That Arden would be in a place I never see and don't
want to go." My frown deepened. "I see this road all the
time."

"Then anything new should stand out like a beacon in a storm."

He was right. I knew this street. I walked it twice a night, at least. I remembered the way Devin hid Home from mortal eyes, using a misdirection spell anchored to a piece of Coblynau metalwork. Whatever magic Arden was hiding behind had to be something similar, and that meant she didn't need to be in a knowe, or even a shallowing. She could be anywhere.

Tybalt held out his arm. I took it, leaning close in an effort to borrow some of his body heat. I needed to replace what the Shadow Roads had taken. Together we walked side by side down Valencia Street.

It was a beautiful morning. Most of the shops were open or opening, and the foot traffic was still sparse, leaving the sidewalks wide open. Dire as the situation was—goblin fruit killing changelings, missing princesses, my impending banishment and all—it was nice to just walk with him, knowing that together, we could handle anything the city wanted to throw at us. It had taken us a long time to reach the point where moments like this were possible. I wanted the moments to last a lot longer . . . all of which made it all the more important not to get my changeling ass tossed out of the Kingdom of the Mists.

I glanced down at the firefly on my jacket. It was glowing steadily, like a tiny Christmas light pinned to the leather. Then I glanced back up again, and stopped dead.

Tybalt took another step before the sudden drag of my arm on his pulled him to a halt. He stopped and frowned, following my gaze to the nearest storefront. "October, I love you, and I understand that we all have our quirks. I'm even willing to wait while you acquire the coffee you so obviously need. But I do not think that standing here staring at the coffeehouse will cause a beverage to appear."

"You don't understand." I glanced at him, and then back to the storefront, like I was afraid it might disappear. I *was* afraid it might disappear. "I know every coffee shop in a two-mile radius of my house. I know how much they charge, how good their coffee is, and what their hours are like."

"And?"

"And I've never seen this place before." According to the sign in the window, accompanied by a logo that looked like an ouroboros—a red snake eating its own tail—this was the Borderlands Café. I scooped the firefly off my lapel and tucked it into the pocket of my jacket. Hopefully, the little bug was sturdy enough that it wouldn't be squashed. "Can you see anything glowing through my clothes? I don't want to spook the locals if we can help it."

"Hmm." Tybalt stepped back, taking an ostentatiously long look up and down my body. I crossed my arms, raising an eyebrow. He raised a finger to silence any objections I might be preparing and continued his study. Finally, he nodded, looking smug, and said, "Nothing but your sparkling personality."

"You can be a real dick when you want to," I said. "Why am I dating you again?"

"Leather pants," he deadpanned.

I laughed. I couldn't help myself.

"And that, too, is my saving grace: I make you laugh when you spend far too much time wrapped in the shroud of your own dignity." He placed a kiss on my forehead. "If I may be so bold, now would be an excellent time for you to get a cup of coffee."

"Best hiding place ever," I agreed, opened the screen door, and stepped inside.

The Borderlands Café was a long, rectangular room, stretching past the kitchen area to meet with the back wall. The floor was polished hardwood, and the furniture was an eclectic mix of wooden tables, comfortable chairs, and even couches. It was surprisingly busy, considering the hour. People sat with their laptop computers, magazines, books, or in small clusters, sipping their drinks and talking. It lacked the hectic air of many of the local cafés—something that was probably connected to the signs saying "No Wifi." People who wanted to hang out in a coffee shop would stay, people who wanted to get online for free would go find someplace more suited to their tastes.

We approached the counter, where a large blond man in a black T-shirt proclaiming "Carnies Need Love Too" was wiping glasses with a rag. He beamed when he saw us, showing a daunting number of teeth in the process.

"Hi!" he said, setting the glass aside. "Welcome to Borderlands. What can I get you?"

I glanced at the menu on the wall. "A large coffee."

"Two large coffees," amended Tybalt.

The blond man nodded, smile fading as he focused on our order. "Here or to go?"

"Here." We needed time to figure out where Arden was, or whether the firefly had sensed my need for caffeine and simply led us to a coffee shop someone had, for whatever reason, decided to hide from most of the city.

"Should I leave room for cream and sugar?"

"Yes on his, no on mine," I said, producing my wallet. "Hey—how long has this place been here?"

"Oh, a couple of years. The bookstore was here first, and then the owner got bored and decided to open a café." The blond man beamed again, showing, if possible, even more teeth than before. "Alan gets bored easy."

I paused. "There's a bookstore?"

"Yeah, next door." The blond man pointed to the wall where the menu was posted. "It's through there. Alan says he's going to open up a door between them any day now, but he's been busy. You know. Owner stuff."

"Right, owner stuff," I said. "You know, I'd love to see the bookstore. When do they open?"

"Oh, they just opened." He beamed. "You have great timing."

"So I've been told," I said, and smiled back. "Could we get that coffee to go?"

Unsurprisingly, it turned out that we could.

NINE

MY COFFEE WAS HOT AND STRONG and gone by the time we'd traveled the five steps between the coffee shop and the bookstore. Tybalt plucked my empty cup from my fingers, replacing it with his own, which was still full. I blinked at him. He smiled.

"I did not 'profane' the coffee with milk or sugar, much as I would have liked to," he said. "Unlike you, I am capable of functioning without artificial stimulants."

"I *like* artificial stimulants," I protested. "They usually mean nobody's trying to kill me. Unlike the natural kind."

Tybalt laughed. I took advantage of the pause to study the front window of the bookstore, where a display of books about robots was arranged alongside a sign advertising the store hours. Inside, tall bookshelves were the order of the day. A woman almost pale enough to be nocturnal stood behind the register, a red kerchief tied over her near-black hair. She glanced up, saw me looking in, and smiled in the tired but welcoming way of early morning shopkeepers everywhere.

Tybalt stepped up next to me. "Have you any idea what comes next?"

"Yeah." I took a long drink of coffee. I actually tasted it this time. "We go inside."

The bookstore was even quieter than the café, probably because it didn't hold as many people. The hardwood floors were older, softened by worn Oriental rugs, and classic rock played from somewhere behind the counter. The woman was still smiling at us.

"Welcome to Borderlands," she said. "Let me know if I can help you find anything."

She sounded like a California native. I smiled back and raised my coffee cup, using the action to mask opening my mouth and breathing in a brief taste of her heritage. Human. I lowered the cup. "Actually, maybe. My sister was here recently, and she said she was supposed to get a call from a lady who works here? Um . . . her name was Arlene or Denise or . . . something, I don't know. My sister's not too organized."

To my relief, the woman grinned. "I'd be willing to bet you're looking for Ardith. Give me a second. I'll see if she's ready to start her shift."

"I'd appreciate that," I said. I'm technically allowed to thank humans. That doesn't stop it from feeling weird. I avoid it when I can.

"Just be glad you came in early—Ardith helps open, and then she's gone until late afternoon," said the woman. She moved out from behind the counter, heading toward a door at the back of the room and vanishing through it.

Her motion, meanwhile, had startled the store's cat, which had been curled unseen on one of the chairs behind the counter. It leaped up next to the register, where it crouched, wrapping its tail around its legs, and considered us with eyes the color of Midori liqueur.

Tybalt recoiled, horror and shock in his face. "What," he demanded, "is *that*?"

"It's a cat," I said. There was a sign next to the register. "It says her name is Ripley. She's a Sphinx. They're hairless cats from Canada. Huh. Who'd have thought hairless cats would come from Canada?" I gave the cat another look. "I wonder if I should get one for Quentin."

"It's *naked*," said Tybalt.

He was right: the cat was almost completely hairless, with only a few stubby, half-curled whiskers and some patches of fuzz on her toes and tail. Her skin was pink blotched with black and orange, like part of her remembered, deep down, that she was supposed to be calico. She was still watching us. I'd been around Tybalt and my own cats long enough to interpret her expression as a smirk.

"She's pretty, in a weird, alien life-form, probably steals souls in the night kind of way," I said. I held out a hand. Ripley sniffed it with the expected gravitas before deigning to butt her forehead against my fingers. "I think she likes me."

"Delightful," grumbled Tybalt.

"You don't get worked up over Manx cats."

"Missing a tail is nothing like missing all your hair," said Tybalt primly.

I snorted laughter, and took another drink of coffee. That was all I had time for before an unfamiliar voice from behind us said, "Oh, you met Ripley. She's granting you a great favor, you know. She doesn't always let first-timers see her. Now what's this about a sister?"

This time, when I tasted the air to feel out the heritage of those around us, I got more than just Dóchas and Cait Sidhe. The flavor of Tuatha de Dannan overlaid them both, strong and very, very close. Lowering my coffee, I turned. Tybalt turned with me.

The voice had come from what looked like a perfectly normal shop girl. She was wearing jeans, and a black shirt with red cap sleeves and the store's logo printed across the chest. Each of her ears had been pieced three times, something that was easy to notice, since we were almost the same height. Her eyes were two different colors, one brown, one so blue it was almost disconcerting, and her hair was chestnut brown, worn long. Her bangs overhung her eyes, and her skin was even paler than mine. She was looking at us with cheerful curiosity, like she couldn't wait to help with our question, and for a moment I hated myself for coming here to drag this girl back into the world she'd clearly walked away from when her father died. I knew all too well what it was to have people putting their expectations of your parents onto your shoulders. It wasn't fair of us to come here and ask this of her.

It wasn't fair for the Queen of the Mists to bring goblin fruit into the city. It wasn't fair for me to be exiled from my home. The Luidaeg was right: Faerie isn't fair. Maybe it was never meant to be.

"There's no sister," I said, talking fast to get the words out before the human clerk came back. "Well. I have a sister, but she's never been here. None of us have. Your charms made sure of that, Your Highness, and I know they've kept you safe for a long time, but it's time to stop hiding. Your Kingdom needs you."

Her eyes widened. Then they narrowed, taking on a calculating cast as she looked from me to Tybalt and back again. "I don't know what you're talking about. Now please leave, or I'll tell Jude you're harassing me, and she'll call the police."

"Princess." Tybalt's voice was a slow rumble. She turned to him, expression melting toward confusion. He has that effect on most women, including me. "I knew your father. He was a good man, and he equipped you with the means to hide yourself for good reason. I was a reluctant Prince, in my own time, and I know the terror of the throne. I claimed mine when to do otherwise would have been to fail my people. Can you owe your people any less?"

"I don't know who you people are or what you want, but you need to leave," she said. "Now."

The store was still empty, and Jude hadn't reappeared. I decided to push things a little farther before giving up. I took a breath, and said, "Your name is Arden Windermere. Your father was King Gilad Windermere. I don't know where you've been or what you've been doing since he died, but the Mists needs you. *I* need you." I reached into my jacket pocket, relieved when the firefly inside responded by climbing onto my fingertip.

The firefly's glow brightened as I pulled it out into the open air of the shop. It rose on only slightly-battered wings to fly to Arden, hovering in front of her startled eyes for a moment before doing a loop around her head and finally landing on her chest like a strange, living jewel.

"We don't have the wrong girl," I said.

Arden looked down at the firefly clinging to her shirt. Then she looked up again, sorrow and despair warring in her eyes. "Don't do this," she begged. "Whoever you are, whatever you want, don't do this. Leave. Walk away. Don't make me refuse you again."

"We can't," I said. "But if you'd like to talk about it in private, we'd be happy to listen."

Her expression sharpened, turning almost feral. It was the sort of wary, assessing look I'd seen on the face of every child Devin had ever brought Home, the kind of look that knew there was no help coming. "How do I know you're not working for *her*?"

There was no question of who Arden meant when she said "her": a Princess hiding in her own kingdom would have no need to refer to anyone with that much bitterness unless she was talking about the person who held the throne that should have been hers. "The Queen of the Mists hates me more than just about anyone else," I said. "Maybe she hates you more, if she knows you exist, but I don't know. What I do know is that I'm not her creature. If you need proof of that, well. She banished me last night. I have three days to get out of the Kingdom."

"I am a King of Cats," said Tybalt. "My loyalty is first to my people, second to my lady, and lastly to myself. The Kings and Queens of the Divided Courts have no power over me."

Arden shook her head. Then she turned to the office and shouted, "Jude, I need to spend some more time with these folks, okay? Tell Madden I'll be downstairs if he needs me."

"Okay . . ." Jude's answering call sounded dubious. Arden clapped a hand over the firefly on her chest just before the mortal woman emerged from the back room, wrapping her fingers around it. She put her hand behind her back, offering Jude a sickly smile. Jude blinked and then frowned, giving us a suspicious look. "Ardith? Is everything okay?"

"I'm fine. I just have the things I promised to give to her sister downstairs." Arden shot me a panicked look as she realized she didn't know what to call me.

"I'm October, by the way," I said, to Jude. I tried to make it look like a normal introduction. I probably failed.

Tybalt, naturally, was cool as ever. "Rand," he said, smiling. "It's a pleasure to make your acquaintance."

"Uh-huh," said Jude. She was looking more suspicious by the second. "Ardith, are you sure you don't want me to keep your friends company up here while you go get whatever you need from the basement?"

"I'm sure," Arden said. "Just tell Madden where I am."

"Right." Jude stepped behind the counter. Her smile did not reappear.

"Come on." Arden gestured for us to follow her with the hand that wasn't full of firefly. She led us to a small door near the front of the shop and opened it, revealing a narrow flight of stairs descending beneath the building. She started down, leaving us no choice but to follow. Tybalt went last, and closed the door behind himself, cutting the light to almost nothing. Only almost: the firefly in Arden's hand was glowing brighter than ever. The light seeped through her fingers, lessening the darkness just enough to make it navigable to fae eyes.

Arden didn't speak as she walked down the stairs to the basement below. It was a large, cavernous room that appeared to exactly mirror the bookstore over our heads. Support pillars broke up the space, explaining why several hundred paperbacks weren't crashing down on our heads. Everything smelled of fresh sawdust and old dampness, the clean kind that naturally built up underground. It spoke of growth and potential, not decay.

"Shield your eyes," Arden said, and flicked a switch on the wall. Bulbs came on overhead, almost blinding after the darkness. She opened her hand, letting the firefly free, and released her human disguise in the same motion.

Her magic smelled like redwood bark and blackberry flowers. Her hair was the color of blackberries, so black it was virtually purple, with strange, glossy undertones. Her eyes stayed mismatched, but instead of brown and blue, they were polished pyrite and shifting mercury silver. No wonder a somewhat alien blue had been the best she could do. Those were eyes designed to resist concealment. Her ears were delicately pointed, and her bone structure had changed subtly, but those things were almost afterthoughts. Nothing human had those eyes.

She glared at us as the firefly circled her head and came to rest once more on her chest. "Who sent you?"

"The Luidaeg." I pulled the flask of fireflies out of my jacket pocket, holding it up. Arden gasped. "She thought we might have trouble finding you, so she gave us these."

Arden's surprise quickly faded into wariness. "I don't believe you."

"Of course you don't." I tucked the flask away again as I released my human disguise. I smelled pennyroyal, and knew without looking that Tybalt was doing the same thing, both of us trying to convince our reluctant Princess that we meant her no harm. We didn't look like the Queen's guards. I was wearing an increasingly dingy ball gown, and Tybalt was the wrong species. "We haven't been properly introduced. My name is Sir October Daye, Knight of Lost Words, in service to Duke Sylvester Torquill of Shadowed Hills." I didn't identify my race. The human in my background would be easy enough for her to see, and for the moment, it was better if I didn't try to explain the situation with my mother.

For once, my name brought no flicker of recognition or reminder of things I hadn't necessarily intended to do. Arden just frowned, and said, "I remember Duke Torquill. He was a nice man."

"He still is."

"I am Tybalt, King of the Court of Dreaming Cats," said Tybalt. "I knew your father."

"So you said, but what makes you sure he *was* my father?" Arden focused her frown on him. It was a bit of a relief to see her glaring at someone else. "I never said I was your girl. Maybe I just took you guys down here because I didn't want you talking crazy in front of Jude. She doesn't know."

"That's good; mortals shouldn't," I said. "You didn't have to say it. The fireflies know."

"You have your father's eyes," added Tybalt. "It's no wonder you had to work so hard to hide yourself. Anyone who knew the King would have looked at you and known you for his child. I am so sorry for your loss."

Those words seemed to seal any hope Arden had that we could be convinced she was really Ardith, bookstore clerk, and not Arden, Princess in the Mists. Her face crumpled, tears springing up in her mismatched eyes. "No one said that to us," she said. "No one knew how much we'd lost. Father was gone, and Mother . . ."

Understanding hit me. There was an element we'd missed, someone who should have either whisked the children safely out of the Kingdom or backed their claim to their father's throne. "What happened?"

"She was one of his servants at the Court," said Arden. She sniffled. "It was how they made sure no one was suspicious about them spending time together. It was like a game they played. They made sure we knew the rules, so we wouldn't get mad at Father for refusing to acknowledge her, or mad at Mother for letting him ignore her. It was even fun, sometimes, when she brought us to the Court and made us wear disguises and pretend we were changelings, or servant-children, or fosters. We learned about hiding." She reached up, touching the corner of her silver-mercury eye, and added, "We had a nursemaid to spin our illusions for us, back then. We didn't have to depend on our own."

"That makes sense," I said, not wanting to interrupt the flow of her story, but not wanting her to think I wasn't listening.

"When the earthquake came . . . things were falling

everywhere. Nolan's leg was hit when some rocks came out of the wall. I went running, looking for Mother. We weren't supposed to talk to her when we were at Court. I broke the rules." For a moment, her expression was a child's, filled with the quiet conviction that breaking the rules somehow caused everything that followed. "The earthquake was still happening. I found her in one of the bedchambers, where she'd been changing the sheets. She was already . . ." She closed her eyes. "She was gone."

I blinked. "Wait. She was dead? Did something fall and hit her?" Some of the chandeliers I'd seen in noble knowes could crush an adult, if the chandelier was falling and the adult was unlucky.

"No." Arden opened her eyes. "Her throat was slit. She was murdered. My father was, too. There's no way he died in the quake. He was Tuatha de Dannan. He was a *King*. He would have died saving his people, if he died at all. Instead, they said he was crushed. Just crushed. That's not possible. That's not my father. Someone killed them, and they would have killed Nolan and me if Marianne—our nursemaid—hadn't taken us away before anyone realized who we were. So, yes, you found the missing Princess in the Mists. Now please, save my life, and leave."

"Oh, oak and ash," I whispered. People had always suspected that King Gilad was assassinated; Oleander de Merelands was in the Kingdom at the time, and her presence combined with his death was too convenient to ignore. This was as close as we could get to proof without questioning the night-haunts. Arden had been orphaned, and her parents had been murdered. "I'm so sorry."

"It was a long time ago," she said—but her tone made her words into lies. Her voice was shaky and raw, like the deaths had happened only days before. She'd been deferring her grief over a century, and grief deferred can turn toxic. "But that's why you have to leave. You can't be here. You can't ask me to claim the throne. I have nothing left to lose."

I paused, a sudden thought striking me. Arden wasn't an only child. Her brother, Nolan, might not have been

Crown Prince, but he was with her during the earth-quake, and he went with her into hiding. So why was she only asking us to save *her* life by leaving? "Arden, where's your brother?" I asked.

"You're very young, aren't you?" Her reply seemed nonsensical until she continued, saying, "You think you're the first ones to track me down. Like *that* could happen. Our parents did their best, but there were always rumors. The lost Prince. The missing Princess. It was a fairy tale waiting to happen, and you know how we love our fairy tales." She spun on her heel, stalking toward the back of the basement. After four steps, she paused, looking back, and demanded, "Well?"

"We're coming," I said, exchanging a glance with Tybalt. We walked after her, approaching the rear wall.

The closer we got, the stranger it looked. It was like someone had painted a perfect replica of the actual wall, and then hung the picture in place, using it to hide the fact that the room wasn't all there. Arden slipped her hands into a fold in the air, pulling the illusion open like a heavy canvas curtain. It was a gesture much like the one Tybalt used when he was accessing the Shadow Roads, but with less natural ease: this wasn't her spell.

"Marianne's work," she said, holding the illusion open for us. "She was Coblynau. She left us with everything she knew we'd need, and then she disappeared."

That explained the quality of the illusion. Tuatha de Dannan are passable illusionists, but they're barely in a league with the Daoine Sidhe, much less the masters. Coblynau are good, and more, can bind their spells into objects. That long-gone nursemaid saved her charges' lives with the things she'd given them. She had to know it, too. It was the only reason someone who loved the children she was tasked to protect would have left them. Her presence was a danger, and her gifts were the shield her body couldn't be.

We stepped through the curtain. Arden followed us through, letting the illusion fall closed again. Viewed from inside, it really *was* a curtain, a heavy canvas sheet with a slit cut down the middle. A narrow slice of the basement showed through the gap. Arden pinched it closed, sealing us inside.

The space on the other side of the illusion was small, about the size of my bedroom back at the old apartment. A bunk bed was flush with the basement wall. The bottom bunk was a welter of sheets and handmade quilts, and a reading lamp was set up there, gooseneck bent toward the piled-up pillows. Mismatched bookshelves lined the walls, piled with books, DVDs, even VHS and Betamax tapes. There was a stereo system and a television, which was on, quietly playing an episode of some television drama that I didn't recognize. There hadn't been any sound from the other side of the curtain.

A heavy wardrobe took up almost a quarter of the living space, made from what looked like redwood, with a pattern of blackberry vines and dragonflies carved into the doors. It was the nicest piece of furniture in the room, and as such, it immediately caught and held our eyes. It also raised the question of exactly how much Arden could transport when she teleported. That thing had to weigh two hundred pounds, easy.

She followed my gaze and scowled "It was my mother's," said Arden. "You wanted to know why I don't want your help reclaiming my throne? Tempting as the idea sounds? Come here." She walked to the bunk bed, where she stepped onto the lower bunk, holding the upper rail in both hands. I walked after her, and at her silent urging, climbed the ladder so I could see what she was looking at.

In a way, I already knew what I'd see. But some things must be seen in their own time, and in their own way; some things can't simply be said. As I looked down at the sleeping body of Prince Nolan Windermere in the Mists, I knew that this was one of those things. He looked almost enough like Arden to have been her twin. He had the same blackberry hair, and the same faintly olive Tuatha skin. His clothing was out of date, making him look like he'd just stepped out of a production of *The Great Gatsby*.

"Nolan didn't like what that woman had been doing to our father's Kingdom," Arden said. "He wanted us to come forward during the War of Silences, but we were too young to rule, and we were so afraid. I convinced him to wait a little longer, and see if she'd get better. Maybe she'd turn into the kind of Queen our father wanted me to be, and then it wouldn't matter that the throne wasn't mine. As long as someone was caring for the Mists, it would be all right."

"But she didn't," I said quietly.

"No. She got worse, and after Silences, she started changing the rules. Our father was never a great advocate for changeling rights," the look she cast my way was almost apologetic, "but he believed they were a part of Faerie, and they deserved to be treated fairly. When he was alive, Oberon's Law was applied to the changelings of his Kingdom. He let them hold titles, as long as they never aspired to claim anything greater than a Barony. He was . . . he was fair."

I stared at her for a moment before looking back down at Nolan. "That's not the world I grew up in," I said.

Tybalt's hand landed on my shoulder, squeezing once. I descended the ladder, putting my hand over his and holding him there as Arden began speaking again.

"Father maintained ties with the Undersea and the Sky Kingdoms. He insisted we treat the Cait Sidhe with respect, because Oberon wouldn't have given them dominion over themselves if they weren't worth respecting. He did all those things, and she did none of them. I was scared. Marianne—our nursemaid—was so clear about how important it was for us to hide, and I'd seen Mother's body. Nolan never did. He wanted us to come out of hiding. He wanted us to take back what was supposed to be ours. He wasn't *scared*." From her tone, she wished he had been.

"What happened?" I asked.

"He said we had to go to the false Queen and demand our Kingdom back. I told him he was being foolish, that all he'd do was get us both killed. But Nolan never listened to a word he didn't want to hear. He slipped out of the boarding house where we were living while I was at work. The pixies led me to him two days later. He was in the bushes in Golden Gate Park, with the arrow still in his chest. They'd used it to leave a note." A tear ran down her cheek, falling onto the pillow next to Nolan's head. It probably wasn't the first.

"What did it say?"

"That I was lucky they'd only used elf-shot; that if they saw either of us, ever again, they wouldn't be so merciful." She looked up again, eyes hardening. "They would have killed him. I *know* they would have killed him. But they needed me to know I'd be a fool to stand up to them."

"No," I said. "I'm sorry, Arden, but no. They didn't need you to know. They weren't being merciful. They needed you to be *afraid*. If they'd really wanted to show you that you were too weak to defeat them, they would have killed your brother. They left him alive because they wanted you scared, not angry. The War of Silences happened in the 1930s, and judging by his clothes, that's how long he's been asleep. That means he'll wake up soon. Do you want to tell him they won? That they made you sit out the fight because they told you had things would happen if you didn't?"

Arden looked at me solemnly. Then she looked down at her brother, reaching out to wipe an imaginary smear of dust away from his cheek. "Father did everything he could to protect us," she said.

"It's time for you to pay him back," I said. "It's time for you to protect his Kingdom."

"*Your* Kingdom," said Tybalt.

Arden shook her head. "We've been safe because we've been invisible. We have no allies. We have no resources. My brother's been elf-shot. Where could we possibly go?"

I blinked. And then, slowly, I smiled. "Princess," I said, "I know someone who would very much like the opportunity to meet you."

TEN

THE REDWOOD-SCENTED PORTAL closed behind us as Arden and I stepped into the darkened hall of Goldengreen. Arden staggered, looking winded. I offered a hand to steady her.

"Easy," I said. "It's been a while since you've had to take passengers." Not to mention the strain of teleporting into someone else's knowe, where the wards wouldn't recognize her. We'd probably just broken half a dozen rules of etiquette, as well as a few prohibitions against trespassing, but I wasn't as concerned about that. Dean would understand once he saw who I was bringing with me. We wouldn't have been able to get inside at all if I hadn't been the keeper of Goldengreen at one point— and most teleporters couldn't have made the journey without knowing their destination. She was strong.

I hoped that was going to be a good thing.

Arden shrugged off my hand, looking around us. "Where's my brother?"

"He and Tybalt should be right behind us," I said. It had been hard to convince Arden to take me while Tybalt carried Nolan, but the division was necessary. No matter how strong she was, she couldn't open a portal big enough to get four people safely across the city. The trouble was, since Nolan was asleep, he wouldn't know not to breathe on the Shadow Roads. That meant taking the long way around, through the Court of Cats, to give him time to thaw.

A swarm of pixies raced down the hall, scattering off in all directions to avoid hitting us. Rather than flying on, they clung to the walls and tapestries, scolding in shrill, bell-like voices. A female whose wings and body were glowing a bright daisy yellow stopped to hover in front of my nose, shaking her finger and scolding me in a high, chiming voice.

"Hey, I couldn't ask permission before we came," I protested. "Don't worry. Count Lorden will approve once I have a chance to explain."

"I'm glad to hear you're planning to explain," said a voice.

"Hi, Marcia." I sighed with relief, turning my back on the pixie as I faced her. "I'm sorry to burst in like this, but we couldn't go outside; the Queen's guards know what my human disguise looks like. Tybalt should be arriving with another guest any minute now. Again, sorry for the lack of advance warning. Things have been a little crazy." I paused, blinking. "Marcia?"

The quarter-blooded changeling was staring at Arden, blue eyes gone so wide and normally rosy cheeks gone so pale that for a moment, I was afraid she was going to pass out. Then she shook her head, smile returning, and stepped forward to offer her hand. "I'm sorry. I didn't catch your name."

Arden took a breath, and said, "I am Princess Arden Windermere, rightful heir to this Kingdom, and I am about to be sick." She sounded apologetic about that last part. I suppose princesses aren't supposed to puke. "Do you have a bathroom I can use?"

Not the most regal greeting ever, but Marcia took it in stride, offering Arden her arm. "Right this way, Your Highness, and while you're settling your stomach, I'll tell the Count you've arrived." She cast a half-panicked look over Arden's shoulder at me. "He'll be surprised to hear that he's hosting such a royal guest."

I shrugged, mouthing "Sorry."

"I'm not particularly royal anymore." Arden took Marcia's arm. Apparently, now that Marcia knew her real name, she fell into the category of "trust, because there's no other option." It was pragmatic of her, although it may have had something to do with her apparently urgent need to vomit. As she was led down the hall, I heard her ask, "Do you have any crackers?"

Half the pixies followed them. The other half stayed with me, still ringing in strident annoyance. I sighed and dug my phone out of my pocket. Scrolling quickly through my contact list, I found the name I needed and pressed the button to complicate the situation even further.

After the second ring, Etienne's calm, overly cultured voice said, "Hello?"

I sighed with relief. "Hi, Etienne," I said. "Can you put His Grace on for me? I sort of have a situation."

There was a pause while Etienne considered my request. We go way back, Etienne and me, and my part of our relationship has traditionally consisted of giving him headaches and creating messes he has to clean up. That changed a few months ago, when I saved the life of the teenage daughter he hadn't even known he had. Etienne had always possessed a certain grudging respect for me. Saving Chelsea may have finally made us friends.

"Is this one of those situations where the less I know, the happier I'll be?" he asked.

"Absolutely. I absolve you of all involvement, at least for right now. Just please, please, get me the Duke."

"Hang on," said Etienne. There was a thump as he set the receiver down. It wasn't loud, but it was loud enough I might have missed the soft sound of Tybalt's footsteps, had they not been accompanied by the pennyroyal and musk scent of his magic—and the maddened shrieks of the pixies, who were clearly unhappy about the ongoing invasion of their territory.

I turned. Tybalt was behind me, holding Nolan in a fireman's carry. He was winded, and as I watched, he lowered the unconscious Prince to the floor, half-propping him against the wall. "Remind me, next time I agree to something like this, that I am an idiot and should not be trusted to make these decisions," he said, wheezing.

I grimaced. Before I could reply, the phone was picked up, and Sylvester said, "October? What's wrong?"

Moment of truth time. I took a deep breath, and answered his question with a question. "If I had reason to believe one of our local nobles was holding their demesne illegitimately, would you want to know?" That should be vague enough that he wouldn't jump straight to "you mean the Queen." I hoped.

Silence until, finally, he asked, "October, where are you?"

"I'm at Goldengreen." I paused before adding the next piece of the night's news. I didn't want to upset him, but he needed to know. "Oh, and the Queen of the Mists has sort of exiled me from her Kingdom."

His sharp intake of breath was audible even through the phone. Then he said, "Please come to Shadowed Hills at your earliest convenience. And to answer your earlier question . . . I would absolutely like to know." The phone went dead.

I lowered it, closing the lid as I turned to Tybalt. "Sylvester's on board and wants us to drop by later. Now we just need Quentin."

Tybalt raised an eyebrow. "How's that?"

"He's my squire, he should be here to watch me rail against the monarchy."

Tybalt sighed. "Give me your phone."

"What?" I blinked. Of all the things he could have requested, that one was near the bottom of the list.

"I will call Raj, who has recently taken to carrying one of those damnable machines. Raj will go get Quentin. They're similar in size, and it's time my nephew started transporting others through the Shadow Roads. He needs the practice."

". . . right." I handed my phone to Tybalt, trying not to

think about the fact that I was signing up my squire as a test case for a Prince-in-training. "I'm going to go see if I can find Dean and get help carrying Nolan to a better napping spot." Hopefully, Dean would be okay with the fact that his knowe was becoming party central for the anti-Queen action. The fact that his parents were together in part because of Arden's parents might help. If I was lucky.

"I'll be right there," Tybalt assured me, and began to dial.

I turned and walked toward the courtyard. That was my best hope of finding Dean fast. If I was going to run this fire drill, I wanted to run it *right*. Maybe it was cliché to hide the Crown Princess of the Mists in the only County in San Francisco whose regent had ties to the Undersea, but this was my first planned rebellion against the throne, and I was flying by the seat of my pants. Those pants said "go where she's likely to find allies."

Even if this didn't work out, I had little doubt the Undersea would be happy to take Arden and Nolan in, hiding them where the Queen could never reach them. I snorted with suppressed amusement. Me, October "I was a fish for fourteen years" Daye, advocating that someone go hide with the mermaids. I guess some traumas get better with time. That, or they wind up buried under newer, bigger problems.

Dean was running across the courtyard when I stepped inside. His eyes widened when he saw me, and he stumbled to a stop. "What's going on?" he demanded.

"Do you want the long version or the short version?"

"The pixies and bogeys are going out of their minds! I don't really understand them—"

"Who does?"

"—but Marcia ran off when they started freaking out, and she hasn't come back, and now you're here! What's *happening*?"

I took a deep breath. "Marcia is in the bathroom with one of your unexpected guests, who needed to throw up after teleporting us both across the city. Tybalt is in the hall with another, who isn't throwing up, largely because he's been elf-shot."

"Tybalt's been elf-shot?" asked Dean blankly.

"No, the other guest has been elf-shot. Tybalt's fine. He's calling Raj to pick up Quentin and bring him here. Sylvester is also on the way."

Dean frowned. "Anyone else?"

"No, that's it for now. Only you should probably call your parents back, because they're going to want to be here for this particular debriefing."

Dean's frown deepened, growing more suspicious. "Why is that?"

In for a penny . . . "Because the guest in the bathroom with Marcia is Crown Princess Arden Windermere in the Mists, and the elf-shot man in the hall is her younger brother, Nolan. They're here because we need—*I* need—Arden to take her throne back, and she has good reason to be afraid for her life if the Queen hears about her. I figured we might find allies in Goldengreen. Or, if not, we might at least find a fast ship to very, very far away."

"I hate sailing, and I'm supposed to close the bookstore tomorrow. Jude's going to be pissed if I don't show up," said Arden. I turned. She was standing in the doorway. Marcia was a few feet behind her, still looking pale. Arden, meanwhile, smiled wanly and walked forward to offer Dean her hand. "I'm told you're the Count who currently holds this demesne. We appreciate your hospitality." She cast a glance my way. "I'm definitely going to need to hear the story of what happened to Countess Winterrose. I thought that old spider would be squatting here until the stars burned out."

"She died," I said.

"Short story," said Arden. She turned back to Dean. "I'm sorry to barge in on you like this. October said this might be a safe place to go, and we never went out into the open. No one could have seen us."

Dean blinked, first at Arden, and then at the hand she was offering him. Finally, he took a step backward and bowed. His form wasn't what I'd have expected from a courtier raised on land, but his posture was good, and his spine curled in the perfect mixture of deference and civility. Courtly manners aren't identical throughout Faerie. They're still recognizable, whatever form they take.

"If you are who October indicates you to be, I am your servant," he said, straightening. "If you are not, you are still welcome here. Any friend of hers is a friend of Goldengreen."

Arden blinked mismatched eyes in visible surprise before withdrawing her hand. "I guess I'm a little out of touch."

"A hundred years among the mortals will do that, I understand," said Tybalt, walking in behind us. He was carrying Nolan slung over his shoulder like a sack of slumbering potatoes. "Where might I deposit this gentleman? I am loath to drop a potential Prince a second time, but he is *remarkably* heavy for one who has not eaten in decades."

"Marcia." Dean looked to his seneschal. "Please prepare a guest chamber for the Princess' brother. Meanwhile—" Whatever Dean was intending to say was lost as two teenage boys burst through the doorway, both of them moving at a speed that was probably unsafe when there were other people involved. Quentin managed to skid to a stop, his shoes making an unpleasant scraping noise on the cobblestones. Raj seemed like he was on a collision course with Arden until Tybalt reached out with his free hand and grabbed his nephew by the scruff of his neck, bringing him to an abrupt halt.

I didn't bother hiding my smile. "Hi, boys," I said. "Welcome to our party."

"Did you really find the Princess?" Raj demanded, twisting in Tybalt's hand as he tried to get a better look at Arden. "Let me down, I want to see!"

"He was never this willful before you came along," said Tybalt mildly.

"Liar," I replied. Raj was a Prince of Cats. "He's always been this bad. Raj, calm down. There's enough stupid political intrigue for everybody."

Raj stopped squirming. Tybalt let him go, and he brushed himself off, going from hyperactive kitten to feline royalty in an instant. He turned to Arden. "Hello," he said. He didn't bow. Cait Sidhe bow to members of the Divided Courts only when they want to, and a wayward Princess he'd only just met didn't rate. Instead, he looked at her, taking her measure with his eyes.

Arden might not have remembered all her courtly manners, but she clearly knew how to be looked at by a cat. She crossed her arms, raising an eyebrow, and eyed Raj right back, giving as good as she got. Like Quentin, Raj was growing like a weed, although she wouldn't appreciate that the way that I did. When I first met him, he was a half-starved refugee in Blind Michael's lands. Now he was a tall, thin teenage boy who somehow managed to avoid "gangly" in favor of looking like he was going to be snapped up to model jeans at any moment. His hair was russet red tipped with brown, like an Abyssinian cat's, and his eyes were the green of leaded carnival glass. He looked nothing like Tybalt—they weren't blood relatives—but after spending so much time around the Cait Sidhe, there was no way for me to look at him and not see the subtle marks of power that labeled him as a Prince.

"Hello," said Arden finally. She extended her hand again. Unlike Dean, Raj took it. "Arden Windermere."

"Raj." He shook once, then reclaimed his hand and looked to Quentin, apparently waiting to see what was going to happen next. I followed his gaze. I was as curious as he was.

Much to my surprise, Quentin neither bowed nor offered his hand. Instead, he cocked his head, studying Arden. His gaze was franker than Raj's had been, like he was looking for something specific. Finally, he asked, "Was King Windermere your father?"

"It was a long time ago, so I never got a paternity test, but as far as I'm aware, yes," she said. She looked almost amused. "My brother looks just like him. We both have his eyes. Our mother always swore we were his fault. So I'm assuming he was my father."

"Okay," said Quentin. He bowed—not as formally as Dean had, but with a goodly measure of propriety. "It is a pleasure to meet you, milady."

"This is my squire, Quentin," I said. "Let me know if he bothers you. I'll slap him upside the head until he stops." I paused before adding, "Raj is also sort of my squire, but mostly, he's Tybalt's heir. I also have slapping rights where he's concerned."

Raj wrinkled his nose. Tybalt looked amused.

Dean, meanwhile, rubbed the back of his neck, and said, "This all seems a little, well. Lighthearted. If we're actually doing what I think we're doing."

Marcia stepped back into the room. I hadn't even seen her leave. "I've prepared a room for the Prince," she said. "My Lord, your parents are on their way. They should be here shortly, if you wanted to receive them in the cove."

"That's a good idea," said Dean. He rubbed the back of his neck one more time before asking, "Tybalt, can you . . . ?"

"I will join you by the water," said Tybalt, and turned, following Marcia out of the room. I watched him go. Nolan's head banging against the middle of his back only detracted a little bit from my customary admiration of his ass.

I turned back to the others. Dean met my eyes and grimaced.

"You really don't have a plan, do you?" he asked.

"Not as such," I admitted. "But I have a Princess, and that's better than I was doing a few hours ago. Let's go see your folks."

The walk to the cove-side receiving room was less disorienting this time, since it was no longer totally unfamiliar. Raj and Quentin, on the other hand, gaped. They'd both essentially lived in Goldengreen while it was mine, and they'd done more exploring than I had, since, well, they were teenage boys and I wasn't. For them, the existence of an unfamiliar hallway was both a delight and an insult to their skills.

Arden walked more slowly than Dean and the boys. I fell back to pace her, walking alongside her in silence for a little while before I asked, "Are you okay?"

"Yes," she said. Then she laughed unsteadily. "No. No, I am not okay."

"You want to talk about it?"

She waved a hand, indicating the walls. "When I got up this morning, I wasn't planning my return to Faerie to be quite this . . . now. Or ever. You're all very nice, and I'm sorry if this seems rude, but you haven't shown me anything that makes me think we can take the throne. You've got what, a King of Cats, a couple of kids, and some changelings? No offense."

"None taken," I lied. Ahead of us, Dean stiffened. He'd clearly heard Arden lumping him in with the "kids." "Look. We're sorry to drag you into this. But aren't you tired of hiding?"

"Yes," she admitted. "That doesn't mean I'm tired of *living*. The one seemed like the best way to accomplish the other."

I sympathized with her, I really did. There was a time when I did my best to get the hell out of Faerie—and my best was never anything close to Arden's, which removed her from our world for the better part of a century. Maybe longer, depending on how involved she'd been before Nolan got elf-shot. Faerie is huge and complicated and frankly scary if you've been living in the mortal world, where the laws of physics don't change from hour to hour and the inanimate doesn't take sides.

But that didn't mean I'd let Arden walk away from her duty. Maybe that was ironic—me, October Daye, the woman who once said destiny could go screw itself if it insisted on trying to make me play its reindeer games—but I didn't care. Arden was the Princess in the Mists. Unless she took the throne, nothing was going to change, and I was going to be banished. Neither of those things was okay with me, and that meant she was going to do her job.

I didn't scold her. Instead, I said, "We have more allies

than you think. I sort of collect them. You might be surprised by how much of the Kingdom will side with us once they know who you are."

"You're going to need an army," said Arden, a note of well-worn bitterness in her tone.

Her voice carried. As we stepped off the stairway into the receiving room, Dianda Lorden, Duchess of Saltmist, stood from where she'd been sitting at the edge of the water. The scales covering her tail fell away, replaced by legs wrapped in blue canvas trousers. She was dressed like a pirate preparing to board a merchant ship. No romance here; just solid, serviceable clothing. Patrick stood next to her, his own clothes quietly echoing hers . . . and behind them stood what looked like a regiment of seafolk. Merrow and Selkies, Cephali and Naiads, and beyond them in the water, the vast forms of the Cetacea.

"Will this army do?" asked Dianda.

Arden's widened eyes provided all of the answer we needed.

ELEVEN

BRINGING THE UNDERSEA INTO THE PICTURE
meant another round of introductions, none of which
managed to top Arden meeting Dean for awkwardness,
although all of them came with some measure of sizing
up. Arden looked uncomfortable, the Undersea guards
looked murderous—nothing new there—and Dianda
looked murderously hopeful, like this was the opportunity she'd been waiting for since King Gilad died. I
guess it's not every day you get invited to overthrow
the ruler of the neighboring Kingdom and get away
with it.

"At least I hope we get away with it," I muttered, picking at the ribbons snarled in my hair. I had retreated to
stand near the wall while Dianda introduced her people
to Arden. This was Dean's County, not mine. Let him
handle the tricky political bits. I just didn't want to get
dripped on by the admittedly damp representatives of
the myriad Undersea races.

Where I went, Quentin inevitably followed. It's been
that way for years, so it wasn't a surprise when he trailed
after me. I elbowed him as best I could with my hands
full of hair.

"Don't you want to hang out and learn about the politics and stuff?" I asked. "Hell, it's an opportunity to get

to know a Princess. Isn't that supposed to appeal to your inner romantic or something?"

Quentin snorted. "If you're going to ask two questions in a row, could you not end them with 'stuff' and 'something'? It makes you sound ..." He stopped, apparently realizing there was no good way to end that statement. Finally, he mumbled, "Princesses aren't that exciting. I've met princesses before."

"Uh-huh." I balled up a ribbon, flicking it at him before starting on the next one. "Where did you meet a Princess?"

"Not here." He folded his arms, looking back to the gathering.

That meant that he'd probably met a Princess somewhere in Canada, and that telling me would give away too much about where he came from. Pressing the subject would have been rude, and so I didn't try, asking instead, "What did you find at the Library after we left?"

"Lots of stuff about the history of the Kingdom of the Mists. The Kingdom was founded by Denley and Nola Windermere; they had two children, a daughter, who died before she could be named—a curse was suspected, but never proven—and Gilad, who was basically raised in a bubble."

"They probably felt like that was the only way he'd live to take the throne." I shook my head. "Does *anyone* royal ever die a natural death?"

"Statistically speaking, no," said Tybalt, stepping out of the shadows beside me. I didn't flinch. Years of putting up with his sense of humor even before we started dating have left me surprisingly desensitized to people sneaking up on me that way. It's probably going to get me killed one of these days.

"What do you mean?" I asked.

"I was not in the Mists before Gilad's reign, but it was common knowledge that his parents had been murdered. I would not be surprised if it was done to make room for someone else's political agenda. Gilad was a young King. He had not been given sufficient time to prepare before he took his place." He moved to stand behind me, pushing my hands away as he began delicately unwinding the ribbons from my hair. "The trouble with killing old Kings in hopes that young ones will be more easily controlled is that young Kings are frequently headstrong and angry over their change in status. They refuse to listen to reason, and they are not always as weak as they are expected to be."

"Did anything indicate that King Gilad was involved with the conspiracy that killed his parents?" I asked, dropping my hands to give Tybalt room to work.

Quentin shook his head. "Kind of the opposite. Apparently, the High King had to coerce him into taking the throne, because he didn't want to rule in the Kingdom where his parents had died. And then, once he was in charge, he was a *good* King. Not everybody liked him, but everybody agreed he was as fair as it was possible for him to be."

"Faerie isn't fair," I said, automatically. My eyes strayed back to the water, where one of the Cephali was bowing to Arden. She looked discomforted by the whole situation. I guess having an octopus person bow to her wasn't a normal thing back at the bookstore. "Did the books say anything about him having children?"

"They said he was really private. He didn't like anyone knowing what he was doing, or where he was going when he didn't have to be formally before the Court. Some people said he was arrogant, but most of them thought he was sad. He was all alone. He never had any lovers the Court knew about." Quentin followed my gaze to Arden. "But there was nothing to say that he *didn't* have children."

"She does look like her father," said Tybalt. "Even if I had not known, I would have suspected, once I saw her eyes." He pulled another ribbon from my hair. "The question becomes, is she prepared for what lies ahead?"

"I don't know," I said. "She looks pretty unhappy to me."

"Where did you find her, anyway?" asked Quentin.

"There's a bookstore on Valencia," I said.

"I know. Dog Eared Books."

"No, there's another one. It's called Borderlands. They have a café." I paused before adding, in my most portentous tone of voice, "It sells coffee, and I had no idea it was there."

Quentin turned back to me, eyes going very wide. "Wow. Whatever spell she's been hiding under, it's a doozy."

"I know, right? She's been hiding in plain sight this whole time. Hiding and hoarding all the coffee." I shook my head. Tybalt's fingers promptly snagged in my hair, and I winced, going still again. "She's been living in the basement with her brother. He's upstairs now. The Queen had him elf-shot sometime in the 1930s, and any chance Arden was going to lead an uprising on her own died when he went to sleep. I guess we could wait another decade or two for him to wake up, but somehow, I doubt the Queen is going to put up with me lurking around the borders of her Kingdom until then." Not to mention all the changeling children who'd become addicted to goblin fruit before that could happen—and once they were addicted, they were as good as lost.

No. It had to be Arden. The Queen was part of the problem, not part of the solution. I couldn't do anything if I was banished from the Kingdom of the Mists. Quentin would have to find a new Knight, and Tybalt . . .

That wasn't even worth thinking about. I sighed, and continued, "Arden didn't want to come, we didn't really give her a choice, and now we have to talk her into a revolution. If anyone can do it, it'll be Dianda." The Undersea Duchess looked positively gleeful about the entire situation. I couldn't hear them from where I was standing, but handing her the opportunity to overthrow the Queen of the Mists was probably just shy of her personal Christmas.

"The Lordens are a good choice," Tybalt agreed. "They knew her father well."

"Yeah. For now, we need to go put in an appearance

where the Queen's men can see me." Both Tybalt and Quentin looked at me blankly. I swallowed the urge to roll my eyes, and said, "If I disappear completely, she's going to assume we're up to something. Since we *are* up to something, it's important we keep her from thinking that."

"Ah," said Tybalt. "Misdirection."

"That, and having me around isn't going to help Arden make up her mind. Getting out of the way and letting her talk to people who remember her father just might." I held out my hand. "Can I have the ribbons, please?"

"Certainly." Tybalt handed them to me. "If I may say so, the style does not exactly suit you. Perhaps if you were a trifle more staid . . ."

Quentin snorted.

"I'm not going to put them back in my hair, and you," I pointed to Quentin with my free hand, "no commentary from the peanut gallery, you got me? I'm going to go get Raj, and then we're getting out of here." I turned and walked toward the group gathered near the water, where Raj had joined the others in studying our lost Princess.

Patrick saw me coming and smiled. "You know, October, I'm starting to think you'd be a dangerous enemy to have. You have a disturbing tendency to find what people don't want you looking for."

"I can't take all the credit this time; I'd never have done it if the Luidaeg hadn't pointed me in the right direction," I said, and turned to Arden. "Are you going to be okay here for a little while? I need to go be seen in public so the current Queen doesn't start an inquisition looking for me."

Arden blanched. "Is that a risk?"

"Only if I don't go. There's no way she followed us here, and you'll be safe with the Lordens. They're some of the best people I know." Assuming "best" meant "most potentially deadly if thwarted." "Your brother is safe here, and we're going to be looping back to the Library of Stars. I'll see if there's anything about waking up elf-shot victims early."

"I'm not sure . . ." said Arden, still looking uncomfortable.

I tried to smile. "Look, you've known us, what, an hour longer than you've known everyone else here? And you're a Tuatha de Dannan. Worst comes to worst, you can teleport yourself straight home. Please. Stay, and listen to what everyone has to say."

There was a long pause, where I was afraid Arden might insist on coming with us rather than staying in this strange new place, surrounded by strange new people. Finally, she nodded, and said, "If I'm not here when you get back, don't look for me."

"I won't," I said. I turned to Raj. "Ready to go?"

"I was thinking I'd stay here." He snuck a glance back at Tybalt and stepped closer to me before saying, softly, "I want there to be more than one person who can move fast without going into the water." He shuddered at the very idea.

It made sense, tactically. Arden couldn't teleport more than one or two people. That didn't mean I had to like it. "If there's a problem, where will you go?"

"Shadowed Hills," he said. "I can carry someone there if I have to, I think. Or I can do short jumps and lead the way for the Princess."

"All right," I said, finally. "But be careful."

He grinned, showing over-long incisors. "That wouldn't be any fun at all."

"Yeah." I turned to Dean, who had moved to stand next to his mother, and bowed. "My Lord, I must take my leave. I'll be back as soon as it's safe. Do you have my phone number?"

"I do," he said. With a faint smile, he added, "If we can pull this off, we're even."

"A rebellion for a rescue? Works for me." I held up the handful of ribbons. "Do you mind if I borrow some of your pixies?"

He blinked. "They're not mine to loan, but if they want to go with you, sure."

"I appreciate it." I glanced toward the Lordens. "Nice seeing you, Patrick, Dianda."

"Always a pleasure," said Patrick. Dianda just smirked, which somehow seemed like the perfect answer from her.

I walked back to Tybalt and Quentin. "Let's go upstairs. I have some pixies to bribe."

"It is a terrible thing that this statement seems completely reasonable to me," said Tybalt.

We walked back up the spiral staircase to the hall upstairs. Marcia was there, viciously sweeping the pristine-looking floor. I stopped, blinking. I hadn't realized she wasn't downstairs with the rest of us. In the crowd, it had been hard to see who was and wasn't there.

"Marcia?"

She jumped, expression seeming oddly mired between guilt and terror as she whipped around to face us. Then she relaxed, somehow forcing herself to smile. "Toby. You scared me. Are you leaving so soon?"

"For a little while. Dean has everything taken care of with Arden, and I need to keep moving, or the Queen's going to get suspicious. Speaking of which . . ." I held up my handful of ribbons. "Do you know where the pixies are? I have a business proposition."

Marcia blinked, blue eyes going puzzled within their protective mask of fae ointment. "What kind of proposition?"

"Simple: I want them to take these ribbons and scatter them around the city. That way, when the Queen sets her men on me, she'll be able to find traces of my presence *everywhere*, not just where I've actually been." I shrugged. "If she's going to insist on transforming my clothing without my consent, she can deal with the consequences."

"That's . . . actually pretty clever," said Marcia.

"I try," I said, and watched as she raised her broom and rapped it against the rafters. Tiny, multicolored heads popped into view as the pixies that had been lurking overhead checked to see what was going on. I offered them a little wave. "Hi. You guys want to do me a favor?"

The pixies left the rafters in a swarm, surrounding us. Some landed on my shoulders and head. More hovered in front of my face, waiting to hear what the "favor" would constitute.

"I need to mess with the Queen," I said. "Can you take these ribbons and scatter them around the city, so she can't tell where I am?"

One of the pixies rang in a questioning tone.

"I'm prepared to pay you three bags of cheeseburgers from the fast food joint of your choosing." They'd choose McDonald's, if the swarms of pixies around the dumpsters were anything to go by, but that was no big deal. There are several in the city, and they'd all seen stranger things than a woman buying half her bodyweight in food.

The pixie rang again.

"Three bags a week for the next month," I amended.

A third ring.

"With fries."

That seemed to satisfy her. She turned to the other pixies, ringing turning strident. I held out the fistful of ribbons. Pixies darted in from every direction, each snatching a single ribbon before darting away. A few even went for my hair, fishing out ribbons Tybalt had missed. It was like being at the center of a very accessory-oriented swarm. I didn't move until they were done. Neither did Tybalt and Quentin. Pixies are nowhere near as harmless as they look. If I didn't keep up my side of the bargain, they'd begin invading the house, and their homemade spears were frequently tipped with poison. I made it a rule never to break a bargain with a pixie.

After the last ribbon had been whisked away and the last pixie had vanished down the hall, I turned back to Marcia and said, "We're going to take off. You okay here?"

Marcia worried her lip between her teeth before she nodded. "I'll be fine. I'm just not sure how Dean is going to handle all this. He's only been Count for a little while."

"He'll be fine," I said. "He's had way more preparation than I did, and I didn't get us all killed. Besides, he has you to help."

"That's not as encouraging as you think." She flapped her free hand at us. "Go. We'll call if there's any trouble."

"Okay. Can you also call if Arden decides to cut bait and run? I need to know if I should start packing my things."

"We will," she pledged.

"I know she's in good hands," I said.

She smiled a little. "I do my best."

We could have kept on saying good-bye for hours, since none of us were in a hurry to go back into the Queen's line of sight. With a sigh, I turned away from her, offering Tybalt a wan smile, and asked, "Shadowed Hills?"

"I've been waiting for that particular request, since I know the Queen will be expecting you to be seen there," he said. "May I suggest, instead, that we return to your house? Once there, you can drive yourself and Quentin to Duke Torquill's domain, and I can handle certain necessities at the Court of Cats before I come to collect you."

Moving the car would certainly lend credence to the idea that I was desperately racing around the Bay Area, looking for a way out of my banishment. And Tybalt didn't need the strain of transporting two people along the Shadow Roads for more than a few miles twice in one night. I nodded. "Works for me."

Quentin and I each took one of Tybalt's hands, and together, we stepped into the dark, leaving the warm, uncomplicated halls of Goldengreen behind us. It was a shorter passage through the darkness than many of them, maybe because we were traveling such a short distance, maybe because we were moving from one familiar location to another. Whatever the reason, we stepped out into my living room not much later.

I wiped the ice from my eyelashes and called, "Hello, the house!" A rattling noise answered me as Spike—my resident rose goblin—woke up and jumped onto the back of the couch, making a puzzled mewling sound. I leaned over to scratch behind its thorny ears. "Hey, buddy. Where are May and Jazz?"

"Jazz is getting some sleep, and it's my turn to keep watch," said May, stepping into the living room with a cup of coffee in her hand. She held it out to me. "She's gone to bed. We'll switch off in an hour or so. Where's Raj?"

"We left him at Goldengreen," I said, taking the cup. "What are you up to?"

"I did laundry, I cleared some things off the TiVo, and I waved to the men the Queen has lurking around the edges of the park, trying to look unobtrusive." May grinned. "I mean, to be fair, I probably wouldn't have known they were there if I weren't, you know, a Fetch, but wow, did I freak 'em out."

May's fae abilities were something of a guessing game, since no Fetch had ever existed this long before. One of the first things we learned about her powers was that she was virtually impossible to sneak up on, especially if your intentions weren't good. I frowned. "How do you know they're freaking out? I thought you couldn't see through illusions."

"Oh, I can't *see* them—I just know where they are, and every time I wave, they run around and get into new hiding positions, like that's going to fool me somehow." May looked entirely too pleased with herself. I couldn't say that I blamed her. "*Hours* of enjoyment. Seriously."

"Well, we're about to take your pretty toys away." I sipped my coffee as I outlined the plan, using as few words as possible. Tybalt and Quentin chimed in a few times, but mostly left things to me. That was probably for the best; it was confusing enough as it was.

May waited until I was finished before nodding and asking, "Is there anything I can do?"

"Start packing," I said. "I'm sure some of the Queen's men will stay to watch the house, even if most of them go after me. Make it look like we're planning to leave the

Kingdom if we have to, while I try to convince them I'm frantically looking for a loophole. Hopefully thus concealing the one loophole we *have* managed to find."

"Arden," said May. "It's risky."

"What about this hasn't been?"

She sighed. "Right. Well, just be as careful as you can, okay? I don't think Sylvester will let me keep the house if you get yourself slaughtered."

I laughed. "I love you, too. I just need to get some more coffee in me, and then I'm good to go. Quentin, if you need anything from the house, now would be the time."

"Okay," he said, and turned to head off toward his room. May followed him, running a hand through her hair as she walked. It was a gesture she'd borrowed from her memories of being me, rather than any of the other people who made up her patchwork lifetime. She still made it entirely her own.

Tybalt touched my shoulder. I looked back at him and smiled.

"Hey."

"Hello," he replied. He raised an eyebrow. "You're in surprisingly good spirits for someone who's been given every reason to be furious with the world. Should I be checking to be sure you're not your own Fetch in disguise?"

"Nope," I said. "You'd smell the difference. And I'm in good spirits because things are actually . . . I don't know. I'm starting to think this might work." I had good allies on my side—and better, I had family.

Tybalt leaned in and kissed me before taking his hand away. "Optimism suits you," he said. "I'll do my best to see that it endures—but for the moment, I must be on my way."

"I know," I said, before kissing him. Turnabout is fair play, after all. "We'll be at Shadowed Hills when you're done with whatever needs doing."

"I'll come for you there," he promised, and then he was gone, stepping into the shadows by the wall and fading into nothingness.

Finding myself alone in the living room, I checked the flask of fireflies in my pocket and started for the kitchen. I already had my knives, and for once, I'd managed to leave the house and come back without getting my clothes soaked in blood, ichor, or anything else. My dress wasn't restricting my motion, and the fact that I was still wearing it would look good to the Queen's men. It meant I was too distraught to bother getting changed.

"Quentin, hurry it up!" I shouted, as I capped off my thermos. Coffee would make everything all right. "We're burning daylight." It felt like half of the Kingdom was staying awake during the day on my account.

"Coming!" He came half-trotting into the kitchen. He hadn't visibly changed, but I was sure he'd filled his pockets with something, even if it was only beef jerky. "I'm ready."

"Good." I waved a hand, grabbing the necessary magic to weave myself a human disguise. Quentin did the same, finishing several seconds before me even though he'd started after I did. I wrinkled my nose at him. He grinned.

"Being Daoine Sidhe has to come with *some* advantages."

"Brat," I said, without rancor, and opened the back door.

I didn't see any of the Queen's guards in the park, but I trusted May's magic: they were there, and they were no doubt watching as Quentin and I got into the car. I started the engine, resisting the urge to wave as we drove past the spots with the best cover. There was no point in taunting them for doing their jobs. The fact that they had to deal with the Queen of the Mists on a daily basis was punishment enough. I even felt a little bad about what had happened to the guards who had been assigned to watch the Luidaeg's place. They couldn't have known what they were getting into, and I couldn't imagine the Queen being someone who'd willingly accept a letter of resignation.

Sometimes living in a feudal society stinks. I focused

on driving while Quentin fiddled with the radio, finally settling on one of the modern country stations he liked so much. We were both tired; it had been a long night, and it looked like the day wasn't going to be any shorter. We drove in silence across the Bay Bridge, the Pacific Ocean stretching out like a blue satin sheet below us, and onward into the East Bay.

Driving in the morning after rush hour is peaceful. Having a boyfriend who can transport me without needing to worry about finding parking is nice, but I was glad to be making this trip by car. I'd been driving this road for literally decades, and no matter how much everything else around me changed, the road remained essentially the same.

We pulled into the lot at Paso Nogal Park in Pleasant Hill a little over an hour after leaving the house. Quentin was the first one out, as always, speed-walking to the base of the nearest hiking trail before turning to wait for me with ill-concealed impatience.

"Well?" he said.

"I'm coming!" I took my time locking the car, enjoying the mild frustration on his face. Quentin had lived at Shadowed Hills for years before he moved in with me. Coming back was exciting. Homecomings always are. I started toward him. "Just hold your horses."

I was halfway to the spot where he was waiting when a male voice said, "Hey, lady, you got a quarter?"

"Sorry, no," I said, automatically looking over my shoulder to assess the voice's owner for signs that he might be a danger.

He was a skinny mortal man in a long black trench coat—or at least, that's all I saw before he pulled his hand from behind his back and was suddenly next to me, crossing the intervening distance at a speed that was anything but human. I reached for my knife, but I was too slow, too slow to do anything but open my mouth in preparation for a shouted warning. Then the pie he was holding was slamming into my face, filling my mouth and nose with sticky sweetness.

Wait. Pie?

Quentin shouted something as I clawed the pastry from my face, wiping fruit and chunks of crust away from my eyes. My attacker was gone, leaving the parking lot empty except for me, Quentin, and the pretty floating lights that were dancing a slow quadrille around us.

Oh.

I looked down at my pie-covered fingers. I should have recognized the smell, if not the taste—and why would I have recognized the taste? I had always been so *careful*. I had never tasted goblin fruit before in my life.

"Quentin," I said. I wasn't quite sure why it was important that I tell him what was going on—the lights seemed a lot more pressing—but he was my . . . he was my brother? My son? My squire. He was my squire, and that meant telling him I was going to be unavailable. "I think you should get Sylvester."

"Toby?"

He sounded scared. Why should he sound scared? This was *wonderful*. I raised my head and beamed. He was beautiful. Everything was beautiful.

"I think I'm going to be sick," I said, and passed out in the parking lot.

TWELVE

KAREN WAS SITTING ON THE foot of the bed, and the bed was the one I'd had when I lived with Cliff, a yard sale special bought for five dollars and the manual labor it took to carry it up the stairs to our shitty second-floor apartment. I'd hated that apartment, but I'd loved that bed. Gillian was conceived there, my beautiful baby girl. I smiled at Karen and stretched to my full length, luxuriating in the simple pleasure of having my bed back again.

"Hi, sweetie," I said. "What are you doing here?"

Karen frowned. She was thirteen now, no longer the gangly eleven-year-old I'd once rescued from Blind Michael's lands. Her hair had continued to pale as she aged and was now an interesting shade of birch-bark white, although the tips were black, matching the tufts of fur tipping her dully pointed ears. She was wearing purple cotton pajamas, and looked profoundly displeased.

"I'm here because Quentin called me," she said. "He said you needed me because you were dreaming, and you wouldn't stop."

I looked at her blankly. Karen was an oneiromancer, capable of interpreting and traveling through dreams. But that left one important question: "Who's Quentin?"

"You don't mean that, Auntie Birdie." She slid off the

bed, grabbing for my hands. "Come on. Get up. You need to get up."

"I don't want to." I snarled one hand in the blankets, refusing to be moved, and scowled. "Didn't your mother ever tell you not to yank your elders out of a nice, comfortable bed?"

"Why don't you come with me, and you can tell her what I did?" Karen asked the question like it was entirely reasonable, punctuating it with another tug on my hand. "Come on. Get me in trouble. I *want* you to get me in trouble."

"Wait a second ..." I squinted, trying to puzzle through my increasing confusion. Finally, I said, "You're not Karen."

That seemed to startle her. She stopped pulling. "What?"

"Karen's a teenage girl. Teenage girls don't want to get in trouble. You want to get in trouble. That means you're not Karen." I pulled my hand effortlessly from hers. Her grip had lost all strength once I realized she was just a figment of my imagination. "You have no power over me. Now shoo."

Karen blinked at me again before looking up at the ceiling and saying, "I tried. I'll try again, but she's too far gone right now." Then she disappeared, leaving me alone.

Well. That was rude of her. I yawned and rolled over in the bed, trying to find a good position for a nap. Everything was comfortable. Everything was *wonderful*, and weirdly, that was the problem. I wasn't used to being so content. I didn't know how to sleep through it. I closed my eyes, hoping that would do the trick.

Instead, I felt the mattress shift as someone sat down next to me, and Connor said, "You know, you're never going to be totally happy here. This isn't where you're supposed to be. Also, this is a *really* ugly duvet."

"Connor!" I opened my eyes, rolling onto my back again so that I could see him better. My Selkie lover looked just like he always had, silvery hair, drowning-dark eyes, handsome without being intimidating about it. So much of Faerie tried to turn beauty into a weapon. It was nice to look at a man who was just easy on the eyes, no supernatural strings attached.

Maybe that also explained my attraction to ... my smile faded, replaced by a puzzled frown. My attraction to who? I was lying in my bed—my big four-poster bed, the one Mother had put in my room at her tower, with the pillows piled so high they were almost a pre-made fort, and the sheets spun from wind and thistledown—and I was looking at Connor, so why was I trying to think about another man? It didn't make any sense.

Connor rested one webbed hand against my cheek, frowning. "You need to wake up."

Now it was my turn to frown. "You, too? Come on, Connor, I'm not asleep. I'm here, with you." It felt like I hadn't seen him in forever. I sat up in the bed, looping my arms around his shoulders, and leaned close enough to smell the sweet saltwater scent of his skin. "Kiss me."

"No." He pulled away. "Toby, fight it. You have to fight it."

"Fight what?" My frown turned puzzled. "Come on, Connor. Kiss me. Don't you love me anymore?"

He laughed, a sharp, barking sound that gave away his Selkie nature almost as much as his appearance. "With all my heart, but, Toby, I lost the right to kiss you on the night that I died. Remember? I died in the shallowing in Muir Woods, when we went to bring Gillian home. You saw me among the night-haunts." He gently removed my hand from the back of his neck and moved it to press against his chest. "Remember?"

Dampness beneath my fingers, dampness flowing up through the fabric of his shirt. I pulled my hand away, and it was red with something I wanted to pretend was wine, but it wasn't wine, no, it had never been wine. The smell of blood was suddenly heavy in the room, so similar to seawater, so unmistakably not. I raised my head to stare at Connor.

He shrugged, looking sheepish and sad. The blood was spreading rapidly through his shirt, dyeing it a deep, almost purple shade of crimson. I wanted to look away. I hate the sight of blood. "I'm sorry, Toby," he said. "I died. You were there. You loved me, and I died, and I can't kiss you anymore, because I'm not the one you're meant to be kissing. I would have stayed with you forever, if I'd had the chance. I would have given you a million kisses. But that didn't happen. I died, and all those kisses died with me."

"What . . ." The room suddenly seemed wrong. I hadn't lived in my mother's tower for years. Connor had never been there at all, not the first time we were dating, and not the second time, either. I looked down at myself. I was wearing a long black T-shirt with the logo for the Bourbon Room on the front. I hadn't owned that shirt in twenty years. I didn't even remember what had happened to it. "What's going on?"

"You need to wake up now, Auntie Birdie." Karen again. I raised my head, unsurprised to find her standing there. Equally unsurprising was the fact that the room had changed. Now it was my room at the house, comfortable in a way that neither the apartment nor the tower had been, because it was *mine*. It was the home I had made, not a home that had been made for me.

"What do you mean? I didn't go to sleep." My fingers were sticky. Unthinkingly, I wiped them on the blanket.

Karen's eyes followed the gesture. "Even in dreams, blood has power for you," she said.

It was clearly a suggestion. That didn't make it an appealing one.

Still: if I was hallucinating and Karen was telling me to wake up, maybe whether or not something was appealing didn't get to matter just now. I licked my palm, filling my mouth with the coppery taste of Connor's blood—although, because this was a dream, it brought no memories with it. The blood was just blood, empty of anything but power. I shuddered, swallowed, and licked my hand again before looking around me, trying to force the situation to start making sense.

The room didn't change. Maybe that meant the blood

was helping: things were actually letting me look at them now, instead of shifting as soon as I tried. I slid out of the bed, standing unsteadily. "What's going on? Karen, why do you keep saying I need to wake up?"

"Because you're dreaming, even though you didn't go to sleep." Her expression was grave. "You have to wake up. This is what she wants. I've walked in her dreams. I know this is what she wants. You can't give it to her."

"What who wants?" I rubbed my face, trying to clear it. The taste of the blood in my mouth was changing, saltiness turning sweet, until it filled everything. Until it filled every little crack and crevice and . . ., oh. *Oh*. I lowered my hand, looking at it. The blood was gone, replaced by the dark purple stickiness of jam. There were seeds under my fingernails, like proof that a crime had been committed.

When I raised my head again, the room was dark. Everything was gone, except for Karen, standing in the nothingness. I took a step toward her. She remained just as far away.

"The pie . . ."

"Yeah." She grimaced sympathetically. "You need to wake up now."

"Quentin. Is he all right?" I looked around, trying to tease details out of the dark. "Oh, root and branch, where is he? And where's Tybalt?" I remembered him leaving me to go to the Court of Cats, but had that really happened, or was I trying to imagine him safe and far away?

"Wake *up*," commanded Karen. She took a step toward me, her eyes seeming to glow white through the gloom. When she moved, we actually wound up closer together. "You want answers, you can't find them here. Wake up, now, before it's too late. Wake *up*."

She was close enough to touch me, and she did, reaching out with both hands and shoving me. I wasn't braced. I fell, arms pinwheeling as I struck the spot where the floor should have been and then kept falling, down, down, down into the darkness that seemed like it would never end. I screamed. It didn't change anything. I closed my eyes, taking a deep breath—

—and I wasn't falling anymore. I was flat on my back on what felt like a feather mattress, and I wasn't moving at all. My mouth still tasted like berry juice and blood, a mixture of salty and sweet that was disturbingly reminiscent of Chex Mix. I cracked open one eye, wondering what room I was dreaming myself into now.

It was one of the guest rooms at Shadowed Hills. The walls were painted white, and the single window looked out on the eternal twilight of the Summerlands sky. This wasn't the first time I'd woken up here; as I opened my other eye and sat up, I looked down at myself. I was wearing a cotton nightgown with the Ducal arms stitched on the right breast. Then I raised my head, and collapsed back into the bed as the room began to spin.

"Oh, Maeve's *ass*," I groaned. My voice came out weaker than I liked. I groaned again, and rolled back into a sitting position, waiting with my head bowed until the room was still.

So far, so good. I swung my feet around to the floor and stood. The room remained still. Emboldened by my success, I took a step toward the door and promptly collapsed, like my skeleton had been replaced with pipe cleaners. There wasn't time to roll with the fall; I hit the floor hard, absorbing most of the impact on my knees and palms, although I also cracked my forehead. The hot smell of blood filled the room again, now emanating from my skinned hands.

The spinning of the room was joined now by the throbbing in my head, but I had just enough remaining coherence to bring a hand to my mouth and start sucking on it, trying to get as much blood as I could before the wound healed. My thoughts cleared as soon as the blood hit my tongue. Not enough for me to stand, but enough for me to realize that the last thing I wanted to do was stop drinking my own blood. I was prepared to reopen the wound on the floor if I needed to . . . but I didn't seem to need to. I was still bleeding.

Huh. I rolled onto my back and stared at the ceiling, still sucking. I was definitely awake this time—asleep didn't hurt this much—and the pie that I'd been hit with in the parking lot was definitely baked with goblin fruit. Nothing else explained my dreams, or my disorientation.

Which meant I was now addicted.

"Shit," I mumbled, against the flesh of my own hand.

Footsteps came running down the hall outside my door before it banged open. I tilted my head back and saw a woman I didn't recognize standing there, hands braced against the doorframe. She had the body of a 1940s pinup girl and the hair of a Disney princess, platinum blonde, shoulder-length, and just wavy enough to make it interesting to animate. She also had a pair of frantically beating mayfly's wings growing from her shoulders.

"Toby!" she shouted. She hurried forward, helping me off the floor. Her wings provided just enough lift to make the process possible. I doubt she could have moved me on her own.

"Hi, Jin," I said, leaning on her and allowing myself to be moved. My knees still hurt, and my palms were still bleeding. That didn't strike me as a good sign. "Recent molt, huh?" Jin was an Ellyllon, a type of hedonistic fae who often worked as healers, since they were better acquainted with the body than almost anyone else. That meant, among other things, that she periodically changed her entire physical appearance. She didn't have any control over the process, but the results were always interesting.

"It's been a long time since I've been blonde," she said, taking her arms away once she was sure I was steady. "How are you feeling?"

"Like I've been hit in the face with an evil pie." I opened my eyes, panic lancing through me. "Where's Quentin? He was with me."

"He's here," said Jin. "I made him wait in the ballroom when he wouldn't stop pacing. Sylvester came back from Goldengreen once we realized what was happening to you. He's been with your squire in the ballroom since."

As the Duke's personal physician, Jin was one of the few people who could order Sylvester Torquill around his own knowe.

I nodded shakily, looking down at my bleeding palms. "This is bad, huh?"

"You could say that." Jin placed the back of her hand against my forehead. "You're not running a fever. That's a good sign."

"What are you talking about? It's a drug, not a disease."

"Yes, except that your body seemed to treat it as a combination of the two. Goblin fruit is tricky, Toby, and you have the power to make it . . . better . . . for yourself."

From the way she said "better," I didn't think she was referring to the process of kicking my unwanted habit. "What do you mean?"

"Humans enjoy goblin fruit more than fae do. It's part of why it kills them. It's why it kills changelings, too, although it takes longer. You may be the only changeling who's ever tasted the stuff and had the power to make things . . . more enjoyable."

I stared at her.

Slowly, Jin nodded.

"Oh, no. No, no, no." I grabbed a hank of my hair and pulled it in front of my face. It was a colorless brown, the noncolor of tree bark and faded dye jobs. "No." Dropping the hair, I felt for my ear, and breathed a sigh of relief. It was still pointed. Less than it should have been, but enough that I knew I hadn't turned myself completely human.

"It'll be okay," said Jin awkwardly. She patted me on the shoulder. "We'll figure something out. We always do."

"So what, I'm addicted to something that's killed every changeling who's ever tasted it, and my body is trying to turn itself human so it can enjoy dying more, and we're going to 'figure something out'?" I glowered at her, glad to have *something* to focus my ire on. "How's that going to work?"

"I didn't say it would be easy, now, did I?" Jin stood.

"I'm going to go let everyone know that you're awake. When you decide to get dressed—against my recommendation, but that's never stopped you before—there are clean clothes in the top drawer of the bureau. But I really wish you'd stay in bed." With that, she was gone, shutting the door behind herself.

Jin was probably right: I needed to stay in bed. I needed to keep moving even more. The Queen had sent the man who hit me with that pie. I knew that was true, even if the Karen I'd seen in my dreams turned out to have been a goblin fruit-induced hallucination. The Queen was scared of me. It was the only explanation. And as to why she hadn't killed me . . .

Killing me would have been like killing Nolan. Elfshot took an opponent out of the picture for a century. Getting me addicted to goblin fruit proved that I was incapable of resisting temptation, turning me into someone to be pitied, not rallied behind. She didn't want a martyr, and so she was trying to discredit me in a way my critics would believe.

"To hell with that," I muttered. I licked my palm again, worrying the last flecks of drying blood loose with my tongue, and reached as deep into myself as I could, looking for the place where my fae and mortal heritages met. It was hard, slow work, like trying to swim through quicksand, but I found it, an intangible line drawn across the substance of myself.

I had done this before. Never intentionally to myself, but on Gillian, when I turned her mortal, and on Chelsea, when I turned her fae. I knew how the process worked. Reminding myself of that as firmly as I could, I gathered the tatters of my magic and wrapped my mental hands around the line, yanking hard.

The pain was immediate and intense. The line didn't budge, but I did, falling off the bed as I screamed, clawing at my own head in an effort to make the hurting stop. It didn't help. I kept screaming, and was still screaming when the door slammed open and Sylvester was there, gathering me into his arms.

"October!" He cradled me, looking back toward what I could only assume was Jin. "What's wrong with her? Fix her!"

"I can't." Jin stepped into view behind him. I barely noticed. I was too busy screaming. "The air smells like her magic. Just a little, but enough that I think I know what happened. Toby! Did you try to shift your blood?" My screams must have been answer enough. "She only stopped sliding toward human when she got too weak to change herself that way. If she tried to do it on purpose . . . no wonder she's screaming. She doesn't have the strength to do that, especially not with the goblin fruit still in her system."

"So get it out of her system!"

"Your Grace, if I knew how to do that, I would be rich beyond even your wildest dreams, and have a Duchy of my very own."

Then she was stepping past Sylvester, and her fingers were grazing my temple, as gentle as spiderwebs. The pain dropped away, and I dropped with it, falling back into the dark.

THIRTEEN

I WOKE AGAIN TO FIND SYLVESTER sitting next to my bed. He smiled when my eyes opened, but there was something forced about it, like he was smiling because the alternatives were too unpleasant to be considered. I'd known him long enough to see the screaming in his face.

"Hi," I rasped, and stopped, surprised by the sound of my own voice. I'd screamed my throat raw, and I wasn't recovering the way I expected. This "healing like a human" thing was going to take some getting used to.

"Welcome back," he said. He started to reach for me and hesitated, looking uncertain.

Sylvester has always been one of the few people in this world who could make me feel completely safe. I sat up, opening my arms, and whispered, "Please? I really need a hug."

That was all the encouragement he needed. He gathered me close, and I smelled the faint, familiar dogwood and daffodil scent of his magic. It was barely there: one more sign of how human I suddenly was. I barely had time to register it before he pressed his face against my hair, holding me like a father holds a child. He'd been holding me like that for most of my life.

"Oberon's grace, October, I am so sorry," he said, voice muffled by my hair.

"Don't be sorry yet," I said. "We can beat this." We had to beat this. We didn't have a choice.

"Toby?"

I looked past Sylvester to the doorway. Quentin was there, looking anxious. I managed to force a smile, despite the pounding in my head.

"Hey," I said. "Did you carry me up the hill? Kiddo, I gotta tell you, I'm impressed . . ." I stopped as I realized his eyes were brimming with tears. Disentangling one arm from Sylvester, I gestured. "Come on. Get a hug."

Quentin all but dove for the bed, and for a few moments, it was just the three of us clinging to each other, looking for a shred of hope in the comfort of one another's arms. Hope seemed to be in short supply at the moment. My throat still hurt, and I could feel the beginnings of hunger twisting in my stomach. Hunger that wouldn't be satisfied by anything from the mortal world. A slice of pie, on the other hand . . .

I shoved the thought aside, squeezed Sylvester and Quentin a little more tightly, and then pulled away. It was difficult to do, because none of us wanted to let go. They were my stability in a chaotic world, and I was more scared than I could allow either of them to see. It wouldn't have been fair.

Speaking of stability . . . I frowned, suddenly realizing who was missing. "Where's Tybalt?"

"Um." Quentin let go, taking a step back from the bed. "He . . . he doesn't know."

"What?!" I hadn't realized my torn-up throat would let me yell until I had already done it. I regretted it immediately. Glaring, I repeated, "What?" in a raspy whisper.

"There was nothing he could have done by being here, October, and I'm sorry, but his temper isn't precisely steady when it comes to you. When he came, we sent him away. Told him you were finally getting some rest, and he should go about his business." Sylvester looked at me with genuine apology in his expression. "I wanted you awake before we told him of the . . . situation."

"What, you mean the part where I'm a jam-junkie now, and oh, right, I tried to turn myself human so I could enjoy it more while it's *killing me*?" I shook my head, shoving the covers aside. "Where are my clothes? Where is my *phone*?"

"October, please."

I whirled, fighting a wave of dizziness as I pointed at Sylvester and snapped, "Don't you 'October' me. He is my *family*. Even if you couldn't respect that, I don't understand how the hell you got Quentin to go along with you."

"I was so scared," said Quentin quietly. I turned to him. He met my eyes without flinching. That may be the only thing that kept me from yelling. "I didn't know what was going to happen, and Jin needed us to stay away so she could work, and Tybalt . . . there wasn't anything he could do. The Duke sent him away. I didn't interfere."

I took a deep, slow breath, holding it as long as I could before I blew it out through my nose and said, "This isn't over. But right now, I need my phone."

"You need your rest," said Sylvester.

I swung back around to face him, grateful to have a target again. "This isn't your fault—if it's anyone's, it's mine—but I'm not going to sit back and play invalid while you all wring your hands about how horrible it is. I'm going to find a way to *fix* it. Because I'm a hero. And that's what heroes *do*. Now where. Is my. Phone?"

"I'll get it," said Quentin, and stood, scampering to the dresser with a speedy grace I envied. Even under my dizziness and steadily growing hunger, my body felt clumsy and strange, like I was moving through cotton.

It was almost funny. When Amandine changed the balance of my blood—I'd been elf-shot, and I would have died if she'd left me as I was—I'd wound up feeling like my body wasn't mine anymore. It was too quick, too strong, and too *fae*. Now, I'd managed to shift myself in the opposite direction, and I was having the exact same problem. This body, *my* body, didn't feel like home anymore. It felt like I'd been transformed into a stranger. And it was something I was going to have to deal with, because it wasn't going to change any time soon.

Quentin came back with my phone, pressing it into my hand without a word. I flipped it open, punching in the number for home on something that was just barely this side of autopilot.

May picked up on the first ring. "I told you, she's not *here*."

"Hi, May," I said shakily. "How's it going?"

"Toby!" Her voice was like an ice pick in my ear. It was all I could do not to drop the phone. "Oh, thank Oberon. Did Sylvester finally wake you up? Did they spike your drink or something? Because I gotta tell you, girl, this was *not* a good time for an all-day nap."

"All-day . . . May, what time is it?"

"About eight o'clock. Tybalt's been skulking around here since they threw him out of Shadowed Hills, and when he's not skulking here, he's visiting Goldengreen or making annoying phone calls to find out whether I've heard from you. Can you maybe ask Sylvester *never to do this again*? Because while I like Tybalt and all, having an agitated Cait Sidhe checking in every twenty minutes isn't doing anything for my nerves."

"Yeah, see, normally, I don't think Sylvester would have asked Tybalt to leave the Duchy while I was unconscious." I rubbed my face. "There were extenuating circumstances."

"Extenuating circumstances meaning . . . ?" she asked.

"Meaning I got hit in the face with a pie."

"A pie?" Now she just sounded dubious. "Was it an evil pie?"

"Yeah. Yeah, it was."

There was a horrified pause as May worked her way through the implications of that statement. Finally, she whispered, "Oh, oak and ash, Toby, are you okay?"

I laughed, high and shrill, before I could stop myself. "No, not really. Anyway, next time Tybalt checks in, can you ask him to get over here? We need to talk about what happens next." And I needed to tell him his girlfriend was now both mostly mortal and addicted to goblin fruit. That was a conversation that was practically guaranteed to not go over well.

"Okay," May said, voice barely above a whisper, and hung up.

I lowered my phone, hope and anger warring for control of my emotions. As always, it was easier to let anger win. I turned back to Sylvester. "You threw him out?" I asked, in a low, dangerous tone. "I was asleep for almost eleven hours, and you threw him *out*?"

"October, I told you we had asked him—"

"No. 'We asked him to leave so you could rest' only works if I was asleep for four hours, or six, or maybe, *maybe* eight, although me sleeping for eight hours when I'm not injured or drugged is such a perishingly rare event that he should have been sitting next to the bed with a bowl of popcorn. Do you understand me? I was *poisoned*. This stuff is *poison* to changelings, and the man I love wanted to be with me, and you *sent him away*. You kept him away from me for eleven hours, and you didn't tell him what was going on. I know you meant well. But can either of you tell me how in the hell you could believe that was *right*?"

Sylvester's mouth moved silently as he struggled to respond. Finally, he bowed his head, and said, "No. I am sorry. I was scared. We were both . . . we were *all* scared. And I apologize for this, October, but I didn't have the energy to deal with his fear while I was fighting with my own. I may not love you the way he does, but I love you as if you were my own daughter, and I would have done the same had you been my flesh and blood."

I glared at him for a few seconds more, but the first heat of my anger was already dying, replaced, however reluctantly, with understanding. What he'd done wasn't right. It was still the only thing he could think of to do. In his position, I might have done the same thing.

"I'd like you both to leave now, please, so I can get

dressed," I said. "Tybalt will be here soon, and then we're going to need to get moving. I don't have a lot of time."

"October—"

I raised my hand. "Please. Not now. I just want to get dressed, so that I can leave."

"Okay," said Quentin quietly. He started for the door. After a painfully long moment, Sylvester followed him. They both looked back at me before stepping out of the room. I didn't say anything. Yelling at Sylvester had been emotionally exhausting on top of everything else, and I simply didn't have the energy to deal with them any further.

"We'll be right outside," said Sylvester, and shut the door.

This time, when I stood, I did it slowly, letting my body adjust to its condition before I tried to move. The room swayed a little, but it didn't spin, and I didn't fall. That was going to have to be good enough, for now. Still taking my time, I walked to the dresser and opened the top drawer, revealing a pair of jeans, fresh undergarments, and a cable knit sweater made of dark gray wool. My sneakers and jacket were there, too, scrubbed clean of traces of goblin fruit.

My stomach growled at the thought of goblin fruit, a thin ribbon of hunger snaking through me like the root of some poisonous flower. I put a hand against my belly, willing the hunger away. It didn't do any good, and it wasn't going to. I may be renowned for my stubbornness, but if "stubborn" was all it took to kick goblin fruit, it wouldn't be a death sentence. I was going to get hungrier and hungrier, and I was going to give in.

The thought made me furious. I welcomed the anger. Half the things I've accomplished in my life have been because I was too pissed off to realize that they weren't possible. I yanked my borrowed nightgown off and dropped it on the floor, beginning to pull on the clothes that had been left for me. My knife was at the bottom of the drawer, along with a new belt to hold it. I strapped it into place, wishing I had a rubber band or something for my hair. Well. Beggars can't be choosers.

I was turning to leave when I heard a loud sound from the hallway, like, say, a six-foot-two Daoine Sidhe being slammed into a wall by a furious King of Cats. I somehow found it in myself to run to the door, wrenching it open to see Tybalt holding Sylvester off the ground by the front of his shirt. Several of the Ducal guards were there, hands on their swords, but they weren't moving. Sylvester had his hand raised, gesturing for them to stay back.

I didn't move. I couldn't. My fear was a hard knot in my throat, mingling with my growing need for more goblin fruit. Tybalt hadn't seen me yet. His lips were drawn back from his teeth as he snarled at Sylvester, holding my liege like he weighed nothing at all. He hadn't noticed my hair, or realized how human I'd suddenly become.

What if he didn't want me once he knew? Of all the endings I'd envisioned for our relationship—and there had been more than a few—me turning mortal was never on the list.

Quentin glanced toward the door. He was holding the flask of fireflies the Luidaeg had given me, and he looked miserable. He relaxed a little as he saw me. "Tybalt?" he said.

Tybalt snarled, starting to turn, and froze when he saw me. I fought back the urge to wrap my arms around myself and retreat. Instead, I met his eyes, bit my lip, and waited.

Slowly, Tybalt lowered Sylvester to his feet and stepped away from him. The guards moved in, helping the Duke stay upright. Sylvester raised a hand to his throat, coughing. Tybalt didn't seem to notice all this commotion behind him. He was focused on me, and only on me. He took a step forward.

"October?"

He sounded puzzled, not disgusted. That was a start. I nodded, saying, "In the too, too solid flesh." A bubble of laughter rose unbidden to my lips. It probably made me sound slightly unhinged as it burst into the air. I managed to swallow before it could happen again, and said,

"I'd quote 'Goblin Market' if I knew the words, but all I can remember is the part that goes 'we must not look at goblin men,' and it's too late for that . . ."

Then, to my shame and surprise, I started crying.

Tybalt didn't say a word. He closed the space between us in two long steps, gathering me into his arms and holding me as close as if none of this had happened. I clung to him and cried, not caring who saw me. I was past giving a damn if someone wanted to say that I was a weak little changeling who couldn't handle her own affairs. If there had ever been a time when I needed allies, this was it.

Finally, the tears slowed, and I pulled myself away. Tybalt let go reluctantly, and kept one hand against the curve of my waist, providing me with an anchor. I blinked up at him, waiting to hear what he would say. He narrowed his eyes, looking at me. I bit my lip.

"Have you done something different with your hair?" he asked.

This time, my laughter sounded a lot more normal. I smiled through the last of my tears, and said, "Yeah. Do you like it?"

"I could grow accustomed to it, if you chose to keep it this way." His gaze swung back to Sylvester, going cold. "I might already *be* accustomed to it, if I had been allowed to come to you sooner."

"You have my apologies, Tybalt, and there will be no action taken by myself or by my household to answer your attack upon my person," said Sylvester, rubbing his throat. "I was wrong to keep you away."

"You should never have allowed her to be endangered in the first place!" snarled Tybalt, fangs showing and eyes glinting a dangerous green. "Do not forget, *sir*, that she was fine in my company."

"Except for the whole 'getting banished' thing, and all those times in your company when I've been stabbed or gutted or poisoned or whatever," I said, interjecting myself before they could make the situation any worse. "Please. Can you stop? We don't have time for this. Please."

Sylvester looked away. Tybalt remained where he was, and didn't say anything.

I sighed. "This is going to be a *great* night. Sylvester, where's Jin? Am I cleared to leave? Because I'm leaving either way, but it would be good to have a medical release."

"I wish you wouldn't," he said.

"I don't care. But I'm leaving the car here. I'd bet you a dollar the Queen figures you're going to keep me locked up while you try to figure out how to wean me off goblin fruit without losing me, and this is the one place in the Kingdom that I'm officially allowed to be after my deadline. So let her assume she's taken me out of commission." I bit back a bitter smirk. "I barely even need a human disguise to go out in public right now. Her men won't recognize me."

"You don't need one at all," said Quentin softly.

"What?" I turned my attention to him, and paused, seeing the grief and, yes, terror written on his face. This, right here, was what he'd been afraid of since I started my one-woman crusade against goblin fruit on the streets of my city: I was addicted, I was mostly mortal, and he was going to lose me.

"If you keep your hair over your ears . . . they're not even that pointy. You don't need a human disguise at all."

The words were like blows. I'd known that I looked human, but not that I was *that* far gone. I looked to Tybalt, searching his face for confirmation.

He nodded.

"Oh, ash and pine." I closed my eyes, taking a shaky breath. "Fine. So the Queen's guards won't be able to track me by my magic. Let's see this as a good thing, and go."

"Where to?" asked Sylvester.

"The Library, to start with. Maybe there's something there about helping a changeling kick a goblin fruit addiction." If not . . . I had already asked Mags to pull any books on hope chests. I'd been trying to understand how my magic worked. Maybe I could use any information she had for me as a way to find another hope chest and put myself back to normal when I couldn't do it on my own.

"I will take you anywhere you need to go," said Tybalt.

"I'm coming with you," said Quentin.

I wanted to argue with him. I couldn't do it. With my magic essentially out of commission for the moment, I was going to need all the backup I could get, and he was my squire. He had as much right to be by my side as anybody else, and more than most. "It's going to be dangerous," I said.

"That's nothing new," he said. "Besides, my knight is pretty stupid when it comes to danger, and she's the best role model I have for dealing with the stuff."

I smiled a little. "Just so long as you're aware."

"I am."

"Okay." I turned to Sylvester. He looked so miserable, standing there next to the wall, watching us make plans to go away and leave him. He'd lost me more times than anyone else in this room. He'd watched me walk away, and he'd never stopped me, not once. He let me grow up. He knew that he had to give me that much.

Pulling away from Tybalt, I walked over to Sylvester and hugged him. This might be the last time we saw each other. I wasn't going to let my anger and his well-intentioned betrayal be the last things he remembered. No matter how deserved that might be, or how wrong he'd been, I loved him too much for that. I always had.

"Please be careful," he whispered, before kissing the crown of my head. "I wish you wouldn't go."

"I'll be as careful as I can," I said, and stepped back. "Tell Jin where I went, and that I'll have my phone if she comes up with any brilliant ideas about how to get me through this."

"I will."

"Quentin, come on."

My squire walked over to me. Tybalt took my right hand and Quentin's left, and we stepped into the shadows, and were gone.

FOURTEEN

WE DIDN'T STEP OUT OF THE SHADOWS: we fell, all of us dragged into an ungainly heap by my collapse. Tybalt wasn't letting go of me, and Quentin wasn't letting go of *him*, and the end result was a total train wreck. I, of course, wound up on the bottom of the pile, but I would have been in bad shape either way. The run had been too much for me. My eyes were frozen practically shut, and I was struggling to breathe.

"October!" Tybalt rolled off me, shoving Quentin out of the way—I heard his faint grunt of protest—before gathering me into his arms. "Breathe, dammit," he commanded, cradling me close as he tried to warm me with his own body heat. "Toby! *Breathe!*"

I coughed, breaking the frozen seal on my mouth, and began to take great, choking gasps of air. I didn't even pretend to be sitting up on my own. I just let Tybalt hold me, and kept focusing on trying to thaw my lungs.

"Is she okay?" Quentin, somewhere off behind me.

"I forgot how badly the Shadow Roads used to treat her." Tybalt sounded guilty, like this was somehow his fault, and not the Queen's for sending someone to hit me in the face with a pie full of goblin fruit.

A *pie.* Sweet Oberon, could we get any more slapstick if we tried?

Giggling made breathing harder, but it made me relax, which helped. I sat up straighter, scraping the ice from my eyelashes. "I'm okay," I said, the wheeze in my voice revealing my words as lies. I coughed again before offering my hands to Tybalt, letting him pull me off the floor. "Really. I'm okay."

"Are you sure?" he asked. I realized with a start that I couldn't make out his expression through the gloom. Humans aren't equipped to see in the dark the way fae are. I really was running blind.

"I'm sure," I said, looking around the defunct bookstore. It was, if anything, even more decrepit-looking in the dark; the shelves were just blurs. Even the pixie dust was gone. Its faint glow would have been a real blessing, but humans can't see pixies, either. Not without fae ointment. Maybe Marcia would give me some. "Quentin, can you get the door? I'm never going to find it on my own."

"On it," he said, and moved past us, a pale smudge against the dark bookshelves.

Tybalt took my arm. I didn't pull away. In my current condition, I needed the help.

"Are you truly sure that you're all right?" he murmured, pitching his voice too low for Quentin to hear.

"No," I whispered back. "But for right now, I have to be. So let me be all right. Please."

"Ah." He sighed, hand tightening on my arm. "As you say."

I flashed him a smile—he'd be able to see it, even if I couldn't see him—and let him guide me to where Quentin was waiting for us. I could see the bookshelves behind him, but no matter how much I squinted, there wasn't even the glimmer of an illusion.

"Here," he said.

"Yeah." I stopped walking, pulling Tybalt to a halt. "Tybalt, you'd better pick me up."

"Why?" I could hear his frown.

"Because I can't even tell there *is* an illusion here, which means it's probably going to be really hard for me to walk through the spell that covers the doorway. Faerie doesn't like it when humans wander in willy-nilly. It'll be easier if you carry me."

There was a moment of silence as we all considered the ramifications of my current condition. I was just this side of out of Faerie. Then Tybalt shifted his hold so that his arm crossed my back, and hoisted me up into something uncomfortably close to a parody of a bridal carry. I closed my eyes. He stepped forward, and the world did a sickening dip and weave around me while what felt like thousands of gnats gnawed at my skin, creating an itching, stinging sensation that made me want nothing more than to rip myself free and run like hell.

I wanted to run more than I wanted another bite of goblin fruit. That realization was a relief—I could still find things I wanted—and I held to it tightly as he took another step, carrying us out of the thin barrier zone between the mortal world and the Summerlands. Then we were inside the knowe, and the biting sensations stopped, replaced by the familiar disorientation of breathing air that had never been touched by the Industrial Revolution.

At least it was better lit here, even if I couldn't see a direct source of the illumination. That meant pixies, or witch-light, or something else my eyes couldn't handle. Tybalt put me down without being asked. I kept hold of his elbow as we walked, afraid of being lost in the stacks. Somehow, I didn't think the Library would be very open to helping me. Not now. Not as I was.

We stepped out into what I couldn't help thinking of as the Library's living room. Mags was there, sitting on a stool that allowed her to fan her wings without worrying about hitting them against anything. She was flipping through a photo album, but looked up when she heard our footsteps. Heard *my* footsteps, really; Tybalt was silent, and Quentin was only a little louder. Her eyes widened and she set the photo album aside, sliding off the stool.

"What *happened*?" she breathed, staring at me.

"I got hit in the face with a pie," I said.

Mags stopped, blinking. "You got . . . hit in the face

with a pie," she repeated. "I . . . what? I'm sorry, but I've been in charge of this Library for a long time. I've seen a lot of really ridiculous things. I lived in *Wales*. And there is no way being hit with a pie should have turned you *human*."

"It was a really evil pie," I said. Mags looked at me blankly. I shook my head. "It was a goblin fruit pie, and it turns out that since goblin fruit is more addictive and effective for humans, and lucky me, I come from a race that can change the balance of fae blood—normally, anyway, I can't do a damn thing right now—so since I'm part human, I turned myself *more* human while I was drugged out of my mind, in order to enjoy the goblin fruit more. Now I'm stuck. I'm addicted, I'm *starving*, but the idea of trying to eat anything but goblin fruit makes me want to throw up. We could really use a miracle right about now."

"Miracles aren't exactly a Library specialty," she said. "Could you . . . what do you mean, can change how human you are?"

"Remember that thing about Mom being Firstborn?" Mags nodded.

"That's what I got out of the deal. I'm Dóchas Sidhe. We're blood-workers, to the point where we're basically living hope chests. Only Mom never taught me anything, so I was hoping you'd have a book on hope chests that could help me understand what I do and how it works. I guess that's more important now than ever, since I need to *find* a hope chest. If I don't get less human in a hurry, I'm going to have problems." I already had problems.

"Oh." Mags took a step backward. "I pulled the book for you earlier. Let me get it." Then she was gone, running into the stacks. I knew that she had to be leaving a trail of pixie-sweat behind her, but I couldn't see it, and part of my mind kept trying to insist that her wings were fake, just cellophane over pipe cleaners. That wasn't good. The human mind instinctively rejects Faerie, because it's safer that way. Only if *I* started rejecting Faerie, I was going to be in a world of hurt.

"We need to find me some fae ointment," I said, directing the comment toward Tybalt. "Can you go to Goldengreen and—"

"No." The word was said flatly, and with absolute conviction. There was no getting around it. "I will not leave you again. Do not ask me. When we are done here, I can take you there. But I will not leave you."

"Okay." I touched his arm. "I'm sorry."

"No." Tybalt shook his head, and for a moment, I wished for the dimness of the bookstore. At least there, I wouldn't have been forced to see the anguish in his eyes. "I'm sorry. I should never have left you."

I was trying to formulate an answer to that—one that would explain how wrong he was without making light of his obvious distress—when Mags came trotting out of the stacks, a blue volume in her arms. "Found it!" she called. "Sorry about the wait. I had it in your pull, but well. Sometimes the books migrate when they feel they've been out of their sections for too long, and then I have to figure out where they've shelved themselves."

"It's okay," I said. "Also, I wish that didn't make sense." I took the book she offered to me, looking at the cover. There was no illustration. There wasn't even a title. It was just plain blue silk—no. I rubbed my thumb over the spine. Plain blue *samite*. Metallic threads wove in and out of the blue, adding liquid glints of platinum and silver. "Who's the author?"

"Antigone of Albany. She was one of the Firstborn, before they took titles in place of names. I don't know which one she became. The histories are very unclear on that period."

"Huh. Okay." I started toward the couches. "I guess I have some reading to do."

"Would you like me to go get some coffee?" asked Quentin.

"No, I'm good," I said, without thinking. Then I froze, and turned to look into the horrified faces of Tybalt and Quentin, both of whom were staring at me like I'd said the unthinkable. In a way, I had. "Crap," I said, intelligently.

For possibly the first time since I discovered the bittersweet blessing that is caffeine, I didn't want a cup of coffee. Normally, I didn't just drink the stuff: I practically *breathed* it, using it as a substitute for everything from a balanced diet to sleep. I could drink — and had drunk, on more than one occasion — a pot before I even opened my eyes in the afternoon. And I didn't want any. Worse than that, the thought of putting coffee in a cup and raising it to my *mouth* filled me with revulsion, like it was the most disgusting idea anyone had ever had.

"Goblin fruit replaces everything you love," said Tybalt. There was a tremor in his voice, the sort of thing I would have dismissed once as a trick of my imagination. I bit my lip as I looked at him. He didn't look away. *"Everything,"* he repeated.

"That's a big word," I said. It included my family, my duty . . . and him.

"I know."

"Then we'll have to finish this fast." I sat down heavily on the couch, sending dust puffing from the cushions. "Mags, do you have any other books that might help us? Like, maybe the rehab guide from *Goblin Fruit Anonymous*?"

"I can look," she said.

"Quentin, go with her, see if she needs help carrying anything. Maybe we'll get lucky." I didn't bother telling Tybalt to go. He wouldn't have listened, and I didn't want him leaving me. Not when he had that tone in his voice, like he should have known better than to believe anything could go right for very long.

"Okay, Toby," said Quentin, and handed the flask of fireflies to Tybalt before following Mags into the stacks. I opened the blue book and started to read, not looking up even when Tybalt came and sat beside me, curled so close that I could feel his body heat. He placed the fireflies on the table, where they added just that extra edge of light. I leaned slightly to the left, just enough that my shoulder was resting against his, and continued reading.

The first chapter was a history of the hope chests —

when and why they were made, and why Oberon thought they were necessary. He made the first as a gift for Titania, to allow her to manage her own Court. The others had been created later, and their makers were lost to history. It was all stuff I'd heard before, and none of it was particularly relevant until I got to the end.

I sat up a little. Tybalt tensed beside me.

"What is it?" he asked.

"Listen to this," I said, and read, "'When the last of the hope chests was crafted, Oberon gathered them, and gathered also his children, and the children of his Queens, to ask what they would do with such power as those chests contained. Five were given to the best of them, and five to the worst of them. One was given to the author of this book, for safekeeping, and one to her direst enemy, for sake of balance. The hope chests exist to keep Faerie in balance. Forget that at your peril.'"

Tybalt frowned at the page. "I don't see why this excites you."

"Oberon gave the hope chests to the Firstborn, right?"

"According to this text, yes."

"Well, we have more Firstborn around here than you can shake a stick at. Maybe someone we know has a hope chest, and we've just never asked." Not Mom. She was too young, as Firstborn went, and she didn't need one. Acacia, maybe, or the Luidaeg . . . "Maybe there's an index that says who got which chest." I flipped to the back of the book.

"You never could have been a scholar, could you, little fish?" Tybalt toyed with a lock of my hair, his voice turning contemplative.

I kept flipping. "I never wanted to be. Research is boring if it doesn't end in hitting—ha! There *is* an index. Oberon bless the Type A personalities of the world." I ran a finger down the list of names, looking for one that I knew. Then I stopped, and blinked. "Whoa. That's weird."

"What is?"

"The Mists is a pretty recent Kingdom, right? It's younger than Mom, and she's younger than the hope chests."

"I believe that to be correct, yes."

"So why is Goldengreen listed in here?" I flipped forward in the book again, stopping when I got to the page indicated by the index. It was an illustration of a hope chest that I knew all too well. It was the only one I'd ever seen, and the intricacy of its carvings weren't something I'd forget any time soon. Feeling dazed, I lowered the book to let Tybalt see.

Fig. XIX: Goldengreen.

For a moment, we both sat quietly, considering the picture. Finally, in a soft voice, I said, "The key didn't have anything to do with the knowe."

"What?"

"When Evening died, I rode her blood. That's how I found the hope chest in the first place. I let her tell me where to go." The experience damn near killed me. Her blood was too strong for me, and I was too human to handle it. I glanced at my hand, lips pressed into a flat line. I was more human now than I was then. No blood magic for me. "One of the things she, um, 'said' was that the key would open my way in Goldengreen."

"I see," said Tybalt, sounding puzzled.

"No, you don't, and neither did I until now. Tybalt, the hope chests have *names*, and the key did nothing to help me get into the knowe, or to guide me while I was there." I twisted to face him, the book still open in my arms. "The key got me to the hope chest, because it was taking me to Goldengreen. *This* is Goldengreen." I gestured to the illustration.

"They named the knowe for the treasure it contained?"

"I guess so." I turned the page, and read aloud, "'The seventh chest to appear was Goldengreen, made of oak, ash, rowan, and thorn, carved by no fewer than seven hands, and no more than thirteen. The exact number is unknown, but it is unique among the hope chests in that no trace of apple or rosewood was used in its making, nor willow, nor pine. The wood was soaked in blood before it was lain into place, and the hope chest itself does not sit easy in the hands, making some suspect the crafters died in the making of it' . . . charming.''

"Who was its bearer?" asked Tybalt. "Perhaps we can determine where the others might be by eliminating at least one of the possibilities."

"Let me see . . ." I turned a few more pages before I found a passage I wanted. "This says it was given to Eira Rosynhwyr for safekeeping. Why do I know that horribly unpronounceable name?"

"It's Eira Rosyn*hwyr*, and if you've heard of her, it's because she's the Daoine Sidhe Firstborn," said Mags, emerging from the stacks with empty hands. My heart sank, and only rose slightly as Quentin came into view behind her, carrying several books.

"Okay," I said. "Is she one of the ones who's still around? Do we have a directory or something?"

"No, there's no, ah, 'directory' to the Firstborn, and as for Eira, I don't know. Maybe she's alive, maybe she's not. There are no records of her death, and even if there were, it might not have stuck. Her particular parlor trick had to do with playing Snow White."

"She hung out with Dwarves?" I guessed.

Mags smiled. It didn't reach her eyes. "She never stayed dead for long. Firstborn are notoriously hard to kill, and Eira was always the hardest of them all."

"Okay." I looked back at the book. "So she was the Daoine Sidhe First, and she left the hope chest with her descendants. Maybe we can find the others by figuring out which races they parented, and then going door to door."

"I'm not sure you're physically prepared for a search . . ." Tybalt began.

I cut him off with a tight shake of my head. "Don't say it. Please. I am begging you. Don't say it." My stomach growled. I pressed my hand against it, trying to silence the need, and cast a pleading look at Mags. "While I'm begging . . . please tell me you have a suggestion about what might make this a little easier to bear. Just long enough for me to find a hope chest."

"We could put you into an enchanted sleep . . ." she began.

"No," I said, before she could continue. "Elf-shot kills humans just as dead as goblin fruit does, and anything else would take too long to put together. I can't just sleep this off."

"I don't have any other suggestions. What I do have is books." She gestured at Quentin and the books that he was holding. "This is the sum total of what we know about goblin fruit. I'll begin looking for any sort of treatment known to work for humans. If anything has ever been written down, I'll find it."

"I'll help," said Quentin. I blinked at him, and he looked at me, finally letting all his anguish and terror show. "I shouldn't have walked ahead. I should have been there. This is something I can do to help you. Please. Let me help."

"Of course." I held up the book on hope chests. "Go through this, too. See if there's anything that might help you figure out where these damn things are now. So far, I've got nothing. The index tells me who had the chests when they were divided, but it uses names, not titles, and the only Firstborn I'm on a first-name basis with is my Mom." And Acacia, but she was beyond my reach at the moment. If the Shadow Roads were hard, the roads it would take to get to the skerry where she lived would probably kill me.

"Okay," he said. Then he smiled, a little awkwardly, and said, "You're not really on a first-name basis with her, are you? You call her 'Mom.' "

"See, now you *really* understand why I need you going through this book. We're going to go see the Luidaeg. I may not be on a first-name basis with her, but I don't think that matters. Maybe she knew this Antigone lady, and can point us in the direction of another hope chest. But first . . ." I shook my head. "We're going to go to Walther first."

"Walther?" asked Mags blankly.

"He's a friend of mine. An alchemist. He's been trying to find a way to make goblin fruit less addictive, or at least come up with a treatment for the people who are already addicted." Walther was a pureblood Tylwyth Teg alchemist masquerading as a human chemistry professor at UC Berkeley. He'd been trying to isolate the addictive properties of goblin fruit, working under the assumption that since the addiction was magical, the treatment would be too. I'd been supplying him with the goblin fruit I confiscated from the dealers I cleared off the streets. I was happy to do it. At least I knew that whatever I gave to him was removed from circulation for good.

"And you think he can help you?"

I shrugged. "It's a long shot, but so is everything else. He's been working with the goblin fruit for months, trying to find something to cut the craving. It's time for us to see how far along he really is."

Quentin nodded. "I'll call you when we find something helpful. And I'll call Goldengreen if I need a ride anywhere. Raj can come and pick me up."

"It'll give him something to do other than hanging around making Arden uncomfortable." I turned back to Mags, opening my mouth to speak, and stopped as I saw her staring at the flask of fireflies. "The Luidaeg gave those to us," I said, perhaps unnecessarily. "She thought they'd help us find King Gilad's missing kids. They did, so I guess she was right about that."

"They're from Annwn, aren't they?" She drifted closer, a wondering look on her face. "I used to chase sparks like this across the moor when I was a child, before I'd ever seen the human world—or ever seen a human, even. Back when we lived in Annwn, and everything was going to be wonderful forever . . ."

Watching Mags approach the fireflies felt weirdly intrusive, like this was something I wasn't supposed to be seeing. I cleared my throat and stood. "Yeah," I said. "They're from Annwn." I decided not to mention that we'd been to Annwn ourselves, not that long ago. From the way she was looking at the fireflies, hearing that might break her heart.

"That's amazing."

"Well, we don't need them right now, and it's probably best if we're not carrying anything extra, so why don't I leave those here with Quentin? That way you can keep looking at them, after you finish looking things up."

Mags was close enough to touch the glass of the flask with one trembling fingertip. She looked up, and nodded. "Yes, that sounds like it would be wonderful. I promise I won't let anything happen to them. They're so *beautiful . . .*"

"Yeah, they're pretty neat." I glanced to Quentin. "You sure you want to stay here?"

"Tybalt doesn't need to be carrying us both right now," he said. "I'll be fine. And it's like I said, if I need you, I'll call."

"Okay, kiddo. Just stay safe." I wanted to hug him. I wanted to tell him he'd always been an amazing squire, and one of the best kids I'd ever known. He was definitely better than I deserved, on both counts. But that felt too much like saying good-bye—maybe because saying good-bye was exactly what it would have been—and so I didn't say anything. I just turned, offering Tybalt my hands, and let him pull me first into his arms, and then down, down, into the dark.

FIFTEEN

TYBALT DIDN'T LET ME RUN with him this time. He hoisted me into his arms as soon as we were on the Shadow Roads, carrying me through the darkness. I didn't protest. I knew as well as he did what we were up against, and if we were going from San Francisco to the UC Berkeley campus, I needed all the help I could get. Instead of fighting, I just curled there, trying to borrow what warmth I could from his body, and held my breath, waiting for it to be over.

I hate being helpless even more than I hate being hurt. I spent too much of my life thinking I couldn't take care of myself, and having that condition thrust upon me was not making me a happy girl. The steady rumbling in my stomach wasn't helping. If this went on much longer, I was going to be just like every other goblin fruit addict in the world: out of my mind with wanting, ready to do anything for a fix.

My lungs were burning by the time Tybalt stepped out of the shadows and into the cool night of the mortal world. I coughed, wiping the ice from my face, and tried to scramble down. He bent to make it easier for me. I cast him a grateful look before catching myself on the nearest surface — a brick wall — and vomiting. I didn't have anything in my stomach, but that didn't seem to matter to my body. It was unhappy, and it was going to make sure I knew it.

Tybalt put a hand on my back, resting it in the space between my shoulder blades. "Are you all right?"

"Not on this or any other planet." I straightened up, looking around. We were under the old bridge spanning the creek that cut through the middle of campus. I sighed. "See, if I'd just realized where we'd come out, I could have thrown up in the water. Less mess."

"Yes, but won't you think about the frogs? I'm sure they receive enough unwanted vomit from the student body."

I blinked. And then, to my surprise, I laughed. Tybalt smiled toothily.

"Good," he said. "You're still you."

"You're stuck with me," I said.

His smile faded, replaced by a quiet uncertainty that I'd come to recognize an inch at a time, picking it out of his more common expressions like a secret that was just for me. Kings of Cats aren't supposed to be weak; they're not supposed to be uncertain or worried. Those are emotions for people who don't have Kingdoms to run.

Or for people standing alone with their suddenly mostly-human girlfriends, wondering if they put off saying, "I love you" for too long. I put my hand against the side of his face. This was the first time we'd been alone since I woke up. If I couldn't afford a few seconds for this, it was already too late. I was already lost.

"Hey," I said. "I mean it. You're stuck with me. I'm not going *anywhere*. If there's an answer, we'll find it. And if there's not an answer, we'll *create* it. We're going to talk to Walther, and then we're going to ask the Luidaeg if she knows where to find a hope chest, and we're going to fix this. I'll be back to normal before you know it."

"Your life is in danger. You're stubborn, pigheaded, and refusing to admit the gravity of your situation. I'd say you're normal right now." His tone was light, but it couldn't disguise his relief.

"Don't make fun of me while I'm in the middle of a crisis."

Tybalt peeled my hand away from his face, holding it as he stepped closer. There was no space left between us. "My sweet little fish. If I refused to make fun of you simply because you were in the grips of a crisis, I would never have the opportunity to make fun of you again."

"I'd be okay with that," I said.

He laughed and started to lean forward, clearly intending to kiss me. I raised a hand, stopping him. He blinked at me.

"I just threw up," I said.

"October, given the circumstances—"

"All I can possibly have had in my stomach was goblin fruit. I don't need to deal with you going on a magical mystery tour while I'm trying to cross campus. Let me rinse my mouth, and then you can have all the reassuring kisses you want, okay?"

Tybalt sighed. "Loath as I am to acquiesce to your request, it does have merit."

"You could have just said 'okay,' you know."

"Ah, but then, would you have smiled?"

I laughed, and held his hand as we walked out from under the bridge, heading for the dirt trail cut into the hillside by generations of students coming and going. The campus was mostly deserted this late at night. A few students walked the pathways, but they were few and far between, as were the homeless people sleeping in the shelter of the school's patches of carefully preserved natural vegetation. I realized with a shiver that I couldn't tell whether the people remaining were human or fae, and walked a little closer to Tybalt. My current condition could come with a lot of nasty surprises if I wasn't careful.

"Are you cold?" he asked, looking down at me.

"Just facing a few unpleasant realities," I said. "Walther's office is this way."

As a junior faculty member, Walther rated a proper lab less because he was valuable, and more because he had a tendency to cause unexpected and odd-smelling explosions. I was pretty sure he'd used some persuasion spells, and maybe a glamour or two, to convince the administration to give him as much leeway as he had. He was in a better spot than some people with much more seniority, and nobody seemed to mind.

Then again, this was Walther. They probably just assumed he'd blow himself to kingdom come and they'd get his space without having to waste precious political favors.

The back door to the chemistry building was never locked, to accommodate the hours kept by the graduate students and some of the faculty—again, Walther. Tybalt and I walked through the empty, echoing building to the one door with a light shining through the glass. I knocked.

Something clattered. Footsteps followed, and then the door opened, revealing a tall blond man with disturbingly blue eyes only half-hidden by a pair of wireframe glasses. He was wearing a welders' apron over his carefully professorial slacks-and-button-down-shirt combination, and he looked confused.

"Hello?" he said. Then he paused, squinting at me. Tybalt didn't normally visit, or deign to wear a human disguise; my usual human disguise actually looked a little less human than I did at the moment. Still, some things carried over, because Walther said, incredulously, *"Toby?"*

"We sort of have a problem," I said. "Can we come in?"

"Sure. Jack's not here." Jack Redpath was his very friendly, very human grad student. Without him, the lab was clear.

I walked inside, Tybalt close behind me, and promptly froze, swaying on my feet. Tybalt was right there to grab my shoulders, preventing me from lunging for Walther's workbench.

"What in the world—?"

"If you would be so kind as to put the goblin fruit away, we can discuss the current situation," said Tybalt, in a tight, clipped voice.

It took everything I had not to fight against his hands. The smell from the open jars of goblin fruit filled the room the way blood normally would, obscuring and over-powering everything with need, need, *need*. I *needed* to fill myself with sweet fruit and sweeter dreams, forgetting all this nonsense about a lost Princess, a banishment, all of it. The goblin fruit would take it all away. Everything would be wonderful if Tybalt would just let me go—

I was held captive by a mad Firstborn once. Blind Michael, whose magic was a lot like goblin fruit in the way that it could remake your perception of the world. I fought him, even if I couldn't beat him. I did it with my own pain and with the smell of blood in the mist. "Tybalt," I managed, gritting the word out through my teeth. "I need you . . . to scratch me."

"What?"

"Just . . . pop your claws and . . . break my skin. Please. I need you to hurt me."

He hesitated, his grip slackening as he warred against himself. The hungry part of me saw that as an opportunity. I ripped myself halfway out of his hands before he clamped down, claws coming out as an automatic response. They drew a thin line of pain across my left wrist, and the smell of blood was suddenly hot in the room, overpowering the smell of the goblin fruit. That may have been because Walther was frantically capping the jars, but I didn't think so.

"Let my left wrist go," I whispered. "Just that. Hold tight, but give me that."

Cautious now, like he was afraid I would run again at any moment—and he was right to be cautious, because I was ready to bolt—Tybalt released my left wrist. I raised it to my mouth. He hissed when he saw me bleeding, but I ignored him, clamping my mouth down over the wound so my lips created a virtual seal. Blood filled my mouth, hot and salty and so absolutely *real* that I wanted to cry. I didn't cry. Instead, I swallowed, and swallowed again, and kept on swallowing until Walther turned to face us.

"Sorry about that," he said. He had thrown a sheet over the goblin fruit, apparently trying for "out of sight, out of mind."

"'S okay," I mumbled, around a mouthful of my own wrist. The bleeding had almost stopped; the scratches weren't deep. Reluctantly, I pulled my hand away, swallowing one last time before I said, "We didn't call first."

"Still." Walther removed his glasses, dispelling the hasty illusion that made him look human at the same time. His eyes were even bluer this way. All Tylwyth Teg have eyes like that, making it seem like they're looking straight through you. "What happened?"

"The Queen sent someone to hit me in the face with a goblin fruit pie," I said. "Well. We're assuming it was the Queen. That much goblin fruit is going to be expensive, and she's the one with the most interest in seeing me discredited, instead of just dead. If any of the jam dealers I've been hassling had decided to go after me, they would have hired an assassin instead of wasting perfectly good product." The thought of the pie I'd been hit with made my head start spinning again. I raised my wrist and started sucking on it again. The taste of blood was faint, but it helped.

"Ah, the good old days, when men tried to kill you with guns and I could simply eviscerate them," said Tybalt.

Walther snorted. "Any questions I had about who your companion was have just been answered. Can you drop the illusions?"

"No," I said. "I'm not wearing one."

He paused. Beside me, the faint smell of musk and pennyroyal ghosted through the air as Tybalt removed his human disguise. Finally, Walther said, "That's what I was afraid of. Let me guess: you got hit with the goblin fruit, your body went 'oh, this is nice,' didn't recognize it as a poison, and tried to adjust things to get the maximum amount of enjoyment. Only since I'm going to bet you were overdosing at the time, you weren't awake to consciously control the urge, and so you wound up dialing yourself almost all the way human before you ran out of oomph."

I blinked, lowering my wrist. Tybalt blinked. Walther grinned, a little wryly.

"Did you think I put 'Professor' in front of my name

because I wanted to get respect from college girls? I *am* actually capable of analytical thought." He paused, cocking his head. "You were ready to beat me down to get at the goblin fruit a minute ago. How are you feeling now?"

"Sore," I said. "Tired, annoyed, hungry . . ."

"But not like you want to take me on if it gets you a fix?"

I eyed him warily. "Not as such, no."

"Good. Good. Your instincts are usually right, when you let yourself trust them. For you, blood will almost always be the answer." He grabbed a suspiciously convenient roll of gauze from the desk, lobbing it at me underhand. I caught it, only fumbling slightly in the process. My fingers were too thick and clumsy, and they didn't want to do as they were told.

Well, they were going to learn. Until I could get hold of a hope chest, they were what I had to work with. "Do I even want to know why you had this sitting there?"

"I work with sharp things, and some of us don't heal like superheroes," said Walther. He paused, blanching. "I didn't mean . . ."

"It's okay." I shook my head. "Although if you have a scalpel or something that I can borrow, that would be good. I don't want to depend on getting Tybalt to claw me when the craving gets too bad."

"I would prefer to avoid that myself," said Tybalt.

Walther frowned. "How much do you know about anatomy? Physiology? Where the major arteries in the humanoid body tend to appear?"

"Wow, you know, most people would just go 'where the major arteries are,' " I said, trying to make him smile. It didn't work. I sighed. "Very little. But that isn't my main concern right now."

"When you're bleeding out because you sliced yourself wrong, it will be," said Walther.

"And when I'm so high I can't think, much less act, I might as well be bleeding out," I snapped back. "At least then, I'd die knowing that I was trying. Look, I'll avoid any visible veins, I'll cut across instead of cutting down, but I *need* easy access to blood. Unless you've managed to cook up a cure while we weren't looking?"

"Not yet," said Walther. "I'm still trying. But there are better options than scalpels."

"Like what?"

He turned his back on us, opening one of the long drawers in his desk to produce a leather-wrapped bundle. When he unrolled it, he revealed a variety of old-fashioned-looking surgeon's tools, including a syringe that could probably have been used to extract blood from a Bridge Troll. I blanched.

"That is *not* a better option than a scalpel," I said.

"I've been a chemist for a long time," he said, picking up the syringe. "That used to include a lot of the duties humans have transferred to doctors."

"You practiced bloodletting?" asked Tybalt.

"For about eighty years. Syringes and leeches, that's the way to keep food on the table. Toby, pick up that bottle of rubbing alcohol and come over here. Let's see if we can't find a way to keep you from damaging yourself to get the blood out." He paused before adding, "It's the bottle labeled 'rubbing alcohol,' next to the bottle labeled 'H2SO4.' Don't grab the wrong one."

"Why not?"

"Because the other bottle is sulfuric acid, and you'll die."

"Oh, because that's safe," I grumbled. Grabbing the bottle that *wasn't* going to kill me, I walked over and offered it to Walther.

"Good," he said. "Tybalt, get me one of the ice cube trays from the freezer?" He picked up a cotton ball, dousing it in rubbing alcohol. "Toby, arm, please."

Hanging my leather jacket on the nearest chair, I held out my right arm. Walther swabbed a square of flesh about an inch wide clean and drove the needle home before I could tense up. Eighty years of practice had left him pretty good at gauging the location of a vein: the syringe in his hand began to fill with blood as soon as he pulled back the plunger.

No matter how advanced my blood magic has become, the sight of blood has always made me nauseous. Not this time. I couldn't take my eyes off the glass as it filled. My stomach grumbled again. If I couldn't have goblin fruit, apparently blood would do perfectly well. "Great," I said, sounding dazed even to my own ears. "Now I'm a vampire."

"There's precedent," said Walther. "There are some old records that claim Daoine Sidhe changelings last longer once they've become addicted than most others, because they can take sustenance from the blood of beasts. You're just cutting out the middle man."

"I could hunt for her?" asked Tybalt.

"You could, but I think this is more hygienic, and probably more effective. Pass the ice tray?"

"Here." Tybalt stepped up beside me, holding a bright green plastic ice tray.

For some reason, that struck me as unutterably funny. I put a hand over my mouth, but not quickly enough to smother my smile. Walther just smiled, taking the ice tray from Tybalt's hand.

"If you're smiling, there's hope," he said, and put the tray down on the counter before picking up another cotton ball. "Hold this to the wound while I determine whether we need more blood."

"Yay," I deadpanned. "Holding my blood inside my body is always my favorite part of crazy alchemy adventures."

He pulled the needle out. A bead of blood welled up before I slid the cotton into the place. The smell of copper still filled the air, relaxing my nerves further and causing my stomach to rumble again. It felt like I was trading one form of addiction for another. At least this one came naturally, and might eventually make me better, instead of making me worse.

Walther turned to the ice cube tray, squirting blood from the syringe into each of the tiny squares. He ran out of blood with only half the spaces filled. Turning back to me, he said, almost apologetically, "Other arm, please."

"You could at least buy me dinner first," I said, bending my right arm to keep the cotton in place as I extended my left.

"Tybalt would gut me if I tried," said Walther. Again, he slid the needle into my vein; again, the glass chamber began to fill with blood.

"See, that kind of attitude is never going to get you anywhere with the ladies." I sighed, watching the blood flow. Then I paused, and asked, "Shouldn't I be dizzy? Blood loss is supposed to make you dizzy."

"Right now, I think your body is too distracted for dizziness." Walther pulled the needle out again, putting another puff of cotton in place. "Bend your arm."

I did as I was told. "That doesn't sound very scientific to me."

"Says the girl with the goblin fruit addiction and the tomcat boyfriend, to the alchemist who's about to do something really impressive," said Walther. He emptied the freshly-drawn blood into the last of the little squares, put the syringe aside, and reached for a saltshaker filled with what looked like paprika. "You may want to step back."

"Why?" I asked.

"Because there's a fifty-fifty chance this is going to explode."

I stepped back. So did Tybalt, who positioned himself slightly to my left, where he could push me clear if something actually blew up, without seeming like he was hovering. I appreciated his concern, even as I resented the need for it.

Walther sprinkled the paprika-looking herbs over the squares of congealing blood before waving his hands and beginning to chant in Welsh. The air in the lab chilled by about eight degrees in as many seconds, the faint ice and yarrow scent of his magic surrounding us. He kept chanting, lowering his hands toward the blood. The air got even colder. Then the magic burst like a popped balloon, and Walther turned to face us, grinning broadly.

"I am a genius," he announced. "You may lavish praise upon me at your leisure. But don't take too long, I haven't got all night."

"I'll start lavishing praise when you tell me what you did," I said. The air wasn't warming as quickly as it had cooled. I shivered and hugged my arms to my body. "Can I put my coat back on now?"

"If the bleeding has stopped, yes." Walther produced a cookie tray and a roll of parchment paper from the mess on the counter. He spread the paper across the metal, then reached behind himself for the ice cube tray. "Voilà."

"Walther, seriously, you need to tell me what I'm supposed to be getting excited about, because I honestly don't have a clue."

Walther tipped the ice cube tray over the parchment paper. The "ice cubes" fell out . . . but they weren't ice cubes, not even bloody ones. Instead, a shower of what looked like polished garnets landed on the parchment paper. They ranged in size from Tic Tacs to throat lozenges almost an inch long.

I blinked. "That's my blood."

"Yes."

"You turned my blood into . . . what, exactly?"

"These are like M&M'S; they melt in your mouth, not in your hands." Walther picked up one of the mid-sized "stones," offering it to me. "Try."

"If you say so." I took the chunk of solidified blood and popped it into my mouth, where it immediately dissolved on my tongue. The growling in my stomach stopped, replaced by a sudden feeling of fullness. It didn't even leave the taste of blood behind; instead, my mouth tasted like mint and lavender. I stared at him. "What . . . ?"

"It's a simple preservation spell, with a little herbal mixture to make the taste more palatable." Walther turned to the counter one more time, this time producing a plastic baggie. "If you take one of these whenever the craving gets too bad, you should be able to keep it under control, for a little while. I'll keep working on a more general treatment. This is just a short-term solution."

"What do I do if I run out?"

"Try not to run out." Walther swept the artificial jewels into the baggie before pressing the zip-seal closed. "This is . . . I'll be honest, Toby, I have no idea how your body is sustaining itself. You're the source of this blood. It shouldn't give you any nutrition you didn't lose in creating it. At best, this is like dancers eating ice chips to convince themselves that they've had an actual meal. At worst, it's not even that much. You're going to starve if this goes on too long, and I'm concerned that bleeding you more than once would wreak havoc on your system when it's already overtaxed. Do you understand me?"

"Do I understand that this is a stay of execution, not a cure? Yeah. But it's more than we had when we got here." It might be enough to get me to a hope chest—or to Mom, although that seemed less likely. I picked up my leather jacket, shrugging it back on. "You do good work, Walther."

"Yeah, well, I came to the Mists for the tenure, I'm staying for the excitement." Walther smiled a little as he turned to hand me the bag of gleaming red stones. It didn't reach his eyes. "Please try to be careful. And Tybalt, if she seems to be running out of stamina, don't let her argue. Get her out of whatever she's doing and back to someone who can take care of her."

"I will have her at Shadowed Hills before she can utter a word of protest," said Tybalt.

"Hey, right here, remember?" I protested. I took the bag from Walther, tucking it into the inside pocket of my jacket. The urge to eat another stone—just one—was strong. I forced it away.

"Yes, and we'd like to keep it that way." Walther shook his head. "I know too much about goblin fruit, and not enough about Dóchas Sidhe. Be careful."

"I'll try." That was all I could promise him. That was all I could promise anyone, myself included. This wasn't the sort of situation that allowed for much in the way of "careful." But there was "less stupid," and maybe that would be enough.

It was going to have to be.

SIXTEEN

TYBALT PICKED ME UP before stepping onto the Shadow Roads. I huddled against him, holding my breath and squinting my eyes tightly shut. Better a few frozen eyelashes than a pair of frozen eyeballs. Before I got hit in the face with an evil pie, I would have joked about my eyes growing back. Now . . . well. Until we got things sorted, these were the only eyes I was going to get.

The thought was morbid enough that I clapped a hand over my mouth to stop myself from laughing. Given how little air I had left, that would have been a terrible idea.

Then we were stepping out into the warm, still air of the San Francisco night. I coughed as Tybalt put me down, steadying me with one hand while I wiped the ice from my face. Finally, I opened my eyes and said, "That's it. You're nice and all, but I need something with a little more horsepower if I'm going to be running back and forth across the Bay Area."

He quirked a faint smile. "Are you dumping me for your car?"

"Come on. You always knew it was coming." I coughed again, grimacing as my cold-chapped lips threatened to split. "But seriously. I can't keep taking the Shadow Roads everywhere we go. If it means the Queen can track me, so be it."

"Ah." Tybalt paused, indecision clear. "I suppose this would be a bad time to point out that your vehicle remains in Pleasant Hill."

"We'll work it out." I started walking toward the Luidaeg's apartment. None of the Queen's men were lurking this time—at least, none that I could see. There was always the chance that . . . wait. I stopped dead in my tracks.

"October?" asked Tybalt. "What is it?"

"I'm an idiot," I said.

"Yes, frequently, but what now?"

"The Luidaeg said I'd be able to see through any illusion while I had the fireflies, and so what did I do? I left them in their damn flask, and then I left the damn thing at the Library." I started to walk a little faster now. "I need my car, and I need those fireflies, at least until I can get my hands on a hope chest. You know, I did *not* sign up for a crazy fairy tale scavenger hunt this week."

"Yes, you did," said Tybalt, pacing me. I shot him a sharp look. He shrugged. "You got out of bed. The universe does seem to take that as a personal affront."

The urge to call him something unforgiveable was strong. I settled for glaring and walking faster until we reached the Luidaeg's door. It looked the same as always. I'd never been able to see through her illusions anyway. Raising my hand, I hammered against the water-damaged wood loudly enough to wake the dead. Then I stepped back, and waited.

It wasn't a long wait. The door opened just a crack, revealing the scowling, suspicious face of the Luidaeg. She blinked when she saw me, suspicion fading first into puzzlement, and finally into raw shock. Allowing the door to swing the rest of the way open, she said, "Toby?"

"Yeah," I confirmed.

"Bullshit."

I blinked. "Okay, that's not the reaction I was expecting. Look. I have my knife, I have my jacket, I have my sarcastic tag-along . . . what else is required for the position? Because I'm way too tired to stand out here and argue about my identity any longer than I need to. I need your help."

"What you *don't* have is a hell of a lot of fae blood," the Luidaeg said. Her hand shot forward, grabbed my upper arm, and hauled me into the apartment. Tybalt followed, not protesting her rough treatment of me. Even Kings of Cats have to come with *some* sense of self-preservation.

"Ow!" I protested, trying—and failing—to pull myself out of her grasp.

She raised her head, eyes narrowed, and turned toward Tybalt. "Close the door," she said. Then she started walking, hauling me toward her bedroom.

I had time to note that the illusions normally filling her apartment were gone, leaving the place visibly impeccable. She knocked three times when she reached her bedroom door—she almost always did that, and I never knew why—before opening it to reveal the dark, candle-filled cavern of her bedroom. The walls were lined with saltwater tanks. I couldn't make my eyes focus on half of them, although I knew their contents: that one held hippocampi, brightly-colored as reef fish and the size of my hand; that one housed a pearl-eyed sea dragon the length of my arm. His name was Ketea, and the Luidaeg once used one of his scales to turn me into a Merrow.

"Sit," she commanded, shoving me toward the large bed. I stumbled backward, barely managing to avoid hitting my hip on one of the carved wooden posts that held up the canopy. She planted her hands on her hips, eyeing me. I squirmed, but didn't say anything. It seemed better not to. Finally, she said a single word: "How?"

"Someone hit me in the face with a pie," I said.

The Luidaeg blinked, expression going slack. The candlelight threw strange shadows over her cheeks, and made my stomach clench. I don't like candles. "That's . . . wait . . . *what*? You're almost human because someone's been watching too many damn Bugs Bunny cartoons?"

"I don't know whether I should be horrified or impressed that you know who Bugs Bunny is." I leaned back to rest most of my weight on my hands and said, "It was a goblin fruit pie. Jin at Shadowed Hills thinks my body liked the fruit so much that it wanted to experience the stuff more strongly, and so it shifted itself around without consulting me. I was sort of overdosing at the time."

"And you can't turn yourself all the way human," said the Luidaeg grimly. "Thank Dad for that."

I blinked at her. "I didn't know that."

"Faerie protects itself, and good thing, too. If you didn't have that particular failsafe built into your powers, you'd be mortal, and we'd be screwed."

"But couldn't we find a hope chest and . . ."

"You've said it yourself, October: you can't make something stronger when it's not there. If your body had been capable of chasing the goblin fruit all the way into mortality, you'd be off the playing field permanently. Have a nice life, all sixty or seventy years of it, and try not to remind your old enemies who you are. It can be done *to* you, but it's not a thing you can do to yourself." She reached out and grasped my chin, turning my face roughly one way, and then the next. "Right now, you're basically a merlin. Ten, maybe fifteen percent fae. Even when Amy was fucking with you as a child, she never jobbed you as good as you've just jobbed yourself. Gold star, moron."

"Is there nothing that can be done?" asked Tybalt. I pulled my head from the Luidaeg's grasp and turned to see him standing near the open bedroom door.

"There's plenty, assuming you can keep her alive long enough to do it." The Luidaeg snapped her fingers, pulling my attention back to her. "Hey. Look at me, human girl. How bad is the craving? How many of us would you stab for a jar of jam?"

"It's not bad right now," I said. "We went to Walther before we came here. He figured out a stopgap that I should be able to use long enough for us to figure out something more permanent."

The Luidaeg raised an eyebrow. "Methadone won't work."

"I'm not even going to ask why you know what methadone is, but no." I pulled the baggie of blood gems out of my inside jacket pocket. "He made these from my blood. They dull the wanting for a little while." But not for long. I could feel it starting to twist in my gut again, telling me that nothing in this world mattered half as much as seeing the beautiful things the goblin fruit had to show me.

"Your little alchemist does delight in surprises, doesn't he? May I?" She didn't actually wait for permission before snatching the bag out of my hand, opening it, and removing one of the larger blood gems. She held it up so that it glittered in the candlelight. "Hmm. Good work. I couldn't have done better."

"Seriously?"

"Seriously." She dropped the blood gem back into the bag. "I'm not an alchemist. What he's done is tricking your body into believing that it's being fed. That's flower magic, like illusions, and he gets that from his connection to Titania. I'm all blood and water. I could turn you into a turtle so you'd die a little slower, but I couldn't make your mind into a turtle's mind."

"That's a charmingly specific distinction." I reclaimed the baggie, tucking it back into my pocket. "I need help."

The Luidaeg snorted. "Tell me something I don't know."

"I can't stay this human. The goblin fruit will kill me. I'm not sure how to call my mother—and given what she wanted to do to me before, I don't know whether calling her would do any good."

"Ah," said the Luidaeg softly. "I guess I can see where that would be a concern."

"Yeah." When my mother first changed my blood, she wasn't trying to make me more fae; she was trying to turn me human, to protect me from whatever lunatic destiny she was afraid lurked for our bloodline. And maybe we *have* some sort of destiny. I've had more than a few soothsayers and prophets predict that I'm going to be involved in something big, whether or not I want to be. She thought that turning me human would save me, and maybe she was right; I don't really know one way or another. But I do know that when I was elf-shot and would have died immediately, she'd changed the balance of my blood to make me more fae.

I just wasn't sure she'd be willing to do it again.

"What were you hoping I could do for you? I don't have Amy's gifts. I can't make you any more or less mortal than you are right now." The Luidaeg grimaced. "I could wrap you in a Selkie's skin, but that's a step that can't be taken back. You'd never be Dóchas Sidhe again."

My eyes widened. For the Luidaeg to even offer . . . "No. I don't want that. I was hoping you'd be able to tell us whether there were any hope chests in the Kingdom other than the one the Queen is holding."

"Ah." The Luidaeg looked relieved. I couldn't blame her. The Selkies were skin-shifters, and the skins they wore had been flayed from the living bodies of the Roane. Every Firstborn had his or her own descendant races. The Roane had been hers.

The Luidaeg's relief faded quickly, and she shook her head. "I'm sorry, Toby, but no. The only hope chest in this Kingdom is the one you surrendered to the Queen. If you want it, you need to get access to the treasury."

"And we're back to insurrection." I sighed. "That's still the plan, mind you, but I was hoping to be a little more indestructible when I pulled the trigger. Also, alive. Alive figures heavily in my long-term plans." As human as I was at the moment, I wasn't even sure the night-haunts would come if I died. The thought filled me with a new form of sick terror. Faerie lives on in the night-haunts. They're the closest we can come to actual eternity. I've never been in a hurry to join them, but the idea that I might not join them at all was . . . unsettling.

"So what's next?"

"There's a book at the Library. No title, bound in blue samite, written by Antigone of Albany. It has records of where the hope chests went after they were handed out—including the one the Queen has now. Got any ideas on where we could find her? Maybe this Antigone lady can give us some suggestions on where to get our hands on an alternative."

The Luidaeg stared at me for a long moment. Then, mirthlessly, she laughed. "Oh, how quickly they forget. Yeah, Toby. I know where to find Antigone."

"Great!" I moved to stand. "Where—"

"That's the name my parents gave me, after all."

I jumped the rest of the way to my feet. "What?"

"Oh, Toby, Toby, Toby." The Luidaeg reached over and pushed me gently back into a sitting position. "You didn't think Maeve looked at me in my cradle and went 'let's name her Luidaeg,' do you? My name—my given name—is Antigone. I was born in Scotland. We called it 'Albany' at the time. To be honest, I like that name a lot better, but what kind of vote do I get? I moved out centuries ago."

"You—I—what?"

"All Firstborn have names, Toby. We chose to hide them behind titles a long time ago, when we realized it was time for us to take a big step away from Faerie. Even the strongest of our descendants were weak compared to us, their parents and originals. We didn't have to leave. But we did have to create a barrier, to remind the children of our children that we were something more than tools to be used."

"Blind Michael," I said, softly.

"Yes. And Black Annis, and Gentle Annie—her name was Anglides, before she shortened it and turned it into a warning. The Mother of Trees." The Luidaeg looked at me levelly. "We took titles as a warning. 'Stay away. Here there be monsters.'"

"So you can't help me," I said quietly.

"I didn't say that." She held out her hand. "Give me one of those chunks of blood."

I pulled out the bag, eyeing her warily. "Why?"

"Because I asked you to, stupid."

"Right. Do not argue with the woman who could take your head off." I pulled one blood gem from the bag and dropped it into her palm.

"See, if you were always that smart, we'd have a better working relationship." The Luidaeg closed her hand. "I'll be right back." She turned and left the room, leaving the two of us alone.

Tybalt moved to sit down next to me on the bed. I scooted over so that my leg was pressed against his, and rested my head on his shoulder. He sighed, a sound that was somewhere between exhaustion and relief, and raised a hand to stroke my hair.

"We will come through this," he said. "If I have to find your mother myself, and drag her kicking and screaming from whatever hole she is currently hiding in, we will come through this."

"And if we don't?" I twisted so I could see his face. "What if it's me, and chunks of frozen blood, and a human grave? What then?"

"Then I stay beside you for as long as we have." He kept stroking my hair. Cats like to be petted. Cait Sidhe like to pet. "October, I meant it when I told you I was not leaving you. I will *never* leave you while both of us are living. You were not quite this human when I met you, and you were far less human when I finally allowed myself to love you. But the essential core of your being has remained the same no matter what the balance of your blood."

"How is it that you always know the exact right stupid romance novel thing to say?" I asked, leaning up to kiss him.

He smiled against my lips. When I pulled back, he said, "I was a student of Shakespeare centuries before the romance novel was even dreamt. Be glad I do not leave you horrible poetry on your pillow, wrapped securely around the bodies of dead rats."

"Cait Sidhe romance," I said, and laughed. "It's definitely different."

"I simply wish to ensure you are never bored."

"Toby doesn't do 'bored,'" said the Luidaeg, walking back into the room. She was carrying a baggie of her own. This one was smaller, and contained what looked like a handful of black cherry cough drops, larger and darker than the blood gems I'd gotten from Walther. She thrust it toward me. "Here."

"What—?" I took the bag.

"I can't transform your blood into something that can sustain you, but I can freeze mine. If things get desperate, try one of these. Just . . . make sure things are bad, okay? They're going to have a hell of a kick."

I looked at the lozenges with newfound respect, and more than a little wariness. "You froze your own blood?" My magic drew power from blood—any blood. But the blood of a Firstborn wasn't something to mess around with. I could do myself some serious damage with her blood, if I took too much of it, if the power overwhelmed me.

And that was a risk worth taking, if the Luidaeg really thought that it would help.

"I have plans for you, October Daye. They don't include you dying human of a stupid addiction." The Luidaeg shook her head. "I can't help you get a hope chest. I can't even necessarily help you find your mother—although I can go looking for her, and I will, as soon as you people get the hell out of my bedroom. Don't come looking for me. I'll find you."

"On that terrifying thought . . ." I stood, tucking the bag of lozenges into my jacket. Both my inside pockets were filled with solidified blood now: mine and the Luidaeg's. I just hoped I wouldn't confuse the two. "Tybalt, you good for a trip back to my car? It's time for me to go back onto the grid, and stop wanting to pass out every time we move from point A to point B."

"Or you could call your friend the taxi driver," said the Luidaeg. "Don't exhaust your allies, Toby. You're going to need them before the night is through. Now get out."

I considered asking what she meant, but knew I

wouldn't get anything but vague implications of danger to come and maybe some profanity I hadn't heard in a while. So I just nodded, and said, "I'll call if anything changes," before following Tybalt out of the bedroom and heading for the front door.

I was about to step out when a hand descended on my shoulder. I looked back to see the Luidaeg standing behind me, concern written baldly on her face.

"You're fragile right now," she said. "Try to be careful, okay? You're the only niece I'm actually speaking to these days. I'm not in the mood to see you dead."

"I'll try," I said.

She scowled. "Next time, say it like you mean it. Now *out*." She pushed me over the threshold, slamming the door behind me.

Tybalt blinked.

I looked at him, and smiled. "She really does care," I said, before digging my phone out of my pocket. I flipped it open, scrolled through my contact list, and raised it to my ear. A few seconds later, I said, "Hello, Danny? It's October. I need a ride . . ."

SEVENTEEN

DANNY'S CAB SCREECHED around the corner at a speed somewhere between "unsafe" and "suicidal." He got extra points for driving that fast through the thick fog that had risen to shroud the entire block while Tybalt and I waited for him to arrive. I hoped it was the Luidaeg trying to give us a little extra cover, and not some sort of nasty present from the Queen. Standing there in the chilly night air, I was very aware that the Queen—illegitimate or not—was part Sea Wight, and I had no idea whether she had access to Sea Wight weather magic.

Then the cab door was slamming shut, and the mountain that was Danny McReady was storming toward us through the fog. "Somebody call for a— Oberon's scrotum, girl, what did you do to yourself *this* time?"

"Hi, Danny," I said, the ghost of a smile on my face. I couldn't see his expression, but I knew that tone. He'd be looking at me with raw, almost offended incredulity, like he was sure he could figure out the trick if he just stared hard enough. "You like my new look? I'm calling it 'mortality chic.' "

"It is a good thing fashions change so quickly these days," said Tybalt. He raised a forefinger. "A point of order—did you just swear by Oberon's *scrotum*?"

"Situation demanded it." Danny stepped closer, and

now I could see his face. The incredulity was there, mixed in equal measure with concern. It was like being worried at by a statue. "You okay?"

"Just don't hug me, and I'll be fine," I said, reaching out to rest a hand against his arm.

Danny McReady is a Bridge Troll—eight feet tall if he's an inch, with skin the color and consistency of granite, and the sort of natural strength that would allow him to fling a Buick, if he wanted to. A hug from him would probably have resulted in my mostly-human guts coming out of my mostly-human eyes. And nobody wanted that.

"Yeah." Danny frowned before taking an exaggerated step backward, like he'd just realized how fragile I really was. "You guys needed a ride?"

"We do," I confirmed, and started for the cab. Looking displeased about the whole situation, Tybalt followed. I smiled at him, and smiled again when I saw that the cab was blessedly free of Barghests. "You left the kids at home!"

"I was taking some mor—I mean, I was picking up hu—I wasn't workin' with a Barghest-friendly clientele." Every self-correction made Danny look more miserable, until his face was practically a grimace. "Aw, shit, Tobes, don't listen to me. I run my mouth."

"It's okay, Danny. Honest." I got into the front passenger seat. Danny was going to need an update on the situation, and it would be easier if I wasn't shouting from the back of the cab. "Tybalt, do you want to ride in cat form, or do you want to be a part of this conversation?"

"I want to shift into something smaller more than you can possibly know," he said, getting into the back with exaggerated offense. "Sadly, the smell of Barghest is near-overwhelming with my nose in its current configuration. If I were to become more sensitive, I fear I would black out from the stench."

"Don't cats lick their own assholes?" asked Danny mildly, as he wedged himself behind the wheel. Despite the fact that he had to weigh several hundred pounds, the car didn't even shift. Danny's cab was so tricked out with charms and customizations by his Gremlin mechanic that it probably handled better with the ballast. "I'm just sayin'."

"I will not dignify that with a response," said Tybalt.

Danny snickered as he started the engine. He sobered quickly, glancing to me as we pulled away from the curb. "Where we going?"

"The Library of Stars, to get Quentin—I have directions, and the Librarian promised it wouldn't move until we were done—and then to Shadowed Hills, if that won't take you away from your fares for too long. I need to pick up my car."

"Nope," said Danny imperturbably.

"What?" I blinked at him.

"I'll take you to the Library, but I'm not taking you to your car. I'll take you to Shadowed Hills, if you want. Maybe you could do with checking in, I dunno. Doesn't mean you're getting your car back."

"What are you talking—Danny." I folded my arms. "Tell me you're not refusing to take me to my car because you think I'm too human to drive."

"Can't. I don't lie to friends." He took a sharp turn. "You don't need a car, Tobes, you need a driver, and muscle to keep you from doing whatever ass-crazy thing pops into your head. You're too used to being invincible, and right now, you're not. Me, I sort of *am* invincible, as long as you're not coming at me with dynamite and blasting caps. Let me be invincible for you. I can stand between you and the shit that's trying to make you stop breathing."

"Much as I hate to add to the size of our company, he has a valid point," said Tybalt. "I would gladly take a bullet for you. I would even more gladly stand behind a man of living stone and allow him to take the bullet for the both of us."

"This is macho bullcrap," I said sourly. It wasn't—it actually made sense—but I didn't care. I hated the idea of needing protection.

"So is getting yourself killed to prove that you're still

unkillable," said Danny. "I ain't taking you to your car, and that's final. Now what in Maeve's name *happened*?"

The fact that he'd managed to go this long without asking was something of a miracle all by itself. I took a breath, and began, "We found a dead changeling girl lying in an alley . . ."

It took most of the drive for me to explain what had happened since we found the dead girl in the alley, especially since I kept having to pause to give Danny directions. Tybalt interjected when necessary, mostly to make dire predictions about the Queen's reign and Sylvester's future health. I didn't ask him to stop threatening my liege. Maybe I should have, but Sylvester should have known what he was getting into when he barred my Cait Sidhe boyfriend from my bedside. In the future, he might think twice before doing something that stupid.

Silence fell over the car when we were done. Danny kept driving, his brows knitting into a rocky shelf above his eyes. Finally, he took a breath, and passed judgment:

"Damn."

"I know."

"I mean, seriously . . . *damn*."

"Yeah."

"When you decide it's time to up the ante on getting into deep shit, you don't mess around, do you? You're just like, hey, what's the worst that can happen? That's the worst that can happen? Great. Let's do that."

"That's not fair," I protested.

"Says the more-mortal-than-not girl with the goblin fruit addiction she got from being hit in the face with a *pie*," Danny shot back. "You sure that chick from Dreamer's Glass hasn't been playing with your luck again?"

"I'm sure," I said. My stomach grumbled. I dug the baggie of blood gems out of my pocket as I added, "There haven't been enough disembowelments. Li Qin's luck manipulation really focused on getting me disemboweled." Trying to hide the motion as much as I could, I pulled one of the larger stones out of the bag and popped it into my mouth, where it dissolved into the taste of lavender and mint. My stomach stopped growling.

Thank Oberon.

"Yeah, well, there's not going to be any of *that* while I'm with you," said Danny, pulling the cab to an abrupt stop in front of the bookstore that housed the Library of Stars. "Disembowelment is pretty fatal, and I don't like fatal. We're here."

"I see that." I opened the door. "You want to come in?"

"Nah." Danny shook his head. "I don't like leaving the cab unguarded, and from what you were sayin', the Queen's guards might try to mess with it if I did. I'll wait. Take your time, I got a book."

"We will be respectful of your time," said Tybalt—as close to a thank you as he could really get. He slid out of his seat more quickly than my too-human eyes could follow, moving to offer me his hand. "Come, little fish. Knowledge awaits us."

"Yippee," I said dryly, letting him pull me from the cab. "Back soon, Danny."

"I'll be here," said the cabbie.

Knowing that he had my back was even more reassuring than I would have guessed. Feeling almost relaxed for the first time in a while, I kept hold of Tybalt's hand as we walked into the dusty bookstore. When we approached the point where the entrance to the Library of Stars was hidden, he swept me smoothly off my feet and into his arms. I squeezed my eyes shut, letting him carry me through the door I couldn't see.

"I hate this," I muttered, as softly as I could.

His lips brushed my ear. "I know," he murmured, and set me back on my feet.

I sighed and opened my eyes, sticking close as we walked through the darkened stacks to the small open space where Mags and Quentin had been when we left. I could hear voices before we got there, one male, one female.

"—not that anyone's found." Mags. She sounded

frustrated. This argument, if that was what it was, had clearly been going on for a while. "I've pulled out all the books, I've even pulled out books where the footnotes might have been relevant, and there's *nothing*. No one has ever found a treatment for goblin fruit addiction in humans. No one has really even *looked*."

"Merlins, then. Or Selkies. They're both almost human, and they're both powerful enough to do their own research." Quentin. He didn't sound frustrated. He sounded angry, and determined—and yes, a little bit scared. If I hadn't known him for so long, I wouldn't have been able to hear that part. "Maybe they know something."

"The merlins don't have any answers," said Mags. "You're grasping at straws."

"Yeah, and the Selkies don't know anything either," I said, stepping out of the stacks. Mags and Quentin were sitting across from each other. They still both jumped when they saw me, looking like they'd been caught in the act of doing something wrong. "I just got done talking to the Luidaeg. She'd know if the Selkies had a treatment for goblin fruit, and since she wants me to stay among the living, I sort of figure she would have told me. She didn't—she didn't even hint—so I'm guessing there's nothing."

"You're looking . . . well," said Mags, clearly unsettled.

"You mean I'm not totally lost in DTs and screaming for a fix? Yeah, I'm pretty impressed with that, too." I crossed my arms. Tybalt was a comforting presence behind me. "How's the research going? Have you two found anything of any use?"

"No," said Quentin. "There are some treatments for three-quarter changelings, but they're all hit-or-miss. There's nothing that works on half-bloods, much less . . ."

"Much less whatever the hell I am right now," I said, finishing his sentence for him. "Okay, we stick with the plan. We kick the current Queen off the damn throne that wasn't hers in the first place, get Arden confirmed, and get the hope chest out of the royal treasury so I can shift myself back to normal. And we hope that we can do it really fast, before this stuff gets the better of me. Does anybody have any objections?"

Silence.

"Does anybody have any better ideas?"

More silence.

"Great. Quentin, get your things. Danny's waiting outside, and we should get over to Goldengreen. Arden doesn't know it yet, but the timeline on our insurrection has just been moved up by circumstances beyond our control." I shook my head. "We're going to fix this."

"How?" whispered Mags.

I shot her a glare. Stalking over to the coffee table, I snatched the flask of fireflies and tucked it back into my jacket pocket where it belonged. She looked mournfully after it. "Does it matter? As long as it gets fixed, I'm willing to call it good." I turned to go.

"Wait," said Mags.

I stopped, looking back at her, and raised an eyebrow.

She stood, wings vibrating nervously, and asked, "Did the Luidaeg know anything that might help you find a hope chest? I'm happy to keep researching while you do whatever you feel needs to be done." She indicated the stacks around her, a wry smile briefly painting her mouth. "It's not like I'm exactly crawling in company. This is the most excitement I've had in decades. I want to help."

"The Luidaeg doesn't know where any of the hope chests are right now, except for the one the Queen has," I said. It seemed somehow too ... personal ... to tell Mags that the Luidaeg *was* Antigone of Albany. The Firstborn traded their names for titles for a reason, and I would respect that, as long as I could do so without making things even worse. "Since the Queen isn't going to let me borrow it, we need to get moving. We're on a deadline here."

"I'm ready," said Quentin, trotting over to stand next to me.

I had to look up slightly to meet his eyes. I wrinkled

my nose. "Who gave you permission to be taller than me?"

"You kept feeding me," he said, relief evident in his voice. If I was still making jokes, however bad, there was still a chance that things would be all right.

My stomach rumbled at the mention of food. I put a hand across it, trying to be subtle, and turned my attention back to Mags. "If you want to help, we're happy to have you. Keep looking for anything about curing goblin fruit, or at least mitigating its effects for extended periods. And if you happen to find a convenient map to the hope chests of the world, I'd love to see it."

"All right," said Mags. "I'll call you if I find anything."

"Great. We look forward to hearing from you." There wasn't anything else to say—I couldn't thank her—and we had far too much to do. I turned, beckoning for Quentin to walk with me. Tybalt turned as well, pacing us as we walked out of the Library to the bookstore.

The transition was just this side of painful, like walking through a curtain made of Pop Rocks. I stopped, gasping a little. Tybalt put a hand on my shoulder to steady me, looking alarmed.

"October?" he asked.

"Toby?" asked Quentin.

I bit my lip before I could snap at them. In that moment, I saw my future if I couldn't fix this. My allies—my best friends, my *family*, the people I loved more than anything else—would never adjust to me being this breakable. They'd treat me like I was made of glass until we could change the balance of my blood. Maybe they were right to feel that way. Humans without protectors have never had much of a life expectancy in Faerie. It still made me want to scream.

"Quentin, why don't you go let Danny know we're almost ready?" I asked.

"Okay . . ." said Quentin, frowning as he looked from me to Tybalt and back again. I raised an eyebrow. He went.

Tybalt removed his hand from my shoulder as the

bookstore door swung shut behind my squire. "You're . . . unhappy," he said, cautiously.

"True, but that's not why I sent Quentin away." I sighed, raking my hands back through my hair. "Tybalt. I need you to do something for me. It's something you're not going to like, and I'm sorry about that. It's still important."

His expression went blank, features smoothing out until, for a moment, he looked like the impassive King of Cats who used to lurk in alleys for the sole purpose of annoying me. "You are going to attempt to send me away," he said. "What in this world or any other could convince you to try something so foolish?"

"Tybalt, please."

"Did you fail to notice that the *last* time I allowed myself to separate from you, you wound up in your current condition? Why would I step aside and allow the chance that something even worse might happen? It is too dangerous. No. I refuse."

"*Tybalt!*"

My voice was impossibly loud in the tight confines of the bookstore. He stopped talking. Even through the gloom, I saw his eyes widen.

I took a shaky breath. "We can't do this."

"I don't know what you—"

"Just . . . just listen to me, okay? Tybalt, I *love* you. I don't want to leave you. I don't want to die on you. But I can't have you trying so hard to protect me that you won't even let me tell you what I need. That's not the relationship we both agreed on. That's not who you are to me, or who I am to you. We save each other, remember? This isn't supposed to be one-sided." I raked my hair back again, harder this time. "I need your help, but you're so wrapped up in the idea of protecting me that you're not even letting me explain."

Tybalt opened his mouth like he was going to protest. Then he stopped, going still for several seconds before he sagged, seeming to grow smaller before my eyes. "You say you can't have me protecting you. I understand that,

I do. But I can't stand by and let you risk your life. It is already taking everything I have not to carry you to your mother's tower and lock you inside until we can fix this."

"See, the fact that you admit to wanting to do that, but didn't actually try it? That's why we're here, having this conversation. I love you, Tybalt. I don't want to leave you."

"Then what, little fish, would you have me do?" He took a breath before raising his hand to my cheek. "In this matter, I am yours to command."

"I need you to go find my mother," I said, putting my hand over his and holding it against my face. "The Luidaeg offered to try, but I know you did it once before, when you weren't sure I was really myself. I know you *can*. And if we don't find a hope chest, she may be our only option."

"You told the Luidaeg . . ."

"Yeah, well." I allowed myself a tight smile. "If Mom tries to turn me all the way human, you'll have your fingers around her throat before I can start screaming. She's not stupid. She'd never have lived this long if she were stupid. So please? Will you do this for me?"

"I am . . . not comfortable with the idea of leaving you alone."

Judging by the tightness of his tone, that was the understatement of the year. I loved him even more in that moment. What I was asking him to do was as necessary as it was unfair. The fact that he was even willing to consider it was a testimony to how much he wanted this to work—and how much he wanted to save me.

But if I gave in, if I played the damsel in distress and let him stay with me, I wouldn't be me anymore. I couldn't do that.

"I know," I said. "I'm not too happy sending you away. But Danny will be with me. You know, the mountain that walks like a man. And Quentin will be there. And we're heading for Goldengreen, which means the armies of the Undersea will be there to back me up if anything goes wrong."

"And should something happen, I won't be there to stop it."

"I know. But that also means you won't be fighting to protect me when I don't want to be protected. We have to find a balance between what I am and what I'm supposed to be, and that means I need you to do this, Tybalt. Please. For me."

"For you, and against my better judgment," he said, and leaned in, and kissed me.

I didn't pull away. There are kisses shared in passion, and kisses shared in anger. Some are sweet, and others are bitter. This one was sad, and frightened, and it tasted like tears—his and mine, although I hadn't seen him shed any. He took his hand away from my face, wrapping his arms around my waist and pulling me close. I went willingly. There was no telling how many kisses we had left, and it would have been cruel to both of us to try to turn this one aside.

My human senses meant the taste of pennyroyal and musk was almost completely absent. In a way, that was nice, because it meant I could focus purely on the physical: his chest pressed against mine, his skin hot under my hands, and his heart, beating rapidly enough that I could feel his pulse through my entire body.

The kiss lasted less than a minute. It felt like it lasted forever, and when he pulled away, I found myself feeling strangely lost. I wanted to kiss him again. I wanted to tell him I had changed my mind; he couldn't go, not now, not when there was no telling what would happen next. Maybe I would die, and I'd do it without kissing him ever again.

There is always a last kiss. Sometimes we're just lucky enough to know when we may have had it.

"I love you," I said. This time, I was the one who put my hand against his cheek; this time, he was the one who covered my fingers with his own. "Now, please, go find my mother. Give me another way of getting out of this."

"I love you, too, October. There is no other reason I

would allow anyone to ask something so cruelly unfair of me."

He stepped backward, leaving my hand to hang in the air as he turned and dove into the nearest patch of shadow. I stayed frozen for a few more seconds, blinking back tears. Then I lowered my hand and walked toward the door.

I had work to do. And I didn't know how much time I'd have to do it.

EIGHTEEN

QUENTIN WAS IN THE BACKSEAT of Danny's cab when I emerged from the bookstore. I walked around to the front passenger seat and practically threw myself inside, digging the flask of fireflies out of my jacket before my butt even hit the seat. "We're good," I said. "We need to get over to Goldengreen. Danny, you know the way?"

"I do," he rumbled, watching me uncap the flask. "Where's kitty-boy? And what are you doin' with the bugs?"

"Tybalt is running an errand for me," I said. I stuck a finger into the flask, asking, "Does one of you want to help me?" A firefly lighted on my fingertip. I pulled it out and placed it against my chest, managing not to shiver as the glowing insect walked onto my collarbone, finally settling against the hollow of my throat. Its tiny legs tickled against my skin.

My instinct had been right: as soon as the firefly settled, the car seemed to snap into sharper focus. The colors became brighter and the details more distinct, despite the lingering darkness. The rocky planes of Danny's face stopped looking like an extremely well-made mask. I was seeing Faerie again.

"And the bugs?"

"As long as I have one of these on me, I can see things

the way I'm supposed to." I blinked rapidly, trying to keep myself from starting to cry again. I hadn't realized how much of a relief it would be to see the world properly. "We should still ask Marcia for fae ointment, just so I'll have a backup, but for right now, everything looks the way it's supposed to." I recapped the flask and tucked it back into my jacket before fastening my seatbelt. "Let's go."

"You're the boss," said Danny, and hit the gas.

My stomach rumbled as the car pulled away from the curb. I dug the baggie of blood gems out of my pocket and popped one into my mouth. The rumbling decreased, but didn't stop. That was . . . not a good sign, definitely, but not terribly surprising. My body wanted goblin fruit. Blood might cut the craving for a little while; that didn't mean it was going to work forever.

"What are those?" asked Quentin.

"Walther made them," I said. "They're . . . nutritional supplements, I guess."

"Made them out of what?"

"My flash-frozen blood." I could move on to the lozenges the Luidaeg had made for me, if I had to, but I didn't have to be an alchemist to know that once I started taking the strong stuff, I wouldn't be able to go back. It was better to stick with my own blood for as long as I could, and save the Luidaeg's for when I really needed it.

Quentin made a face in the rearview mirror. "That's gross."

"You know, we have got to get you a blood magic teacher after all this is taken care of. You're Daoine Sidhe. You shouldn't share my aversion to blood."

Danny snorted. "Best blood-worker in Faerie—'cept your ma, and she doesn't count, since she hasn't done any blood-work in years—and you still can't stand the sight of the shit. Doesn't that strike you as a little ironic?"

"Please don't start an argument about what ironic means right now," I said, replacing the baggie of blood gems in my pocket before sagging into my seat and closing my eyes. "Let's just get to Goldengreen without any problems."

"You're the boss," said Danny again, and hit the gas even harder.

I couldn't stop myself from cracking open an eye and watching the city falling away in the side-view mirror, waiting for the moment when an enchanted motorcycle or a black horse with flaming hooves would loom up behind us. The Queen knew Danny was one of my allies. He'd defended me to her face once, even though it could have gotten him into serious trouble. It would make sense for her to have had the car followed.

Danny caught what I was doing and snorted, sounding amused. "Don't worry about it, Tobes. She ain't following us."

"What?" I sat up, turning to face him. "Why not?"

"'Cause we're in a moving car that's been enchanted seventeen ways from Sunday to keep the iron in the frame from bein' a problem. Plus my mechanic doesn't like it when I get tickets, since paying those off sort of cuts into my disposable income, so she's got a bunch of don't-look-here and hide-and-seek and nope-not-yours charms in here. Queen might be able to find us when we're sitting still. Dunno. But when we're moving, we're invisible to anybody doesn't know just what they're looking for. So relax. It's cool."

"How is Connie, anyway?"

Danny grinned, a little sheepishly. "She's good. Real good."

"How's her schedule looking? I may want to ask her about making some of these modifications to my car. It would sure be nice to be able to drive around without worrying about being tracked."

"Yeah, that's a good point. I'll check and see if she has any big jobs comin' up."

Quentin leaned forward, bracing his hands against the back of the seat. "So, have you asked her out yet?"

Danny couldn't really blush—rock isn't much for showing subtle changes in skin color—but he scowled like a champion. "None of your business, pipsqueak."

"You should, you know. She's smart, she's funny, she

has her own business . . . she could do way better than you. If you don't jump, she's going to find somebody who will."

"Kid's right." I smirked at Danny. "Connie's pretty much got it going on. What's the problem?"

"I may take romantic advice from the kid, but I ain't listening to you," Danny said. "You had to nearly die before you'd listen to me and get with the big kitty. Didn't I tell you ages ago that you should?"

"Yes, you did, and now we're telling you to get with Connie. Besides, she's a Gremlin. For her, fixing your car is about as intimate as it gets. And she didn't give *me* a bucket of bonus concealment charms."

Danny sank lower in his seat, grumbling. "I don't like you ganging up on me." There was a note of relief to his complaint. He liked seeing things trend toward normal as much as I did. Wasn't that the trick, though? Life was one long series of efforts to reach the golden mean, where everything was the way that it was supposed to be. Where we could tell jokes with our friends and tease them about their love lives, and no one had to die for it to happen.

I wanted normal back. And that meant seeing this through.

It was late enough that the parking lot was almost empty when we reached the San Francisco Art Museum. The few cars that remained gleamed faintly, revealing the presence of concealment charms. I glanced fondly down at the firefly that was resting on my collarbone. "You're awesome, little guy," I said.

Maybe it was my imagination, but the insect seemed to glow a little brighter after that.

"I'm not sure the cliff-side entrance would be a good idea right now," I said, getting out of the cab. "I mean, it might work. Or it might decide I'm too mortal to be allowed inside the knowe and dump me into the ocean. Drowning doesn't sound like a good time to me."

"You pushed May off that cliff once," said Quentin.

"May is indestructible; I'm not," I said. "Can you get us in through the shed?"

He nodded. Danny and I followed him out of the parking lot and into the weeds that grew on the stretch of unlandscaped field next to the museum.

Quentin led us on a looping route that seemed to follow no pattern or trail, until we reached an old, rust-covered shed that looked like it should have been demolished years ago to make way for something newer and less likely to give tetanus to tourists. There was a large padlock on the door. Oak trees grew all around it, their branches spread above it like a canopy. It wasn't visible from the parking lot. Somehow, no one ever seemed to find that strange. It was just another part of the museum. The human tendency not to ask questions when the fae don't want them to has served us very well over the centuries.

Voices seemed to whisper from the tall grass as we approached the shed. They were softer than I was accustomed to them being, more believably tricks of the wind blowing off the water. They were accompanied by a feeling of "you should turn back" that was stronger than normal, like the spell had adjusted itself to match my heritage. The more human an intruder was, the less they'd hear the voices, but the more they'd hear the whispered threats.

Quentin walked to the door, where he bent and said something to the lock. The voices stopped, and the wind seemed to still. If I strained, I could catch the faintest hint of steel and heather perfuming the air. Then the stillness passed, and the door swung open, despite the padlock remaining in place. "I love that trick," he said, sounding pleased with himself.

"You can have a cookie when we get home," I said, and walked past him, into the knowe—

—only to hit the hallway floor on my knees as the transition between the mortal world and the Summerlands struck me like a hammer. I gagged. It hadn't been that bad at the Library, but Libraries were special cases, built in shallowings and designed to move when necessary. Goldengreen was a permanent structure. Its roots went deep, and it was not a place where humans belonged.

Massive hands slid beneath my arms, lifting me back to my feet with a surprising gentleness. I slumped against Danny's chest. It was an unyielding surface, but it was better than the floor. My lungs felt like they were three sizes too small, and my head was spinning.

"That *sucked*," I said.

"I've never seen you fall down like that," said Quentin. I turned toward him. His eyes were so wide that I could see the whites all the way around his irises. "Are you okay?"

"Yeah, I'm fine. It's just . . . yeah." I'd seen Marcia make the crossing a dozen times without problems. It must have been the goblin fruit making things even worse—that, or the fact that I was currently even more human than she was. I coughed into my hand and straightened, steadying myself against Danny before taking my hand away. "Let's go find Dean."

A group of pixies rushed by overhead, their wings chiming like bells. They vanished through the door that led into the courtyard. I blinked.

"Pixies usually go where there's food," I said. "I guess everyone came upstairs for lunch?" It would have made more sense to stay down at the beach, where the Undersea army would be more comfortable, but this wasn't my invasion to plan.

We walked down the hall to the courtyard, me trying to pretend I didn't notice how closely my companions were sticking, them trying to act like they weren't waiting for me to fall. Then we stopped, all of us staring through the open door as we tried to make sense of the scene.

Dean was there, in close-held argument with Marcia, both of them making tight, quick gestures with their hands. Patrick was sitting on one of the low walls that supported the flowerbeds, his head cradled in his hands. Dianda was nowhere to be seen.

And neither was Arden.

I cleared my throat. All three of them looked toward

us. Their expressions only drove home the idea that something was terribly wrong. Patrick looked numb; Dean, panicked; and Marcia, who had served as my Seneschal and knew me better than either of the other two, relieved. Then her relief flickered, turning into bewilderment as she really *saw* me, and realized I wasn't wearing a human disguise.

"T-Toby?" she said uncertainly. "Oh, oak and ash, what happened?"

"I think I need to ask the same question," I said. "What's going on? Where's Arden? Where's Dianda?"

"Arden ran," said Dean. His voice sounded hollow. I wasn't sure he'd even registered the change in my appearance. "After the Queen arrested my mother, Arden ran."

"What?!" It felt like the word had been ripped out of me by unseen hands. I stared at him, unable to wrap my mind around what he was saying. "What do you mean, the Queen arrested Dianda? On what grounds?"

"Sedition and conspiracy to incite rebellion," said Patrick. He sounded a little better than his son. I guess after years of watching the Queen's policies chip away at the relationship between the Kingdom of the Mists and the Undersea, he'd stopped hoping for anything better. "She came in here with a dozen guards and said she had proof that Dianda was at the head of a campaign against her. She took my wife to be imprisoned until the Queen of Leucothea could be contacted." A weary smile creased his lips. It was the sort of expression a convicted man might wear on the way to the gallows. "I suppose it's a good thing I recanted my title when I chose the sea over the land. The Queen ignored me completely."

"Me, too," said Dean, sounding confused.

"Yeah, which just proves this is a farce," I said. Saltmist was a part of the Kingdom of Leucothea, the nearest Undersea demesne. But Goldengreen belonged to the Mists. "This is *your* land, Dean. If she was arresting people on charges of sedition, you should have been the first against the wall." He looked sick. I wrinkled my nose. "Sorry about that, and if it helps, I have no idea how she found out. I don't know how she found out any of this. Did the Queen really come here? The actual Queen, not a representative?"

"It could have been a Gwragen under an illusion, but I don't think it was," said Marcia. Everyone turned to her. She shrugged, touching the thin layer of faerie ointment that gleamed around her eyes. "I can't always see through illusions, but I can almost always tell when someone is wearing one. The woman who came here looked like the Queen; commanded like the Queen; scared the crap out of the pixies like the Queen; and she wasn't wearing any disguises. I don't think we're worth that much trouble. Not Goldengreen." She paused before adding, "And she was singing. No one could move while she was singing."

That sealed it. The Queen was part Siren: her songs had the power to command. It also explained how she'd been able to take Dianda with an Undersea army right there. Unless they'd had a Siren of their own to deploy, the Queen could have walked in and out without meeting any real challenge.

"Goldengreen is worth more than any other noble holding in Golden Gate," I said, surprised by the venom in my words. I looked toward Dean. "I am sorry. I am sorry to have brought this on your house, and on your family, and I will do my best to get your mother freed."

"Don't be." He straightened. "The Queen of the Mists is a bad regent, and right now, she's in control of my lands and my people. That means she needs to be deposed. Mom is an Undersea noble. She was committing sedition, even if the Queen had no right to arrest her."

"So what are you committing?" asked Quentin. It was the first time he'd spoken since we stepped into the courtyard.

Dean smiled. "Treason."

"Okay. Just as long as we're all on the same page," I said.

"We're not," said Patrick. He stood. "Pardon my language, October, but what in the name of Titania's ass happened to you?"

"It's a long story," I said. It didn't help: Patrick continued looking at me expectantly, waiting to hear my answer. Dean and Marcia were doing much the same thing. I sighed. "The Queen arranged to have me exposed to goblin fruit. I think she was hoping she could discredit me by getting me addicted to the stuff. Turns out that because of my particular . . . talents . . . I was able to turn myself almost human in the pursuit of a better high."

"Why only almost?" asked Dean.

"Because that's when my magic got too weak for me to keep going. Now I can't turn myself back without either a hope chest or my mother to help me." My stomach rumbled. I ignored it. "Did the Queen see Arden? Or did Arden just run?"

"She—the Queen—came in through the cliff entrance," said Dean. "We were all down by the cove. She and her men used the stairs to get down to us, and they went straight for Mom. Arden was at the back of the crowd. I don't think the Queen saw her, but after the guards took Mom away, Arden was gone."

"Okay. So she got spooked. It happens. Has anyone checked the guest room where Nolan is sleeping?"

Blank looks told me that they hadn't thought of that. I bit my lip before I could say something I'd regret later. Dianda was Dean's mother and Patrick's wife. They could be forgiven for being a little off their game. I would normally have expected Marcia to be more on the ball, but seeing the Queen was never easy on changelings. She had the kind of beauty that stopped hearts, and the more human you were, the worse it was.

If I saw her in my current condition, I'd probably drop dead on the spot. Not a pleasant thought, given that she was the one who had the thing I needed to *cure* my current condition.

Please, Tybalt, find Mom, I thought, not dwelling on the fact that somewhere along the line, I had started thinking of humanity as something to be cured. "Nolan, her brother? The reason she's been in hiding since her father died? That guy? We put him in one of the guest rooms when we first arrived, remember?"

Marcia paled. "I didn't even think to check."

"That's what I thought you were going to say." I looked back to Danny. "Wait here. I don't think the Queen is going to come back, but if she does . . ."

"I start shoutin' about how I'm so honored by her presence and does she need a ride anywhere," said Danny. "They'll be able to hear me in Shadowed Hills."

"Good." I smiled before turning to Marcia. "Lead the way."

Marcia nodded, looking anxious, and walked quickly out of the courtyard. The rest of us followed her, me and Quentin at her heels, Dean and Patrick bringing up the rear. None of us spoke. Until we knew whether Nolan was still in Goldengreen, conversation would be a waste of time.

The guest room Marcia had chosen for the slumbering Prince was at the back of the knowe, small but nicely appointed, with a large, comfortable, and above all else, empty bed at the center of the chamber. I stopped in the doorway and sighed. "Damn."

"He was right here!" protested Marcia.

"I know." I turned to Patrick and Quentin. "I need your help."

Both of them blinked. Patrick spoke first, asking, "What do you need us to do?"

"Look: right now, my magic is basically nonexistent. My body is using all its resources just keeping me on my feet. Either Arden teleported to this room and left with her brother, or the Queen brought a teleporter and used arresting Dianda as a cover for her real goal."

"The Prince," said Quentin, sounding horrified. "If she knows about him, she wants him."

"Yeah." I nodded grimly. "I still don't know how she knows about *any* of this, but we have to assume she may know we've found Arden and Nolan. So what I need to know is who took him."

"There's no blood," protested Patrick. "I can't do blood magic without blood."

"Ah, but you *can* look for traces of other spells. Daoine Sidhe aren't as good as Dóchas Sidhe, maybe, but you're better than anything else Faerie has on tap. So come on, you two. Dig deep, and use what Titania gave you. Tell me who took the Prince." I stepped to the side, motioning them into the room.

Patrick squared his shoulders and stepped past me. Quentin hesitated.

"I'm not sure . . ."

"Quentin. You're my squire. You've followed me into Blind Michael's lands. You've survived being shot, being transported to Annwn, and riding in a car with May. I've overseen your education gladly, and I've been perpetually amazed by the man you're growing up to be. You can do this. And if you refuse to even try, I'll kick your ass." I put a hand on his shoulder, shoving him after Patrick. He stumbled, but not for long. Glancing back at me, he smiled anxiously, and then hurried to join the other pureblood.

I took a step backward, getting out of the way. What came next would have nothing to do with me, and everything to do with the two of them. Marcia and Dean moved to flank me.

"Do you really think this will work?" asked Marcia.

"I don't have a damn clue," I said. "I also don't have a better idea." I dug the baggie of blood gems out of my pocket almost without thinking about what my hands were doing and popped one into my mouth. It dissolved like the others, but my stomach didn't stop growling. I pulled out another one. That dulled the hunger, and replaced it with a new, gnawing worry.

Walther said these wouldn't last forever. Just how short was "not forever" going to be?

"What are those?" asked Dean.

"All that stands between me and wasting away for want of goblin fruits," I said, tucking the bag back into my pocket. "So let's hope this gets taken care of fast, shall we?"

Inside the guest room, Quentin was pacing, while Patrick was standing frozen at the center of the floor. His eyes were closed, and his chin was tilted back, allowing him to sniff the air. Quentin, meanwhile, was peering at every crack in the wall and every bit of pixie dust on the tapestries. It would have been a comic scene if they hadn't looked so damn serious. This wasn't a game. People were going to get hurt if we didn't figure out where Nolan was. This was my strength: tracking people through their magic. And I was benched for the duration.

Patrick spoke first, saying uncertainly, "I smell . . . clover."

"I have dry grass," said Quentin. He looked toward me. "I don't know what kind."

"Okay," I said. "Focus, both of you. Patrick, is there anything special about the clover?"

"No. I'm not you, October. I can't sniff the air and go 'oh, it smells like red clover from the cliffs of Oregon.' That's your line. All I can give you is 'wet clover,' and that's almost guessing."

I smiled, just a little. "See, Patrick, you're better at this than you think you are."

He frowned. "Come again?"

"Wet clover, and dry grass. We're looking for a Tuatha teleporter. But not Arden." My smile died as fast as it had come. "Arden's magic smells like blackberry flowers and redwoods. She didn't take Nolan. That doesn't mean she won't be looking for him." My fingers itched with the almost undeniable urge to punch something. Arden had hidden for decades. She'd kept her brother safe and out of the Queen's reach. And I, in my efforts to fix things, might as well have handed him to the very thing his sister had been trying to avoid.

"So what do we do now?" asked Quentin.

I took a deep breath. "Patrick, I need to ask you for the sort of favor that isn't just unreasonable: it verges on obscene. Will you please not hit me until I can explain?"

"You want me to keep the news of my wife's arrest from the Undersea," he said.

"Yes," I said, meeting his cold gaze with my own pleading one. "For now. Just long enough for us to find Arden. If we can give her the throne . . ."

"You understand that this could get me banished."

"You understand that a war, right now, serves no one's interests but the Queen's."

Patrick took a breath, as if to object. Then he stopped and slowly nodded. "I will talk to the soldiers we brought with us. They're still in the cove, waiting for instructions. If I can convince them, I will do so. But I make no promises."

"That's all I can ask for." I turned to Dean. "The next part is yours. I'm asking your father to help me avoid a war. I'm asking you to plan for one. The Queen will take Goldengreen if she has to. Don't let her."

Dean frowned. "What are you going to do?"

"Me? I'm going to find Arden and convince her there's only one way this can end well for any of us. We're going to find her brother. We're going to get him back. And then we're going to take the throne of the Kingdom of the Mists and give it back to the Windermere family, because it's pretty damn clear that the current government isn't working out."

"But you're *human*," said Dean.

I looked at him, trying to project a calm I didn't feel. "Only mostly," I said. "I guess the universe decided it was time the Queen had a fighting chance. Now if you're with me, it's time to kick her ass out of this Kingdom." I extended my hand. After a moment's pause, he took it.

Dianda was the only one who'd been arrested; she was the only one viewed as a threat. The Queen should have thought bigger. Because as long as any of us were free, she was finished.

Hopefully. Assuming we could all stay alive that long.

NINETEEN

"WHERE ARE WE GOING?" asked Danny. He didn't slow down the car; he just kept going, rocketing out of the parking lot at a speed that made his previous unsafe driving seem like child's play. I clung to the oh-shit handle above the door, trying to keep my ass in contact with the seat. Quentin was rattling around in the backseat like a bouncy ball.

Oh, well. He was a teenage boy. A few bruises were good for him. "Valencia," I said. "We want a bookstore you've probably never noticed before, across the street from an Irish pub that you probably have."

"Dog Eared Books isn't across the street," protested Danny, taking a corner sharply enough that I would have sworn the back tires actually lifted off the pavement. "It's down the block a ways."

"Yes, but we're not *going* to Dog Eared Books," I said. "We're going to a place called Borderlands."

"No such place."

I gave him a sidelong look, or as much of one as I dared when we were moving that fast. "Danny. You're a Troll, driving a cab. Yesterday, I was a superhero, and today I'm addicted to jam. *Jam.* Do you really think we get to pass judgment on what does and does not get to exist? There's a bookstore on Valencia that you've never seen. I promise."

"If you say so," he muttered, and eased off the gas.

"I do," I said, breathing a near-silent sigh of relief. Finding Arden wasn't going to do us any good if we got pancaked in the process.

Silence from the backseat reminded me that Danny wasn't the only one who'd never been to Borderlands. I twisted to see Quentin looking at me dubiously.

"You want to say something?"

"Yeah . . . are you *sure* there's a bookstore there?" He at least had the good grace to look faintly abashed as he continued, "You might have dreamt it."

Anger rose in my throat like bile. I swallowed it back down and said, "I can understand why you might be concerned about that, but Tybalt and I went to Borderlands *before* I was hit with the evil pie." No matter how many times I said "evil pie," it never started sounding normal. "The store is there, it's just hidden from anyone who claims allegiance to the Mists. Arden has been hiding there for a while. It may not be where she went to ground, but it's the best lead we have."

"And if she's not there?" rumbled Danny.

Her magic smelled like redwood trees and blackberries. So did the place where I had heard her name spoken to open a shallowing that had been holding itself closed for decades. "If she's not there, we head for Muir Woods," I said, "She's connected to the shallowing there, somehow. She might try running for it. It seems like less of a sure bet, but again. We take the leads we have when we're dealing with something like this."

"I don't like it," said Danny.

"Join the club," I replied.

We were in the strange hours of the night, where traffic became unpredictable, here heavy, there nonexistent. The route Danny was plotting took us straight through San Francisco, ignoring the daily logic of the city in favor of a more personal approach. He never slowed down. Somehow, he managed not to run any red lights or hit any pedestrians, either. Those Gremlin charms were worth their weight in whatever he had paid for them.

When we reached Valencia, he took his weight off the gas, reducing our speed until we were almost obeying the law. "Now where?" he demanded.

"Hang on." I took the flask of fireflies out of my pocket, using my finger to coax one of the brightly-shining insects out. Carefully, I transferred it to his shoulder, where it settled into a pose of apparent contentment. "Look down the street until you see something you don't recognize, and park there."

"What?" Danny frowned at me before turning to scan Valencia. "That's about the dumbest thing I've ever—holy shit, girl, there's a *bookstore* there. What the hell? When did they build a bookstore?"

"Since the building is like a hundred years old, a while ago," I said. "Can you park?"

"I'm on it." He twisted the wheel abruptly enough to make the tires squeal in protest. Somehow, this ended with us wedged into a space that had just opened in front of the Phoenix, the Irish pub almost directly across the street from Borderlands. "We're here," he said smugly, and turned off the engine.

Other things that had happened during our unexpected hairpin turn in the middle of a San Francisco street: my hands were pressed flat against the dashboard, although I didn't remember putting them there, and Quentin was bent almost double, his arms wrapped against my seat's headrest. I forced the muscles in my arms to unlock. It wasn't easy. Adrenaline had everything confused, and my body really wasn't interested in listening to me.

"Danny?"

"Yeah, Tobes?"

"If you kill us trying to protect me, Tybalt will figure out a way to get through that skin of yours and introduce you to your own internal organs. He's Cait Sidhe. He can do it."

To my surprise, Danny laughed. I blinked. He grinned. "See, as long as you're capable of gettin' pissed at me, I know you're gonna be okay. You may not like what comes between here and actually getting to that point, and the rest of us will pretty much hate it, 'cause you can be nasty when you want to, but you're gonna be okay."

I blinked again. Then I smiled. "I didn't think of it that way."

"'Course not. You're the hero. You're never supposed to think about your own mental health." Danny wrapped a human disguise around himself and slid out of the car before I could answer him. Stifling a snicker, Quentin did the same.

I reached for my seatbelt. My hands were shaking too badly for me to undo the latch.

Slowly, I raised them to a level with my face, trying to make the shaking stop. If I really focused, I could stop the worst of it, but a fine tremor remained, like my body was caught in its own private earthquake.

Danny knocked on the window. I jumped.

"You okay in there?" he asked. His concern was visible; he knew something was wrong.

All I had to do was admit it. All I had to do was say, "I'm sorry, I'm done, I'm starting to break down," and he'd take me back to Shadowed Hills. Jin could put me to sleep until Tybalt or the Luidaeg got back with Mom, however long that took, and I'd be okay, or at least I'd have a shot at it, which was more than I had now. All I had to do was say the word.

And Nolan would die, if he wasn't dead already. Because there was no chance that anyone other than the Queen had taken him, and there was less than no chance that she was going to let him live a second time. His life had been the coin she used to buy Arden's silence. Well, Arden wasn't silent anymore. Not even running away would save him now. And then there were all the humans and changelings who would waste away yearning for goblin fruit . . .

I lowered my hands and plastered a smile across my face, hoping the unfamiliar humanity of my features would make it harder for him to know that I was lying. "I got a splinter from the protection charms on your stupid dashboard," I said. "I'll be right there."

Danny didn't look like he believed me, but he said, "If you're sure," before straightening again.

I wasn't sure. I was so far from sure that we weren't even in the same time zone. But I was doing the best I could. I raked my shaking hands through my hair, trying to catch my breath. Then I reached into my jacket and pulled out the second baggie. I wasn't sure about this, either. I didn't see any other way.

Opening the baggie, I reached in, pulled out a frozen piece of the Luidaeg's blood, and dropped it onto my tongue.

There was no taste of mint and lavender this time, no soothing feeling that I was somehow repairing myself. Instead, it felt like my entire mouth was freezing solid, a cold so profound that it actually crossed some unmarked internal line and started to burn. I gasped and folded forward, clutching my stomach.

Somewhere outside the car, Danny and Quentin were shouting my name. I managed to peel one hand free and wave to them, trying to signal that I was okay. It was hard to focus through the burning chill. Slowly, it was replaced by the taste of loam, the smell of bonfires in the night. I tried to pull myself out of the memory I could feel building around me, but it was too late; I was already lost. And then . . .

And then . . .

"Dammit, Amy, you're not listening *to me!" I'm angry with her, and with myself. This is my fault as much as it is hers. She's the youngest. She should never have been given so much freedom, never allowed to make so many poor decisions. But we were scattered, broken by what had happened to our parents, and we left her free for so long. Too long. This is my fault.*

She whirls, blonde hair flying, hands balled into fists, and shouts, "You had no right!"

The Luidaeg's memory was showing me my mother, back when she was vital and engaged and not hiding from the world for some reason she'd never shared with me. I gasped and stopped fighting the blood. If the Luidaeg's memory had been focused on my mother when she was bleeding for me, there must have been a reason. Maybe this would tell me what it was.

And maybe it would kill me. Too late now.

"I had every right, Amy; I had every right. That little girl deserves better than what you were trying to do to her, and you know it."

"She deserves a life!"

"She's not human! No matter what you do to her, no matter how deep you go, Faerie will always know her as its own. Do you understand? You can't free her. All you can do is make her defenseless. She'll belong to Faerie until she dies. You're making sure that happens sooner."

She looks at me, my pretty Amy, and her broken heart is shining in her eyes. Finally, she shakes her head, and speaks. "So be it," she says, and I know.

I know she's given up again.

The blood haze was starting to loosen, and with it, the bands constricting my lungs and gut. I took a great, gasping breath, and the bands loosened further. Scrabbling along the door with one hand, I found the handle and wrenched it open. Only my still-fastened seatbelt stopped me from fully spilling out into the street.

"Whoa, whoa, whoa!" Massive hands were suddenly there to support me as Danny interrupted my fall and hoisted me back into the seat. "What'n the hell was that all about? You need a cup of coffee or somethin'?"

"Coffee doesn't cure all ills, Danny." My hands were steady enough now that I could undo the seatbelt. Score one for the Luidaeg and her weirdly invasive style of magic. Using Danny's arm to steady myself, I stood. "I haven't had a cup of coffee since the pie."

"Huh," he said, looking impressed. "Maybe you can kick caffeine and goblin fruit at the same time."

"I doubt it." I looked across the car to Quentin. He was pale, and his lips were pressed into a thin line—something he only did when he was really concerned. "I'm okay. I just wasn't prepared for the remedy the Luidaeg made me to kick as hard as it did."

He blinked as he looked at me, and said, "Maybe you should fix your hair."

"What?" I reached up to feel it with one hand. "It's my hair. It's fine. It always looks like this."

"Yeah, but your ears don't."

Now it was my turn to blink. I dropped my hand lower, to where the edge of my right ear was just visible through the tangled strands of my hair. It was still mostly rounded . . . but the edge was more pointed than it had been at the start of the evening. "Oh," I said.

"Yeah," Quentin said.

My magic—which was currently way too willing to act outside my conscious control—must have decided I needed help focusing on the Luidaeg's borrowed memory, and so inched a little closer to fae. Not enough closer; I still couldn't taste Danny or Quentin's heritage, and I knew from the depth of the shadows across the street that if I lost the firefly, I'd be fae-blind once again. But enough to stop the shaking.

Enough to buy me a little more time.

"Luidaeg, you are a fabulous monster, and an even better bitch," I muttered.

"What's that?"

"Nothing." I smoothed my hair down over my ears, looking back to Quentin. "Better?"

"Better," he said. "You still don't need, um . . ." He waved his hands, encompassing the length of my body.

I decided to show mercy for once. Taking my hand off Danny's arm, I said, "I'm still human-looking enough that I don't need to worry about a full-body disguise, huh?"

Cheeks flaming red, Quentin nodded.

"Okay. At least we know what we're working with. Come on. Quentin, you need to stay close to either me or Danny, since otherwise I don't think you're going to be able to see the place." I could have given him a firefly of his own, but I was starting to do the mental math, and I didn't like the numbers. I'd started with ten. We lost one finding Arden; I had one on me, and so did Danny. They could fly away at any time. As long as they were my only reliable way of seeing into Faerie, I was going to hold onto the seven I still had with an iron fist.

"Okay," said Quentin, and took my elbow as we jay-walked across Valencia Street.

Jaywalking is common in San Francisco. It's not that there aren't crosswalks—there are—it's just that as a populace, we're all too damn lazy to walk to the end of the block when we can see our destination right across the street. So it wasn't until we were halfway across the street that I realized what was wrong.

There were no other jaywalkers. There were no other pedestrians of any kind, not on the sidewalks, not even clustered outside the Phoenix or the corner store. Even if everywhere else was deserted, there should have been *someone* outside the two nearest sources of alcohol. I stopped, not particularly caring that we were in the middle of the street. "I'm an idiot," I murmured. "Quentin?"

"Um, yeah?" he asked, automatically dropping his voice to match mine.

"I need you to throw up a hide-and-seek spell, and it needs to be big enough to cover all three of us." I started looking around, trying to focus on the places where the shadows were deepest. The firefly was supposed to let me see through illusions. That was fine and dandy, except for the part where I had to *find* those illusions before I could see through them. I hate loopholes.

"Tobes? You wanna tell the rest of us what's going on?"

Doing emergency planning in the middle of the street might seem counterintuitive, but it actually wasn't a bad idea. If anyone tried to sneak up on us, we'd see them coming. That wouldn't stop listening charms. There's always an element of risk. "As soon as the hide-and-seek is in place, grab Quentin and run," I said, quietly. "I'll be running in the opposite direction. I hate to split up, but we're walking into a trap, and I bet the Queen set it. She's trying to find Arden's hiding place."

"Wait wait wait," said Danny. "Why am I grabbing the kid? No offense, but I should be grabbing *you*."

"Because you, and me, we can see where we're going. Quentin can't." I shook my head. "He hides us, we run, we find people. Once we find people, we know we're outside the bounds of this ambush. You carry Quentin back to the you-know-where," I was suddenly unwilling to say the word "bookstore" aloud, "and I'll meet you there."

"I don't like this plan," said Danny.

"I *hate* this plan," said Quentin.

"Well, then, it's a damn good thing I'm in charge, since this is the only plan that's getting us inside without telling the Queen where we're going," I half-snapped. "Now cast the hide-and-seek. We need to get moving."

Quentin sighed. Then he raised his hands, waving them through the air like he was conducting an unseen orchestra, and sang, in a clear, high tenor, "Oh, my name is Captain Kidd, as I sailed, as I sailed, my name is Captain Kidd, as I sailed . . ."

I couldn't smell his magic, but I felt a prickling sensation run across my skin as the spell was cast, causing the small hairs on my arms and the back of my neck to stand on end. Quentin lowered his hands. I looked at him. He nodded.

"All right," I said. "See you there."

Then I turned, and sprinted for the end of the block, still in the middle of the street.

Hide-and-seek spells primarily depend on one thing: the person you're trying to hide from losing sight of you. We hadn't exactly been subtle as we stood on Valencia Street and argued about our next move, but we also hadn't been *moving*. It was my sincere hope that our sudden action would be confusing enough to give us a few seconds' head start. That, and I really, really hoped the Queen hadn't sent any Centaurs. I'm pretty good at running for my life—I've had a lot of practice, when you get right down to it—but there's no way I could outrun someone with four legs and lungs sized to sustain most of a horse's body. A Silene, maybe. A Centaur, no way.

As I ran, I dug my phone out of my pocket and started scrolling through my contacts with my thumb. Why did I have to know so many *people*? It was like having a cell phone made people you hadn't talked to in years come out of the woodwork, demanding you care enough to keep their information handy. I decided I'd delete them all as soon as this was over, and pressed "call" as the list finally reached the name I'd been looking for.

There were cars on the block up ahead. I veered back onto the sidewalk, listening to the phone ringing in my ear. "Come on, pick up," I gasped, already too winded to do much else. "Come on, come on . . ."

"Hello?"

"May!" I swerved to avoid running into a fire hydrant. "Is Jazz there?"

"Toby? Are you running or something? You sound like you can't breathe."

"That's because I'm running! Is Jazz there?"

"Yeah, she's—"

"Tell her I need her, and the flock, to mob at Valencia and 16th Street. *Now*."

"Toby, what—"

"I'm being chased by an unknown number of people," I swerved to avoid a bike chained to a bike rack, with no owner in sight, "and I'm not sure how long I can keep running. I need a mob."

"On it," said May, and hung up.

That would have to be good enough. Hoping Jazz could actually rouse the rest of the city's Raven maids and Raven-men before I had passed the intersection, I put the phone back in my pocket, put my head down, and *ran*.

This is how it is with me and exercise: I have to exert myself, I get winded, I complain about getting winded, I swear I'm going to get into shape, I get distracted, and it never happens. Developing a supernaturally-enhanced healing talent didn't help, since it meant I no longer had to worry as much about outrunning gunshots. So I wasn't in the best shape, endurance-wise, *before* the goblin fruit caused my body to shift me most of the way back toward human. I was moving on momentum and terror, plain and simple, and as soon as one of them gave out, I was going to be in a world of trouble.

It was a good thing I was semi-invisible at the moment, since I knew how strange I would have looked to anyone who could see me: just a woman, running pell-mell down the empty sidewalk, with no one visibly in pursuit. I wanted to stop. My lungs were burning, and my knees had started to ache—a pain from my more mortal days that I'd been more than happy to forget about. The landscape was on my side for the moment, presenting me with a gentle downward slope, but once I crossed 16th, that would stop. If Jazz and the Ravens didn't meet me there, I'd be running uphill.

Come on, Jazz, I prayed, as I dug deep for one more burst of short-lived speed. *I know you can do this. I believe you can do this. So come on, and prove me right. Please.*

My next stride hit the sidewalk just a little bit wrong, and I lost my balance, going head over heels before landing in a painful heap against the base of a nearby wall. Spots danced in front of my eyes. I tried to roll to the side, and found myself looking at a series of koi silhouettes that someone had painted on the sidewalk and building. I laughed, and then groaned as it made my head ache even more.

For the first time, I heard footsteps behind me. I tried squinting in their direction, but there was nothing there, and I realized that the feeling of feather-light feet dancing over my collarbone was gone. I raised a hand and touched my chest, confirming what I already partially knew: the firefly was gone. Either the flight or the fall had dislodged it.

"Then there were seven," I muttered, pulling myself inch by aching inch to my feet. The knees of my jeans were ripped out, and the smell of blood was thick in the air. Good. I raised one scraped palm to my mouth and ran my tongue across it, borrowing what strength I could from my own blood before I snapped, "Well? What are you assholes waiting for? Come on!"

The Queen's guards stepped out of thin air.

There were five of them, all dressed in the Queen's livery, all armed. They had to be allowing me to see them through some sort of selective don't-look-here; those weapons weren't street-legal, and it wasn't like I had the power to see through illusions on my own. The figure at the center of the group was a Gwragen, eyes closed and mouth moving in some silent litany as she maintained the spell that was keeping them concealed and keeping the mortal population at bay.

"You're going to have one *hell* of a headache in the morning," I wheezed, and licked my hand again. Despite the bits of gravel and dirt embedded in the skin, the blood tasted good.

"October Daye, you are under arrest—" began one of the guards, a broad-shouldered Satyr with holes cut in his helmet to allow his horns to curl through.

"Sir," I said, interrupting him.

He stopped, frowning at me. "What?"

"Sir," I repeated. "If you're going to arrest me, you're going to use my proper title. Can't you people remember your own procedures? I mean, come on."

He stiffened, lips drawing into a scowl. I wasn't making any friends with my attitude. But I never do, where the Queen's men are concerned, and all I needed was enough time for Danny and Quentin to get away from whoever might have followed them. Once they were safe, I could get arrested as much as I wanted to.

"*Sir* October Daye," he began, "you are under arrest—"

A vast flock of black-winged birds descended from the sky, talons clawing and wings beating wildly as they mobbed the Queen's guards. In a matter of seconds, inky feathers had obscured them from my view.

I wasn't up for running—my running had been used up somewhere between 18th Street and taking a header into the sidewalk—but I was fully equipped to limp laboriously away. The beauty of the hide-and-seek is that you don't have to go all that far. I stopped on the opposite corner, watching with some satisfaction as Jazz and her flock did their best to recreate *The Birds* with the Queen's guard. As for the guards, they held their positions for almost a minute, which is longer than I could have done. Then they turned and ran, with the ravens in hot pursuit.

One large raven stayed behind, fluttering down to land in the street. It picked its way through the fallen feathers, head bobbing. It cawed, an inquisitive sound. I smiled a little. The raven was Jazz, more than likely, and it—she—couldn't see me. The hide-and-seek was holding.

"Open roads," I whispered, too softly to be heard, before I pulled the flask out of my jacket and freed another firefly, setting this one on my neck, where it would be hidden by my hair. Once that was done and the flask was put away again, I turned and began limping back up the street toward Borderlands. The fading sound of wings and shouting told me I was moving away from the Queen's guards. That was good. I really didn't have a second encounter in me.

It took three times as long to walk the few blocks between me and Borderlands as it had when I was running and—oh, yeah—uninjured. Still, eventually, I found myself in front of the bookstore's closed screen door. I peered through the window. Danny and Quentin were already inside, looking profoundly uncomfortable as they pretended to browse the bookshelves. The dark-haired woman with the red kerchief was behind the counter, handing a book to a woman in a white peasant blouse. Her hair was an odd shade of silvery-red, like red gold. Neither of them seemed to realize there was anyone else in the store. The hide-and-seek was holding.

The redhead turned to leave. I stepped out of the way, letting her open the door for me. I might be hidden by Quentin's illusion, but that was no reason to push my luck by making the woman in the kerchief—Jude, that was her name—deal with a door that was opening on its own.

As the redhead stepped out of the store, I stepped in. Danny turned toward me. Quentin and Jude didn't. I blinked, impressed. The hide-and-seek was clearly better than I'd thought.

Interacting with someone will enable them to see you, illusions or not. I walked over and put a hand on Quentin's elbow, squeezing when he started to jump. "It's me," I said. "Breathe."

He exhaled. "Toby."

"Come on." I gestured for Danny to follow as I led Quentin toward the door leading to the basement. If Arden was here, and hiding, she would be in the makeshift apartment that she'd been sharing with her brother. It was the safest place for her.

Jude didn't look up as we opened the door and started down, shrouded by the hide-and-seek spell. Once the door was closed behind us, I murmured, "Let it go," to Quentin.

He released the spell with a sigh of relief. "Ow," he said. There was a pause, presumably while he got a good look at me. I couldn't see his face in the dark, but I knew the hole that assessing someone's injuries could make in a conversation. "Toby? What *happened*?"

"I think I need a Band-Aid, an icepack, and some new knees," I said. "Danny, get the lights?"

"Sure thing," Danny rumbled.

The light clicked on, flooding the basement with light—and revealing the man from the café next door, the one who had served us our coffee. He was wearing another black T-shirt, this one with the Borderlands logo, and holding a crossbow, which was aimed squarely at my chest.

"Hi," he said, with another tooth-baring smile. "I wondered when you'd get here."

Crap.

TWENTY

THE STAIRWAY WAS NARROW ENOUGH that there was no way Danny could put himself between me and the arrow without both of us plummeting to the basement floor below. That might have been all right a week ago, but as things stood, either he'd land on me—bad—or I'd land on him—almost as bad, since Bridge Trolls aren't exactly a soft surface. I raised my hands, trying to show that I wasn't a threat.

"Hi," I said. "I'm—"

"I know who you are." He snorted. "You take your coffee black, and you have no respect for the beans. You shouldn't gulp it like that. It's *wasteful.*" His eyes narrowed. "I don't know them, though. Troll and Daoine? And you. You didn't smell right before, and you smell even less right now. You smell like blood and mistakes. What *are* you?"

I raised a hand to touch the firefly hidden in my hair, trying to force my eyes to focus. A glimmer appeared around him, marking the boundaries of a human disguise. "What are *you*?" I countered. "I don't know you."

"I'm Madden," he said. "I sold you coffee. Remember?"

He sounded so offended by the idea that I'd forgotten him that it was all I could do not to laugh, despite the absurdity of the situation. "That's not what I meant," I said. "I meant . . . my name is October Daye. I'm a changeling. These are my friends, Danny and Quentin."

"Hey," said Danny.

"Hello," said Quentin.

"You smelled stronger before," said Madden.

"It's been a strange week," I said. "Now please . . . what are you? How could you tell . . . ?"

"Oh!" Madden snorted again before aiming his crossbow at the ceiling. He waggled the fingers on his free hand, and the illusion around him burst like a soap bubble.

The change to his features was subtle. His nose seemed to broaden across the arch and square at the bottom; his eyes grew rounder and took on a golden cast, more wolfish than the honey-gold of the Torquills. The more dramatic change was in his hair, which went from gold to platinum blonde, streaked randomly with blood red. I blinked, and then relaxed.

"Cu Sidhe," I said. "That's why you didn't say anything before. You didn't want to get into a fight with my companion." Cu Sidhe—the faerie dogs—have been fighting with the Cait Sidhe since the beginning of Faerie. Anyone who's ever lived with a cat and a dog at the same time knows that most of the clichés about "fighting like cats and dogs" don't really apply. The same can't be said for the Cu Sidhe and the Cait Sidhe. They've never gotten along. Faerie didn't make them that way.

Madden shrugged sheepishly. "I'm not supposed to fight while I'm at work. Alan looks all disappointed and talks about needing to let me go if I can't mind my temper, and then Arden has to work on him until he changes his mind. She doesn't like doing that. I don't like it when she has to. So even when cats come in, I don't bark. It's not allowed."

"That . . . makes a surprising amount of sense, as long as I don't think about it too hard." I lowered my hands, waiting for him to jerk the crossbow back into position. He didn't move. "My friends and I are here—"

"I know why you're here," he said, frowning. There

was something uncomfortable about being frowned at by a Cu Sidhe. It was like I'd managed to disappoint the universe. "Arden doesn't want you."

"This is why I could never date a dog," I muttered. More loudly, I said, "I know she's upset, but is she here? We need to talk to her. It's important."

There were two steps between me and Danny. Just enough for a body to wedge itself between us. Something sharp was jammed against my back, right over the spot where I judged my kidneys would be located.

"What the fu—"

Danny's exclamation was cut off by Arden saying softly in my ear, "If he squeezes, I see how far into you I can jam this before I stop breathing. I bet it's pretty far. What do you think?"

"Danny, whatever part of her you have, let go of it," I said. I didn't try to turn. The situation was fairly self-apparent, considering the parties involved. I just hoped Arden wouldn't shove whatever she was holding into something I was going to need later before she gave me a chance to explain.

"The bitch has a knife," said Danny.

"Yeah, and the knife is at my kidneys, so *let* her *go*," I said. "It'll be okay."

"Will it?" snarled Arden. "Let's ask Nolan, shall we? Oh, wait. We *can't*."

"That's what I'm here about," I said. "Can we sit down and talk about this like civilized people, instead of standing here and talking about it like people who use knives to get what they want? Please?"

"Hi, Arden," said Madden happily. "I found the people you said might be coming. Well. I found the person." His smile died, short-lived, replaced by confusion. "Two of them aren't who you asked for. Is that okay? Did I do okay?"

"You did great," said Arden, with a note of affectionate praise that couldn't have been faked, even if it was a little forced. I guess "good dog" didn't come naturally in a situation like this one.

"Yay." Madden seemed to remember that he was holding a crossbow; he swung it back down to aim at me.

"There's a knife at my back," I said flatly. "I don't think that's necessary right now."

"Better safe than sorry," said Madden.

"Where is my brother?" demanded Arden.

"That's why we're here," I said. "Please, can we just sit down? We just want to talk. I swear, we're not here to cause any trouble."

"Drop the disguise." Her voice was cold. "I want to see what kind of weapons you're hiding under there."

"Drop the . . . oh. Oh, right." The last time I'd seen Arden had been before the pie, and before I'd turned myself mostly human. "I know this is going to be hard to believe, but I'm not wearing a disguise right now, Arden. This is just me." I gestured toward Madden, and promptly regretted it, as she dug the point of her knife a little deeper. "I'm serious. Ask him what I smell like."

"Madden?" she asked, suspiciously.

"She's human," said Madden. He paused before adding, "Well, mostly, sort of. She smells like people, and like something I don't know, and like blood, and like goblin fruit."

"What?" Arden pushed me away from her, sending me stumbling down the stairs toward Madden. That wasn't a good move on her part. I'd barely gone two steps when she made an outraged squeaking noise. I turned to see Danny's hand wrapped around her head, all but obscuring her face. More importantly, it was blocking her eyes. A Tuatha de Dannan who can't see is a Tuatha who can't teleport. Arden clawed at his hands, still squeaking.

I sighed. "Danny, let her go."

"What?" He frowned over the top of her head. "She can't go anywhere when I got hold of her like this."

"Okay. One, he," I jerked my thumb over my shoulder, indicating Madden, "still has the crossbow. So she's not the only threat here. Two, I'm still technically in charge. So could we please stop arguing *about crushing the Princess' head*, and let her go already?"

Danny blanched. "Oh, hell, I forgot that part," he said, and let Arden go. She stumbled forward before sitting down heavily on the steps and glaring up at Danny. He grimaced. "Sorry, Your Highness."

"I hate you people," she said, climbing back to her feet. She transferred the glare to me. "What are you doing here? Where's my brother? What *happened* to you?"

"We are here because we still need your help, and now, so does Nolan," I said. "The Queen of the Mists has him."

"Bitch took him while she was arresting the Duchess," snarled Arden. She bounded down the stairs to stand in front of me, so close that we were practically nose-to-nose. "Where. Is. He? Tell me. I will get him back, and then you will never see us again."

"This is still your Kingdom."

"And a fat lot of good that's done me!" Arden snarled. "This Kingdom killed my father! My brother's been asleep for so long that I have no idea how I'm going to get him to adjust to this world when he wakes up! This Kingdom has *ruined* my life, and now you're here, stinking of goblin fruit and saying I have a responsibility to it? Screw *that*. Tell me where to find Nolan. We're *leaving*."

"You asked what happened to me," I said. "Let me tell you what happened to me. The Queen? That same Queen who had your brother elf-shot, and who has him now? She sent a man to hit me with a goblin fruit pie."

"I like pie," said Madden.

"What does pie have to do with anything?" Arden glowered at me, looking frustrated. Honestly, I understood how she felt. There just wasn't anything I could do about it.

"When we first met, did you assume that I was Daoine Sidhe?" Arden didn't answer, but then, she didn't need to. Her expression was answer enough. "My mother, Amandine, she's—"

"Wait: *Amandine*?" Arden's expression shifted from confusion to outright disbelief. "You can't be Amandine's kid. You're part human. Juniper and thorn, you're *mostly* human. She'd never bed a human man. Her husband would never stand for it."

Now it was my turn to look confused. "What are you talking about? Mom's not married. She was married to my father, but he's dead now. And before he died, he was human."

A strange look crossed her face. Then she shook her head, and said, "I don't care. I don't care who your mother is, or why that makes pie your weakness. I want my brother back."

"Amandine isn't Daoine Sidhe, and neither am I. It's hard to explain, but when the Queen sent that man . . . I think she was trying to get me hooked so she could destroy my credibility. Maybe that would have worked, except I'm *not* Daoine Sidhe. I didn't just get hooked. I changed the balance of my own blood so that the goblin fruit would be even stronger. I turned myself mostly human."

"So turn yourself back," she said.

"I can't. I need a hope chest."

Arden raised her eyebrows. "My brother is missing and you came to ask if I have something that doesn't exist? Are you *high*? Oh, wait, goblin fruit—of course you're high. There are no hope chests, October. They're a fairy tale."

"Says the lost Princess of the Mists," I snapped. "They're real. Evening had one. I found it after she died."

"So? Then you don't have a problem. Get the hope chest, do whatever it is you do with hope chests, and leave me out of it. I just want to get my brother and get out of here."

"I gave it to the Queen."

Arden barked a short, startled laugh. "Oh, is that what this is all about? You still think I'm going to help you overthrow her? Dream on. I am *done* with insurrections. Find yourselves another Princess."

"That doesn't sound very royal," I said.

"What do any of you know about being royal?" she

shot back. "It's all betrayals and backstabbing and never trusting anyone."

"I know a lot about being royal," said Quentin.

It was a calm statement, made with absolute sincerity. We turned toward him. Quentin stepped around Danny, moving with careful grace, his shoulders locked in a line so precise it could have been drawn with a ruler. His chin was up, and his eyes were fixed on Arden.

She blinked before shaking her head. "Watching them doesn't make you an expert. It makes you a voyeur. You don't know *anything*, kid."

"I know more about it than you do," he said, as he reached the bottom of the steps. He shot me an apologetic glance before turning to face her again.

In that instant, I knew. That look . . . it answered all the questions he'd never been willing to, and put so many statements into a new context. I stared at him, slack-jawed, the urge to shake him and the urge to slap him warring for dominance in my mind.

Neither of them won out. Instead, I stayed where I was, and listened as he said, "My name is Quentin Sollys. I am the Crown Prince of the High Kingdom of the Westlands. And I think I know a thing or two about being royal, no matter what you say."

"I'm going to kill him," I muttered.

Arden just stared. "What?"

"My father is King Aethlin Sollys of the Westlands," said Quentin. "I've been in blind fosterage for the last six years. It seemed like the best way for me to grow up without being treated like a Prince everywhere I went." He glanced at me sidelong, and while there was still apology in his eyes, it was underscored now by amusement. "I can definitely say that I've *not* been receiving the royal treatment for the last several years."

"You people are *insane*." Arden shook her head, apparently shaking off her shock at the same time. "She's not Daoine Sidhe, and a pie turned her human, so she wants me to go through with an *act of treason* so she can get her hands on a fairy tale, and now you're telling me it's okay, because you're secretly the Crown Prince of the Kingdom that *my* Kingdom answers to." She turned, leveling a finger at Danny. "Are you going to tell me that you're really Oberon in disguise? Is that the next piece of the lunatic pie?"

"Nah, not me," said Danny. "I'm just the taxi driver. Also, it ain't treason if you're the rightful heir. Insurrection, maybe. But that's a technicality."

"This is all your fault." Arden swung back around to face me. "None of this would have happened if you hadn't tracked me down. I don't care how much you thought you needed me. You had no right."

"You said 'my Kingdom,'" I said.

"What?"

"Just now. You said Quentin's parents were in charge of the Kingdom your Kingdom answered to." I shrugged a little. "You know this is your fight, Arden, and you know you don't have any other choice. You can hate me if you want—I'm sort of used to the Queen hating me— but you also know that I'm here because it's time for you to step up and do your job."

"We do not have the luxury of choosing our duty," said Quentin, in a tone I'd never heard from him before. In that moment, he sounded like a Prince. "Faerie calls. It is your burden, and your blessing, to answer."

"And while you're doing that, I can go upstairs and save Jude from the people who want to know where you are," said Madden, with blissful unconcern.

We all turned to look at him. "What?" I said, after a few seconds of bemused silence.

Madden shrugged. "There are people upstairs talking to Jude. They're being pretty nasty, since she won't tell them where you are. I don't think she knows."

Shit. "The Queen's guards must have followed us here. But how . . . ?"

"Your shoes." Madden again. Again, we all turned to stare at him.

"What about her shoes, Madden?" asked Arden.

"They're all spelled up. They smell like secrets." Madden pointed at my feet, in case we didn't know where shoes were typically kept. "I think they followed your shoes."

"My . . . oh, Oberon's eyes." I bent, hastily untying my laces before yanking the sneakers off my feet. "I'm an idiot. I'm an idiot and a fool and every other word you can come up with for stupid. Here." I thrust my shoes toward Arden as I straightened—my shoes, which I held by the blood-red laces the Queen had tied them with when she transformed my dress, back at the beginning of this whole mess. I'd been so relieved not to have another pair of sneakers transmuted into high heels that I hadn't stopped to wonder why she'd been merciful. I'd just kept on wearing them.

Arden frowned. "What do you want me to do with these?"

"Teleport as far away from here as you can and dump them," I said. "Aim for Petaluma. If the Queen's guards are using the shoes to track us, they'll go after you."

"This is idiotic," said Arden . . . but she took the shoes. "Madden, don't let them leave."

"Okay," said Madden.

Arden turned, her hand sketching an archway in the air. If I squinted, I could almost see the shimmer on the other side—and then she stepped through it and was gone. Almost in the same second there was a clicking sound from above us as someone started to turn the doorknob.

"Shit," I hissed, and grabbed Quentin's arm. "Madden, Danny, come on!" I didn't look to see whether they were following as I took off across the basement, heading for the painted canvas "wall" separating Arden's makeshift apartment from the rest of the room. If we could just make it through before anyone came down the stairs, we'd be hidden; we might be able to evade the guards, and Jude wouldn't get hurt. She didn't *deserve* to get hurt.

But when Faerie and the human worlds collide, someone always gets hurt. That's just the way things are. I was a fool to think that it could ever be any different.

I touched the firefly hidden in my hair as I ran, trying to force myself to see the gap in the illusion. *Come on, come on . . .* I thought—and there it was, a narrow crack in what should have been empty air. I reached out and pulled it open wide enough for me to fit through, hauling Quentin in my wake. Danny was close behind us. Once he was through, he grasped the two pieces of canvas and pulled them shut, holding the seam tight with his massive fingers.

"Where's Madden?" I whispered.

"He didn't move," Danny whispered back.

The sound of footsteps on the stairs cut off any further questions. "—there's anyone down here," said Jude dubiously. "Ardith didn't come in today, and Madden is on his break."

A dog barked joyful greeting.

"What is *that*?" demanded an unfamiliar male voice.

"That's Madden's dog, Buddy," said Jude. "We let him stay down here sometimes, when Madden's working short shifts. Hi, Buddy. Who's a good boy, hmm? Who is it?"

Madden barked again, apparently asserting that he was, in fact, a good boy. Claws clacked against the basement floor. I've known enough canines in my time that it wasn't hard to picture him jumping up on the Queen's guards, tongue lolling, tail wagging madly.

Cu Sidhe are interesting. Like Cait Sidhe, sometimes they look a lot like Daoine Sidhe with animal characteristics, although they always have that red and white candy cane hair. Unlike Cait Sidhe, they have two distinct dog forms. One, the form most of them are born in, is a tall sighthound with white fur over most of its body, and red at the ears, tail, and paws. The other is, well, a different kind of dog. It varies from Cu Sidhe to Cu Sidhe, but when they're in their second dog forms, there's nothing fae about them. They look like any other mutt enjoying the wonders of the dog park.

Jude seemed to think Madden was a perfectly normal dog. That meant he had to be in his second form—and that we might have a chance at getting out of this unseen.

It all depended on how good the Coblynau illusion hiding Arden's "apartment" really was, and whether getting rid of my shoes would actually make the guards stop following us.

Carefully, I stepped back from the curtain, my bare feet making no sound on the threadbare rug as I moved to sit on the bottom bunk of Arden's bed. Danny remained where he was, frozen in the act of pinching the curtain closed. After a few seconds, Quentin followed me, taking a seat to my right. I put an arm on his shoulder, not looking at him, and listened to the sound of Madden barking and jumping on the guards, whose muttered exclamations were becoming increasingly frustrated—and increasingly close.

"I told you, there's no one down here." Jude again. "I'm not sure why it was so important that you look for your friends in my basement, but I'm going to need to ask you to leave now."

"They're here." This voice, I recognized: the Satyr who tried to arrest me earlier. Apparently, the Ravens hadn't pecked his eyes out after all. Darn.

"They're *not*," said a second female voice. She just sounded tired. "I don't know how, but the bitch figured out she was being followed. This was all just misdirection. We need to get back to the hunt."

The voices were coming from right outside the curtain. No matter how good the illusion was, all it would take was one of them making an over-enthusiastic gesture, and the jig would be up. I closed my eyes and tightened my arm around Quentin's shoulders. Seconds crawled by.

"Fine," snarled the Satyr.

I opened my eyes, startled, and listened to the sound of receding footsteps. Madden barked again, punctuating the sound of those same footsteps climbing the stairs. Finally, the basement door opened and closed again, and the only sound was Madden's barking.

Quentin started to stand. I pulled him back down to the bed. He turned and blinked at me. I shook my head.

If Madden was still barking, we didn't have the all-clear. We'd come too far to blow things by deciding to be impatient *now*.

More seconds crawled past, until finally, one more set of footsteps started in the basement outside. Madden was still barking, so they weren't his. That last pair of feet climbed the stairs, and the door opened and closed one more time.

We waited.

"Okay," said Madden, sounding pleased with himself. "Okay, okay. The bad people are gone now. Everything is wonderful, and I get to have a ginger cookie once Arden gets back. Protect the basement, get a ginger cookie."

Danny rolled his eyes as he turned to look at me. "This guy for real?" he muttered.

"Cu Sidhe," I said, like that explained everything. In a way, it did. They're not stupid—in fact, some great fae scholars have been Cu Sidhe—but they prefer simplicity and joy to complexity and angst. It's a nice change from the rest of Faerie. I stood, releasing my hold on Quentin, and walked to the curtain. "You can let go now, Danny."

He released the seam. I spread the canvas "wall" and walked through, back out into the basement, where a smug-looking Madden was waiting for us.

"They left," he said. "You did a good hide. It was real quiet. I barely heard you at all."

That was high praise coming from a Cu Sidhe who'd been in animal form while we were trying to stay silent. I smiled at him, fighting back the urge to ruffle his ears. "You were an excellent diversion and protector," I said. "You did real good."

He beamed at the word "good." I guess the urge to be considered a good dog is genetic. "Arden didn't want you taken."

"No, she wants to yell at us herself." Speaking of yelling at people ... I turned to Quentin. "Were you serious before?"

He grimaced, looking down at the floor. "I didn't want you to find out like this."

"Quentin."

"You knew I was a blind foster." He glanced back up at me. "I mean, didn't you ever wonder if maybe I was . . . ?"

"*No*! No, I did not! You know why?" I didn't wait for an answer. "Because your parents approved of you being my squire, and there is *no way* the High King would approve of his son and heir being trained by a *changeling*."

"I told him what you said."

That stopped me. "I . . . what?"

"The first time we met—really met, I mean, since you never let me deliver the Duke's messages—you told me his rank gave him the right to command you, and you'd do what he said because he held your fealty. But that was all. You said he wasn't better than you. That he got your attention and your courtesy because you respected him. And that changelings weren't a lesser element to be kept under control." Quentin bit his lip. "I'd never heard that before. Everyone back home said changelings were inferior, and I'd sort of started to believe them."

"Even your parents?" The question was out before I could stop it.

To my relief, Quentin shook his head. "No. But they didn't have time to manage the bulk of my education. That's why *Maman*," he said it the French way, two quick syllables that almost melted together like sealing wax, "said I had to be sent away. I had to learn to be tolerant if I was ever going to be a good . . . a good . . ." He hesitated, seemingly unwilling to finish.

So I finished for him. "A good King. They fostered you to Sylvester and let you be squired to me because having the crap kicked out of you on a daily basis was going to teach you how to be a good King."

Quentin nodded.

I pinched the bridge of my nose. "You're serious. You're actually serious, and this isn't a really poorly timed practical joke. You are the Crown Prince of the Westlands."

"Yup."

"The Crown Prince of the Westlands has seen me wandering around the house in athletic shorts and a tank top on laundry day."

"Yup."

"I've been making the Crown Prince of the Westlands do dishes."

"Yup."

"Are you gonna run through every chore you've ever involved the kid in?" asked Danny. "Because we'll be here all night, and I don't think we've got time for that."

"I'm running through chores in a vain effort to stop myself from running through all the times I've endangered his life," I said. "That's a longer list."

"Bloodier, too," said Quentin. He sounded almost cheerful about it. I shot him a glare. He grinned. There was an element of relief in his expression, like he was glad to finally have everything out in the open. "Don't worry. Like I said, my parents approve of you."

"That worries me even more," I muttered.

"What does?" Arden demanded.

I turned.

She was standing by the base of the stairs, with foxtail briars snagged on the legs of her pants and a distinctly windblown look to her hair. She folded her arms, glared, and said, "Your shoes are now safely hidden on Alcatraz. In the middle of a field. In a hole. Is that good enough, or do you need me to put them somewhere else? After all, it's not like there's anything *urgent* I need to be taking care of."

"We're going to get your brother back," I said. It seemed like the only thing I *could* say. Arden kept glaring. I pushed on. "Right now, the Queen having your brother is a good thing."

Her mismatched eyes widened. *"What?"*

"Hear me out." I raised my hands to ward her off. "She's not going to hurt him. He's bait. She wants you to rush in there half-cocked, so she can arrest you on some bullshit charge. She arrested Dianda for sedition. There's no reason for that, unless she's planning to try and present you as a figurehead. The way I see it, if the Queen gets close enough to offer you a deal, she will: your brother for you publicly renouncing your father. Say you're not a Windermere. Let her keep the throne, and ensure you have no valid claim to it in the future."

"Fine," Arden snapped. "If it gets my brother back, fine."

"And if it gets Dianda convicted?"

"She's a big girl. She can stand on her own two fins."

"You have watched way too many Disney movies." I stepped closer. "If you renounce your claim to the throne, Dianda stays in the Queen's dungeon for however long it takes to set up a trial with the Undersea. I've been in that dungeon. The amount of iron in there will break her long before she sees the open sea again. Her family will never get her back. You want to do all this to save your brother. Think about what that does to Dean's mom."

Arden's glare didn't waver. "She made her choice."

"I know. But what you don't seem to understand is that *you're* not making *your* choice. You're making the choice the Queen is trying to force you into, and that isn't going to be the right choice for you *or* your brother. Where are you going to go, Arden? With Dianda in custody, you can't take Nolan and run to the Undersea. Silences is a puppet government. Angels has its own problems. You could head inland I guess, to Frozen Salt or Skytower, but you'd never be able to stop running. Your parents were assassinated. Do you honestly think the Queen of the Mists is above making sure Nolan doesn't wake up and start this all over again?"

"This is your fault," said Arden quietly.

"Maybe. Or maybe it was always going to happen. The Luidaeg sent me to find you. Someone would have done it eventually, if not me." My stomach was starting to ache again. I had to fight to keep from reaching for the baggie of blood gems. "As long as she has Nolan but not you, he's safe. This is the moment where you step up. This is when you fix things."

She kept glaring for a few more seconds. Then she seemed to wilt before my eyes, her shoulders slumping, her chest collapsing as she stopped holding herself rigidly upright. "I was supposed to protect him," she said.

"This is *how* you protect him," I said. "You protect your family by making the world a better place for them to live. Not by running away."

"I don't know what to do," said Arden. Madden whined and put his hand on her shoulder. She sighed, resting her cheek against it.

And I smiled.

"That's okay, because I do," I said. "Danny, can you drive Quentin back to the house?"

"Not if it means leavin' you here," he said.

"You won't be," I said. "I just don't want Arden going out in public yet. She and I will meet you there."

Arden blinked. "We will?"

"We will," I said. "I have a plan." It was a terrible plan. It was still a plan.

After a moment, Arden nodded. "All right," she said. "What do we do?"

TWENTY-ONE

THE PASSAGE THROUGH ARDEN'S PORTAL was surprisingly easy, especially when compared to my recent trips through the Shadow Roads. One second, we were in the basement at Borderlands, and the next, we were standing amidst the riotous explosion of carefully overgrown flowers that was my backyard.

Arden frowned at the house. "I recognize this neighborhood."

"We're pretty close to the bookstore; you should feel right at home. Dolores Park is right over there." I started up the path to the back door, grimacing as I walked. It seemed like I was stepping on every possible pebble and twig the yard had to offer, and my bare feet didn't appreciate the experience. "I should warn you, I have roommates, and they're a little . . . well, unique."

"I live in a basement with my comatose brother, and one of my best friends thinks a good afternoon is spent chasing Frisbees around the dog park," said Arden. "How unique can they be?"

"Just keep thinking that, okay?" I said, and unlocked the door, stepping into the kitchen. "May! Jazz! I'm home, and I brought company!"

"Toby!" May came hurtling into the kitchen, still holding the remote control in one hand. She ignored both Arden and the open door as she flung her arms around me, pulling me into a hug that was tighter than my lungs approved of. "You're okay! Jazz said she didn't see you when the flock mobbed the intersection, I was *so worried*, don't *do* that to ... me ..." Her voice trailed off as she finally noticed Arden. "You meant actual company."

"I did," I said, and disentangled myself from May's arms. "May, this is Arden. Arden, this is my housemate, May."

"You must be Toby's sister," said Arden, shutting the front door.

"I'm her Fetch, actually," said May, staring at Arden. "I ... forgive me. You look a lot like someone I used to know."

"Fetch?" said Arden, looking horrified.

"It's a long story, and she's not a death omen anymore," I said. "May's retired." May also had the memories of every face she'd ever worn back when she was a night-haunt. The odds that she'd eaten someone who knew King Gilad were more than reasonably high, given how many fae died in the 1906 earthquake. I elbowed her before she could say anything. "Is Jazz here? I wanted to let her know how much I appreciated the assist."

"Um, yeah, she's here, but she had to go back to bed," said May, shaking off whatever memory she'd been trying not to share. "Diurnal, remember?"

"I remember." I started toward the dining room, gesturing for Arden to follow. "We're just here to pick up supplies—and you—and then we have to get moving. The Queen has Arden's brother. We need to get him back."

"Oh," said May, blinking. "Well. That's not good. I'm happy to be picked up, I guess. There's nothing on TV right now anyway. Where are your shoes?"

"Alcatraz."

May looked at me blankly.

"Arden took them there when we realized the Queen

was using them to track me. Remember how she didn't turn my sneakers into high heels? She turned them into tracking devices instead. Remind me never to assume that she's doing anything without an ulterior motive." I paused at the base of the stairs. "Arden, there's stuff for sandwiches in the fridge, if you want one. May, Danny and Quentin are behind me."

"Make sandwiches, got it," she said. Hooking her arm through Arden's, she said, "You can help," and hauled the startled-looking Princess back into the kitchen. I shook my head fondly. Then I turned and walked up the stairs to my room. I needed shoes, and jeans that didn't have gaping holes where the knees used to be.

More than that, I needed weapons.

I used to carry two knives everywhere I went. I still carried the silver one, but I'd been forced to put the iron knife away after Mom shifted the balance of my blood to turn me more fae than human. Well, I was almost human now. That had to come with a few advantages.

The bedroom door was closed. I opened it, reaching inside and fumbling for the light switch. I never found it. Instead, hands grabbed my wrists and hauled me forward, into the darkness. I had time to squeak before a mouth was clamped over mine, and I was being kissed with ruthless firmness. The hands released my wrists, going to my waist, pulling me closer. I didn't fight; my brief panic had passed as quickly as it had come. I couldn't taste his magic—my senses were wrapped in cotton by the change in my blood—but a man can't kiss you as many times as Tybalt had kissed me without becoming familiar.

I slid my hands up his arms to his shoulders, and then into his hair, allowing myself a few precious seconds of melting into his arms. Tybalt pulled back first, his eyes glittering green in the light that bled through from the hall. "Welcome home," he said, voice rough.

"Hi," I said, barely above a whisper. I pulled my hands out of his hair, resting them on his shoulders. He didn't let go of my waist. "Have you been here long?"

"I arrived seconds before you did," he said. "I was going to ask May to phone you when I heard your voice from downstairs." He kissed me again, more softly. Then he stopped, nostrils flaring. "I smell blood. Are you hurt?"

"It's nothing major. I fell down while I was running away from the Queen's guards on Valencia," I said. "I need new jeans and some Neosporin, and then I'll be as good as new. Did you find Mom?"

"Don't evade. Are you aware that 'when I was running away from the Queen's guards' is not a reassuring statement?"

"Who's evading?" I held up my skinned palms, showing him the damage. "I used to hurt myself worse than this falling off the playground swings. I'm fine. But if we want this sort of thing to not be a problem, we need to get me back to normal, and that means finding Mom. Did you have any luck?"

"Her tower gates were closed." He sounded defeated. His shoulders slumped. "I circled, but there was no entry to be found. I called for every cat in the Summerlands who would answer me, and some who would not. None of them had seen her. Your mother has vanished, October, and I know not to where."

"Then we stick with Plan A. We get Arden on the throne, we get access to the treasury, and we hope chest the extra human right out of me." I pulled away from him, turning to flip the light switch.

Tybalt caught my wrist. I turned to blink at him.

"What?"

"Would you return yourself to your former state if it weren't for the goblin fruit?" he asked. "I remember a time when this was what you wanted."

"Would you leave me if I still wanted that? If I still wanted to be human?"

Tybalt laughed a little, shaking his head. "No. But you would eventually ask me to. I am . . . not sure . . . I could stop myself from wanting to protect you. I want to protect you anyway, but normally you can do that on your own. Now . . ."

"I wanted to be human once," I admitted. "I wanted to sleep at night, and age like the people I saw on the street, and not have to worry about being carried off by a Kelpie just because it was hungry and I was in the wrong place to stay out of its way. I mean, the Kelpies would have still been there, I just wouldn't have known, but . . . that's not the point. People change. *I* changed. I have a life in Faerie. I'm not giving it up for anything, and definitely not because of something as stupid as getting hit with a pie." My stomach clenched again. I winced. "Okay. You need to let go of me now."

"October? What's wrong?"

"Seriously, let me go." Tybalt released my arm. I dug the baggie of blood gems Walther had made out of my pocket and popped two of them into my mouth. It barely took the edge off. I didn't care. That was going to have to be enough, because I would need to be in way worse straits before I took another piece of the Luidaeg's blood.

"Toby?"

I raised a finger, closing my eyes as I waited for the snarling in my stomach to subside. Tybalt was watching me with open anxiety when I opened them again. I sighed. "Better, for now. We need to move. Are you sticking with us?"

"Unless you have another fool's errand for me to undertake," he said.

"The only fool's errand I have left is deposing a Queen, installing a Princess in her place, and fixing my," I waved a hand to indicate my too-human body, "little problem." I started for the dresser where I kept my iron knife, safely muffled in a bundle of yarrow branches and silk.

"Have you considered that curing your addiction may result in humanity no longer being an option for you?"

The question was mild. I stiffened but didn't turn as I opened the drawer and started moving sweaters aside. "I did."

"And?"

"And I'd rather not give up my humanity—not yet— but if that's what has to happen, then that's what I'll do."

I untied the cord that held the silk in place and began unrolling the bundle across the top of the dresser. "If I come away from this completely fae, then so be it."

"Ah." Tybalt packed an amazing amount of relief into that single syllable.

The last of the silk came away, revealing my iron knife in all its menacing simplicity. There was nothing splendid about it: it wasn't ornate or decorative. It was just a piece of metal, designed for killing the fae. And it was very, very good at its job.

"What, you thought you'd get rid of me that easily?" I slid the iron blade into place in the holster around my waist, relaxing a little. Using iron against the fae isn't something to be done lightly. Iron dulls magic and causes iron poisoning, which can be fatal. It's the sort of thing you only do when you have to. But if the Queen's guard came for me again, they wouldn't find me quite so helpless. "Sweetheart, you're stuck with me until you decide not to be."

"At this point, if your foul attitude and utter lack of manners were going to drive me away, they would have done so already."

"There, you see? Nothing to worry about." I stripped off my ripped, bloody jeans and pulled a clean pair out of the dresser, stepping into them without bothering to bandage my knees. They weren't bleeding anymore, and at this point, a little pain could only focus me. I was either going to get back to normal or die before infection could set in.

"October, if there is one thing I have learned over the course of my association with you, it is that there is always the potential for something else to worry about."

"Flattery will get you everywhere." My jeans were looser than they would have been even a day ago. My poor metabolism had to be working double-time as it tried to keep me going on a diet of adrenaline, blood, and misery. "Throw me my shoes. We've got a Queen to overthrow, and that means we need to get this show on the road."

Tybalt smiled as he bent and grabbed a pair of sneakers from the floor beside the bed. He lobbed them to me one at a time, and smiled more as I caught them. Catching the shoes stung my scraped palms, but I didn't allow myself to show it. The last thing I wanted was to worry him more after I had just sent him away.

Voices drifted through the open door. I looked back over my shoulder as I pulled my sneakers on and quickly laced them. "Sounds like Quentin and Danny are here."

"Ah, yes," he said dryly. "The cavalry."

"Stand behind the man made of stone, don't get shot, remember?" I stepped in and gave him one more kiss before grabbing the first aid kit off the dresser. "Come on. Let's go."

"As you like," he said, and followed me out of the room and down the stairs, to where the dining room was increasingly coming to resemble a surrealist dinner party. Danny was standing in the doorway, where he was less likely to accidentally break anything. May was setting out a platter of sandwiches; Quentin already had one in either hand and was eating like he was afraid he'd never be fed again. Which was a reasonable concern, given the way things had been going for the past few days.

"Everybody grab what you're going to want, and grab it to go," I said, stepping into the room. "Tybalt, that means you, too. You need to eat something."

"Hey, Tybalt," said Quentin, waving a sandwich.

"Hello, all," said Tybalt. He took a sandwich before offering Arden a shallow bow. "Milady."

Arden frowned. "Hello, King of Cats. Have you come to join this fool's parade, or are you just here to make snide comments before disappearing again?"

"Ah," said Tybalt. "I have so missed people making assumptions about my intentions since my fair October learned I was an ally. We shall have to keep you. You'll provide some much-needed unpleasantness."

"At least that's one thing I can be sure will never change," said Arden. "No matter how much time I spend in or out of Faerie, Cait Sidhe will always be annoying."

She turned to me. "You said you had a plan. What is it? Or was it just 'feed me sandwiches.'" Her frown faltered. "I admit, I don't really see what sort of benefit you'd be getting from the sandwiches, but . . ."

"The sandwiches are a side benefit," I said. "You should eat, if you haven't already. But the plan . . . your father's knowe was in Muir Woods, wasn't it?"

Arden blinked. "How did you know that? The knowe was sealed after his death."

"I've been there, or at least, I've been to the part that's still accessible. It's a shallowing now."

"It's sleeping," she said. "Father said it would wait for us forever."

"And there you go," I said. "We take you to Muir Woods. You reopen the knowe—you reopen *King Gilad's* knowe, lost to us for over a hundred years—and you send out letters to announce that you are the rightful Queen of the Mists." Pixies make a surprisingly good messenger service when bribed, and Muir Woods was swarming with them.

Everyone stared at me like I had lost my mind. Everyone but Quentin, who just nodded, looking thoughtful.

"*In* the Mists," said Arden, without varying her expression at all.

I smirked.

"Are you insane?" asked May.

"She's insane," said Danny.

"The Queen will have to attack immediately or risk granting legitimacy to the challenge," said Quentin. "She won't even have to wait three days. That kind of treason warrants immediate response, if there's any chance that people will take it seriously."

I nodded. "Exactly. And reopening the lost knowe of King Gilad is the sort of thing people are going to take pretty damn seriously."

"What good does it do me to get myself killed?" asked Arden. "I don't have an army!"

"You have the Undersea. You'll have as many men as Sylvester can provide."

"How is this helping me get my brother back?"

"I've been in the Queen's dungeons before." I looked to Tybalt. "Iron isn't really a problem for me right now. So a little jailbreak shouldn't be that big a deal."

He blinked as the full scope of what I was asking hit him. "You want to break into the Queen's knowe. October. Have you lost your mind?"

"You know it's a good plan when it gets *everyone* to ask if I'm crazy," I said amiably. "No, I have not lost my mind. The Queen will have to answer Arden's challenge with as much force as she can muster, and she's not going to be expecting anyone to be dishonorable enough to make a sneak attack."

"There's *nothing* dishonorable about taking back someone who shouldn't have been taken in the first place," snapped Arden.

"That's my opinion, too."

"Uh, not to sound dense here, but how does this fix anythin'?" asked Danny. "Sure, you get the missing dude back, but Arden here is still under attack by Queen Crazy-cakes and her big-ass army, and we're all gettin' banished or killed. I'm not really seeing this as a win."

"We don't have to win. We just have to hold off her forces long enough to contact a higher authority. Getting Nolan out of her knowe is mostly to make sure she won't do anything vindictive and stupid when she realizes that the tide has turned against her." I looked toward Quentin. He met my eyes levelly. "She's held this throne because she was unchallenged, and because no one higher up than she was ever had the excuse to say, 'No, that is not yours.'"

"Arden's claim is good, and supported by the Library," said Quentin. "I'm sure King Sollys will hear your petition."

"Swell. Do you think you could relay that to him, then, preferably before the Queen of the Mists decides to kill us all?"

Quentin smiled crookedly, while May and Tybalt looked at me in bewilderment. "I can do that."

"Good. Because you're going to be staying here."

His eyes widened. "What?"

"You heard me. Someone needs to stay here and make sure the Queen doesn't send people to attack the house. Jazz is asleep. I'd rather she not be ambushed. And we're going to need May to put on some of my clothes, cast an illusion to turn her hair brown, and go with Arden. We need them visibly standing together, both to draw fire—"

"Gee, thanks," said May.

"—and because people will assume that May is me." I looked around the little group. "This is a risky plan. It's complicated and it's convoluted and it's entirely outside of my primary skill set. And it's the only one I have that stands a chance of working. If any of you have something better, now would be the time to bring it up."

No one said anything.

I nodded. "Okay. If any of you doesn't want to be a part of this, now would be the time to leave."

"Pass," said May.

"No way," said Danny.

"I'd love to, but I'm the only one that offer doesn't apply to," said Arden.

Tybalt didn't say anything. He didn't need to.

"I want to make a change," said Quentin.

I raised an eyebrow. "What's that?"

"Instead of staying here—and I mean, I get why you want me to stay here; somebody has to stay with Jazz, and you probably want me to be as far away from actually breaking the law as possible right now—why don't Jazz and I go to the Library of Stars and hole up there? I can call Raj. He can take us, and we won't ever have to go outside." Quentin shrugged. "It won't stop the Queen if she decides she wants to burn the house down, but we couldn't stop her if we were here. I'm not Elliot. I can't create big waves just because I want them."

"And the Library is neutral ground," I said thoughtfully. "Even if the Queen wants to cause problems for you there, she can't. All Mags has to do is refuse to let her into the stacks. Okay. We'll go with that. And, uh, bring donuts or something to apologize to Mags for my exploiting my Library pass."

"Will do," said Quentin.

May looked relieved. "I guess I can take a few head-shots for the cause if Jazz will be safely out of the line of fire."

Arden looked confused. I glanced at her, explaining, "May is literally indestructible. As near as we can tell, she *can't* die now that she's no longer connected to me."

"Oh," said Arden.

It was time for the part that wasn't going to go over so well. I turned to Tybalt, and took a deep breath. "Tybalt . . ."

"Ah." His eyes narrowed. "This is where you once again ask me to leave you for someone else to defend, and trust that I will do it simply because you claim that it is necessary. Really, October. I thought this time, per-haps, your endless assurances that you weren't going to send me away might last a little longer."

"I'm not sending you away. I want us to end up in the same place, because I need you to go break Nolan out with me. I just need you to do something else, first." I tucked my hair back behind one ear, trying to ignore the snarling from my stomach. "I need you to go and ask the cats for help."

He blinked. "You what? October, the Court of Cats cannot fight—"

"No, they can't. This is a matter of succession for the Divided Courts, and it would be completely inappropri-ate for the Court of Cats to get involved. But if they happened to be hanging out in Muir Woods before hos-tilities were formally declared, and accidentally served as an early warning system . . ."

Tybalt blinked, and then smiled, although his pupils remained hairline-thin. "You have gotten trickier. It suits you. I am not happy about this request, but I can see the wisdom in it, much as I might wish not to. I will ask them."

"And since you're the King of Cats, that means they'll do it, right?"

He snorted. "So long in my company, and yet you still know so little of the feline mind. Some will cooperate. Others will find better things to do with their time."

"Fair enough." Even partial cooperation would give us the manpower we needed to make this work out. Of course, there was one other stumbling block to be overcome . . . "Someone needs to explain what's going on to Sylvester."

Now Tybalt's eyes widened. "You cannot be serious."

"I am." I could have called. Sylvester would have listened. But I didn't want them fighting any longer than was absolutely necessary—and more, sending Tybalt would impress on Sylvester just how important this really was.

"He *kept* me from you."

"And now he can pay back a little of the debt he incurred to *me* in doing that. He can come and fight beside us. Please."

Tybalt simply stared at me for a long moment. Then he stepped closer. "You were less trouble before I told you that I loved you." This said, he bowed his head, and kissed me, long and slow and sweet. Despite the fact that we were surrounded by people, I kissed him back.

When he pulled away, he sighed. "Where shall I meet you?"

"Come to Muir Woods," I said. "I'm going to go there with Arden and the others to get the knowe open. Once that's done, it'll be time for you and me to hit the Queen's dungeons."

"Ah," he said. "The simple pleasures." He turned to Arden, offering another shallow bow. "Highness," he said. "May you have the best of luck in claiming the throne you once refused. I know it is a difficult choice to make. I hope you will have as many joys in your place as I have had in mine." He pivoted on his heel, walking out of the dining room.

I turned back to the others, pulling my jacket a little

tighter as I said, "All right, then: we know what we're doing, we know where we're going, and we know this isn't going to be much fun. I'm going to call Goldengreen before we leave here. May, go wake Jazz. Quentin, go call Raj. Arden, eat a sandwich. You're going to need it. Danny . . ."

"I know how to get to Muir Woods," he rumbled, folding his arms. "I'm drivin'."

I smiled a little. "Yeah, you're driving." May and Quentin had already vanished into other parts of the house, leaving me and Danny alone with Arden. I turned to her. "You okay?"

"I can't decide whether you're a genius, an idiot, or one of those people who's only happy when she's making everything up as she goes along," said Arden. She paused before adding, "And I'm starting to believe we can pull this off. It's . . . a little bit weird."

"Welcome to life with Tobes," said Danny, clapping her on the back.

Arden stumbled forward a few feet before getting her balance. "She hasn't killed the rest of you yet, so I guess that's something," she said. She looked at me. "Can we swing by the bookstore and pick up Madden? If we're going to need all hands on deck for this, I want him with me. He's one of the best men I know, and I'm not leaving him out."

"Absolutely," I said. "When it comes to committing treason, the more the merrier." I pulled my phone out of my pocket. "Now if you'll excuse me, I'm going to go call Goldengreen, and then we can leave."

"We'll be here," said Danny.

I made it into the kitchen—and even managed to close the kitchen door—before my stomach clenched so tight that I could no longer stay upright. I grabbed the edge of the counter and hung there, suspended by my white-knuckled fingers, while I waited for the pain to fade.

It seemed to take forever. It could have taken seconds. It was hard to tell. The pain was bad enough to twist my perception of time. I eventually hauled myself back to my feet, shaking, and wiped the sweat from my forehead. I could hear Arden and Danny talking quietly in the dining room. I couldn't have been incapacitated for too long; they'd have noticed my absence, and come looking for me.

I popped three more of Walther's blood gems into my mouth as I dialed the number for Goldengreen, slumping against the counter in the process. The bag was almost empty. This had to end soon. One way or another, it had to end soon.

I just hoped and prayed that it was going to end with everyone still standing.

But I no longer quite believed that was possible.

TWENTY-TWO

DRIVING AWAY FROM THE HOUSE and leaving Quentin and Jazz behind was one of the hardest things I'd done all week. I sat in the backseat with May, twisting around in my seat so that she could apply Neosporin and strips of gauze to my scraped-up palms. Her fingers were trembling, and she kept stealing glances through the rear window, watching as our house receded into the dark. I felt a pang of guilt. As hard as it was for me to leave my squire behind, leaving her girlfriend had to be even harder for her.

"I'm glad you're here," I said.

"Hmm?" May's attention focused on me. For a moment, it was like she wasn't even seeing me; she was still looking back, watching one more life fade into the distance. Then she shook her head, mustering a smile, and said, "I'm glad you asked me to be. I've been feeling sort of left out lately."

"I'm sorry."

"Don't be. I mean, I'm your death omen. I don't exactly have the right to demand to be a part of your life." We pulled up in front of Borderlands, visible now that Arden was with us. She hopped out, trotting toward the darkened storefront. May tracked Arden's movements, her smile fading. "She really does look just like her father. It's weird. I never thought I'd see those eyes again."

If we survived this, May could tell Arden what she remembered about King Gilad; Arden was going to find out where Fetches came from eventually, if she didn't already know. It occurred to me that I didn't have any idea what she did or didn't know about Faerie. She'd been young when she went into her self-imposed exile, and her education seemed to have been centered on keeping herself and her younger brother safe. How much time would that have left for learning how everything else in our world worked? We might be putting a completely unprepared woman in charge of one of the largest regional Kingdoms in the Westlands . . . and to be entirely honest, I didn't care. Ignorant or not, Arden was smart; she could learn. And anything would be an improvement over the Queen we were living under.

"Did you know him?" I asked.

"Yeah." May sunk down in her seat. "I *wasn't* him, or anything—that would be too weird—but I was one of his servants, or I remember being one of his servants, a little. She's patchy. Too many other memories overwrote hers. But I remember seeing Arden in the halls. She was always so serious. She and her brother haunted the knowe like little ghosts. They were so sad, and Gilad would never talk to them when he knew anyone else was around."

"But that didn't always include the servants," I guessed.

May shook her head. "No. He was a good man, but he was still a King, and Kings sometimes forget that servants are people. We knew who she was, and we all kept his secret, because we understood why it was important."

The cab door opened, and Arden slid into the backseat, forcing May to move into the middle. "The secret is out now," she said. We looked at her guiltily before May turned to resume bandaging my hands, trying to act like she'd been doing that all along.

"Arden—" I began.

"I heard enough," she said, cutting me off. "I'm not

going to ask what it all meant, because this isn't the time. But once we're finished taking back my Kingdom, you're going to explain *everything* to me. Do you understand? *Everything.*"

"I hope you have a lot of time to kill," said May.

I offered Arden a sheepish smile. "Sorry. Things get chaotic around me sometimes."

"You don't say."

The front passenger door opened. Madden flung himself into the seat, beaming. "Hi!"

"Hi, Madden," May and I chorused dutifully.

He turned a hopeful expression on Danny. "Can I . . . ?" he asked.

Danny chuckled. "Sure thing," he said, and started the cab. "Just don't jump out the window while we're moving, okay?"

"Okay!" said Madden, and shimmered, replaced by a large white dog with red-furred ears. His eyes were surrounded by matching circles, giving him an almost panda-like quality. Danny hit a button. Madden's window rolled down, and he stuck his head outside.

"Dogs are weird," I said.

"Says the woman who voluntarily travels with a cat," said Arden, turning back to me. "Will all those people you named before *really* come to help us?"

"I know the Undersea will; they're going to want Dianda back, and this is a way to accomplish that without *actually* going to war this week. Not that they'd be opposed to a good war, but that's something I'd rather avoid. Shadowed Hills . . ." I paused, trying to find the words for my complicated relationship with Sylvester Torquill. I settled for saying, "My liege holds Shadowed Hills, and he's never failed to come to my aid when I truly needed him. I absolutely believe he'll be there for me now. And he likes the current Queen about as much as I do."

"An' Toby hates her," said Danny.

May sighed. "Danny. Don't explain the joke."

"Sorry." He turned off Valencia, heading for the freeway. "Muir Woods is about an hour away."

"That gives Tybalt time to notify the cats and get to Shadowed Hills so Sylvester can start mobilizing the troops," I said. Muir Woods was close to the ocean, with a beach technically inside the boundaries of the park. I was assuming the Undersea would come largely via the water, which meant they never had to set foot, fin, or tentacle on land that belonged to the Queen. Sylvester could get his people there, and Marcia and the others from Goldengreen who couldn't swim but didn't want to stay there could take their cars. We were going to be on time.

Too many of my allies were scattered, unprotected, around the Bay Area: I knew that, even as I knew that there was no way to call them all to safety, and no safety to call them to if we tried. Walther would be better off on campus, far away from fights of succession. Mitch, Stacy, and the kids would be safer at home. April O'Leary couldn't move without the necessary hardware, and Li Qin Zhou was just as likely to kill me with her luck as she was to save me. The Luidaeg might have been able to help us ... but then again, she might not. Rayseline Torquill had proven that the last time the Luidaeg tried to get involved in person. She couldn't raise a hand against any descendant of Titania, and that included at least half the Queen's guards.

So no. This wasn't everyone I could have called, but in this instance at least, it was everyone I *should* have called. My stomach rumbled. I stuck one of my freshly-bandaged hands into my pocket and pulled out the baggie of blood gems from Walther, trying not to think about how few were left.

May followed my gaze to the baggie, and said, "I have a suggestion, but you're not going to like it."

"Those words are right so much of the time that it makes my teeth itch just hearing them." I looked away from the too-tempting chunks of frozen plasma and met the pale gray eyes of my Fetch. It occurred to me that my eyes were darker than hers for the first time. What a funny world we lived in. "What is it?"

"Goblin fruit isn't hard to find right now. Maybe if you had a little . . ."

"May!" I stared at her. "I can't believe you'd even suggest that."

"Toby, addiction isn't a personal failing. It's a thing that *happens*, sometimes because you made a mistake, sometimes because of, you know. Evil pie." She made a pie-tossing gesture. I scowled. She sighed. "You know I'm right. I mean, this is the longest you've gone without coffee since you discovered its existence. If it weren't for the goblin fruit, I'd expect you to be climbing the walls over caffeine withdrawal. And if you can't even kick coffee cold turkey, why should you think that's the right way of dealing with something a hundred times more addictive?"

"Maybe because goblin fruit messes me up so badly that I'm useless? I need to be able to take care of the situation, not just lie around watching pink elephants dance around the room."

May shrugged. "That's why you should just have a little bit. Just enough to calm your body down for a while, but not enough to make you start hallucinating. We don't have to do this for long, right? We're fixing things."

What she was saying made sense, and I hated it. I hated it right down to the bones of me. Most of all, I hated how much I wanted to give in.

"I—"

"She's right," said Arden. I looked past May to find her watching me, a serious expression on her face. "If you're starting to get shaky from goblin fruit withdrawal, you need to have some. Otherwise, you're going to wind up useless to me, and I'm sorry, but I can't allow that." My shock must have shown, because she smiled. "You said you wanted me to be your new Queen. Well, that means you have to listen to me. As your Crown Princess and presumptive regent, I am *ordering* you to have some goblin fruit."

"Look, even if we had some here—which we *don't*—

you don't know what it's like," I said. "You can't know. You're not a changeling."

"I can't know what it's like for you, but I do know what it's like. Being a Princess doesn't make you immune to temptation, especially when you're a Princess in exile in your own country, and you're too scared to run because running would change everything, would start something you're not sure you're ready to finish . . ." Arden shook her head. "Father hated the stuff—he said it was cheap and unfair—but I was lonely and scared, and I knew better than to play around with mortal drugs. So I got some goblin fruit. And you know what? It helped. I don't really remember most of the '60s . . ."

"Neither does anyone else," said Danny.

"Not helping," said May.

Arden continued. "But it really did help, and Toby, I know withdrawal when I see it. You're one sharp noise away from flipping out and climbing the nearest tall building with a sniper rifle, and that's not going to get my brother back. You need some goblin fruit."

"It doesn't matter what you think I need," I said flatly. "We're not stopping to find a street corner drug dealer, and I don't think Danny's been running goblin fruit out of the glove compartment. So I'm going to just keep on the way I have been, if it's all the same to you."

"No, you're not," said May, in a very small voice.

I turned to frown at her. "May?"

She didn't say anything. She just reached into her purse and pulled out a plastic baggie with a sandwich inside. It was white bread, cut into quarters; the crusts had been trimmed off. My eyes widened.

"May, no, don't—"

She opened the seal, and the smell of goblin fruit flooded the car. Without my having consciously decided to move, I was taking the baggie away from her and cramming the sections of sandwich into my mouth. There was barely a teaspoon of jam in the whole thing, making it just a thin layer of sweetness between the slices of bread, cheese, and ham, but I somehow managed to stop myself from ripping the sandwich apart to get at what I wanted faster. The small part of my brain that was still capable of making rational decisions knew that this was the only way I'd get the calories I needed to rebuild what my body was burning.

That part of my brain was in the minority. Most of me had been transformed into pure wanting, and it wasn't until I was sucking the crumbs off my fingers that my head cleared enough for me to realize what I'd done.

"Oh, root and *branch*," I swore, woozily. The car was getting blurry around the edges as the goblin fruit kicked in. I fumbled for the knives strapped to my waist, not really caring which one I grabbed, as long as I got something I could use to cut myself.

May shouted something, trying to pull the knife out of my hand. The car was already starting to fade from view, and it felt like my blood was carbonated. I couldn't feel my own fingers.

But I could feel hers.

"M'sorry," I managed, and stabbed her in the arm.

May shrieked. Arden swore. Danny briefly lost control of the car in the commotion, sending us swerving across two lanes of traffic. I ignored them all as I clamped my mouth down over the wound I'd created.

Her blood tasted like her magic, cotton candy and ashes, as well as the copperier, more expected taste of the blood itself. The fact that I could taste her magic at all was a change, although I wasn't sure whether it was a good one or a bad one. A stream of faces and flickers of memory tried to rise in my mind's eye, and I forced them away, refusing to look at them. I was too busy trying to hold my focus, forcing it inward and pushing back the bubbling sensation I could feel working its way through my veins.

Arden could talk about the dangers of withdrawal all she wanted, and she could even convince May she was right—although the fact that May had that sandwich ready to go probably meant that my Fetch had come up with this particular harebrained scheme at least partially on her own. And maybe they *were* right . . . for them. They were both purebloods, and neither of them had the kind of magic that could turn them human if given something to work with.

Goblin fruit counted as "something to work with." I ignored the sounds around me, and focused on getting as much blood into my body as I possibly could. It was funny, in a sad sort of way: the goblin fruit was the reason I had to do this, but it was also giving me the strength to counter its effects. The fuzziness retreated to the corners of my eyes, and while Arden's shouts retained an odd echoing quality, they didn't get any stranger. I pulled my mouth cautiously from May's arm, checking the size of her actual wound at the same time.

It was barely more than a scratch. Goblin fruit apparently interfered with my aim in addition to everything else.

May clamped her hand down over her arm as soon as I was out of the way, eyes wide, and demanded, "What in the name of Oberon and his wives do you think you're *doing*?"

"Surviving." I wiped my mouth. It left a red trail on the back of my hand. I fought the urge to gag. "What do *you* think you're doing? Dangling goblin fruit in front of me like that is *dangerous*."

"You *stabbed* me!" She made a grab for my knife. I pulled it back, out of her reach. "Oh, no, give me that You don't get to stab me and then hold onto your knives."

"No, but I *do* get to stab you if that's what it takes to keep from turning myself human." I wiped the blade on my jeans, glaring at her defiantly, before shoving it back into its holster. "Or did you forget that little parlor trick?"

"You said you couldn't turn yourself any more human than you already were," May protested.

"I said I didn't have the strength." I reached up and tucked my hair behind my ears, using the gesture as an excuse to check how pointed they were. They didn't feel like they'd changed at all . . . this time. That was a small

mercy, and one I wasn't going to count on. "I've consumed the Luidaeg's blood since then. So I *had* the
strength to start a change. I needed the strength, and the
focus, to *stop* it."

"You were telling the truth."

Arden sounded almost awed. That was enough to pull
my attention away from May, and back to her. She was
pressed against the door, mismatched eyes wide. "Excuse me?" I said.

"You're not Daoine Sidhe. You weren't lying about
that. Your mother . . . *Amandine* is the Last Among the
First?" She said it like it was a title, each word weighted
somehow, so that they stood separate and distinct from
the rest of the sentence. She said it the way I would have
said "once upon a time," and for some reason, that terrified me.

"Um . . . yeah?" I said, glancing to May for help. She
shook her head, looking as mystified as I felt. "I told you
that, remember? Mom's Firstborn."

"She was here all along." Arden sagged, looking suddenly stricken. "Father could have saved himself."

"What?" I demanded.

"What?" May echoed.

"We're at Muir Woods," said Danny. We all turned to
stare at him. He grimaced apologetically. "Sorry. Just
thought you'd like to know."

"You said we had an hour," I protested.

"You were latched onto my arm for a while," said May.

I groaned, running my hand back through my hair.
"Of course I was. Swell. Arden, you have until Danny
parks this car to tell me what the hell you're talking
about. Talk fast."

"A woman—Oleander de Merelands—came to the
Court a week before the earthquake," said Arden. "She
told Father that the Last Among the First was in the Mists.
She said the Last was going to shake the world down if we
didn't find and stop her. He searched, but there wasn't
much time, and there was nothing to be found. The only
Firstborn even rumored to live in the Bay Area was the

sea witch, and no one finds her when she wants to be left alone. Time ran out. The world fell down."

"And your father died," I said grimly. "I'm willing to bet that had more to do with Oleander than it did with the earthquake."

"It doesn't matter," said Arden. "*Amandine*? Really?"

"That was pretty much my reaction." I looked to May as the car rolled to a stop. "How's your arm?"

"Almost healed. I'm not in your league, but I'm close. It's a Fetch thing." She scowled. "Don't stab me again."

"I wasn't planning to. Don't feed me any more goblin fruit."

"Deal."

"You ladies keep havin' sharing time. I'll be right back." Danny got out, lumbering over to the chained gate into the parking lot. Madden jumped out after him, tail pluming wildly, and vanished into the underbrush.

"Should I be concerned?" I asked.

"No," said Arden. "He'll check for dangers and be there when we get out of the car. You'll see."

"Huh." Cu Sidhe and Cait Sidhe were very different. And yet maybe not. I would have been just that sure of Tybalt. "Uh, so are the two of you . . . ?"

Arden actually laughed. "Me and Madden? No. Even if I was interested, his boyfriend would kill me with a hammer."

"Just asking."

Danny had reached the chain holding the gate closed. He stooped, saying something to the lock. Even with the windows down I couldn't hear him, but apparently the metal of the hasp liked what it was hearing, because it popped open. Danny removed it, pulling the chain free, and opened the gate before walking back to the car and getting in. "Here we go."

"I love Trolls," said May blissfully, leaning forward and hugging Danny's neck around the back of the seat. He didn't say anything, but I could see his smile reflected in the rearview mirror.

Arden was still staring at me with a strange mix of confusion and anger in her eyes. I did my best to ignore her. As soon as the car stopped, I undid my seatbelt and slid out into the cool, redwood-scented air of Muir Woods. Somewhere in the tall old trees an owl shrieked, and something rustled through the underbrush. I felt like an intruder, stepping into a world that was never meant to be mine—and at the same time, I felt like I was coming home.

It was a changeling's dilemma, writ large through every cell of me. The trouble was that this time, I knew what I was missing. I wanted my real world back.

Arden stopped next to me and tilted her head back to look at the trees, eyes filling with slow tears. I didn't say anything as May stepped up on my other side. I just waited. Finally, Arden spoke.

"I haven't been here since Father died." Her tears slipped free, running down her cheeks. "It still looks just the same." Madden came bounding back out of the trees, stopping beside her. He didn't shift back to human form.

"Let's see if that applies everywhere," I said. "Come on."

We walked into the forest. Madden quickly ran ahead, visible only as an occasional glimpse of white between the night-blackened trunks. An owl screeched, protesting this intrusion. Madden barked gleefully back. At least one of us was having a good time. Of the five of us, I was the only one who'd been to the shallowing in the last hundred years, if at all. May walked beside me, her hand resting on my shoulder, where she could pull me back before I went blundering off into the underbrush or walked into a creek. I made my way through the redwoods largely by feel, pausing occasionally to get my bearings.

"Toby . . ." said May.

"I know," I said. "Just trust me, okay? Sooner or later, Arden's going to say—"

"I know where we are." Arden pushed past me, suddenly moving through the trees with purpose. May muttered something that sounded suspiciously like "I hate you," and tightened her grip on my arm, stepping in front of me so that she could haul me after the fleeing Princess. Danny brought up the rear, moving surprisingly quietly for someone his size.

Arden led us up a series of mud and timber steps that had been cut into the side of the hill, breaking into a run when she reached the top. The rest of us followed. When we caught up with her again, she was standing in front of an enormous redwood tree, with Madden sitting near her feet. The trunk was bigger around than my kitchen; you could have hollowed it out and used it as a good-sized living room. She was crying again. That wasn't really a surprise.

"I'm here." She raised her hands, pressing them flat against the tree. "I'm sorry. It took too long, and I'm sorry, but I'm really here. It's me."

Nothing happened.

Arden took a step backward, away from the tree. "It's going to be like this, huh? Okay. I can handle that." She turned to me. "Can I borrow your knife please?"

"Um. Sure." I pulled the silver knife from my belt and offered it to her, hilt first.

"Thank you," said Arden, with ritual formality. Thanks are always serious in Faerie, not least because they imply fealty—in this case, my fealty to her. She was beginning to accept who she was. Not waiting to see how I would respond, she turned back to the tree and ran the edge of my knife across her left index finger, pressing down until she drew blood. I swallowed hard, fighting the urge to look away.

"My name is Arden Windermere," she said. "My father was Gilad Windermere. My mother was Sebille, of no family line. They are gone now, both of them; they have stopped their dancing. I have not. In the name of the line of Windermere, I ask you to open your door to me. Know me, accept me, and welcome me home." She pressed her bloody fingertip against the tree, and smiled. "I've missed you."

What happened next . . . I might have understood it a little better if I'd been more fae at the time. One moment, the tree was intact, and the next, there was a great hollow in its center. That, I had almost expected, based on my previous visit to Muir Woods. What I didn't expect was the door, a huge, ornately-carved thing that filled the hollow. As we watched, it swung open, revealing a vast hall so choked with cobwebs that the ceiling was invisible. Arden's smile brightened, becoming almost painful to look at. She started to step forward.

"This is too easy," I muttered, and lunged forward, grabbing her arm. She stopped, blinking at me. Fortunately, Madden stopped with her. I was quietly relieved. That would have been a complication I didn't want to deal with.

"What are you doing?"

"This is too easy."

"Uh, what? Maybe you're used to bleeding every time you want something to happen—"

"She is," said May.

"—but that was *not* easy," continued Arden, undaunted.

I shook my head. "Just trust me, okay? This was too easy. The doors shouldn't have opened without some sort of failsafe, and if Oleander was here a week before the earthquake, if she knew that it was coming, then she killed your father. And Oleander loved traps. Was this door accessible only to people with royal blood?"

Arden paled. "Oh."

"I thought so." I looked over my shoulder. "Hey, May, come and trigger a booby-trap for us, will you?"

"Why is that always my job?"

"Because you can't die."

"Oh, right." May stuffed her hands into the pockets of her jeans, humming atonally as she stepped through the open doorway into the lost knowe of King Gilad. There was a whistling sound, and a fletched dart appeared in the middle of her chest. She blinked down at it, then shot me an annoyed look. "I better not have just been elf-shot, you idiot."

"Do you feel like passing out for a hundred years?"

"No."

"Then you're probably fine. Keep walking."

May rolled her eyes before continuing on into the darkened knowe. She vanished into the cobwebs. There was a thumping sound, followed by a meaty *thud*. "I'm okay!"

"What happened?"

"Tripwire! But I think I'm supposed to be dropping dead from neurotoxins right about now, so come on in."

Arden looked at me uncertainly. I gave her what I hoped was a reassuring smile. "We do this sort of thing all the time. If May says it's safe, there's a really good chance she's right." I decided not to mention that usually "we" meant "me." There was no point in making things more awkward than they already were.

"All right . . ." said Arden, and stepped into the knowe.

There should have been a fanfare, some sort of glorious celebration of the circle that had been broken when King Gilad died and his children lost their parents and their home in the same night. There should have been *something*. But all we got was a gradual brightening of the room as lights high above the cobwebs came on, glowing golden through the grime of years, and the door swinging closed behind us.

May walked back to join the rest of us, a gray ghost swathed in dust and cobwebs. "There's a big receiving room up ahead," she said. "No more traps that I could find."

"We'll have to check everything twice before we assume it's safe," I said. Then I turned to Arden, who was looking around with wide, too-bright eyes. I dropped to one knee and bowed my head.

"What?" she asked.

A soft thump told me May had followed my lead. A second, much louder thump told me that Danny had joined us.

"Your Highness," I said. "Welcome home." I raised my head, meeting her eyes. "May we reclaim your Kingdom now?"

Arden took a deep, shaky breath before she nodded. "Yes," she said. "Why don't we go ahead and do that?"

TWENTY-THREE

WE WERE ALL CAKED IN GRIME by the time Tybalt arrived. He walked in through the now-open door of the knowe and followed the sound of vigorous decobwebbing to the receiving room, where we were still hard at work. We didn't have brooms, so we were making do with branches gathered from the forest outside. Madden had Oleander's scent from the dart we'd pulled out of May and was following it around the receiving room, barking every time he found something that smelled like a trap. We'd been marking them all with branches, since we also didn't have the equipment to safely disarm them.

Tybalt stopped in the doorway, staying well clear of the cascading filth. "This is a charming hovel. In a few decades, it might actually be worth the effort of maintaining. I doubt it, however."

"Yeah, it's nice, isn't it?" I lowered the branch I'd been using to sweep cobwebs from the wall, smiling at him. The expression felt strained. I had no idea what it looked like, but judging by Tybalt's frown, it didn't look good. "At least we got in without any fatalities. How did it go at Shadowed Hills?"

"I do not believe Duke Torquill and I will be friends any time in the near future," said Tybalt. "Still, he did not eject me on sight, and I did not gut him, so we can both be said to have shown admirable restraint. He is on his way, along with those of his fiefdom who are willing to make an active stand against the Queen. He said they would take an alternate route, and that you would know it."

I stared. "He's getting Luna to open a Rose Road." Sylvester's wife, Luna, was a Blodynbryd—sort of a Dryad who was connected to fields of roses, rather than a single tree. Maybe because she was the daughter of two Firstborn, or maybe because she was old enough to have access to some pretty unusual magic, she knew how to open the Rose Roads, one of the old paths that ran through Faerie like roots through soil. But those roads had their costs, and she'd never opened a Rose Road for more than two people at once in all the time I'd known her.

Tybalt nodded. "They should be arriving shortly."

"And the forces from Goldengreen?"

"Already on their way."

I looked across the receiving room to where Arden was pulling down more cobwebs, revealing hand-carved redwood bas-reliefs all along the walls. "We're really going to do this. We're going to put this girl in charge of a Kingdom."

"Are you having second thoughts?" Tybalt finally moved, ignoring the grime that covered every visible inch of me as he walked over and put his arms around my waist. I relaxed into his embrace, wishing more than anything that I could smell the hot pennyroyal of his magic. I hadn't realized how much I would miss it until it was gone.

And that was why I couldn't be having second thoughts. I shook my head. "No. We're past that now."

"Good. My cats are outside. They won't engage the Queen's forces unless they are challenged; if they are, they'll win." It wasn't a boast. Tybalt was telling the truth as he saw it.

"Okay." I pulled away, gesturing for him to follow as I made my way across the receiving room toward May and Danny.

My Fetch had solved the problem of height by climbing onto Danny's shoulders, and was wielding her redwood branch with a gleeful violence that sent sheets of dust and cobwebs cascading down onto them. The floor, which hadn't been exactly clean when she started, was rapidly turning an undifferentiated shade of ashy gray. She stopped when she saw us approach, although I'm not sure how she saw *anything* through that mess.

"Is it time?" she asked, passing her redwood branch down to Danny.

"Soon," I said.

"Okay." She slid back down to the floor, tucking her dirty hair behind her ears with one hand as she walked toward us. "Hey, Tybalt. How do you like the place?"

"It's charming," he said blandly.

"Don't listen to him," I said. "The Court of Cats is just as bad."

"Sweet Oberon, will you *look* at this place?" The question was asked in a tone of shrill delight, like the speaker couldn't imagine her luck. All four of us turned to see Melly and Ormond in the entryway, mops in their hands and blissful expressions on their faces.

I blinked. "Tybalt, you told Sylvester we'd need more than just the Hobs, didn't you?"

"I did," he said, sounding as bemused as I felt.

Meanwhile, Melly had spotted us. Beaming, she trotted across the dirty floor and seized my hands before I had a chance to step away. "Isn't this just the finest of all fine messes?" she asked. "Oh, October, it's *beautiful*, and you'll see, we'll have it all shipshape in no time!"

Ormond followed her, seeming to move more sedately, and yet somehow crossing the floor in the same amount of time. "Before you go worrying yourself, His Lordship is right behind us, and with four dozen men besides. We were just at the head of the pack, as it were. It occurred to us there might be a mess in need of setting right, and it would have been unfair to leave it any longer than necessary."

"Ah," I said. "Let me introduce you to Arden. This is

her knowe." I started walking, not bothering to check whether the Hobs were following me. Because this was Arden's knowe, they'd need her permission to start cleaning—and there's nothing in this world or any other that Hobs love more than they love to clean. It's their calling and their passion, and a mess like this one was their equivalent of Christmas.

Arden had heard the unfamiliar voices, and had managed to set her makeshift broom aside and at least try to dust off her hands before we reached her. "Hello," she said, with a mildly questioning lilt.

"Melly, Ormond, may I present Her Highness Arden Windermere, Crown Princess and rightful Queen in the Mists," I said. "Arden, meet Melly and Ormond. They're from Shadowed Hills. They'd really appreciate being allowed to mop your floors."

"And wipe your windows, and scrub your stonework, and polish anything that needs polishing," said Melly, sounding dazed. Then she curtsied. "Your *Highness*."

"Highness," said Ormond, with a much more restrained nod of his head. "We're here to set your house in order, if you'll let us."

"Please," said Arden fervently. "This place is . . ."

"It may be booby-trapped," I interjected. "Oleander was here."

Ormond's expression hardened. "Will that snake never stop poisoning our gardens?" he asked sourly. "Be assured, we'll watch for signs of her."

"Okay. If you find a trap you can't defuse on your own, mark it with a redwood bough." Glancing to Arden to be sure she was all right with what I was saying, I continued, "It'd be best if you could start here, get this room and the entry hall into a presentable condition. Arden, did you have a room here?"

"Yes," said Arden, sounding puzzled.

"Melly, if you can find the Princess' room, you might be able to find her wardrobe . . ."

Melly straightened, all but glowing in her excitement. "Oh, dresses! Yes, of course! Highness," she bobbed another curtsy to Arden. Then she was off, moving almost too quickly for my human eyes to follow as she vanished into the remaining curtain of cobwebs.

Arden blinked. "It's going to take me a while to get used to that."

"Fake it." Footsteps from the entry hall signaled the approach of a much larger force. I turned to see Sylvester stepping into the receiving hall. All his knights and men-at-arms were behind him, even Etienne. Grianne was standing at Sylvester's right, signaling that she was, for the moment at least, his second-in-command. It made sense: without his powers, Etienne couldn't safely move outside the knowe unescorted. It still sucked.

Sylvester paused long enough to look around, assessing our progress, before turning and murmuring something to Grianne. She nodded, and her Merry Dancers—the two globes of living light that accompanied her everywhere she went—rose to ceiling level, lighting up the receiving hall and throwing the grime into sharp relief. I didn't say anything, but I was glad to have the extra light, no matter how nasty it made everything look. Sylvester nodded, looking pleased, and led his forces across the room to where we were waiting. No one said anything.

When he reached us, he drew his sword, placed its tip against the floor, and knelt. "Your Highness," he said.

Arden looked flustered. "You don't have to do that."

"Yes, he does," said Tybalt. She glanced to him, startled. "Accept the fealty you are offered. It is your responsibility, your privilege, and your burden."

". . . right." She turned back to Sylvester. "Thank you."

Acceptance of fealty is one of the few times in Faerie when thanks are appropriate. Sylvester rose, resheathing his sword. He was trying to watch Arden—I knew him well enough to know that—but his eyes still skipped to me, taking in my too-human state and the faint glow of the firefly sitting on my neck.

"We are here to support your claim to the throne," he said, tearing his eyes away from me and looking back to Arden. "Will you have us?"

"Gladly," said Arden.

"I have also brought my housekeepers, as I thought you might need some small assistance in preparing for parley." I was impressed: he managed to say that with a straight face.

"Melly and Ormond are already starting to scrub things," I said. "Don't mess around: the place is a sty. Did you see the Undersea forces at all?"

"They're on their way up from the beach," he said, looking only faintly annoyed by my determined effort to ignore propriety.

"Good. And Goldengreen?"

"Amassing in the parking lot."

"Better." I looked to Arden. "Your army is here. Your knowe is open. This is your time to act."

She took a deep breath, and turned to Sylvester. "Your knight is a Candela, I believe?" she said, indicating Grianne.

"She is," said Sylvester.

"May I borrow her?"

A smile flashed across Sylvester's face, there and gone so fast that it would have been easy to miss. "Please."

Arden turned to Grianne, taking a deep breath as she visibly centered herself. "I'd like you to carry a message to the imposter who currently holds my throne, if you would be so kind."

Grianne cocked her head, waiting.

"Tell her . . ." Arden took another deep breath. "Tell her I will no longer sit idly by while she pretends to my father's name. Tell her the true Queen in the Mists is in her knowe, and claiming that which is hers by right."

"Yes, Your Highness," said Grianne. Her Merry Dancers descended and swirled around her as she turned and ran toward the wall. There was a green glittering in the air. Then she dove into it, and was gone.

Arden stared after her, something midway between hope and horror in her face.

"Well, then," I said. "No turning back now. May?"

"I'm on it." May waved her hands, and while I couldn't

see the casting, I could see the results: in the blink of an eye, she went from herself to me, as I normally was. She even created an illusionary leather jacket, completing the picture. "Now go get that boy and bring him home."

"We will." I turned to Sylvester. He would barely meet my eyes. Our last parting had been hard, on both of us, and he clearly wasn't sure I'd forgiven him for keeping Tybalt away when I needed him there.

Sylvester had been a father to me when I'd had no one else. I leaned over and kissed his cheek, propriety be damned. "Kick her ass," I said. I glanced to Arden. "Stay alive. I'll be back with your brother."

Tybalt was waiting when I turned back to him. He gathered me into his arms without asking, and carried me, grime and all, into the hanging curtains of cobwebs until the light became diffuse enough to count as shadow.

"This will take some time," Tybalt murmured. "I'll come out as often as I can. Just hold on, all right?"

"All right," I said. "I trust you."

He smiled through the growing dark. I took a breath and closed my eyes, and the world went cold around us.

True to his word, we broke back out into warmth just as my lungs were beginning to burn. Tybalt kept running. I gulped down several mouthfuls of sweet, night-warm air before he squeezed my arm, signaling that we were about to step back onto the Shadow Roads. I took a breath and held it as we dove back into the cold.

The transition happened twice more before Tybalt stumbled, dropping me onto a stone floor. I yelped—I couldn't help myself—as I spun head over heels to slam into a wall that somehow felt even harder than the floor. I finished my tumble by hitting my head against that same wall. Yup. It was definitely harder than the floor.

Then I realized that Tybalt hadn't made a sound since he'd fallen.

"Tybalt?" I was aiming for a whisper. My voice came out in a squeak. Trying to ignore my spinning head, I rolled to my hands and knees and crawled toward him. "Are you okay?"

He still wasn't moving. I swallowed a cold jet of panic and crawled faster, finally reaching his side. Maybe it was the pain, and maybe it was the cold inevitability of the situation, but I found myself swaddled in a veil of surprising calm. Things had been going too well. Everyone I loved had to die. That was the way my life worked, and had worked since the day I woke up, wet, naked, and alone in the pond that had been my prison. I was a fool to have thought, for even a few seconds, that this time would be different.

I pressed my fingers against the side of Tybalt's throat, trying to find a pulse, and found nothing. "Come on," I whispered. "Please, just this once, just this one time, forget you're a cat, and come when you're called. Please."

He didn't respond. The muscles in his face were completely relaxed. He looked like he was sleeping; like he'd wake up at any moment.

My head was still spinning. I raised my hand to cup his cheek. "Please, don't do this. Tybalt, you promised. You promised you wouldn't do this."

He didn't move.

I took a deep, ragged breath, reaching up to touch the firefly that was huddled in my hair. I didn't know whether seeing illusions would extend to hearing things that were normally confined to Faerie, but it was worth a try. The firefly's wings buzzed against my fingers. I eased my butt down to the stone floor, leaning against Tybalt, and waited for something to happen. Seconds ticked by, each of them seeming to last an eternity.

And in the distance, I heard the sound of wings.

My heart lurched. I opened my eyes and turned to see the first of the night-haunts descending toward us. No—not the first. The flock normally traveled together, a great swarm of shadowy bodies and ragged, fast-beating wings. There were only two this time, both wearing faces I recognized. My old mentor, Devin . . .

. . . and Connor. They landed several feet away, folding their wings behind their Barbie-sized bodies and watching me warily.

Hope bloomed in my chest like a cruel flower. "He's not dead, is he?" I asked.

"Death is like pregnancy," said Devin's haunt. "A little can go a very long way."

Connor's haunt gave him a reproachful look, but didn't say anything.

"It doesn't work that way," I countered. "You're either pregnant or you're not. You're either dead . . ."

"Or you're dying," said the Connor-haunt. "I'm sorry, Toby, but that's the way it is. Death isn't something that has to be helped along. Once it starts, it generally finishes."

"Then tell me how to save him." They stared at me. I fought the urge to grab them and bash their diminutive heads together. They'd eat me if I tried. "You're the night-haunts. You speak death. Tell me how to save him."

"October—" began Connor's haunt.

The Devin-haunt grabbed his arm, stopping him. "We do not bargain with the *living*," he said. "No matter how much we remember caring for them."

"Not even when the living can make so many meals for you?" I asked. I wasn't going to touch the topic of Devin having cared for me. "Please. I've fed your flock. I saved May, even if I didn't know I was doing it. Please, help me save him." I paused before whispering, "Connor, please."

"We owe you nothing," said the Devin-haunt, releasing the Connor-haunt's arm. "But there is something charmingly perverse about the idea of your being bound to do us a favor. We have not been owed a favor by the living in a very long time." Connor's haunt looked away, falling silent once more. He looked ashamed in that moment. My heart ached for him . . . but he was dead. I had to save my strength for the living.

"I won't kill anyone for you." My lips felt numb as they shaped the words. I meant that—there were some things I couldn't even justify by saving Tybalt's life—but I hated myself for saying it.

"Death is our job, not yours," said the Devin-haunt.

He gave Tybalt a disgusted look. "The cat is not dead, merely drained. The holder of these halls has tightened her wards since the last time the Shadow Roads were used to pierce them, and mortality weighs heavily in that darkness."

"So he hurt himself because he had to carry me through something that wasn't designed to let humans pass." I took a deep breath, swallowing my guilt. "I will owe you a favor."

"Yes, you will," said the Devin-haunt. "And if you default on us, we will take you."

The idea of being eaten by the night-haunts while I was still alive didn't exactly appeal, but I didn't see another way. Not if I wanted Tybalt to live. Reluctantly, I nodded. "I'll do whatever you ask me, as long as I don't have to kill anyone. I won't kill anyone."

"Agreed," said the Devin-haunt. There was a strange weight to the word, like it was binding above and beyond the actual meaning.

Feeling vaguely as if I'd just made a huge mistake, I asked, "How do I fix this?"

"The cat is sore wounded. He used his strength until there was nothing more. He needs power." The Devin-haunt fluttered his wings. "Were you your own self, I would say you could grant it to him, but as you are . . ."

"As I am, I've got nothing."

He smiled. "And yet you could have everything you desire."

I frowned at him before finally looking away from Tybalt and the night-haunts, and taking stock of my surroundings.

We were in the final hall leading to the Queen's dungeons. That was why the wall had felt so much harder than the floor; the floor was just stone, and the walls were laced with iron, to dampen and poison the magic of anyone who tried to escape. That explained why only two of the strongest night-haunts had come: the weaker members of the flock would probably have dissolved as soon as they entered. Torches made of mixed rowan and yarrow burned in sconces set into the wall, sending plumes of smoke up into the air.

We were in the Queen's knowe. We were near the hope chest.

I turned back to the night-haunts. "How much time do I have?"

"The guards at the door heard the sound of wings," said Connor's haunt. "They're not going to come in here until they're sure that we've come and gone. They'd rather not see us if they have a choice in the matter."

A cruel smile twisted the mouth of Devin's haunt. "Fear is a beautiful wall to place between yourself and your enemies."

"Okay. So . . . okay." That didn't give me an *exact* time, but it was a start. I stood, trying to ignore the shaking in my legs. "Can you stay with him?"

"Until you return, or until he comes with us," said the Devin-haunt.

I blanched. No matter how bad I felt, I was doing this on a time limit. "All right," I said. "I'll be back soon."

Connor's wings rattled, and he looked at me, sea-dark eyes sad. "Hurry," he said.

There was a warning in that word that I couldn't deny, no matter how much I wanted to. I needed to hurry; I needed to run through the knowe until I found the treasury. But I was still smart enough to know that I wouldn't make it very far if I tried to do this on my own. Slowly, I turned toward the darkened hall ahead of me. Somewhere down there in the dark was the only aid I was going to find here, in this place controlled by one of my worst enemies. All I had to do was find Dianda, free her, and hope that she was still capable of helping me after being locked in an iron-laced cell. And I had to do it before my boyfriend died.

"No pressure," I muttered, and pulled a torch from its sconce before I limped onward into the dark.

TWENTY-FOUR

I'D NEVER BEEN ON THIS SIDE of the cells before while I was in a position to look around. The air was thick with smoke, making it difficult to see even in the light cast by my borrowed torch. I limped from door to door, peering through the hatches set into them at eye level. The first four cells I passed were empty. When I opened the hatch on the fifth door, a brick rebounded off the grill.

"Whoa!" I yelped, barely managing to fling myself out of the way of the flying stone chips. "Dianda? Is that you?"

"Come a little closer and find out for yourself," she snarled.

". . . definitely Dianda," I muttered. Louder, I said, "It's me, Toby. Can you please not throw anything else? I'm here to get you out of there."

There was a pause before Dianda said suspiciously, "Prove it."

I moved back in front of her cell's hatch. She was standing at the center of the room in bipedal form, a brick in one hand, glaring. Her tunic was ripped and stained with blood and rust. She wasn't wearing any pants, or shoes.

She scowled when she saw my face. "You're not October," she snarled, and pulled back her arm, preparing to fling the second brick.

"Whoa, whoa, hold up!" I said. "I *am* October, I just had a little accident with a goblin fruit pie and sort of accidentally turned myself mostly human." The sheer ridiculousness of that statement hit me as soon as it had left my mouth. I winced. "Okay, let me try again . . ."

"There's no need. No one else would say something that dumb and actually mean it." Dianda lowered the brick. "How did you get here?" She seemed to be trying to look past me to the hall. The reason was revealed when she asked, "How many guards did you bring?"

"I brought a force of one, and he's in trouble. I need you to help me find the treasury so I can fix myself, because I can't fix him until I do that." I drew my iron knife. The hilt was heavy and familiar in my hand. "Hold tight. I'm going to get you out of here."

"Hurry." Dianda wrapped her arms a little tighter around herself. "The air in here burns."

"I know." I dropped to one knee, wincing, and studied the lock. The fact that Dianda was still standing, and still strong enough not to revert to her natural form, was sort of awe-inspiring. Iron saps strength, and the more fae someone is, the faster iron will start affecting them. Dianda was purebloBlooded. She should have been writhing in agony. Instead, she was just looking for something she could hit.

I knew I liked her for a reason.

The lock was surprisingly easy to pick, maybe because there'd never been much of a reason to make it very secure. The Queen's dungeon was hard to access, and anyone fae enough to know it existed was unlikely to ever make it that far. I twisted my knife to the side and the tumbler popped, allowing me to unlatch the door.

"All right; I'm opening the do—" Dianda burst out of the room, shoving past me, and stopped at the middle of the hallway, breathing so hard she looked like she'd just finished a marathon. I caught myself against the wall. "—or now," I finished. "You okay?"

"My blood is full of stinging jellies and I want to hurt someone," she snarled. "So it's to be treason now, is it?"

"No, it's not," I said. "Arden just announced her regency. Unless she fails, this Queen has no right to hold you."

Dianda blinked, and then slowly smiled. "Wonderful. Now about those people I wanted to hurt . . ."

"We can't." I shook my head, resheathing my knife. "We have something else to do."

"What?" Dianda's eyebrows arched upward in surprise. "I'm sorry. You get to give me orders now? Did I miss the annexation of the Undersea?"

"No," I said. "But Tybalt is dying, and we need to find the treasury if there's going to be any chance of saving him. I can't do it on my own. I need your help."

"A knight of the land Courts asking a Duchess of the Undersea to save a King of Cats," said Dianda, almost thoughtfully. "You live your life in a stew of myths, don't you?"

I glared. "This is no time to stand here quipping. Will you help me, or am I leaving you to find your own way out of here?"

"Of course I'll help you." Her bravado slipped, revealing the wounded, weary woman behind her mask. "Love should always be saved—and I owe the bitch who holds this knowe more pain than I can properly describe. We may as well begin with a little robbery."

"Great." I turned in a circle, finally pointing toward the nearest set of stairs. "That way. That'll get us back to ground-level."

"Where is the treasury from there?"

"I . . ." I stopped, shoulders sagging. "I don't know."

"Well, then. It's a good thing you have me." Dianda started walking. I moved to pace her. She was moving slowly enough that I could, and I didn't get the impression that it was due to courtesy; she was a mermaid who'd been forced to remain in a mostly-human shape for hours. She couldn't have walked faster if she'd wanted to.

Since for the moment, we only needed to climb stairs, I didn't ask what she'd meant: I just focused on putting one foot in front of the other. Midway up, I paused to pop another of Walther's blood gems into my mouth. It barely took the edge off my hunger. That didn't matter, because I wouldn't need them much longer.

One way or another, I wouldn't need them much longer.

Dianda reached the door at the top of the stairs first, and paused, leaning in until her ear was almost brushing against the wood. She held up two fingers. I nodded. Then, since I was the one more equipped to touch the iron laced through the door itself, I braced my shoulder against it and shoved it open.

I had time to see the startled look on the first guard's face before Dianda hit him in the throat, the sort of sucker punch that made it impossible for him to do anything but fall down. I grabbed his spear as he fell, whipping around and swinging it toward the other side of the door. Momentum turned me to face the second guard just as the haft of the spear hit her across the belly. The air rushed out of her as a loud grunt. Dianda promptly punched her three times in the face, and she went down beside her partner.

The door to the dungeons swung shut with a disturbingly final-sounding bang. Tybalt was down there, alone with the night-haunts. We had to hurry.

"Amateurs," scoffed Dianda, and crouched to begin searching the fallen guards. "I've got a short sword here."

"I'll keep the spear," I said.

"Suit yourself." Dianda straightened, belting the guard's sword around her waist as she held up a key ring. "Do you know how to get to the main receiving room?"

"That way." I pointed.

"Good. Which way is the armory?"

I pointed again, in the opposite direction.

"Even better." Dianda started toward the armory, bare feet slapping against the stone floor. "The treasury is likely to be near the place where they keep the weapons, but still reasonably close to where Court is held. That makes it accessible but defensible, and means the dungeon is nice and easy to get to if someone tries to rob you."

"Logic in knowe-building. All right." I followed, watching for signs of attack. The halls were quiet around us, but that didn't necessarily mean anything. Even after years of dealing with her, I didn't have any idea how big the Queen's Court actually was. It could have been huge, staffed on a scale with the knowe she claimed. It could also have been tiny. She usually kept visitors confined to the main hall, and that meant she could have been doing everything with no more than twenty people.

"So Arden's claim is declared, huh? Good. I've been looking forward to a brawl." Dianda's tone was casual, but her cheeks were flushed with spots of hectic red. "How's Dean?"

"He and Patrick are both fine," I said. "The Queen only arrested you."

"Thank Oberon for that." Dianda kept walking. "What are we doing, exactly?"

"We're breaking into the Queen's treasury so I can find the hope chest I gave her when Evening died," I said. "That'll let me change my blood back to normal, so I can save Tybalt."

"I have no idea what any of that means, but it all sounds very epic and important, so I'm sure it'll work." Dianda wiped her forehead with the back of one hand. "And then I'm going to kick that white-haired usurper's ass from here to Atlantis."

"Just hold on to that," I said, watching her anxiously. She was showing the classic symptoms of iron poisoning. Walther could treat that, but only if I could get her to him—and if she keeled over, I wasn't going to be getting her anywhere.

Footsteps up ahead cut off any further conversation. Two more of the Queen's guards came around the corner, stopping when they saw us. I threw my spear at the guard on the left. It bounced harmlessly off his chest, but it was a distraction. It bought us a few seconds. I drew my knives and Dianda drew her sword. Then, with no more civility than that, we charged.

The first guard never got a chance to do anything. Dianda's swing caught him in the side of the head, the pommel of her sword impacting hard against bone. The second guard was faster. I slashed at him and he dodged, before swinging his own sword at my side. It was a good hit, the kind of thing Sylvester had tried—and failed—to teach me to avoid before I learned to depend on my own ability to recover from any nonmortal injury. The blade cut deep before it was withdrawn, and the smell of blood flooded my nostrils.

The guard pulled back for another swing. I summoned every bit of training I'd ever had, using it to dodge the hit that would have ended the fight for good, and pressed my iron knife against his throat. He froze.

"Drop the sword," I said. It clattered to the hallway floor. "Which way to the treasury?"

"I will not betray—" he began.

"She's not your Queen," I snarled. "She's a fake, and the real Queen is finally here. You're betraying *nothing*, and you're saving yourself from death by iron. Oberon's Law doesn't bind me. I'm too *human* for that, and it's your beloved pretender's fault. Now. Which way is the treasury?"

Something in my eyes must have told him I was serious. He raised one shaking hand, pointing back the way he'd come. I nodded.

"How many men are guarding the doors?"

"Two," he whispered.

"Good answer." I let go as Dianda hit him in the back of the head, sending him crumpling to the floor. I nudged his body with a toe. He didn't move. "Did you just kill him?"

"No, but he'll wish I had when he wakes up." Dianda looked at me, and her eyes widened. "Toby, you're bleeding."

"I know. I haven't felt this good in days." I touched my

side and winced, resolutely not looking at the damage. "It won't last. We'd better hurry." I didn't want to stop the bleeding—the smell was helping, and as long as I was bleeding, I didn't have to acknowledge how bad the wound actually was. That didn't mean I could bleed forever without consequences.

Eyes still wide, Dianda nodded. "All right. Come on."

We abandoned pretensions of stealth as we hurried down the hall. We were leaving four fallen guards and a blood trail behind us. All we had on our side was speed, and so we were using it as best we could. Which..., wasn't all that good, considering our respective situations. Maybe it shouldn't have been a surprise when we turned another corner and found six guards standing in front of a pair of double doors, obviously waiting for us.

"Aw, they want to win," said Dianda, and broke into a run, launching herself at the startled guards at the last minute. Her body seemed to glitter in midair as her legs elongated into a muscular, scale-covered tail, and she slammed into the first three men like a battering ram, her momentum and increased weight bringing them all crashing to the ground. Still on top of the first three men, she slammed her tail into a fourth, sending him into the nearby wall.

"Get in here!" she roared.

I got.

Playing nice was no longer an option: I was weak from blood loss and withdrawal, and I wasn't sure Dianda would be able to shift back into her bipedal form, which meant she might be a fish out of water for the rest of the fight. I kneed one guard solidly in the nuts. He crumpled, and I hit him on the back of the neck for good measure. Dianda, meanwhile, was simply hitting her four with her tail over and over again, looking entirely too gleeful about the situation.

"She really did just want something to hit," I muttered, turning toward the final guard. She was clutching her spear with both hands, a terrified expression on her face. I guess she didn't see rampaging mermaids and blood-drenched hoodlums every day. "Hi," I said. "You look like a nice girl. Run away now, nice girl, and we'll pretend we didn't see you go."

I didn't have to tell her twice. She whirled and ran, leaving her spear to clatter to the floor. A wave of dizzy grayness washed over me. I slumped against the wall, putting a hand over the wound at my side. "Yeah," I said faintly. "You better run."

"October?" Dianda's voice was very far away. "Are you all right?"

"No." I pushed myself away from the wall and moved to try the treasury door. It was locked. The thought of trying to pick it made me tired. "I need those keys you grabbed before."

She tossed me the key ring. It clattered to the floor at my feet, and it took me three tries to pick it up with my sticky, trembling fingers. The keyhole was large enough that I was able to eliminate half the keys before I even started testing them against the lock. The first three wouldn't turn. The fourth turned slightly, and then stopped, refusing to go any further.

The fifth key opened the lock.

My shoulders slumped in relief as I pushed the door open, letting the keys fall into the growing puddle of blood at my feet. Dianda was saying something, but I couldn't stop to listen. She would get up on her own. Or she wouldn't, and we'd deal with that when I knew whether or not this was the end of the line. My feet left bloody prints as I walked into the room.

Treasure—both recognizable and strange—was piled up on all sides. Bars of gold and platinum shared space with sacks of beans and jars of feathers. I shuffled forward, trying to spot the hope chest somewhere in the mess. The smell of blood was overwhelming everything.

Blood. I fumbled the baggie full of the Luidaeg's blood out of my pocket and managed to break the seal, spilling blood lozenges in all directions. I let them fall, focusing on the two that I had left in my hand. She knew the hope chests. They knew her.

Please, let this work without killing me, I thought, and put the lozenges into my mouth.

The kick of her blood slamming into me was even harder this time, maybe because I'd taken twice as much. It wanted to own me, and I couldn't let it, or I would be lost. I forced the forming memories aside, trying to focus the energy the blood was pumping through me. "Hope chest," I whispered. "Hope chest, hope chest . . ."

And there it was, a simple wooden box on a plain pedestal that I could suddenly recognize. I stumbled toward it, flashes of the Luidaeg's memories washing over me with every step. The Luidaeg and a blonde woman, kissing on a beach at sunset. The Luidaeg in a bog, watching smoke curl up against the stars, holding a little boy who had Blind Michael's eyes. The Luidaeg in the arms of a man with hair the color of twilight, blackness shot through with glints of gold and red and rose.

Then my hands touched the wood, my blood staining the delicate carvings, and I fell to the floor with the hope chest cradled in my arms, and nothing really mattered anymore. I didn't feel myself hit the floor.

I didn't feel anything.

TWENTY-FIVE

I OPENED MY EYES and found myself staring at the ceiling of my old apartment. "Okay," I muttered, sitting up and looking down at myself. I was in my long black Bourbon Room T-shirt, and I was lying on my four-poster bed from Mother's tower. The room was familiar and wrong at the same time, mixing aspects of my mortal and fae lives with maddened abandon. The shelves groaned with battered paperbacks and random knick-knacks alongside magic swords and jars full of fireflies. One of the windows looked out on the Summerlands, while the other showed a midday parking lot.

"I hate symbolism," I said, sliding out of the bed. At least nothing hurt. My wounds were gone, washed away by whatever process I'd started by touching the hope chest.

I *had* touched it, hadn't I? I couldn't quite remember whether I'd reached it in time. I walked toward the door, fighting the urge to touch my ears and see where my blood was balanced. This place seemed designed to tell me soon enough, and there was no point in rushing the inevitable.

Then I opened the door, and found myself looking at . . . myself. Mostly. The woman in the doorway was clearly a changeling, a little less fae than I had been at the start of the week, a lot less human than I'd been when I broke into the treasury. She was wearing my leather jacket, and had a knife in either hand. Her fingers were wrapped around the blades, hiding them, and their hilts were identical.

"Hi," she said, without preamble. "I'm you."

"I got that," I said, frowning. "What's going on? Am I going to have some kind of messed-up vision every time I need to change my blood?"

"Maybe," she said. "It's not like this is ground that's been walked before. Most blood magic comes with visions of a sort, so you could call this more of the same. How do you feel?"

"Weak."

"That's because you're bleeding to death." She held the knives out toward me, hilt first. "Pick one."

I blinked. "That's it? That's the wisdom of this particular stupid vision? 'Pick one'?"

"The hope chest responds to intent, and right now, you don't have any; you're too far gone," she said, still holding the knives out. "You could actually say that this moment, right here, is both you fighting your own blood, and you fighting the hope chest. Part of you wants to be human. Let the goblin fruit carry you away on a tide of sweet, sweet dreams that leave you dead. Part of you wants to be fae. Stop making this choice, stop taking this risk. So pick a knife. If you get the silver, you're fae. If you get the iron, you're human. Either way, you'll have made a decision—you'll have given the hope chest the intent it needs to work."

"Are you messing with me?"

She shook her head. "No. I'm offering you a fifty-fifty chance at survival. And that's better than you'll have if you don't pick a knife soon. There's only so much blood in your body, and you're not regenerating. Come on. Choose while there's still time for it to matter."

The knives were identical, and she was holding them the same distance from her body. Nothing about her position hinted at which one I should take.

"What do I do after I have it?" I asked.

"Stab yourself."

". . . of course I have to stab myself," I muttered. "This day just gets better and better."

"Don't stall," she snapped abruptly. I blinked. She scowled. "If you bleed to death, I die with you. So stop messing around and fix this. I don't want to die. I'm not ready. I have too much left to do."

"But if I pick the wrong knife—"

"If you pick the wrong knife, Faerie had better find a new hero."

I stared at her for a few precious seconds before turning my attention to the knives in her hands. They gave no external clues, nothing that might help me know which one I wanted.

But then, I've never been very good at choosing just one. I reached out and grabbed both knives before she had a chance to react, pulling them from her hands. The motion left her fingers cut and bleeding, freeing the smell of blood to invade the room. I took a deep breath, letting the blood strengthen me, turned the knives around in my hands, and drove them into my stomach in a single gesture. I never did see which was which. It didn't seem to matter.

The pain was sudden and immense, expanding to fill the entire world. The last thing I saw before I fell was my own face smiling at me from the doorway. She looked approving. I wanted to yell at her. If there was a right choice, why couldn't she just tell me that and skip the stupid riddles? But falling seemed much more important than arguing. I hit the floor on knees I could barely feel through the pain washing through my body.

The knives. The knives. I needed to . . . I needed . . . I yanked the knives out of my stomach before the blackness could take me. And then I closed my eyes, letting myself go limp. Dying hurt. I did not approve. I did not—

A hand closed on my shoulder, fingers surprisingly solid despite the remaining haze. "Toby? October? Are you all right?" Dianda sounded worried. I couldn't blame her. From the smell of things, there wasn't much blood left *in* me, but there was a lot of it *around* me. "Hey. Don't be dead. I'm pretty sure it'll count as a declaration of war if you're dead."

"No such luck," I rasped. Until I spoke, I hadn't been quite sure I still had a mouth. It tasted like blood, just like everything else. I swallowed, trying to clear the taste away, and opened my eyes to find Dianda—still finned and scaled—on the floor next to where I'd fallen. I blinked. "Did you crawl here?"

"I need water before I can shift back," she said. "Are you all right?"

"I . . . I don't know." I sat up, waiting for a flare of pain. Nothing happened. I reached for my side, slipping my hand through the cut in my clothing to feel smooth, un-damaged skin. Sitting up a bit straighter, I pulled my hand free, wiped it on my jeans, and reached up to brush my hair back.

My fingers hit the sharp edge of my ear. Not pure-blood-sharp, but the angle I was used to. I took a deep breath, swallowing the urge to shout with joy. "I think I'm—" I began, and stopped as pain shot through my left side. I doubled over, clapping my hands over the wound I knew had to be there.

They found the hilt of my iron knife. Fighting to focus, I wrenched the blade from its scabbard and flung it across the room. It clattered against a pile of golden coins before vanishing behind them. I pulled up my shirt and pulled down the waistband of my jeans. There was a welt where the knife had been close to my skin, and un-like the rest of my injuries, it wasn't healing.

"I'm *definitely* back to normal," I said, and stood, tucking the hope chest under my arm. Maybe more than normal. I felt less human than ever before, although I'd managed to hang on to some of my humanity. I knew the balance of my own blood well enough to be sure of that.

Worrying about what I'd done to myself could come later. For the moment, I had allies to worry about. "I'm going to get you some water," I said.

To my surprise, Dianda shook her head. "No. There's bound to be something in here," she waved a hand to indicate the treasury, "that makes water out of nothing, or never dries up, or whatever. I'll find it. Go save your cat."

Tybalt. Fear washed over me, and I nodded. "All right," I said. "I'll be back as soon as I can." I didn't wait for her response. I was off and running, my feet squelching through the blood trail I'd left earlier. Even in her current form, Dianda could fight off any guards that came for her. She was a Duchess in the Undersea; they based titles off the ability to hold them. She'd be fine. Tybalt needed me.

How long had it been? How long had it taken me to change my blood back to normal, how long for Dianda to pull herself across the treasury floor to where I was huddled around the hope chest? How *long*? I ran, heading as fast as I could for the dungeon door. My feet slid on the blood-slick stone floor. I slammed my hip against a corner and kept on running, feeling the pain first spread through me and then recede, pulled back by the power in my blood.

I couldn't properly enjoy my body being my own again. I was too busy running, my mind already playing through the worst possible scenarios. Most of them were terrifyingly simple: I'd get there and the night-haunts would be gone, and the next time I saw the flock, there would be a diminutive figure with Tybalt's eyes among their number.

The door to the dungeon was unguarded; the guards Dianda and I had taken down were gone. Whether gone meant "away" or "down," I didn't know, and didn't care. I yanked the door open and ran into the dark without care for how badly I might hurt myself. It didn't matter. All that mattered was getting there in time to save him.

The door to Dianda's cell was open. That was a good sign: if the guards had been down here, they would have closed it. I kept running until I turned the final corner and stopped dead. The bottom seemed to drop out of the world, leaving me alone in the darkness. Tybalt was there, unmoving, lying in exactly the position he'd been in when I left him.

But the night-haunts were gone.

Moving slowly now, like the air had been replaced by thick goo, I walked toward him. He still looked fae. Night-haunts usually replaced the dead with human-seeming shells. Would they have bothered with that here, in a knowe, where his body would never be seen by the mortal world? It didn't make sense, from a logical stand-point—but since when was Faerie logical? Maybe they'd left one just to mess with me.

"It isn't fair," I whispered.

"It never is," replied Devin's voice. I whipped around to find the two night-haunts hovering behind me. Connor's haunt wouldn't meet my eyes.

I managed to fight the urge to slap them out of the air. "Is he alive?"

"For now," said the Devin-haunt, looking me up and down. "I see you've found yourself again. Our part in things is done. Whether he lives or not, you owe us."

"I know," I said, and turned my back on them. I walked the last few steps to Tybalt, kneeling beside him on the cold stone floor, and reached out to stroke his cheek. My fingers left bloody trails behind them. "Hey," I said. "Hey, you need to wake up. It's time to save the Prince, defeat the evil Queen, and go on a vacation. I hear Hawaii is nice this time of year. I'll go there with you. I'll go anywhere with you. Come on, kitty-cat. Wake up."

He didn't respond. I glanced over my shoulder to the night-haunts. They were hovering there, watching me. Connor's haunt made a small gesture with his hand, like he was pulling power out of the air. That was all.

My power has never been in the air. I turned to Ty-balt, taking a deep breath, and raised my hand to my mouth, licking the blood off of my palm. There was enough there that I didn't need to cut myself. My magic responded instantly, thundering down on me in a cascading wave of cut grass and bloody copper. I gathered it all, holding it like a snake that wanted to escape, and bent to press my lips to Tybalt's.

Directing a spell means telling the magic where you want it to go. This time, as I kissed him, I told the magic I wanted it to go into his body. I gave it freely and without restraint, trying to push it away from me as hard as I could. *Come on, Tybalt,* I thought, half-begging, half-praying. *Take it. Please, take it, and open your eyes. Come on . . .*

Even with the blood, my magic wasn't limitless. I kept forcing it away from me, but there was only so much I could do, and the end was nearing. I gathered what strength I could and pushed it into him. *Please.*

With a choking gasp, Tybalt started breathing.

His arms rose, closing around me, and my one-sided kiss became something more as he kissed me back. I sighed with relief as I let the last of my magic go, fading into the dungeon air. Finally, I leaned in and let my forehead rest against his. His eyes were open. I had never seen anything so beautiful.

"Hi," I said.

"Hello," he said. Then he blinked, and frowned. "You are *covered* in blood. And your eyes . . ." His eyes widened. "Your eyes are your own. October, did you find it?"

"I did." I pulled away, holding up the hope chest. "I couldn't find the user's manual that goes with it, but I think I did okay. Are *you* okay?"

"Tired. Sore. What happened?"

I climbed to my feet, offering my free hand. "The Queen tightened her wards after our last jailbreak. The strain of carrying me through them nearly killed you."

"Ah." He took my hand and stood. "Then it's a good thing you found the hope chest on your own."

"Not entirely on my own. Dianda's in the treasury."

He blinked. "Why did she not return here with you?"

"She's sort of a fish from the waist down at the moment. And she's got a moderate case of iron poisoning, so she needs water before she can shift back."

"I miss so much when I'm unconscious," he said.

I laughed, turning to lead him out of the dungeon. I was unsurprised to see that the night-haunts were gone. Together we walked back to the stairs and up into the hall. One of the Queen's guards was waiting there. I didn't see Tybalt move. One moment, he was standing beside me, the next, he was holding the guard off the floor by the throat.

"You really like that move, don't you?" I asked, continuing to walk. The guard thrashed as Tybalt cut off his oxygen supply. "Just don't kill him. We're not breaking Oberon's Law today."

"You are *covered in blood*," Tybalt said again, stressing the words harder this time. "It makes me tense." There was a thud as the guard hit the floor, and Tybalt returned to my side.

"Wow. You must be tense a lot."

He sighed. "You have no idea."

I thought of how terrified I'd been when he wouldn't wake up, and shook my head. "I think I have *some* idea," I said, and kept walking.

No more guards appeared as we walked toward the treasury. A large floral display was set up on one of the small tables in the hall. I grabbed it, dumping the flowers on the floor. If Dianda hadn't been able to find water in the treasury, maybe this would be enough.

The reason for the lack of guards became clearer as we neared the treasury. Angry voices were coming from the room, and several sets of tracks ran through the blood trail that I'd left behind me. Tybalt and I exchanged a look.

"*Please* don't kill anyone," I said.

"I will do my best," he replied, and ran ahead of me into the treasury. The angry voices promptly acquired a note of panic. I guess adding an angry Cait Sidhe with some aggression he needed to work off had changed the character of their party. I didn't bother hurrying. Those poor guards were already in enough trouble.

When I stepped inside, I found four guards on the

floor, two more trying to reach Dianda without being hit by her expertly-swung tail, and another being held off the floor by a snarling Tybalt. I stepped around the bodies, stopping just outside of Dianda's hitting range and holding up the vase. "I found you some water," I said.

"Oh, good." She slammed her tail into one of the guards. He toppled over. She took aim at the other. "Hold on to it for right now, I'll get it in a second."

"Okay." I turned to survey the guards on the floor. Two of them appeared to be conscious. One was wearing a very fancy tunic. That probably made him part of the chain of command, although I couldn't have guessed at his rank. I knelt beside him, smiling. "Hi."

His eyes widened. Being smiled at by a bloody, too-calm woman in the middle of a pitched battle was probably a little disconcerting. "You are under arrest in the name of Her Majesty the Queen," he said, his voice shaking.

"Mmm, no, I'm not," I replied. "Her Majesty, Queen Arden Windermere in the Mists, sent me. This is an illegal holding. The Queen who's been doing business here? Turns out she's a fake. Who knew, right?" I leaned closer. "Your mistress has gone to answer Arden's challenge. This is your chance. Change allegiances now, stop attacking us, and we'll tell Arden you helped. Don't ..." I glanced over my shoulder at Tybalt. He had grabbed Dianda's other attacker, and was slamming her against the wall. I turned back to the guard. "Well, you can see what happens if you don't."

The guard looked at me for a few long moments. I looked back, not allowing myself to break eye contact. I was gambling on his loyalty to the Queen being weak — something that wasn't much of a stretch, given the way she treated everyone I'd ever seen her interacting with.

Finally, he said, "Help me up."

"Are you going to try to take me hostage?" I asked, as I took his hand and helped him climb awkwardly to his feet. "Because that would really be a lousy move on your part."

"I know who you are, daughter of Amandine," said the guard. He let go of my hand, turning to the rest of the room. "In the name of Her Majesty, the Queen of the Mists, I order you to stand down."

"Your Queen is a fake," said Dianda, propping herself up on one elbow and glowering.

"My fealty is sworn only to the throne, not to she who sits upon it," the guard replied. "Long live Queen Arden Windermere of the Mists."

The other guards—the ones who were still conscious, anyway, which wasn't most of them—turned to stare at him. Tybalt kindly stopped using his guard as a basketball, releasing the woman to stagger back to her feet and frown at her superior officer.

"How many troops did the Queen leave to hold the knowe?" I asked.

"Thirteen," said the guard. "I am the ranking member of the guard still here."

"Good. Then you can let the rest know that there's been a regime change." I smiled thinly, aware of just how ghoulish that had to look, considering my current condition. "If the old Queen tries to retreat, she's going to find herself with nowhere she can retreat *to*."

"Impressive as it is to watch you erode the loyalties of everyone around you, can I get that water now?" asked Dianda.

"Of course." I walked over and handed her the vase. Dianda dumped its contents over her head, washing away some of the blood—and all of her scales. Her tail disappeared as the water ran along her body, replaced by bare, bloody legs.

"Much better." She dropped the vase to the floor. It shattered. She climbed to her feet and said, "As the ranking noble—no offense, Tybalt—"

"None taken." He sounded amused.

"Good. As I was saying, as the ranking noble currently present, I claim this knowe in the name of Arden Windermere, rightful Queen in the Mists. Do not challenge me. I am out of patience, and I have *such* a headache."

"That'll be the iron," I said. I turned to the guard. "We need an alchemist. She's been in your dungeon long enough to get sick, and since she's not committing treason by backing the rightful monarch, that's technically a declaration of war against the Undersea."

"You people are certainly fond of declaring war against the Undersea by mistake," said Tybalt. "I am pleased the Court of Cats has not managed to do this during my tenure."

"We live in interesting times." I moved to stand beside him. The guards were groaning as they woke up. "We found the hope chest and Dianda, and we technically just conquered the Queen's knowe."

"Yes. Not to mention the rest of it." Tybalt ran a finger along the sharpened peak of my ear.

I smiled. "Yeah, there's that, too. I'm hungry, even." And not for goblin fruit. I wanted a steak. Rare, if not raw. My body had a lot of blood to build back up. "So let's find Nolan while Dianda gets patched up, grab a sandwich, and then head back over to Muir Woods. We have ourselves a war to win."

Tybalt looked surprised. Then, slowly, he smiled back. "Why, October," he said. "I thought you'd never ask."

TWENTY-SIX

FINDING NOLAN MEANT RETURNING to the dungeons. It hurt this time, the iron in the walls singing to my blood and sending a bruised ache through my entire body. It probably hurt when I was going back for Tybalt, too, but I'd been too panicked to notice. Stress is helpful that way. When I need to ignore something unpleasant, I just work myself into a fine frenzy and charge. I realize it was stupid later, when I have time.

Dianda stayed in the treasury while Tybalt and I followed one of the Queen's guards—or former guards, if they were serious about defecting, and not just trying for a double-cross—into the dark. There's not much iron in the Undersea. She was putting on a stoic face, but I knew it had to be hurting her, and more exposure wouldn't have done anyone any good.

As for the guard, he looked uncomfortable about the fact that I hadn't wiped the blood off myself. It was drying in a thick, slightly tacky film. I could feel it cracking at the corners of my mouth every time I spoke. As long as I didn't have to look at it, it didn't bother me. I might need it, and I didn't feel like cutting myself again if I was already conveniently coated in gore. Besides, this was one of the men who'd imprisoned me—and Dianda—without hesitation when he was given the order.

Faerie is a feudal society. That doesn't mean I have to like it.

Tybalt matched my stride. I glanced at him out of the corner of my eye, trying to assess his condition. He'd apparently been waiting for that. He met my gaze, giving a small, imperious lift of one eyebrow. I smiled wryly, the blood around my mouth cracking again.

"Sorry," I said. "I'm a little, you know. Shaken."

"It's good for you to sample your own medicine from time to time," he said. "Perhaps the memory of your current feelings will motivate you to run heedlessly into danger with a bit less frequency."

I thought about that as we walked. Finally, I shook my head. "No, probably not."

Tybalt smirked.

Further conversation was cut off as the guard at the lead of our small procession stopped. There was a narrow, iron-banded door on the other side of the hall. "We're here," he said.

"Where's here?" I asked, frowning at the door. "This isn't a normal cell."

"No," he said. "The Queen's . . . I'm sorry, I don't know what else to call her. My former liege's instructions were very clear. The prisoner was placed in seclusion, to prevent his plotting further insurrection."

"Um, one, Dianda was a lot more likely to plot insurrection, since she was pissed off and also technically isn't under the jurisdiction of *any* Queen of the Mists, and two, Nolan's been *elf-shot*. He can't plot anything, unless it's a really epic snore." I glared at the guard. He squirmed. I glare well. I glare even better when I'm covered in blood. "What's down there that makes it worse than the cells up here?"

"That is where prisoners who must be kept . . . calm . . . are confined," said the guard. "The room keeps them . . . calm."

He looked so uncomfortable, and so unhappy, that I yielded, asking, "You weren't happy about putting him down there, were you?"

"Milady, had I been given any other alternative, I would have taken it."

I nodded. "Arden may be more forgiving because of that, *if* we get her brother back alive. So what, exactly, is down there that keeps people euphemistically 'calm'?"

Looking more miserable by the second, the guard said, "Iron."

The whole dungeon was dripping with iron. My skin crawled even standing here, and I was part human. I frowned. "That's not a sufficient answer."

"*Lots* of iron."

He was standing as far away from the door as it was possible to be while still existing in the same stretch of hall. I frowned again before eyeing the door.

"How much iron are we talking here?"

He didn't answer.

Oberon's Law says purebloods aren't allowed to kill each other. But that law is enforced by the purebloods, and they've had a long time to find loopholes. It says nothing about torture, for example, or about accidental death—say, from an overdose of iron. "How did you get him down there?"

"The Queen retains changelings on her staff for matters such as these."

I didn't bother correcting him on the former Queen's status. Seeing her get her ass handed to her would be correction enough, and I had other things to worry about. "I don't believe I'm doing this," I muttered, and handed the hope chest to Tybalt. "Don't let anyone touch this."

He frowned. "October . . ."

"My father was human. I can do this."

"Your father was human, but less than half your blood remembers that. Can you carry Nolan on your own?"

"We're going to find out, because you're *not* going down there." I pointed to the door. "You were damn near dead before. I can handle that once in a night—I nearly die on you all the time, turnabout is fair play—but

I *can't* do it twice. I'm stronger than I look, I can get him into a fireman's carry, and most importantly, I stand half a chance in hell of making it back alive."

Tybalt shook his head. "Insufferable woman," he said, and leaned forward to kiss me, ignoring the blood smeared around my mouth. I kissed him back, but only for a few seconds; just long enough to show that I meant it, not long enough that it turned into wasting time.

"Wish me luck," I said, pulling away.

"If there is one thing I have never known you to need, October, it's luck," he said.

"There's a first time for everything." I turned to the guard. "Open the door."

"I don't think you understand—"

"Look. Tonight, I have changed the balance of my own blood, brought my boyfriend back from the brink of death, and helped a mermaid kick all your asses," I snapped. "And that's just since I *got here*. You want to see me annoyed? Then go ahead, explain how dangerous this is. But if you want the nice, incredibly irritated woman to stop making you the target of her anger, you will open. That. Door."

"Yes, milady," he said, and moved to unlock the door. Tybalt snickered. I didn't dignify that reaction by looking at him.

Besides, if I had, I'd probably have started snickering, too, and that would have undermined the aura of badass that I was trying to project.

A wash of cold air smelling of iron and rotten straw rushed out as the guard pulled the door open. It made the air in the dungeon hallway seem fresh by comparison. I choked, trying to wave the smell away, and turned to see what the way down would look like. Then I stopped, blinking.

"What in the name of Oberon's ass is *that*?" I demanded.

"The stairs, milady," said the guard. Now that the door was open, he was back on the other side of the hall. I couldn't blame him. I wanted to join him, really, but that option wasn't available at the moment. "There is only one cell, at the bottom."

At least I wasn't going to be descending into the dark again. The stairs on the other side of the door were white marble that matched the main receiving hall, with a polished copper banister. They curved gently down into a stairwell that would have been dim before I used the hope chest, but now seemed reasonably well-lit. If not for the rancid, iron-soaked air rising from the bottom of the stairs, I would have thought it was just another hall.

"I've always wanted to try this," I said, to no one in particular.

"Milady?"

I think Tybalt realized what I was about to do as I started running for the door. I heard him groan. Then my foot was hitting the top step, and I no longer had the attention to sparc. I grabbed the banister, and slung my leg over the smooth copper path. I looked back as I started to slide. The last thing I saw as I accelerated down the stairs was the guard, staring at me in bewilderment, and Tybalt, shaking his head in obvious amusement. Then I turned, and focused on what was ahead of me.

Riding a banister down an unknown number of steps is more nerve-racking than I'd ever guessed it would be. I clung onto it with both hands, using the friction from my fingers to slow myself as much as I could. It wasn't much. Gravity had me now, and gravity wanted me to pay for my sins.

Whatever they were, I hoped I'd be done paying for them soon. The sliding uncontrollably down into an iron-filled dungeon was unique enough to be interesting, but I'd be carrying Nolan back up every one of those stairs. Plus, I had no brakes. I was just going to have to wait for the moment when something stopped me.

"I hope it's a wall," I muttered. The wind generated by my slide whipped my words away, and I slid on in silence. I was just starting to think I'd made a serious mistake when the banister came to an cnd. For a few dazzling seconds, I wasn't falling anymore—I was *flying*.

And then I slammed into the floor, cracking my head against it, and the world went away, replaced by a field of dazzling white agony. I groaned, struggling to sit up. My palms pressed flat against the floor, and a sizzling sound hit my ears a second before the pain raced up my arms. I scrambled to my feet, finally fully registering the hellish scene around me.

The room was made entirely of iron.

The stairs were marble, as was a narrow path wending from the bottom step to the room's single door. Everything else, the walls, the floor, even the chandelier hanging above me, was made of iron. I dove for the path.

"What in name of the root and the branch?" I whimpered, taking only a trickle of comfort in the profanity. This much iron wasn't cruelty; it was a passive assassination attempt. No pureblood could have survived the fall I'd just taken, even if they healed with my preternatural speed. The iron would have damaged them too much, and they'd never have made it back to the path. As it was, my head was throbbing, and my cheek felt like it was starting to blister. The iron in this room was thick enough that I wasn't healing.

That just meant I needed to get out of here. Keeping my feet within the narrow bounds of the marble path, I started for the door.

"This is stupid," I muttered. "This isn't even good stupid. This is Bond villain stupid. This is *Willy Wonka* stupid. Who keeps a pit full of their personal Kryptonite in their own damn *house*? It's stupid. If we weren't already deposing her, I'd be tempted, just because this is so *stupid*."

Muttering helped. It was easier to stay angry when I muttered, and staying angry helped keep me from focusing on the pain that was threatening to consume my entire body. My lungs hurt, too, aching from the iron I was pulling in with every single breath.

The door wasn't locked. I suppose there was no good reason it should have been. Anyone who'd been in this place for more than an hour wouldn't have had the strength to get up and open it.

The chamber on the other side was small, and like the room before it, was completely encased in iron. The marble path extended into the chamber, stopping and widening slightly at the center, into a circle almost large enough to let a human-sized bipedal adult sit down comfortably. Danny would have been forced to stand or burn if he'd been thrown in here.

Ironically, Nolan's elf-shot condition had put him into a better state than most. He was still asleep, and was stretched out on the path, with his head on the marble at the center of the circle. "Let's go," I muttered, grabbing his ankles. He could have died from iron poisoning. He still might, if he didn't get care. But by not depositing him directly on the iron, the Queen's men retained enough deniability that neither they, nor their mistress, could be charged with a breach of the Law.

It was conniving and spiteful, and I was going to have one hell of a time not hitting someone when I finally managed to get Nolan up the stairs.

My head was spinning from the iron, and dragging him along the marble path was a slow, difficult process, made harder by the fact that I was starting to have trouble breathing. I let go of him as soon as we were back in the main room, putting my hands against my knees and bending double as I struggled against the dizziness and gray blurriness threatening to overwhelm me. Everything was turning fuzzy, and my head was still throbbing. My foot had gone numb. That was probably a blessing in disguise.

"Think, October." What did I have? I had a silver knife. I had a leather jacket. I had the remaining blood lozenges. I had—

Blood lozenges. The blood in my veins was thick with iron, but Walther had frozen some of it before I was exposed. The blood gems might be tainted with goblin fruit. That was okay. I had the hope chest now; I could fix it. I withdrew the baggie from my pocket, undoing the seal. I couldn't seem to make my shaking fingers close on a single gem. Finally, I shook my head, muttered, "Fuck it," and dumped the remaining contents of the baggie into my mouth.

As before, the blood gems dissolved when they hit my tongue, leaving behind the taste of mint and lavender. That was the only thing that was like before, because then, I'd been trying to keep myself standing. I'd been mostly human. Now, I was more fae than I'd ever been, and I was looking for strength. The blood, dilute as it was, was happy to give it to me.

Feeling flooded back into my feet and hands as the bruises from my impact with the floor healed. Unfortunately, since no amount of blood could make me immune to iron, the feeling consisted mostly of pain. I didn't have time to worry about that. I could feel the blood flowing through me, strengthening me. I could also feel how little time I had. More of my strength than I'd realized was going toward keeping me upright against the onslaught of iron.

"Come on, Sleeping Beauty," I said, and bent, struggling to hoist Nolan into a fireman's carry. He was a relatively short man, only a few inches taller than I was, and he was slender—spending a few decades asleep is a hell of a diet plan, even for the immortal. That didn't make it any easier to deadlift him from the floor onto my shoulders.

When he was finally in place I turned, staggering, and hissed as the edge of my foot slipped off the marble path onto the iron. I pulled it back, regarding the stairs with the sort of loathing customarily reserved for my worst enemies. In that moment, I hated them more than I'd hated anything else in years.

"You'd better be worth it, Your Highness," I said, and started to climb.

It said something about the oppressive weight of iron at the bottom of the stairs that I actually started to feel a little better as I climbed. The air was still chokingly laced with the stuff, and it would kill me if I stayed too long, but it was better than what we were walking away from.

"Arden needs to fucking bury this place," I muttered, forcing myself to take another step, and another step after that. Every time I put my foot down was agony, like I was walking through a field of broken glass. I kept going. I hadn't come this far, and fought my way through this much, to fall to something as passively dangerous as a room full of iron and a Prince who seemed to be getting heavier by the second.

I didn't know how long I'd been climbing, or how far I had left to go, but I knew this much: I was getting tired. "Hello?" I called, as loudly as I could. "A little help here?"

"October?" Tybalt's answering shout sounded distant. Too distant. "Are you hurt?"

"No, I'm having a damn vacation!" The amount of iron exposure he could get by coming down and helping me carry Nolan the rest of the way would be negligible compared to what I'd already subjected myself to. "Help!"

"I'm coming!"

"Good," I muttered, and kept plodding on. It was less a matter of thinking I could meet him halfway and more the simple fact that if I stopped, I wasn't sure I'd be able to start again.

I'd gone ten steps when Tybalt came around the curve above me, the hope chest still tucked underneath his arm. He paused, swore, and moved to take half of Nolan's weight onto himself with his free arm, relieving my burden enough that I was able to straighten up for the first time since, oh, the ground floor.

"Hey," I said. "Took you long enough."

"I was waiting to be invited." Tybalt adjusted his hold on Nolan, shifting the Prince's weight a bit more, and matched my stride as we walked together up the remaining stairs. "You do get cranky when I insert myself into your life-threatening situations without consent."

"It's a character flaw." The blood I'd borrowed from my past self was running out, and it was getting hard to breathe again. "How far are we from the top?"

"About fifty steps."

Judging by how many I'd already climbed, that meant we were still a little more than halfway down. "Swell," I muttered, gritting my teeth, and climbed.

The next forty steps passed without incident, either good or bad. Tybalt turned pale and started to sweat as the iron wore away at him. I managed to keep walking, but my breath was growing shallower, and every time I exhaled, I was afraid I wasn't going to be able to find the strength to inhale again. It was all I could do to keep putting one foot in front of another.

We rounded the final curve to see the man from the Queen's guard standing in the open doorway, staring down at us.

"Hey!" I called. "Come down here and help us carry this guy!"

"Some of us remember the meaning of loyalty," he responded.

The iron was clouding my reactions enough that it took me a few precious seconds to realize what he was saying. "No!" I shouted, and lunged, trusting Tybalt to keep Nolan from falling back down to the bottom of the stairs.

I was too slow, and the distance was too great. I reached the door a split second after the guard—who was still the Queen's man after all—slammed it shut. As I impacted with the wood, I heard the small, terrible sound of a key turning in a lock.

We were trapped.

TWENTY-SEVEN

"**H**E LOCKED US IN HERE," I whispered. "Oh, sweet Oberon, he locked us *in*." I was dimly aware that Tybalt was trudging up the stairs behind me, but in that moment, I didn't have the capacity to care. If he needed help, he would ask for it, and I . . . I needed to think. I needed to find a way out of this. The lock. I could pick the lock, I could—

There was no keyhole on this side of the door. No one sealed inside was ever intended to make their way out under their own power, and anyone who was sent to retrieve a prisoner would of necessity have a team of people waiting to pull them out if they succumbed to iron poisoning. There was no reason to put a keyhole *inside* the prison.

"*Now* they get smart about their dungeon design?" I turned to see Tybalt stepping onto the landing. "We're trapped. He double-crossed us, and we're trapped."

"I know," he said. He sounded calmer than I did, but I could see the panic gnawing at the edges of his composure. If he was keeping it in check, it was only because he knew that letting go would result in completely losing control. Like most cats, he didn't like being boxed in.

Boxed in . . . "Tybalt, can you access the Shadow Roads from here?"

"No. There's too much iron." He walked past me to prop Nolan against the wall. This high up, it was just iron-laced stone, no more dangerous than the air. Then he turned to me, holding out his free arm in a mute plea.

It was one that I was more than happy to answer. I stepped forward, and he wrapped his arm around me, kissing my forehead before resting his head against my shoulder. We stood there, shivering, holding each other up.

I don't know how long we'd been standing that way when he said, "I need you to do something for me, October."

"What?"

"The hope chest. I need you to use it on yourself."

I pulled away from him, eyes wide. "What?"

"I asked you this the last time I saved you from this dungeon: please, for me, make yourself human." He let me go in order to hold out the hope chest. "The iron can't kill you if it can't hurt you."

"Tybalt, no."

"Please—"

"I said *no*!" I held up my hands. "Oak and ash, we just spent how long turning me fae, and you want me to undo everything so you don't have to watch me die? You think I should have to watch *you* die? Was there a contest somewhere along the way to decide who loved who more, and I lost? I won't do it. I'm not going to change myself just to survive a little bit longer."

"But we know you can use the hope chest," he said, pleading. "You don't have to turn all the way human. Just enough to buy yourself some time, and let you figure out another way . . ."

"If I tell that chest I want to be human, it's not going to stop," I shot back. "I've never touched it when I was this weak. I won't be able to control it, and it'll burn the fae right out of me. We don't even know if the goblin fruit is still in my system! Maybe I'd just be condemning myself to an even worse death, with no escape clause. And it doesn't matter, because I won't do it. I won't leave you like that. I can't. Stop asking me."

"Oh, October." He pulled the hope chest away again. I've never been so relieved by such a little gesture. Then he chuckled. "Sometimes I wonder if we're good for one another."

"Are you kidding?" I asked, forcing a smile. "We're *great* for one another. Who else would show you awesome things like the Queen's secret iron torture room? Admit it. I'm the best girlfriend you could ask for."

"You are definitely the only girlfriend I have asked for in a long time," said Tybalt. He put his head back down my shoulder, sighing. "This seems like a very anticlimactic death. I am afraid I do not approve."

"Yeah. Me neither." I closed my eyes. We were all going to die in here. A Cait Sidhe, a Dóchas Sidhe, and a Tuatha de Dannan, and there was nothing we could do to save ourselves.

My eyes snapped open.

"I can do this," I breathed, and pulled away, pulling the knife from my belt in the same gesture. Tybalt looked at me in alarm. I shook my head. "No, not that. I mean, I'm not going to stab you. I mean . . . look, if this works, be ready to move."

"October?" he asked, bemused.

"No time." I knelt next to Nolan, grabbing his hand and turning it, palm upward, in mine. Then, as carefully as I could under the circumstances, I slashed a line across the meaty part of his thumb and clamped my mouth down over it.

A red veil slammed down over my perceptions as Nolan's memories overwhelmed my reality. *Arden doesn't want to challenge for the throne, but she's wrong. This woman isn't our sister, and she'll lead the Kingdom into ruin. If Arden won't listen, I'll go myself. For Father's sake, and for my sister's sake, because this so-called "Queen" will never leave us in peace—*

There was nothing there that I didn't already know, and so I forced my way past it, trying to filter through his disjointed, dreaming memories. I'd never done anything like this before, but I'd moved through memories, and the principle was the same: all I had to know was what I was looking for.

I found it buried in a memory of Nolan and Arden playing hide-and-seek through Muir Woods on a beautiful starry night years before I was born. They were chasing each other from tree to tree, and every time one of them was about to be tagged by the other, they would disappear, Arden leaving the scent of blackberry flowers and redwood bark in her wake, Nolan leaving the scent of fresh blackberries and sap. I grabbed the memory of that moment as hard as I could, clinging to it. This was just like pushing strength into Tybalt, or letting May guide me through changing one of the Queen's transformations. I could do this. I *could* do this.

Gathering every ounce of strength I could find in myself or borrow from Nolan, I raised my hand and transcribed a circle in the air. The smell of blackberries and sap followed my fingers, faint but there. I pulled my mouth away from Nolan's hand, and whispered, "Now."

Tybalt grabbed me a split second later, somehow managing to lift both me and Nolan off the floor as he leaped. He didn't have to hold us for long. The world dipped and wove—

—and we were landing hard, in a pool of something viscous and sticky. The smell of it hit me a moment after the floor did: blood. My blood, to be specific. We were in the treasury. Groaning, I pushed myself onto my elbows and opened my eyes to find Nolan sprawled a few feet away and Tybalt climbing to his feet. His eyes were wide. He looked stunned. I was proud of myself for that. It's hard to really shock Tybalt.

"What did you *do*?" he asked.

"Magic is in the blood. Nolan's magic includes teleportation," I said, holding out my hands. Tybalt tugged me to my feet. "I just borrowed it for a little bit."

"That is absolutely terrifying."

"Tell me about it." I turned to look at the room around us, my head throbbing in time with the motion. "This is a treasury. This is where you put rare and important things. If you had something that could treat iron poisoning, this is where you'd put it." The gray spots at the edge of my vision were intruding again, threatening to block everything out. I ignored them in favor of pulling my phone out of my pocket.

"What are you doing?"

"I'm calling information."

The phone was answered on the fourth ring. "Hello?"

"Li Qin, hi," I said. "Remember when you called the Library to ask if I could come in? I need that number."

"Toby? You sound terrible!"

I looked around the bloody, trashed treasury and fought the urge to laugh. That would have been taking black humor too far, even for me. "Things have been a little messy here."

"Is there really a challenge to the Queen's throne?"

I pinched the bridge of my nose, closing my eyes. "Okay, Li, I would *love* to explain everything right now, but I honestly can't, because I'm about to keel over from iron poisoning, as is Tybalt, as is the Crown Prince in the Mists. Please, *please*, can you just give me the number for the Library?"

"No," said Li.

"What?!" I opened my eyes to find Tybalt staring at me, apparently startled by my outburst.

"I'm sorry, but I can't—the Library doesn't have a number in that sense. But I can have Mags call you."

"Please," I said, swallowing the urge to yell. "Now." I hung up before Li Qin could ask any more questions. In my current mood, I would have started screaming, and that wouldn't have done either of us any good. Losing my temper would be just one more complication.

Speaking of complications . . . I looked around the treasury, feeling the pit drop out of my stomach, and finally voiced something that had been nagging at the edges of my awareness since we escaped the dungeon. "Where's Dianda?"

"There are two possibilities," said Tybalt. "Either she is unaware of the guard's duplicity and calmly awaiting our return, or she has been overpowered. No matter which it is, we will do her little good in our current condition."

"I know, but—" My phone rang. I answered without hesitation. "Hello?"

"Toby?" This time the voice was less familiar, and had a British accent. I let out a relieved breath, taking a split second of comfort before snapping back to business.

"Mags, Tybalt and I are in the royal treasury. We've both been exposed to a *lot* of iron—I'm not sure how we're still standing, but I don't think it's going to last much longer. Is there anything in here that we could use to treat the symptoms? Anything you've heard of the Queen confiscating, or that was traditionally in Gilad's custody?"

Mags paused. "You know, I don't usually get questions this interesting."

"I'm thrilled to have made your day more fun, but my day is the opposite of fun. Please. What should I be looking for?" If she said "nothing," that was it; we were done. The fuzziness was spreading, and we needed medical care if we wanted to avoid collapsing in the Queen's knowe and missing the fight completely.

"Um . . . there should be a gray earthenware flagon somewhere in there. The current Queen confiscated it from the reigning monarchs of the Kingdom of Silences when she overthrew their government. There will be a cruet with it."

"Hang on." I lowered the phone, turning to Tybalt. "Look for a gray earthenware flagon, and something called a 'cruet.' What the hell's a cruet?"

"A smaller pitcher, of a very specific design," said Tybalt, already moving away from me, toward the shelves. "Ask if they match."

I raised the phone. "Do they match?"

"Yes."

"They match!" I called. Into the phone, I said, "What do we do once we find them?"

"Fill the flagon from the cruet," she said. "It should be a thick green liquid. Drink it."

"That's always the answer when we're talking about thick green liquids, isn't it? Okay. We'll get right on that. If Quentin asks, tell him we're fine."

"Will I be lying?" Mags asked dubiously.

"Right now, I don't know. Open roads." I hung up before she could ask any more questions, turning to scan the room. It was a mess in here, a disorganized jumble of stolen treasures and unique artifacts that hadn't been well organized before we had a major fight in the middle of everything. There was a heap of what looked like old vases in one corner. I picked my way toward them, leaving bloody footprints behind me.

"It's not here," said Tybalt.

"Keep looking." I reached the vases and began moving them one by one, trying to reach the back of the pile. Something this important wouldn't be right out in the open. "Mags says it was confiscated from Silences. That would mean she took it, what, about five years after King Gilad died? Dig deeper."

He didn't say anything, but I heard things clatter behind me as he kept looking. I moved vase after vase, and was on the verge of giving up and looking somewhere else when I pulled the last vase away and revealed the base of what looked like a bookcase. It was covered by a gray silk sheet that had seemed somehow beneath notice until I actually focused on it. "Poor man's cloak of invisibility," I muttered, and pulled the sheet aside. Then I stared. "Holy . . ."

The bookcase the sheet had been concealing was the sort of thing that wouldn't have looked out of place in a royal bedroom. It was made of redwood, carved with a pattern of blackberry vines. "It matches Arden's wardrobe," I said, mostly to myself, and stepped closer to study the assortment of small, strange items piled on its shelves. There were gleaming jewels and jars of oddly-colored liquids . . . and on the third shelf from the bottom, there was a gray earthenware jug that I was willing to call a flagon, with a smaller, vase-like jug next to it. "Tybalt! Over here!"

I picked up the cruet with shaking hands, locking my fingers tight to keep from dropping it, and peered inside. It was empty. In Faerie, that doesn't necessarily mean anything. Leaning forward, I tipped the cruet onto its side over the flagon. Thick green liquid the color of radioactive wheatgrass poured out. It smelled like a mixture of maple syrup and overcooked broccoli. I wrinkled my nose and kept pouring. Tybalt stepped up next to me.

"Is that it?"

"I sure hope so," I replied, continuing to pour. "We're supposed to drink it."

Tybalt wrinkled his nose. "Delightful."

"It's better than dying." The flagon was full almost to the top. I righted the cruet, setting it back on the shelf before picking up the flagon with both hands. "Here goes nothing," I said, and raised it to my lips.

The liquid tasted worse than it smelled, adding library paste and overripe banana to the mix. I gagged but forced myself to keep drinking . . . and as I did, I felt my hands stop shaking. The throbbing, bruised feeling that filled my body faded, taking my headache with it. I kept drinking. The taste of the liquid changed, becoming sweeter. As the throbbing stopped, I swallowed a mouthful of what tasted like sugared raspberries and champagne.

I lowered the flagon, holding it out to Tybalt. "When it starts tasting good, you know it's working. I think. It feels like it worked."

"It worked," he said, and touched my cheek, smiling. "Your color is better, and you're breathing normally. It worked."

"Good." I held the flagon out more emphatically. "Now drink. I'm going to check on Nolan."

Tybalt nodded, finally taking the flagon. I stayed where I was long enough to see him start to drink—and to see the color start coming back into his cheeks—before walking back across the blood-splattered floor to Nolan. He was only half-lying in the pool of blood, I noticed, which wasn't going to stop Arden from freaking out when she saw him. I crouched, checking for a pulse. He still had one. That was something, anyway. He also had a vicious case of iron poisoning, if the taste I'd gotten of his blood was anything to go by.

"Bring that over when you're done," I said, shifting to maneuver Nolan into a sitting position. "We need to pour some of it down this guy's throat before he dies on us."

There was a pause while Tybalt finished swallowing. Then, as he walked toward me, he asked, "Is it safe to give liquids to an elf-shot victim? I'd fear drowning."

"Drowning is a possibility, death by iron is a guarantee. Hell, maybe we'll get lucky, and treating iron poisoning will treat elf shot, too." I held out my hand for the flagon. "Open his mouth."

"All right." Tybalt crouched on Nolan's other side, putting the flagon into my hand before reaching over and prying Nolan's mouth open.

"I don't know how aware you are, but please try not to drown," I said, and pressed the flagon to his lips, pouring just a little into his mouth before gesturing for Tybalt to close it. "Tilt his head back, see if he swallows."

Tybalt tilted Nolan's head back.

Nolan swallowed.

"Well, how about that," I said. "Okay. Let's do this."

Working together, we were able to feed Nolan the rest of the liquid in the flagon. Hopefully, that would be enough, and if not, he'd at least be able to hold up until we were in a position to offer further treatment. He didn't show any signs of waking up, either during the process or after. Guess that was too much to hope for. I put the cruet into my pocket and tucked the flagon under my arm before helping Tybalt lift Nolan off the floor. Now that we weren't dealing with an entire room full of iron, carrying him was a hell of a lot easier.

"Where now?" asked Tybalt.

"Find Dianda, punch the asshole that locked us in the dungeon, get the hell out of here," I said, and started walking.

The hall outside the treasury was deserted, but it wasn't difficult to know which way to go: Dianda hadn't been wearing shoes in her bipedal form. Her footprints were the only ones that were both bloody *and* bare. We followed them through the halls of the Queen's knowe, until we came to a pair of slightly-ajar double doors. There was only silence from the other side.

Cautiously, I pushed one of the doors further open, and found myself peering at a stretch of the Queen's receiving hall.

"*There* you are." It was Dianda's voice. She sounded perfectly fine. Restless, but fine. "I was getting bored."

I turned toward her voice, and blinked. She was sitting on a plain wooden chair, with seven of the Queen's guards behind her. The one who'd been the first to swear fealty to Arden was among them, I noted. Six more, including the man who'd tried to leave us for dead in the dungeon, were unconscious and tied up on the floor in front of her.

". . . okay, that works," I said. "We have a treatment for iron poisoning, and we have the Prince. We need to get moving. Does anybody have a car?" Treatment or not, I wasn't trusting the Shadow Roads until I'd seen Tybalt have a good night's sleep, and I doubted my ability to make Nolan teleport me more than a short distance. His control wasn't good when he was asleep.

"I do," said one of the guards, a diminutive female Glastig with a faint Welsh accent.

"Okay, we have a car. What's your name?"

"Lowri."

I paused, looking at her assessingly. "Were you recruited out of Silences?"

"After the fall, yes." She met my eyes without hesitation.

"Great." If she was a former member of the guard in Silences, she was a lot less likely to be loyal to the Queen, and that made it safer to get into a car with her. "Come on, guys. Let's blow this Popsicle stand."

Dianda frowned. "What's a Popsicle?"

I sighed. "Okay, see, that would have been a dramatic exit, but you had to go and spoil it. Come on. We need to get to Muir Woods before the fighting ends."

"Why?" asked one of the guards.

"I figure either they need us, or I'll get to see the bitch whose house this is," I indicated the room, "getting her ass handed to her. Either way I win."

"I'm out of things to hit anyway," said Dianda, and stood. "Let's go."

Leaving the six guards behind with their former fellows, Dianda, Tybalt, and I followed the Glastig out of the hall, still carrying Nolan between us. It was time to get to Muir Woods. It was time for us to end this.

TWENTY-EIGHT

LOWRI LED US OUT of the receiving hall and through the familiar rocky cave to the beach. We trudged across the beach to the parking lot, where only a few cars had stuck out the night without being ticketed or towed. I glanced toward the horizon, which was only just beginning to brighten with false dawn. Tybalt followed my gaze.

"We should have time to reach the woods," he said.

"If we don't hit traffic," I agreed.

"This is me," said Lowri, drawing our attention to a battered brown station wagon that looked like it had been manufactured sometime in the mid-1970s. Electrical tape held the back and front bumpers in place, and patched a large hole in the rear passenger-side door.

"I don't know *much* about human-world cars, but I'm pretty sure that's not a good one," said Dianda dubiously.

"Her Highness doesn't allow her guard to take jobs in the mortal world," said Lowri, digging keys out of her pocket. The human disguise she had crafted for herself concealed her hooves and goat-like ears, and made her royal livery look like jeans and an old green sweater. I wasn't sure where the pocket was on her actual clothing, and for once, I had the sense not to ask. "Surprisingly, most mechanics don't accept payment in dewdrops and moonbeams."

"But it runs?" asked Tybalt, eyeing the car.

"I can usually talk somebody who understands cars into a freebie when things get bad," she said. "It runs." Glastig are masters of persuasion. If Lowri focused on a mortal mechanic, they'd have no chance of telling her no.

Somehow, I couldn't find it in myself to judge her. We do what we have to in order to survive in this world. When your regent won't let you work, you find another way to keep body and soul together—no matter how unethical that may seem.

"Help me get Nolan into the back," I said, dragging the unconscious Prince the last few feet toward the car. "Dianda, can you ride with him?"

"Sure." She eyed Tybalt speculatively as she opened the car door. "Where's he going to ride? In the way back?"

"He's not going to ride at all," I said. "He's going to take the Shadow Roads to Muir Woods and find out what's happening there. That way, we're not walking in blind."

Tybalt shot me a look that was half gratitude, half annoyance, grabbing Nolan's knees and helping me hoist him into the backseat. "When were you intending to tell me I was doing this?"

"When you saw the car and realized you were too tired to deal with this shit." I guided Nolan into a seated position, fastening the belt across his waist. He slumped sideways. Dianda, who was in the process of getting into her own seat, pushed him upright again. "Taking the Shadow Roads alone shouldn't be too tiring. You can meet us at the parking lot with an update."

Tybalt eyed the car for a moment. Then he sighed. "I suppose some early reconnaissance would not be amiss. If she," he indicated Lowri, "proves to be another turncoat, please dispose of her before she can dispose of you."

"I promise," I said, and shut the car door. "See you in Muir Woods."

"Indeed." He turned and walked away, vanishing into the shadows at the edge of the parking lot.

I turned back to the car to find Lowri watching me. I shrugged. "He gets protective."

"It's not that," she said. "It's . . . I'd heard rumors that you were involved with the King of Cats? But I didn't credit them. Not because you're a changeling," she added hurriedly. "I've just never known a Cait Sidhe monarch to court outside the, um, well, Court."

"We're a special case," I said, getting into the car. "Do you know the way to Muir Woods?"

Lowri nodded.

"Good. Then drive."

It was late enough that the beginnings of the morning commute were trickling onto the roads, making the freeway a hit-or-miss proposition. I handed the flagon and cruet back to Dianda, telling her how to use them to treat her iron poisoning. Lowri drove like a native, choosing side streets and back alleys over congested intersections, and I closed my eyes, starting to relax. I was exhausted. Maybe some people can suffer a mortal wound, use a hope chest on themselves, get iron poisoning, and manipulate someone else's magic in a single night without getting tired, but I'm not one of them.

"Is this woman's claim to the throne really legitimate?"

Lowri sounded anxious enough that I opened one eye, and replied, "Yes, it is. She's King Gilad's daughter. She looks like him. His knowe opened for her. She's the real Queen in the Mists, and she's claiming her crown. The guy in the back is her brother. He's been asleep for a while, thanks to the lady you used to serve. Taking him was sort of the last-ditch attempt to make Arden back down."

"She has the support of the Undersea," said Dianda. "In case that matters."

"I served the current Queen because my family died in the War of Silences," said Lowri. "I lost my liege, my home, my family . . . everything. I had nowhere else to go. But I never gave her my loyalty. Just my service."

"We're not the ones you have to convince," I said. "As long as you don't drive us off a cliff, I'm good."

"We'd hit the water, so I'm good either way," said Dianda.

"I want my normal sidekicks back," I said.

She smirked at me in the rearview mirror. We kept driving.

Lowri turned off the road leading to the Muir Woods parking lot as the first rays of dawn were starting to tint the sky. True to his word, Tybalt was waiting at the gate, which was standing open for us. He stepped aside as Lowri pulled into the first available space, and she killed the engine just as the sun crested the horizon and dawn slammed down on us like a hammer. All the air went out of the world, taking the illusions that made us seem human with it. In that moment, we were defenseless.

I scrabbled for the door handle, finally managing to open the door and lean out into the fresh morning air. It had the distinct ashy taste of dying magic, but that didn't matter; it was a little easier to breathe, and I was willing to take what I could get.

Then dawn passed, and I could breathe again. I pulled in a great whooping gasp, choked, and did it again, more slowly this time. "Everyone all right?"

"I'm good," said Dianda. She left the flagon and cruet in the back as she got out of the car. I nodded my approval. I didn't want to risk them getting broken when we might need them later.

"Yes," said Lowri.

"There are human rangers in the gateway building," said Tybalt. "I've found another route through the woods."

"Oh, yay," I said flatly, and got out of the car. "Tromping through the woods carrying an unconscious man is my *favorite* way to start the day."

"That's good, because that's what you're about to do," said Dianda.

I sighed. "And apparently, the Undersea doesn't have sarcasm. All right. Let's move."

"I can get him," said Lowri. We turned to look at her. She shrugged. "I'm stronger than I look."

Glastig are essentially part goat. Even the weakest among them could win a human weightlifting competition. I nodded. "Okay. Lowri, you carry Nolan. Tybalt, you're on point; Dianda, guard the rear. Now let's move before the rangers come to see whether we need help."

Working together, we were able to lever Nolan out of the car. Lowri hoisted him into a fireman's carry. Tybalt gestured for us to follow him into the trees, and the five of us melted into the brush. For once, I wasn't the loudest as we walked toward the knowe: that honor went to Dianda, who couldn't seem to avoid stepping on every twig and branch we passed. Tybalt moved like a shadow, and Lowri was almost as quiet, her hooves finding easy purchase on the uneven ground. I was somewhere in the middle, not pureblood silent, but not a walking advertisement for our position, either.

Tybalt slowed to match me, murmuring, "I fear we may be walking into something."

"That's not encouraging. Didn't you check the knowe?"

"The door is guarded by the Queen's men. Either Arden has swayed them to her side . . ."

"Or we're about to walk into a trap, got it." I looked back over my shoulder at Dianda. "You want to cut down to the beach and see what's going on with the Undersea?"

"No. I want to punch your former monarch in the throat until she sees starfish. But I'll go. We may need reinforcements, and I'm not sure how much longer I can stay on my feet." She grimaced. "I mean that literally. My knees are starting to go wobbly. I need to get into the water."

"Send whoever you can. We'll see you soon."

"Kind tides," Dianda replied, and turned, hiking off in a different direction. I didn't question whether she'd know where she was going. Merrow can always find the sea.

The rest of us kept going. The air shimmered around us as we stepped from the well-traveled walkway onto the final approach to Arden's knowe, and the open door in the gnarled old tree became suddenly visible. Two of the Queen's men were standing there, flanking the opening. I looked to Lowri. She was frowning.

"I know them," she said. "There's no way they've turned against the Queen."

"Okay." I turned to her. "This is where I trust you, and you either prove me right, or you betray us the minute our backs are turned. I want you to stay out here with Nolan. Guard him with your life. Can you do that for me?"

Lowri blinked. Then, sensibly, she asked, "What's in it for me?"

"If Arden wins, she's going to need a guard. I'll praise you to the skies. And if she loses, you're in the perfect position to either tell the old Queen you were on her side all along, or run like hell. You can't lose if you don't walk through those doors. So will you do this?"

"If Arden doesn't take the throne, I'll run," said Lowri, and nodded. "I'll be here."

"Great. That's a start." I turned to Tybalt. "Now let's go for the finish."

We stepped out of the bushes, walking toward the doors to the knowe. The Queen's men turned to face us, dropping their spears into position. I ignored them, continuing to walk.

"Halt," said one.

"Bite me," I replied.

"In the name of Her Majesty, Queen of the Mists, I command you to halt," said the other.

"In my own name, I refuse," said Tybalt.

The two guards exchanged a look, clearly puzzled. Then, to my surprise, they raised their spears. "Then pass," said the first.

I blinked. Normally, getting past a guarded door isn't as easy as going "nuh-uh" when you're told you can't come in. "Oooookay," I said. Eyeing the guards warily, I walked to the door. They didn't stop me. I pushed it open and stepped through, with Tybalt at my side. The guards didn't say a word as they closed the door behind us.

The Hobs had clearly been hard at work: the cobwebs

that had choked the hall when we first entered were gone, revealing a vaulted ceiling of polished redwood and stained glass. It was beautiful. It was also empty.

"I don't like this," I murmured.

"Neither do I," said Tybalt.

We kept walking. At this point, there didn't seem like any other option. The people had to be in the knowe somewhere; two conflicting armies, however small, don't just disappear . . .

My head was starting to throb again. I shook it, hoping I could will the pain away. It got worse, and I realized I could hear humming from the receiving room. "Oh, crap. Tybalt." I grabbed his arm. He kept walking, dragging me with him for almost a foot before I let go. He didn't seem to notice. He just kept going.

"I'm sorry," I whispered, and turned, running back the way we'd come.

The guards blinked when I burst through the door. "Don't mind me," I said, grabbing the nearest fallen redwood branch. It was sticky with sap, clinging to my fingers like glue. Good. "Carry on," I said, and went charging back inside. They might have stopped me if I'd given them time to realize what I was doing, and I couldn't afford that.

Once I was back in the knowe, I scraped off as much sap as I could, rolling it between my fingers until I had a thick ball. I pulled it apart and jammed it into my ears, grimacing. The throbbing in my head stopped instantly. I closed my eyes. "Well, crud," I whispered.

I'd guessed right when I heard the humming: the Queen was part Siren, and we'd backed her into a corner. We should have stopped to think about what that might mean. And now it was me and a knife versus her and all my allies.

"Isn't this the best damn day." I opened my eyes and started walking again, not quite running, but not wasting time as I made my way down the hall to the reception room. The scene that waited for me there wasn't a surprise. I'd still been praying for something different.

The Queen was draped languidly over the throne that was rightfully Arden's, wearing a long white gown that looked like it would get dirty if you so much as thought the word "mud." Her lips were moving, probably in some vicious comment about my timing or my appearance. I couldn't hear her. The redwood sap was doing its job. That was one threat down—but only one, and I was about to have a hell of a lot more to deal with.

The receiving hall was full of people who should have been my allies. Sylvester and his guards lined the walls. Danny loomed above the rest. He'd never seemed menacing before. He was managing it now—and so was Tybalt, who stood at the Queen's right hand. Arden was at the Queen's left. All of them were looking at me with the same blank-eyed stare and no signs of recognition.

"This is gonna suck," I muttered. Louder, I said, "You didn't have to go all supervillain and take over the whole room. You could have just ceded your throne and walked away."

The Queen's mouth moved. It was a relief not to know what she was saying.

"No, seriously. Let everyone go and get out. Leave the Mists now, and we won't come after you. I give you my word."

She threw back her head, and I didn't have to hear her to know that she was laughing. Then she pointed at me, and May walked out of the crowd of Sylvester's men, a long dagger in her hand. She moved to the exact center of the room and stopped, staring into the distance.

The Queen opened her mouth, not speaking this time—singing. In a flash, I knew what was about to happen, and I didn't move.

I'm sorry, May, I thought.

May—who the Queen must have chosen because she was politically useless, but still important to me—raised the dagger and slit her own throat. Blood cascaded down her front like a waterfall, and her eyes widened, understanding coming back into them for a split second before she collapsed to the floor. I walked forward and knelt beside her, picking up the dagger and checking for a pulse at the same time. She didn't have one.

"She's dead," I said, struggling to keep the horror and revulsion out of my voice. She would be fine—she had to be, she was a Fetch—but she was my friend, and her face was my own. I was going to be seeing that moment in my dreams for years. I raised my head and looked at the Queen, who was smirking at me. "You killed her. You violated Oberon's Law, and for what? To make a *point*? You *killed* her. You know what I have to say to that?"

The Queen cocked her head to the side, saying something I didn't hear. I smiled bitterly. She frowned. Apparently, that wasn't the reaction she'd been expecting.

"You started it," I said, and charged.

The Queen stared at me for a few precious seconds, too stunned to sing her next command. Then she opened her mouth, and the people around her moved.

Good. That was what I'd been hoping for. The Queen could command my allies, but she couldn't grant them any free will—not if she wanted to keep her hold on them. That meant they were limited to the tactics she could think up. Sylvester had a brilliant military mind. He'd won his Duchy fairly. And now he was marching toward me like a windup soldier, sword raised, ready to start hacking.

At the moment, he wasn't my primary concern. That honor went to Danny, who could crush me if he managed to get hold of me. I'd heal, but it would hurt like hell, and it would slow me down until my bones managed to set. Keeping away from him was my first priority. Getting to Arden was my second. Grianne reached me first. She drew her sword and swung for me with none of her normal grace. I ducked under the swing, letting her momentum carry her into Sylvester's path. The two collided. I kept running.

Danny was charging toward me, the floor shaking with every step he took. On the plus side, this was causing the Queen's other puppets to scatter in order to avoid him, which kept them from forming a shield wall between me and her. At the same time, this meant there was nothing between me and the homicidal Bridge Troll.

I turned and ran. "I hate this I hate this I hate this," I chanted under my breath. Madden lunged out of nowhere, his teeth bared in a snarl. I grabbed Melly's discarded broom from the floor, sparing a half-second's thought for where Melly herself might be, and slammed the point of the handle into his exposed belly. He yelped and fell back. I kicked him hard in the muzzle, and he went down. Guilt swept over me. I was going to be apologizing for this fight for a while.

But I was almost there. Arden was right —

Tybalt. Standing in front of me, his incisors showing and his hands curled into claws as. I skidded to a stop. I couldn't hear a damn thing, but I was certain he was snarling, that low, almost subsonic sound that served as the last warning before a Cait Sidhe attacked.

"You don't want to do this," I whispered.

He leapt.

TWENTY-NINE

THERE WAS NO WAY FOR ME to get out of the way once Tybalt was in motion; Cait Sidhe are almost too fast to see when they pounce. I had a split second to decide what I was going to do—and in that split second, I lowered both my knife and my stolen dagger, letting him crash into me. His claws found my neck, ripping through skin and muscle as if they were paper. Only the fact that I was slightly turned kept him from ripping my throat out.

I dropped the dagger, aware that I was mirroring May the way she'd always mirrored me, and clapped a hand over the wound. There was no way to stop the gushing blood, and so I didn't try. Instead, I took a staggering step forward, trying to look like I was about to collapse. It wasn't hard. With the amount of blood that I was losing, even my body was having trouble putting itself back together.

I could feel the flesh growing back beneath my fingers. I kept my hand clamped down, keeping the Queen from seeing my recovery. She didn't know how fast I healed. Why should she? I was her little changeling enemy, and I was no threat, especially not now, wounded, still staggering toward her like there was a damn thing left for me to accomplish.

Arden hadn't moved. I reached out with the hand that

held my knife, trying to make the motion look like a supplication. And then, before the Queen could react, I sliced a narrow cut across Arden's shoulder, grabbed her, and pressed my lips to the wound.

Using Nolan's magic while he was asleep had been hard. Using Arden's while she was enthralled was a cakewalk by comparison. I had enough time to see the Queen start to rise, an expression of shock and fury on her face, before I was falling into the hole I'd forced Arden to open, hauling the Princess with me—

—and landed on my ass, Arden still clasped firmly in my arms. She began to struggle almost immediately. I didn't let her go, instead looking around to try and figure out where we were.

The fight was nowhere to be seen. I was sitting in the middle of a freshly-polished hardwood floor. There was a four-poster bed nearby, carved to match the wardrobe I'd seen in Arden and Nolan's basement home. Arden's flailing nearly caught me in the chin. I let her go, rolling to my feet, and raised a hand to check the status of my wounded throat. It didn't feel pretty, but at least it felt nearly intact.

Arden was shouting something. I shook my head. "I can't hear you, I have sap in my ears." Digging it out with bloody fingers was no easy matter, but I managed.

"— that *bitch*, she just started singing and we were all putty in her hands," Arden snarled.

"That's what Sirens do," I said. My voice sounded strained. Tybalt's claws must have nicked my vocal cords. That said something truly disturbing about how deep they'd gone. "She's part Siren."

Arden paused, eyes going wide. "Oh, sweet Titania, your sister . . ."

"Will be fine. May can't be killed, remember? She's probably totally recovered by now." I wasn't as sure of that as I was trying to sound. I'd never known her not to have a pulse before. "We can't worry about her now. I have Nolan, and he's safe, but we have to stop the Queen. Can you help me?"

"That depends on whether or not we're letting you leave here breathing," said a sweet, familiar voice behind me. I turned. Melly and Ormond were standing there, armed with a mop and a broadsword respectively.

It says something about Hobs that I was more worried about the mop. "You got away!"

Melly's eyes widened. "October, your *throat*."

Only Ormond remained completely calm. "Prove it's you."

"I'm the one who stole all the peppermint brownies before the Midwinter Festival," I said, without hesitation.

"Which year?" Ormond shot back.

"Uh, every year."

To my relief, he chuckled and lowered his sword. Melly did the same with her mop. "You *are* you. But October, your throat . . ."

"The Queen seized control of everyone else." I frowned. "Why didn't she get the two of you?"

"I ran when I heard the singing start, and I dragged young Melly with me," said Ormond. "We're deep enough into the knowe that she can't reach us here, and we cleared the branches off as many of the remaining booby-traps as we could."

"So anyone trying to follow won't know where they are," I said. "Slick." Also damned dangerous: the Queen was controlling our friends and allies. If she controlled them into one of Oleander's traps, they'd probably wind up dead.

"I'm really sorry to interrupt this reunion, but we need to be reclaiming my knowe and my Kingdom right about now," said Arden. "October. What is it that you wanted me to do?"

"We need to block your ears with something," I said, and held up my own ball of now-bloody sap.

"We have sealing wax," said Melly.

"Good, that should work even better than the sap I scraped off the trees outside." I shook my head, fighting the urge to rub my throat, which itched as it healed.

"Once you're safely unable to hear, I need you to gate me back into the receiving hall. Do you think you can land us behind the throne?"

"Why? You're not going to kill her, are you?" Her mismatched eyes narrowed. "Because that would be too easy, after what she's done."

It was comforting to know that that was her only argument. "No, and I promise, what I *am* going to do isn't very nice."

Melly stepped toward Arden, bobbing a seemingly automatic curtsy as she held out a small tin of sealing wax. "For milady."

"Cool," said Arden, smiling her thanks as she dug out a ball of wax and stuffed it into her ears.

"Ready?" I asked, tucking the sap back into my own ears.

Arden looked at me uncomprehendingly.

"At least I know she can't hear me," I muttered, before flashing an exaggerated double thumbs-up at her.

This time, Arden nodded her understanding and began to transcribe a circle in the air. Melly caught my arm as I started forward.

"Be careful?" she mouthed, voice muffled by the sap.

"I'll try," I said, and kept going. The smell of Arden's magic rose around us, and together, she and I stepped through the gate.

Her aim was good: we appeared behind the throne, where the Queen was standing, gesturing wildly at her thralls as her mouth moved in silent instruction. May was still lying facedown on the floor. I hoped she was just playing possum, although there was no way for me to check.

"Hey," I snapped, stepping around the throne and grabbing the Queen by the arm. My fingers left spreading red prints on the sleeve of her gown. "Miss me?"

The Queen turned to stare at me, moonstruck eyes gone wide with surprise and a note of genuine fear. She yelled, probably demanding someone come and save her. I ignored her, raising my other hand to my mouth and sucking the still-damp blood from the space between my thumb and forefinger. Then, before she could pull away, I pulled her close, locking my arm around her neck, and drove my knife into her shoulder.

She held me like that once, when she was threatening my life. But she didn't actually stab me, and she certainly wouldn't have started kissing the wound if she had. My magic rose around us and she screamed, putting every bit of her Banshee heritage into the sound. It was loud enough that I heard her even through the sap.

That still wasn't loud enough to matter.

The only way to break a Siren's spell was to remove the Siren. There were two ways I could do that. I could break Oberon's Law, and kill her ... or I could pull the Siren out of her and set them all free. It seemed like a terrible choice to make for someone else. She hadn't left me any other options. Reaching deep into her blood, I found the pieces of her heritage, the places where Banshee and Siren and Sea Wight collided. And I began to work.

The threads were so tangled that it was almost impossible to find the place where one ended and the next began. There was more Sea Wight than anything else, and so I started with that, pulling and stretching the shape of it as I pulled the Siren away. There was Banshee in the mix, and I hesitated. Removing that would have made her harmless ... but it would have taken this from a necessary invasion to a violation. I left her Banshee blood intact, and kept working.

The Queen screamed, struggling against me. I'd done this twice before, but both times, my subjects had been willing. The Queen was fighting me, in every sense of the word. That didn't matter. That *couldn't* matter. Now that I'd started, I had to win. I still felt bad for her. Having your blood changed is always painful.

The last threads of Siren were tangled deep. I took a breath, bracing myself, and got a mouthful of her blood—something I'd been trying to avoid, even as I mingled her blood with mine.

She'll kill me when she knows; she'll kill me, and this changeling bitch won't even care . . .

I forced the veil of her thoughts aside, grabbed the last threads, and pulled. The fight went out of her; the Queen went limp in my arms. She felt smaller somehow, frailer. I raised my head, spitting to try to clear away any traces of her blood before I could be hit with another wave of her memories. Then I looked around the room.

Everyone was staring at me.

"What?" I dug the sap out of one ear with my free hand. "Haven't you ever seen that trick before?" I spat again. "Anybody have any mouthwash?"

"October . . ." Tybalt approached cautiously, looking like he expected me to cut and run at any second. I swallowed back a sudden twinge of fear, remembering his claws at my throat.

"Hey. Take her, will you?" I pushed the unconscious Queen toward him. He caught her easily, hoisting her onto the throne. My assessment had been correct: it looked like she'd lost at least a foot in height, becoming slimmer and even paler, impossible as that seemed. What little color she'd had must have come from the Siren side of the family. "Has anybody checked on May?"

"Jin is with her now," said Tybalt. "Toby . . ."

"Good." I turned to scan the room. Everyone seemed to be in one piece—mostly, anyway. "Can you go and get Lowri and Nolan? I think Arden's going to want to see her brother."

"All right," said Tybalt, sounding defeated.

I glanced back to watch him walk away. And then I moved toward Arden, who was still standing behind the throne, looking stunned. "She violated Oberon's Law, even if it didn't stick," I said. "She attacked you in your home."

"What did you *do* to her?" she asked.

"I made her stop." I shrugged. "It's what my line is good for. We're like hope chests with thumbs."

Arden started to respond, but stopped as she looked past me, eyes widening. "Nolan!" she cried, and took off running. I turned. Tybalt was dragging the Queen's guards who had been at the door. Lowri was carrying Nolan, her hooves slipping in the pools of blood that covered the floor. The receiving room looked like a slaughterhouse. Between me and May, we'd basically bled our way into a private abattoir.

This was my life. One compulsion-induced torn throat didn't change that. I ran after Arden, veering off at the last moment to bring myself into collision with Tybalt, rather than with Lowri and Nolan. Tybalt blinked at me, clearly startled. There was a moment of hesitation, a shadowed fear in his eyes. Then he beamed and dropped the guards onto the bloody floor, catching me in his arms as I flung myself at him and kissed him like the world was on the verge of ending.

There was a lot of cleanup left to do, both literally and politically. The former Queen would have to be contained, and Arden's claim to the throne would have to be formally recognized. I needed to find out where Tybalt had put the hope chest, and return it to the Luidaeg, who should have had it in the first place. Comfort would need to be given, questions would need to be answered, and wounds would need time to heal. But right here, right now, it was over.

Tybalt locked his arms around my waist and kissed me again, and everything was right with the world.

THIRTY

MAY HUMMED AN OLD ENGLISH FOLKSONG about decapitated women as she fussed with her hair, which was streaked with white, blue, and electric green for the occasion. I eyed her before going back to checking the fit of my own spider-silk gown in the mirror. I didn't need to bother—the dress fit like it was made for me, and always would, because that's what spider-silk *does*. It was the most formal dress I owned, black with gold and silver highlights, cut straight across the chest and with a knee-length skirt. I'd worn that dress the night I first met Patrick and Dianda Lorden. It was my "try to avoid a war" dress. It seemed appropriate to the occasion.

"You weren't decapitated, you know," I said. Stacy had done my hair, curling it gently before pulling it off to one side with a ribbon. Somehow, it didn't make me look like an escapee from a 1980s teen comedy. It was elegant, simple, and perfect.

"Close enough," said May. Her dress was rainbow taffeta, likely rescued from a thrift store somewhere in the Mission District. It didn't match the black velvet band she had tied around her throat. She was healing, but slowly. It would be months before she could go out in public without either fabric or illusions covering her.

There was a knock at the door. I turned to see Sylvester standing there, in full formal regalia, looking embarrassed to have interrupted. "Are you ready?" he asked. "I'm trying to gather everyone who needs to be on time."

"I'll catch up," said May.

"Then I'm ready." I walked over and placed one gloved hand on Sylvester's arm, allowing him to lead me from the room.

A week, and all the Hobs from the old Queen's knowe—under the ecstatic instruction of Melly and Ormond, who felt they had first claim—had worked wonders. The Windermere knowe was a gleaming showpiece, all polished wood and glossy floors. The less public areas would need more time, but it was already suitable for habitation, which was a good thing, since Arden, Nolan, and Lowri hadn't left since the old Queen was defeated. Lowri was serving as the head of Arden's guard, which was made up half of defectors from the old Queen and half of recruits who had shown up looking for a place to serve.

Faerie is like that. Create a vacuum, and we'll rush to fill it. Just in time, too. In the confusion of our allies waking from the Siren song and our enemies figuring out whether they were still our enemies, the old Queen had escaped, aided by loyalists who had managed to sneak in, hidden amongst the more sincere defectors. We needed the extra security now if we wanted to be sure of Arden's safety.

We stepped out of the hall and into the receiving room, which was filled almost to capacity. Sylvester's Court was in full attendance, as was the portion of Dianda's that could survive on land. Tamed Lightning and Dreamer's Glass had sent emissaries, as had many of the other smaller fiefdoms. I didn't recognize everyone. I knew enough of them to know that some were here to curry favor, and some were here to see what they believed would be a righting of past wrongs. The Luidaeg wasn't present. I hadn't heard from her since she'd gone looking for Mother's tower. One more thing to worry about; one more thing to deal with later.

Arden was on her throne, wearing a simple green

gown and chewing on her thumbnail. I let Sylvester pull me through the crowd to a spot at the front, where Quentin and Tybalt were waiting.

"Hey, you," I said, kissing Tybalt on the cheek. Then I ruffled Quentin's hair. "Also, hey, you. You nervous?"

"A little," he admitted. "I haven't seen them in years."

"I'm terrified. I've been worried about meeting your parents for years."

"Pretty sure I couldn't have come up with anything bigger than crowning a new Queen to bring them here."

I paused. "That's actually a reasonable answer."

The final step to any challenge to a throne being deemed acceptable was approval by the High King. Normally, that approval came at a distance, handed down without a physical appearance. This time, due to the circumstances surrounding Arden's ascension, the High King and High Queen had decided to come in person. No pressure.

An aisle had been kept clear along the middle of the room. The reason why became obvious when a faint shimmer appeared in the air and a portal opened, allowing four guards in the livery of the High Throne to walk through. They stepped to the side, and two Daoine Sidhe stepped through the portal, which closed behind them. Everyone in the room, save Tybalt, immediately bowed or curtsied, as low as we possibly could.

"You may rise," said High King Aethlin. His accent was pure Toronto. I straightened, getting a good look at him. He was tall, with hair the color of hammered bronze and features that said a lot about what Quentin would look like as an adult. The woman next to him—High Queen Maida—had hair like molten silver. It didn't make her look old. It just made her even lovelier than she already was.

"Those are your parents," I said faintly. "I think I'm going to throw up."

"Yup." Quentin beamed. "I can't wait for you to meet them."

"Now I *really* think I'm going to throw up."

The High King and High Queen had been walking toward Arden as we spoke. She had remained standing after she rose to curtsy. When they reached the dais holding her throne, she dropped to one knee, bowing her head.

"You claim the throne of the Mists," said High King Aethlin. "Why?"

"By right of blood, my liege," she said. "My father was King before me. I am Arden Windermere, daughter of Gilad Windermere. This throne is mine."

"Prove your claim."

Arden held out her hand, managing to only tremble slightly. King Aethlin drew a slim dagger from within his doublet and pricked her index finger, just deep enough to coax out a single drop of blood. He transferred that drop to his own finger, and raised it to his mouth.

For a long moment, it felt like everyone in the receiving hall was holding their breath. I balled my hands into fists, feeling my nails cut into the skin.

Then the High King spoke.

"Your claim is true. Your crown is untarnished. By the oak, the ash, and the thorn; by the rowan, the yarrow, and the pine, you may rise, Arden Windermere, rightfully Queen in the Mists." King Aethlin smiled. "May all hail your glory."

The room erupted into cheers as Arden stood, looking stunned.

There was so much left to do. We needed to clean up the remaining goblin fruit before anyone else got hurt; I still had a hope chest in my hall closet, along with the flagon and cruet I'd taken from the old Queen's treasury. Arden needed to build a Court, and somewhere along the way, she'd need to start disassembling the puppet government holding Silences. I needed to find the Luidaeg and pay my debt to the Library. Worst of all, I needed to meet Quentin's parents.

All that was for later. Right now, I held Tybalt's hand and put my arm around Quentin's shoulders, and cheered for the new Queen, who was taking her throne at last.

Long may she reign.

As a special bonus in this edition, read on for a brand-new October Daye short story by Seanan McGuire:

NEVER SHINES THE SUN

NEVER SHINES THE SUN

Here never shines the sun; here nothing breeds . . .
— William Shakespeare, *Titus Andronicus*

SAN FRANCISCO. SUMMER, 1959

SEVEN YEARS IS A classic length of time in Faerie. Most enchantments last for seven years, or some multiple of sevens. When people disappear underhill, it's almost always for seven years, no less, no more. Most of all, seven years was long for me to be patient.

It was long enough to wait.

I still felt a little guilty as I settled on the park bench and pulled a bag of breadcrumbs out of my coat pocket. I began scattering them on the sidewalk, trying to look like I was just another part of a perfectly normal scene. Pixies and pigeons swarmed in from all directions and started snatching the food, squabbling amongst themselves all the while. Most of the pixies were content with the bread; a few were clever enough to recognize that it had other uses. They began making a heap of crumbs at the very edge of the feeding frenzy, luring a fat pigeon in their direction. I nodded approvingly. Reducing the pigeon population of the city wasn't going to hurt anything—except for maybe the pigeon in question—and it would teach this particular colony of pixies that being clever could lead to eating better. Given enough time, they might surprise a lot of people.

My attention was only half on the impending slaughter that was being staged in front of me. The rest was fixed on a tall, statuesque figure in a polka dot day dress, her platinum blonde hair pinned back in a sensible bun. She was trudging across the lawn with a picnic basket in one hand and a towheaded little girl running rings around her. Amy would be furious if she saw me. That couldn't keep the smile off my face. Seven years was *more* than long enough to wait. Amy wanted her privacy. That was fine with me. It was selfish and horrible and stupid of her, but it was still fine. I just wanted to meet my niece. I don't have very many of those anymore.

Amy put down her basket, opening the lid and pulling out a battered olive-green army blanket. She spread it over the grass with a practiced flick of her wrists, looking so domestic that it made my chest ache a little. She was living a lie. We both knew it, even if I was the only one who was willing to admit it. But she'd been living it for so *long*, and it was covering up a hurt that was so great . . . how much did that lie really mean to her by this point? How far would she go to preserve it?

The little girl chirped something I couldn't make out, voice high and sweet and shredded by the wind. I heard Amy laugh—she always had the most beautiful laugh; all her lies couldn't change that—and then the little girl, my niece, was running as fast as she could for the playground equipment, her pigtails streaming in the wind. What was her name again?

Oh, right. October. One more page in the ongoing calendar of our tangled lives.

"You never could resist giving that knife one more twist, could you, Amy?" I asked aloud.

The pixies didn't answer. I hadn't actually expected them to.

I dumped the rest of my breadcrumbs out of the bag as I stood, dusting my hands against my legs. My mouth was dry, and my heart seemed to be beating just a little bit too fast. You would never have been able to make me admit it, but I was nervous. Hell, I was bordering on scared. Here was my youngest sister's kid, throwing herself down the slide in a public park like there was no such thing as getting hurt, and I had no clue what I was going to say to her. "Hi, I'm your Aunt" seemed a little weak, and like a good way to bring the wrath of Amy down on my head. All I wanted to do was meet her. I wouldn't introduce myself, I wouldn't interfere, I'd just . . .

I'd just meet her. That would be enough.

Besides, it's not like I've ever been famed for my patience. If something went wrong, Amy was going to have to suck it up and admit that waiting seven years had required a herculean effort on my part. She should be proud of me for even trying.

The grass was springy and slightly damp underfoot, filling the air with the fresh smell of summer. I walked to the play area, careful to avoid any of the really marshy patches. October was still flinging herself down the slide with mad abandon, landing face-first in the sand and then racing to clamber back up the ladder. I stopped at the edge of the sandpit, just watching her for a moment.

She was a pretty little thing, all scabby knees and elbows. Her face was a human-blunted mirror of Amy's. She even had Amy's no-color gray eyes, like the kind of mist that swallows ships whole. Her hair was darker than I'd expected, dirty dishwater blonde already trending toward brown. Maybe blonde hair wasn't going to be a hallmark of the Dóchas Sidhe after all. They were a pretty new race. I was still sorting out what I could use to spot them at a distance.

There was nothing wrong with her eyes. She'd only gone tumbling down the slide twice more when she spotted me and waved, fearless as you please. I hesitated before waving back.

She seemed to take that as an invitation, because she scrambled up and ran over to me. Her feet were bare. I hadn't noticed that before. She dug her toes into the sand and looked up at me, Amy's eyes in a little half-human girl's face, and asked, "Are you lost?"

"What? No. I'm not lost." Shit. I hadn't come prepared with an excuse; I didn't expect her to spot me before I was ready for her. She had good eyes. "My dog is. Have you seen him? He's pretty big and shaggy."

"No," she said, shaking her head for good measure. "I haven't seen any dogs. Did you ask my Mommy?" And she pointed to Amy, who was, blessedly, looking down into the picnic basket. I should have gone then. I should have turned and walked away. But there was something out of place; something in the color of this little girl's hair . . .

I squatted down, resting my elbows on my knees, and studied her as carefully as I could. "What's your name?"

"October," she answered, with prompt and dangerous honesty. "I'm seven."

"Pleased to meet you, October. I'm Annie. I'm a lot more than seven." And I stuck out my hand for her to shake.

There was no hesitation on her part—none at all. She took the hand I offered, and the feeling of her skin on mine told me everything I needed to know.

Seven years wasn't long enough to wait.

Seven years was seven years too long.

The pounding on my apartment door started almost exactly when I expected it to. It had been three days since I had informed Sylvester Torquill of what Amy had been doing; three days since I had "suggested" he take steps to fix things. He was a good man, Sylvester was, and he'd done the honorable thing. October had chosen Faerie. That didn't surprise me—no kid who did that little second-guessing was going to choose humanity—but it was still a relief. The line remained unbroken. Despite everything, there might still be half a chance in Hell.

I waited for a pause in the hammering before I opened the front door and said, very calmly, "Hi, Amy. Nice of you to drop by."

"You—you! How *dare* you!" She shoved her way past me into the hall. It was a mixed blessing. On the one hand, now I could close the door. On the other hand, now she was inside my apartment, and there was a very good chance that she was going to start throwing things.

Amy always was a little temperamental.

"How dare I what?" I turned to face her, cocking my head slightly to the side. "Really. What is it that you think I did? I want to hear you say it."

"You had no right! *None*!" The air around her crackled with the blood and roses smell of her magic as her human guise wiped itself away, revealing Amandine, daughter of Oberon, in all her seriously pissed-off glory. If looks could kill, I would have died at that moment. "I told you to leave me alone. I told you to leave *us* alone."

"I gave you seven years. That was a lot longer than you had any right to ask for." I stepped around her, walking toward the living room. I figured she'd follow me, and she didn't disappoint.

"Do you know what you *did*?" she demanded.

Dad forgive me, but that was the last straw. I whirled around to face her, snapping, "Yeah, I know what I did. I called Sylvester and told him what you were doing to that poor kid, because *he* didn't have the right kind of eyes to see it. I told him he was almost out of time to get her out of there. Fuck, Amy, I knew you wanted out, but I never dreamed—"

"I was saving her!" shouted Amy, balling her hands into fists as the smell of blood and roses thickened in the air around her.

I dispelled whatever she was starting to cast with one sharp slash of my hand. "*You were killing her!*"

Amy stared at me, colorless eyes filling with tears.

It was a trick she'd been using on me since she was born. Littlest sister, getting ready to cry, needing comfort. It usually worked, whether I wanted it to or not. But it wasn't going to work this time. I stepped closer, moving into her personal space as I lowered my voice to a hiss. "You were *killing* her. Every time you twisted that little girl's blood, you took centuries off of her life, centuries that weren't yours to steal—"

"Annie, please . . ."

"No, you're going to listen. Every time you twisted her blood, you took centuries off of her life, and you made her that much more vulnerable. Faerie is *not* going to treat her kindly. Not thin-blooded, and not as your daughter."

She sniffled, trying to lift her head proudly. She almost succeeded. "I was going to make sure Faerie never had the chance to hurt her."

I laughed before I could stop myself: a brief, bitter sound. "You think a lot of yourself, don't you, Amy? You could destroy that little girl. For all I know, you already have. But you can never, *never* save her from Faerie." A thin smile twisted my lips as I added, "It's in her blood. Even you can't change that."

"You never gave me the chance," she whispered.

"You never *had* a chance; it wasn't mine to give," I replied, as kindly as I could. "What you did to her, what you were clearly planning—that's monstrous, Amy. That's Eira's territory."

Her eyes widened. "Don't you compare me to her."

"Then don't you *act* like her. You have to be better than she is. There's no point if we can't be better than she is." As far as I know, Eira Rosynhwyr is the oldest of my still-living sisters. I'd kill her in a heartbeat if I thought I could do it. But she's Titania's eldest daughter, as I'm Maeve's, and if there's anyone in Faerie I fear, it's her.

Amy wiped her eyes, looking at me beseechingly. "I don't know what to do, Annie. Why didn't you ask me before you went to them?"

"Because you would have cried. You would have said you just needed a little bit more time. And I would have given it to you, and by the time I realized I was making a mistake, that little girl would have been completely human, and completely unable to protect herself." I shook my head. "You say I didn't give you a choice. You didn't give me one, either, Amy. The only one with a Choice to make was October, and she's made it."

"She didn't know what she was doing." Amy turned away from me, shaking her head. "I can still change her. I can still save her from all of this—"

"If you touch one hair on that little girl's head, they will never find your body." My voice was low and dangerous, filled with a warning that I knew she would never heed. My poor Amy. She never did learn when to leave well enough alone. "She's not yours anymore. She made her Choice. She belongs to herself."

"You've forgotten what it was to be a mother." A note of smug satisfaction crept into her tone, and I was briefly, burningly glad that I couldn't see her face. If her expression had matched her voice, I might have slapped the smug right out of her. "Children require sacrifice."

"Dammit, Amy, you're not *listening* to me!" It took everything I had to keep my anger in check. This was my fault as much as it was hers. She was the youngest of us, and when she needed me, I wasn't there. She should never have been given so much freedom, never allowed to make so many poor decisions. But the Firstborn had scattered in the wake of losing our parents, and we left her free for so long. *Too* long. This is my fault.

She whirled, blonde hair flying, hands balled into fists. Sudden rage contorted her face as she shouted, "You had no right!"

"I had every right, Amy; I had *every* right. That little girl deserves better than what you were trying to do to her, and you know it."

"She deserves a life!"

"She's not human! No matter what you do to her, no matter how deep you go, Faerie will *always* know her as its own. Do you understand? You can't free her. All you can do is make her defenseless. She'll belong to Faerie until she dies. You're making sure that happens sooner."

She looked at me, my beautiful baby sister, and her broken heart was shining in her eyes like a fallen star.

Finally, she shook her head. "So be it," she said, and I knew.

I knew she had given up again.

"Amy—"

"I hate you," said Amy, the sorrow in her eyes replaced almost instantly by sullenness. She'd been the baby of the family for centuries. We were all too used to giving her what she wanted. "You've gotten so wrapped up in being the Luidaeg—being the all-mighty sea witch—that you've forgotten what it takes to be a sister."

"This may come as a surprise to you, but right now, I don't give a shit what you think of me. I did what had to be done. That's my job. How about you start doing yours?"

Amy's eyes narrowed. "Don't start."

"Little late."

"That's it. I'm done with you. You just stay away from me." Amy shook her head, grabbing fistfuls of the air and flinging a human disguise around herself once more. It was perfect. Her illusions always were. Especially when she was spinning them to fool herself. "Stay away from my daughter."

"As long as you don't hurt her again. If you do, I'll know, and I'll be there." I looked at her coolly, allowing the color to drain from my eyes until they were nothing but white. I had lost a sister by going to the park and betraying her in the name of saving her. I wasn't going to lose my niece. "You've neglected your duties, and I've allowed it. You've refused your purpose, and I've turned the other way. You've been content to play games while Faerie falls apart around us, and maybe that's my fault as much as yours, but you're still the one who did it. I will not let you refuse or fail this child. Am I clear?"

"Crystal," she snapped. "I'll see myself out."

I didn't answer. I just watched her go.

The sound of the door slamming was as loud as the sound of a chain being snapped. I stayed where I was for at least ten minutes, waiting for her to come back and start looking for a way to fix this. A way to put that little girl back the way she was supposed to be, and start doing the things that she should have been doing all along. Faerie never creates anything without a purpose, and that includes the Dóchas Sidhe.

Amy never came back.

Seven years; that's how long I waited before I went to see her, before I went to meet her little girl. And the worst of it is that now, all I can do is wait. I'll wait seven more years, and seven more after that, seven times seven and seventy more, if that's what it takes, until a child of Amandine's line steps up and does what's needed doing for centuries. Mother save me, but I'm starting to be afraid that Eira's going to win. October should have been our best chance. And I waited seven years.

Whatever comes next is on my head as much as it's on Amy's. I will never forgive her for that. But whatever comes next . . . it isn't going to be mine to do. Whatever comes next is October's.

I hope she's strong enough for what's coming.

Seanan McGuire

The InCryptid Novels

"McGuire kicks off a new series with a smart-mouthed, engaging heroine and a city full of fantastical creatures. This may seem like familiar ground to McGuire fans, but she makes New York her own, twisting the city and its residents into curious shapes that will leave you wanting more. Verity's voice is strong and sure as McGuire hints at a deeper history, one that future volumes will hopefully explore."

—*RT Book Reviews*

DISCOUNT ARMAGEDDON
978-0-7564-0713-1

MIDNIGHT BLUE-LIGHT SPECIAL
978-0-7564-0792-6

HALF-OFF RAGNAROK
978-0-7564-0811-4
(Available March 2014)

"The only thing more fun than an October Daye book is an InCryptid book. Swift narrative, charm, great world-building . . . all the McGuire trademarks."

—Charlaine Harris

To Order Call: 1-800-788-6262
www.dawbooks.com